#INFERNO

L.M. STRAUSS

To my family.
I love you.

Wisdom is knowing I am nothing, love is knowing
I am everything, and between the two my life moves.

— Nisargadatta Maharaj

#YOLO

— The Internet

PARIS

Tonight, Bea celebrated turning thirty—she'd see thirty-one if she managed to stay alive until midnight.

From her balcony high above Paris, she looked down toward the historic *Place de la Concorde*. Trees strung with twinkling white lights circled the busy square, and shop windows cast a golden glow, painting the whole scene with a watercolor romance, and quieting the ghosts of twelve-hundred beheadings that once took place there.

Far below her seventh-story hotel rooms, a church bell rang out ten chimes. Two hours to go before she'd be safe.

Bea shivered. For her, the sound of the bell was far more disturbing than comforting. Church bells, kitchen timers, ticking clocks… every one of them a countdown to her ears.

How many chimes had rung out since she'd lost her brother, Dante, nine years ago today? How many more would sound before the cosmic wrong was righted and she caught up to him? How many seconds, how many heartbeats, until the natural balance would be restored—at her expense?

A boyfriend had once asked (in the middle of dumping

her) if she longed for it or feared it, that last grain of sand in her personal hourglass. She hadn't responded at the time because the question was too intimate. But she'd known the answer. It had—and still did—come to her each night when she slipped into bed, when the laptop shut, and the phone screen locked.

She feared it.

Bea moved away from the balcony rail and stepped back inside her suite at the Hôtel de la Reine. A likely-original Louis XVI desk was piled high with her birthday gifts, many from her faceless and devoted followers. Atop the stack sat the one thing in the opulent room that held value—a half-faded snapshot in a cheap wooden frame. A photo of her and Dante during their junior year abroad, the Eiffel Tower rising up behind their silly grins. The last great hurrah of the Allegra twins.

She lifted the frame, smiling at the goofballs in the photo as she ran a finger across her brother's face. He'd been her strong right hand; now... a phantom limb.

She traced his face again. "I'm lost without you."

The door swung open, and her two best friends blew into the room and began taking over every available surface with all their gear.

"Hey, hey, birthday girl!" Melanie said as she popped open her three-tiered makeup kit.

Nadiyah draped Bea's garment bag over a chair. "I can't believe the big night is finally here."

The two women ran her business, and they excelled at it. More, they loved her—and she them. Their excitement whisked away the momentary spot of melancholy and Bea smiled the words '*happy birthday*' to her brother's image as she replaced the frame on the pile. He'd be proud of her tonight.

Nadi opened her tablet. "According to the schedule, you need to get dressed, Bea. We've got to go live with your social feed before we lose prime viewing time in the States." Nadi could have easily become the internet star rather than Bea. With her runway model body, the halo of black curls, and a hint of her childhood Haitian accent, she was a magnet of a personality in her own right, but she preferred a life behind the scenes where she controlled nearly every aspect of the business and never had to deal with trolls.

Bea slipped into the couture gown—a crimson floor-length sheath by the hottest new designer out of Tokyo. The silk felt exquisite as it slid down her skin, and the Louboutin heels that had been sent with the dress made her giddy. For a second, she tossed the thought of her birthday and the deadly countdown aside and lost herself in the sheer joy of wearing such beautiful things.

She grabbed her phone and took one last pre-game selfie to work up her followers' anticipation for the streamed broadcast at midnight, slapping on a few tags and posting for their enjoyment (#mydreamlife #partyinparis #letuseatcake). As an influencer, her life was no longer her own—it was product.

Church bells rang out again. Eleven times.

"Crap, I told you guys we lingered too long at dinner," said Nadi. "We haven't even done your makeup yet, Bea, and I want to do a practice run to check the lighting before the real broadcast. There's little time left."

Bea's moment of joy fled. One hour to go before her live birthday toast.

One more hour to try and beat the Reaper.

As she sank into Melanie's tall make-up chair, Bea studied the lavish suite, searching for potential last-minute death traps to avoid. The edges of the heavy marble coffee table looked mighty sharp, and she was a well-known klutz. Best to stay clear of them while wearing high heels. And that box of Parisian chocolates on the vanity before her posed a choking hazard, or even a previously unknown nut allergy. She leaned forward and shoved the confections far out of temptation's reach.

What if... what if the mascara wand poked Bea in the eye, blinding her and causing her to fly shrieking out of the chair, and as she bumbled around the room, half-sighted and in pain, smashed into a plate glass window and bled out? *(#beautykills)*

"What do you think about the hairstyle, Nadi?" Melanie asked, having now finished her work beautifully and without causing death. "Shall we go with an updo or keep it down?" She gave Bea a little squeeze on the shoulders, a reminder to have fun even though the stakes tonight were high.

This was *the* breakthrough moment of Bea's social media career. Whether she'd continue to get such lucrative and high-profile sponsors as the hotel and fashion designer depended on her success with tonight's shoot. New influencers came onto the scene daily—young, hungry, willing to do whatever it took. Bea had to be better, and this shoot had to be flawless.

"Definitely down," Nadi responded without looking, busy setting up a video light. "Those long dark waves falling over her bare shoulders will be super romantic. We'll tag it 'Italian in Paris'."

Bea took a deep breath and calmed down. She could do this. More than that, she *would* make it to midnight and *live*.

At last, they all gathered what they needed to film the toast and moved out onto the balcony—a dangerous choice of location now that she thought about it.

Bea approached the railing and looked down, expecting the very pits of Hell to open before her, though it was only the colored lights flickering up and down the Eiffel Tower and the yellow glow from within the glass dome of the Grand Palais.

Still, Bea poured her glass of champagne with shaky hands, eyeing the long drop to the street below as Mel stood ready with more powder and Nadi checked all the tech.

"Okay, the post is tagged and we're ready for a test run," Nadi sad. "I'm filming the actual fashion shoot video with the real camera for later editing, but do you want to go selfie-style for the live feed and hold the phone yourself? Or do you want Mel to point it at you?"

"It's more personal to the viewers if you go selfie," Mel said.

Bea waved the phone over, her champagne flute in the other hand as she found what seemed like a safe spot to stand.

"You need to get back further." Nadi pointed to the railing.

Yeah… not so much. She'd prefer to avoid handing herself over to fate on a silver platter.

Still, this job was too important, and Bea stepped to the edge, plastering on sophistication to cover her fear.

Nadi went up on tiptoe, then squatted down, checking the viewing angles. "Can you get a little higher? I don't think you'll get everything in from your spot."

Bea held the phone on the selfie-stick at the perfect height and checked. "I can see the Eiffel Tower and the Grand Palais, but not the Obelisk in the square below. Does that matter?"

"It does if you want to make an 'off with their heads' joke."

She so did not.

"Can you believe people stood on this very balcony during the French Revolution and watched while people were decapitated? Ugh." Nadi gave a little shake of disgust.

Mel pulled a chair to the railing "for a better camera angle," so Bea did as she was told, juggling the phone, the champagne, and balancing on her stilettos as she climbed onto the chair.

The bells rang out the half-hour. Thirty minutes until midnight.

"I can't do it." She scrambled back down. "That's how it'll happen. That's how I'm going to die."

God, what the hell had she been thinking taking this gig? The last nine years of birthdays had been spent firmly planted at home—on her couch—preferably surrounded by a stack of fluffy, protective pillows. Yet here she was, in a foreign country, on a balcony seven floors up, considering standing on a chair *in stilettos*. This was way too far in the wrong direction of being safe.

Even though their eyes had gone wide at her outburst, Mel and Nadi knew the deal. They'd been through years of birthdays with her.

Nadi shook her head, her shoulders dropping. "Listen to me, you are *not* going to die. Just because your twin died on your birthday doesn't mean you will. It's just superstition. Magical thinking."

Bea nodded, wiping away tears… but Nadi was *wrong*. How could the universe allow one twin to continue without the other? It wasn't right. They were… she was… broken in half.

Nadi put a hand on Bea's shoulder. "I miss him too, you know." The sheen in her eyes proved that. "We don't need the chair shot; you look amazing no matter what and I'd rather you appear happy than… tormented."

After a beat, Mel lifted a finger. "Um, I'm sorry, but it's a quarter to twelve and your followers are messaging to ask when we go live."

Taking a deep breath, Bea thanked Nadi and let Mel fix her tear-streaked makeup.

"You got this, girl," Nadi said. "Forget everything else and focus on the celebration. It's your big day. You've worked hard to earn this moment. And your seven-hundred-thousand followers want to toast it with you. Enjoy it."

Her birthday was practically in the bag anyway. Only fifteen minutes left. And Nadi was right, it *was* an amazing moment in her life.

Relief was already washing over her as they turned on the video lights, ready to start the real broadcast. She took her place against the rail with her feet firmly on the ground, and summoned up her professionalism, planting on a broad smile as they went live.

"*Bonjour de Paris*. Hashtag City of Lights. And happy birthday to me!" She paused and took a breath. "But not only to me. Happy birthday to my brother Dante, too. He's… he's no longer with us, and most of you didn't know him, but everything you think you love about me is just a pale reflection of him. He was… the best." She lifted the glass, allowing the lump in her throat to pass. "Here's to us both."

She and her friends—and presumably her thousands of viewers—finally took that sip just as the bells throughout Paris began their midnight song, calling to each other across the city, announcing that, at last, she was safe. *Success*, she thought as comments of love and little red hearts poured into the feed. *I did it.*

"The coast is clear, ladies. Phew!" Bea said as she dragged the previously discarded chair back to the edge. "Nadi, let's get those shots you wanted before so I can pan down and get the Obelisk below. And I need more champagne."

Climbing onto the chair, she proceeded with the balancing act of phone and high heels, not worrying in the least as Nadi snapped more content for posting once they were home in Boston. "I made it one more year," she said, lifting her chin to watch the glittering canopy of stars above.

Mel cleared her throat. "I mean, if you want to get technical, not quite yet."

"Huh?" Bea murmured, only half paying attention as a particularly bright star shot across the indigo sky.

"You were born in Boston, right, not Paris. Your birthday won't actually be over for another six hours, so—"

"Mel!" Nadi shouted. "Shut up!"

"What?" Bea almost fell off the seat as she twisted around.

"Don't worry!" Mel raised her voice as Bea panicked. "We'll tuck you safely into bed right now, and you'll be fi—"

"Get me down!" Adrenaline ripped through Bea's veins as she scrambled to climb off, tipping the chair backward in the process.

7

The champagne flute crashed to ground.

The phone flew from her hand, past her head.

Her hands grasped at nothing but air as she tumbled over the rail into the night.

Someone above her shrieked, and the lights on the Eiffel were a blur as she plummeted toward the flagstones below.

Chapter 2

BEYOND PARIS

Her eyelids fluttered open, only to be hit by a blinding interrogation light.

"Ouch." Her hands flew to cover her face from the painful beam until she acclimated, discovering, not a spotlight, but a glaring hot sky straight above as she lay on her back.

Bea pushed up on her palms, hot dusty stone beneath her fingers, legs stretched out before her on the hard surface, and looked around. She occupied the center of a raised marble platform, a square maybe thirty feet on each side and circled in crumbling pillars. The air was sweltering—like a Las Vegas summer. At midday. During a heat wave. It had to be a hundred and twenty degrees or more. She blinked up at the sky once more. There were no clouds, no blue background, just a sheet of white, all color and texture baked away under the scorching sun.

Standing up, she spun in a circle. "You've got to be kidding me," she said as she eyed the stone steps leading down from the ancient monument to the dry landscape below. Somehow, somebody had transported her unconscious ass to freaking Greece.

Bea did a thorough scan of her body, cleared her throat, tested her voice. Everything seemed in working order— everything except her memory. The last thing she recalled was...

Damn, it must've been a good time whatever it was. Had she passed out at some European summer festival? There were no signs of a celebration. No trash, no leftovers, no other soul in the place with her.

She patted the pockets of the unfamiliar jeans she found herself wearing—no phone. No purse lying around either. Was this some kind of practical joke? Come to think of it, the whole thing was beginning to smell a lot like the publicity-grabbing shenanigans of Nadi and Mel. Though... if they were the orchestrators of whatever this was, they'd seriously leveled up their game—but she was fast losing patience for it.

"Nadi? You guys watching on closed-circuit or something?" She scanned the upper corners of the marble pillars but saw no cameras. "Because, if so, hashtag spoiler alert, I'm over it."

Mel and Nadi... something about them... a champagne flute... a crimson gown...

Bea rubbed her temples, wondering if someone had slipped a drug in her drink. Pressing a hand between her legs, she checked, but felt no soreness or bruising. In fact, nothing on her body showed signs of abuse or even use. Had her boyfriend Angel been with her at whatever this was? It was true they'd been fighting recently, their relationship strained, but he never would've left a party without her and he certainly would've worried had she gone missing.

Moving to the edge of the platform, Bea stopped before descending the cracked and broken steps. She'd been to Greece before, seen all the famous historical spots—the Acropolis, the Parthenon—and spent one glorious week in a villa overlooking the turquoise waters of Santorini, but this little corner of the isles must have been voted least worthy of restoration. It was an ancient shithole.

Ruins in various states of dilapidation were scattered near and far, buildings that had once been temples, amphitheaters, homes, or markets, all either bleached or blackened under the twin terrors of time and heat. They weren't necessarily any less beautiful in their own way than the more famous structures; it was the landscape, really, that changed the whole region into the vacation spot from Hell.

Rocky, barren foothills rose up over gentler slopes that flattened and lead out to what seemed to be a river, but not a single spot of color decorated the earth. No grass, no flowers, no trees except the white skeletal remains of them.

"Abandon all hope, ye who enter here," she mumbled, chewing on a fingernail as she considered what to do next. Wait for someone to show up with answers or go off in search of rescue? She closed her eyes, took a deep breath…

And suddenly was no longer alone.

No footsteps announced the stranger's arrival. Maybe it was a subtle shift in atmosphere, or the slight scent of powder that wafted by that alerted her to the change. There hadn't even been movement in the air, but a woman now stood at Bea's side no more than two feet away.

Bea checked out her new companion. Around the same age as her, with strawberry blonde hair pulled into a careless ponytail, the woman ignored her and studied the shoes on her feet. She wore the same off-brand sneakers Bea had somehow ended up in and was rotating her feet at the ankles. First one way, then the other.

"It's different every time." She spoke without acknowledging Bea, still studying her footwear.

"Excuse me?"

The woman finally looked to her, and Bea stifled a gasp. A few loose strands of hair had broken free from the pony and

11

fell in natural ringlets around her oval face. Pale skin met soft blue eyes and perfect petal pink lips. She radiated both youthful innocence and knowledge of great pain, the whole effect rendering her face a work of art—but those winter blue eyes turned a tight focus on Bea, washing over her from bottom to top like a pair of spotlights illuminating Bea's every flaw. First skin-deep, then soul-deep.

Bea squirmed under the scrutiny, feeling self-conscious as she imagined herself to be as ill-fitting as the unfamiliar garments she had woken up wearing.

Upon finishing her examination, the woman blinked then returned to studying her own feet again, as if the moment of intensity had never happened. "The clothing. It's different with each one."

Bea shook her head. Every minute in this place only brought more mystery. "Each one what?"

Instead of responding, the stranger began a series of high knee marches in place, followed by some deep squats.

Bea giggled—not from humor, more like growing insanity. Was she being punked? Was some reality show producer about to show up and let her off the hook?

The woman finished her calisthenics with a nod, then ran her palms along her jeans—the same generic ones Bea was wearing. As were the plain white t-shirt and shoes. "These will be good. Comfortable. Durable."

Definitely had to be hidden cameras around here somewhere.

Bea stood a little straighter, tucked a strand of hair behind one ear, and offered a smile to the person who was currently her only potential resource. "Hey, so, I know this will sound crazy, but do you know where we are? I'm not even sure how I got—"

"I will explain on the way." The woman reached a hand toward Bea, maybe to shake it, maybe to pull her along. "We should go now."

Bea glanced around once more for the arrival of a familiar face, but finding none, took the stranger's hand and shook it. "I'm Beatrice. Bea."

The woman took her hand back, polite, but verging on imperious. "I know." She started toward the steps, then stopped. "Antonia. I'm Antonia."

The woman had a slight accent—European, but greatly diluted either through time or practice. "I have a cousin named Antonia. I always thought it was gorgeous and so romantic sounding. She goes by Toni, though."

Antonia raised an eyebrow. "Toni." She emphasized the hard vowel sound of the "I". "Sounds like a man's name," she said, and then giggled, showing adorable dimples and gorgeous straight teeth. "Yes. Call me that," she said and began leading their descent from the high ruin.

They stepped off the last stair onto flat ground. It crunched under their feet; dried and cracked under the blazing sun, with potholes and crags oozing yellowish stagnant puddles. Bea covered her mouth and nose—the putrid smell of sulfur permeated the air once they'd stepped down from the higher point.

They weren't alone in this Grecian hellscape. Hundreds of people wandered around. Most appeared to be making their way to the distant body of water she'd seen from the steps... but to what purpose? She held out zero hope she'd find any beachside cafes serving up hummus plates and bottled water.

Water. Why wasn't she thirsty? She couldn't remember the last time she'd had anything to drink, but it had to have been at least half a day. Combined with probable dehydration if she'd indeed been drinking the night before, she should be begging for liquid in this heat.

Bea stopped walking. The thirst issue had just become the most important question she'd ever needed answered. Her skin began to prickle as an inner voice screamed that, somehow, everything that was going on hinged on the answer to this. She knew it without a single doubt.

"Antonia." By now, her companion was a good twenty feet ahead of her. "Antonia!"

The woman turned and strolled—*strolled*—back to Bea. "I much prefer Toni now, I think."

For fuck's sake.

"Tell me what's going on. Where are we? You'd said you'd explain."

"Later. We must make haste."

These brush-off answers had become infuriating, so Bea held her ground. "No, now. I need to make a call. I have no phone."

Toni sized her up again before answering, her nose wrinkling as if at something distasteful. (And perhaps that was fair. It's possible Bea might've stomped a foot to punctuate her complaint.) Finally, Toni cast a significant glance towards Bea's jeans pocket.

"Huh?" Bea looked down, slipped her hand into it then pulled out a phone—an old Moto Razr. "Legit retro, but okay." She flipped it open. No bars, and as she held it up higher, taking a few steps to try and catch a signal, the battery died.

She glared at Toni. "Really?"

Toni shrugged, the ghost of a smirk crossing her lips.

"Enough." Bea tossed the phone and stepped right up into her de facto partner's face. "I want real answers and I want them now. I assume you have them."

Toni's shoulders relaxed, and she nodded, the smirk gone. "Of course."

Bea huffed and opened her arms wide. "Well?"

"First, you must remember where you were before you arrived here. Until you accept what happened, you cannot move forward."

"I've been trying to remember since I woke up back

there." She flung an arm in the general direction of the ancient edifice.

Toni offered a sympathetic half-smile. "No, you've not really tried. Part of you is too afraid. I believe you had some glimpses earlier. You were thinking about your friends at one point, but you dismissed the thoughts."

Bea reviewed her thought process since she'd woken up on the stone platform, not bothering to consider first how Toni could possibly have known what she'd been thinking. "My friends. You mean Melanie and Nadiyah?"

Toni nodded.

"I remember having some fleeting random images." Looking off into the distance, she crossed her arms, rubbing them as if she were chilled even in the scorching heat. "Champagne, and a red designer gown. Gift-wrapped packages, I think. In a beautiful room."

"*Oui.*"

"*Oui,*" Bea whispered back. Then her head snapped up, locking eyes with her companion. "Paris. Oh my God."

"Yes."

Now she really *did* have a chill. She began to pace. "I was in Paris for my thirtieth birthday. We were shooting live, toasting my brother. I'd survived the day and was relieved but then…"

"Yes."

"I..." She grabbed Toni by the upper arms.

Toni stiffened but remained in place.

"I fell."

Toni tilted her head, waiting for more.

"I… died?"

Eyes soft with sympathy, Toni nodded.

"But… but… but that can't be." Bea stepped away, her apparently dead heart nevertheless beating at a frantic pace. "If it's true, what is this place? It makes no sense."

As tears fell, their saline competing with the sulfuric air for the greater sting to her eyes, Toni took Bea's hand and led her to a giant marble head, long separated from its body and lying on its side, one ear eternally listening to the dry, salt-encrusted ground. They took a seat on what was left of the neck.

Bea fought for a rationalization. She now remembered the fall, but she couldn't know for certain she'd died. There was no memory of an actual moment where her life had ended. Maybe she'd landed on an awning and had slid gently to the ground. Perhaps she'd broken every bone in her body but was in a coma in a Parisian hospital, her parents and Angel freaking out at her bedside.

"If I'm really dead, shouldn't there be a bright light and a tunnel? What about all the relatives who are supposed to line up and greet me? My brother?" She searched Toni's face for agreement but found only concern. "Or nothingness. When Dante died, I kept waiting for a sign that he was still around and trying to make contact. I mean, if anyone can communicate from the other side, it would be twins, right? But when nothing ever came, I figured that when we're gone, we're gone. Poof."

"And that's exactly where you might have been headed. 'Poof,' as you say." Toni popped open the fingers of both hands, imitating a dandelion bursting into the wind. "Some people are simply sent back into the ether. Many are sent elsewhere. But, perhaps, you desired to wake up because it seems you've been granted the opportunity."

"The opportunity for what exactly? To not die?"

"To wake up."

Bea blinked once or twice, examining the way Toni's eyes fluctuated between expressions of strength and weariness, hope and despair, as if she were at the same time youthful and ancient, the way she seemed to constantly take Bea's measure. The need this sparked in Bea to be found worthy. "Are you some kind of angel?"

Toni's response was a snort. "I don't know many who would think so." She slid down the statuary and dusted off her butt. "Let's keep walking. The air feels less stifling when we're moving."

By now, Bea knew the conversation had been closed to further discussion. And since the marble head wasn't talking either, she hopped off and followed.

Side-by-side they walked on, moving like lemmings with the rest of the flow of people going in the same direction. Though she felt no hunger or thirst and no calls of nature, she wasn't numb to her surroundings. Her feet grew hot in her shoes, and if she stepped wrong on the uneven surface, her ankle throbbed in response. She wasn't thirsty but was sweating buckets under the broiling sun.

But the lack of bodily necessities was an inconvenient factoid she'd have to find a way to explain. Maybe she was in shock, for example, and eventually her physical needs would kick in. Because, although for the past nine years she'd been convinced she'd one day die on her birthday, now that she was standing in this godforsaken place, everything inside her screamed... *this can't be right*. And while she *could* accept the fact that she'd fallen from the Paris balcony, she was miles from believing she'd actually died and was now hiking through some kind of anti-Elysian Fields.

Bea considered two possible explanations.

One: She was indeed in a coma, and this was all one big dream. But assuming a coma dream was even remotely like a regular dream, her current experience was nothing like that. From the moment she'd woken on the marble platform, she'd been living a chronologically seamless day. No random, illogical jump cuts. No places or people morphing from one thing to another. And she experienced everything in far too much detail, from the sunburn forming on her shoulders to the swarm of gnats that had begun buzzing past her ears.

Two: She hadn't actually fallen the full seven stories and had merely landed on a ledge just below her balcony, knocking herself out. Was it possible she was simply suffering from a broad case of amnesia? If so, maybe she'd booked adventure travel plans as a birthday gift for herself and just couldn't remember. Or maybe Nadi had coaxed her into being on an outrageous, attention-seeking reality show. Something along the lines of *Survivor*. Or, god forbid, *Naked and Afraid*. That would explain the mystery, the lack of luggage, and the grueling environment.

But how had she gotten from Paris to Greece? She'd heard of people with brain damage going hours or days in a fugue state—a sort of walking blackout where they functioned and appeared normal to everyone around them but were totally vacant throughout with no memory of events when they finally snapped out of it. If she had taken a bad fall, the concussion could be all the explanation she needed. And a good old conk on the head with a devilish case of amnesia was a whole lot easier to swallow than discovering that she was, in fact, dead, and her eternity was going to be about traipsing aimlessly through a surrealistic Greco-Roman hellscape with a stranger.

That had to be it; she'd been walking around in a fugue state since Paris—however long ago that had been. God, she hoped she hadn't made a mess of things while living like a zombie. What had she said to her parents during that time? To Mel and Nadi? To Angel—oh crap. Their relationship had already been on shaky ground before Paris. Thank goodness she'd finally woken up here and…

Woken up.

Familiar words. Toni was a piece of the puzzle she couldn't quite place anywhere in her premise. But for now, she'd do what her scientist brother Dante would have recommended—make a hypothesis and set about testing it. She'd operate under the concussion-with-amnesia theory while gathering information and watching for an opportunity to make a phone call and get some answers.

What choice did she have really? Because she was currently in the middle of god-awful nowhere with no resources but the unfamiliar clothes on her back and one odd—but somewhat sympathetic—companion.

Their hike had now brought them within a hundred feet of the river where the mass of people was all funneling toward one point on the bank.

"Are we supposed to be joining this parade?" Bea asked as she merged with the crowd. Most plodded along by themselves. A few walked in pairs or small groups. One couple held hands and spoke quietly. All wore non-descript clothing.

"We are if you want to get out of here," Toni said. "Forward is the only way down."

Forward is the only way *down?*

Bea rolled her eyes behind Toni's back, thinking again about the possibility of a reality show, and wondering if Toni's cryptic words and unusual behavior might, in fact, be scripted. Maybe figuring out puzzles like "forward is the only way down," was part of the challenge. Whatever Bea had signed on for prior to her Parisian disaster, it was bound to be twice as difficult if she couldn't get her memories back.

As they joined the funnel of people, the density of bodies increased along with the density of the gnats, which were bigger and bite-ier near the water's edge. She swatted a nasty one off her shoulder. "Where exactly are we headed? What's up there where everyone's converging?" In truth, she had a thousand more questions than that, but had come to understand that Toni served up answers in only the most meager of rations, and, worse, if they *were* being filmed on hidden cameras for some reality show, Bea had no desire to come across as the biggest fool on the team and, therefore, most likely to be voted off the island first. So she held her tongue.

"A ship, which will take us down the Acheron."

The Acheron. It sounded familiar. Something from her classical studies at university—probably mentioned in *The Iliad* or *The Odyssey*. As long as it wasn't the River Styx, she was okay with it.

She bit back a snort.

As they got closer to the banks, there were vendors lining the path, set up in little booths on piles of rock or crumbled structures. Most sported signs, painted with something disturbingly red, on ripped cloth hung from dried-up tree trunks and branches. And they weren't selling grape leaves or spanakopita. All the vendors displayed the same offering: silver coins about the size of a half-dollar.

One of the salesmen locked eyes with her and shouted. "You there! Come here!"

Okay, so the dude was a bit obnoxious, but maybe she'd get some answers from him. She pulled Toni out of the queue and led her over.

Wearing beige cargo shorts and a woman's pink t-shirt several sizes too small for his massive gut, the man slapped at the bugs torturing his neck and legs. Sweat dripped from his puffy cheeks as he pasted on a grimy smile.

He swatted a gnat on his neck. "Get your tokens here!" he shouted, though she stood right in front of him. The coins he referred to were spread on the ground before him. "They're mandatory to board the ship." He slapped at something on his shin.

Toni brushed away a gigantic horsefly on her own cheek. "Beatrice, we must go."

"But don't we need a couple of these," *slap*, "coins for the boat?" The nasty insects were getting larger and meaner by the minute.

The man glared at Toni. "I'll make you a fair trade. I'm the cheapest of all the sellers here." He swatted a huge iridescent, winged monster off his protruding belly, and Bea noticed the sweat stains around his crotch, at his armpits. She noticed his stink. "I'll take those new shoes you're wearing," he added.

A tall pile of items he'd taken in trade teetered behind him. Shoes, shirts, Moto Razrs.

"We don't need the tokens. Trust me." Toni lifted her lip in a sneer. "The man is an opportunist. Nothing more. Convincing you of a need you do not actually have."

The man stood. "I understand if you don't want to part with your shoes. Just spare me a little bit of paint, if you will. Two tokens for just a thimble of paint. To touch up my sign. You'll never get a better offer than that." *Smack. Slap.*

"Paint? But I don't have any..." Bea glanced up at the vendor sign above his wares, the once wet red paint now dried to a dark copper color. *Copper.* The metallic scent of blood drifted down from the frayed fabric. "Oh. No." Even though she couldn't remember when she'd last eaten, her stomach heaved.

"Come." Toni tugged harder on her arm. "I promise, you do not need what he is selling."

The two women moved back into line, the vendor still slapping at horseflies as they turned their backs. A definite queue had formed, and the press of bodies tightened as they came within twenty feet of their goal.

Bea rose on tiptoe to get a better look. *What the fuck?*

Not a ship at all—the people at the front were boarding a rickety, weather-beaten, ancient-looking Greek fishing boat. No more than ten feet long, it was captained by an equally ancient man who stood at the bow, his long gray beard nearly reaching his toes. With a pole for guiding the boat in one hand, he collected the passengers' tokens with the other, watching them step onto the wobbling craft with a look of utter disdain.

"*That's* the boat we're getting on?" Bea dropped back

onto her heels and continued to inch along. "Jesus, it can't hold more than twenty people or so. If he's got to shuttle each group across and then come back for more each time, we're going to be here a week."

And that was *if* the questionable craft didn't capsize or sink before they got on.

But they kept moving forward, and forward, the crowd before them thinning though the boat never left the dock. Like a reverse clown-car, the more people boarded, the more room there seemed to be. There was no plausible way she could think of to fit the scene playing out before her into the amnesia hypothesis, and sudden fear stopped her feet from moving just as it was their turn to board. People bumped into her from behind as she held up the line.

The river rushed past them with white foamy tips across a rocky bed. Threatening boulders jutted from the depths. Across the way, cliffs rose sharply, the opposite banks shrouded in darkness, the searing sky burning bright only on her side of the river.

Her limbs trembled as the captain thrust his upturned palm at her, glaring with eyes so bloodshot they appeared demonic.

She looked to Toni. "We never got tokens."

Her companion pointed again at her jeans pocket, and this time Bea pulled out a round metal disk. She stared at the shiny object in her hand until somebody shoved her forward.

"Come." Toni stepped up first, calm and collected as can be, onto the tippy boat, then held out her hand for Bea.

Bea chewed her bottom lip, one hand holding the token and the other pulling a tick off her forehead. At least maybe she'd get some relief from the bugs while she was on the water.

Numb from brain to bone, she handed her coin to the ferryman and boarded the impossible boat.

Chapter 3

BOSTON

23 Years Ago

Bea poked at the remains of her strawberry birthday cake. Dante's chocolate cake—and Dante himself—mirrored her from across the table.

They'd turned seven years old today, but the party was now over, their friends dragged home by their parents. An army of balloons still tickled the dining room ceiling. Bright paper plates, half painted in frosting, littered every surface next to crunched up paper napkins and plastic cups filled with the remains of orange punch.

She swung her feet under the table. The brand-new rollerblades she'd just received as a gift from Aunt Stacy were heavy but fit perfectly, and she was anxious to get outside and give them a spin. Turning sideways in her chair, she stretched out her legs for a better look at them, admiring the hot pink wheels and matching long laces. Dante's pair had bright orange wheels with silver flecks. His were super cool, too, but he'd tossed them into a pile of other gifts.

"Dante, come on," she whined, willing him to look up at

her, but his eyes were glued to the chemistry set their parents had bought him. "Let's go outside and skate."

"Not right now," he mumbled, pulling off the cellophane wrapper and reading the side of the box.

It was hopeless. Her brother had probably reached his limit on being around people and wanted to be left alone in his room with that stupid science-y thing. Sure, he had fun with their friends when he wanted to, but it soon drained him every time, and he always had to go hide away for a while after.

Bea didn't get it. Being around people *gave* her energy.

"Go next door and ask Ronna to go with you," he said. "She has skates."

"Dante, go with your sister," their mom said, shoes clacking on tile as she rounded the corner into the dining room. "You could both do with some exercise right now to burn off all that sugar you ate, or you'll keep your dad and I up all night. Besides," she said as she dumped a fistful of party trash into the big plastic bag she carried, "you know our motto."

"Keep an eye on each other," they both drawled as they watched her return to the kitchen.

After a silent moment, Bea rose from the chair, her arms circling and wheels skidding before she finally got her balance, clutching the back of her chair for stability. "You can teach me how to skate backwards," she pleaded, offering him her best smile.

He snorted. "First, you have to learn to skate forward, dork."

She laughed along with him. Because yeah, she wasn't entirely sure how she even planned to get down the front steps without landing on her butt.

In the kitchen, Mom and Aunt Stacy jabbered on while they did the dishes.

"The twins seemed to have had a good time today, don't you think?" Aunt Stacy asked, her voice rising to be heard over clinking trays and running water in the sink.

The faucet switched off and Mom overshot her volume at first. "I think so. Their birthday is always a big hit with their friends. Twice the cake, I suppose."

"Twice the friends, too, right? Twice the partygoers for you to host?"

"Not really," Mom said over the sound of foil ripping. "So far, they've always been a package deal. Their personalities complement each other so well. Dante tells such interesting stories, and he's amazing at games and building forts or whatever the kids get in their heads to create. Bea, of course, is the life of the party and children just seem to flock to her. Between the two of them, they each bring something to the table."

"They're lucky in that regard," said Aunt Stacy. "They're stronger together. Like two halves of a superhero."

Dante's head snapped up at that, his intense gaze tightening on Bea with the same expression he wore when trying to figure out a math problem for school. And she studied him back, a giggle forming as she imagined them in bright matching costumes, a big letter A for Allegra on their chests. Ready to save the world and each other. *Heck yeah!*

A warm sensation of strength and safety filled her heart at the notion.

Her brother was still watching her, his brow creased in thought as she shuffled her way over to his skates like some newborn giraffe struggling to control her legs. She plucked them from the gift pile, and by the time she awkwardly made her way back to the table, he was full-on beaming at her.

"*Two halves of a superhero.*" He formed the words silently, and when she handed him his rollerblades, he grabbed them right up, excitement shining in his eyes. He returned her giant grin. "Let's go skate."

Bea waited as he laced up, and the giggle finally burst from her mouth, because wobbly as she was (standing on wheels), she'd somehow just become utterly… balanced.

Chapter 4

THE FIRST CIRCLE
The Ranch

The mysterious boat pulled to port on the opposite shore, where a wooden dock gave way to a dirt path leading away from the river.

Bea shook her head to clear the mental cobwebs that had formed during their crossing. "How long were we on the water? I'm already forgetting the journey." In fact she was left with only a foggy impression of it in her mind. She glanced back, but the ferry was gone.

"Time and space move differently here," Toni said. "The sooner you get comfortable with that, the better."

Bea rolled her eyes. Dante might've been able to make some kind of sense out of that, but she certainly couldn't.

The ominous skies that had hung over the river now cleared above them, though far ahead in the distance, dark thunderheads boiled against a greenish background. Tornado weather.

Toni and Bea walked side-by-side as their fellow passengers fanned out before and after them, some trotting quickly down the road and others lagging behind. Unlike the bug-infested, salt-encrusted start of her journey, the landscape here was pleasant. Wild and open, the rolling foothills were dusted with fragrant sagebrush, golden wildflowers, and graceful windswept cypress trees. Gone were the marble ruins and ramshackle vendor booths. A few rustic fences were the only sign of civilization.

"Where are we going?" Bea asked.

As they crested a small rise, Toni pointed at the gates of a ranch straight ahead. "Here."

It was the first signs of humanity since disembarking. Yet the other travelers ignored the ranch entrance entirely, continuing their journey on the path as it veered off to the right and around a bend.

Toni motioned Bea toward the slatted-post double gate, above which hung a sign. The wood-burned engraving depicted a circle with the Roman numeral one in the center, followed by the word "ranch." Circle One Ranch.

Bea looked over her shoulder at the crowd moving off down the path. "Why isn't anyone else stopping here?"

Toni followed her gaze with indifference and the usual cryptic response. "Some will be sent back."

As they started to enter, a man slid between them and the gate. He appeared so suddenly, they both jumped back, Toni flattening her palm against her chest with a gasp. Bea couldn't imagine how they'd missed him before. Long, lanky, and sun-darkened, he had to be a good six-foot-four inches tall. Youngish, but too surly to be good-looking, he leaned against the fencepost wearing jeans, a leather vest over a tie-dyed t-shirt with a peace sign in the center, and faded red cowboy boots with matching hat. He held a joint in one hand, the pungent, white smoke tendrils curling in front of his face.

He tipped the brim of his crimson Stetson. "Ladies." Then he jerked a thumb over his shoulder. "You'll need to mosey along now with the rest of your group. 'Fraid I can't let you in without the proper paperwork. You can obtain that down yonder." He pulled a long drag on the joint, held the lungful a moment, then exhaled slowly. "If you're very lucky."

Mosey? Yonder? This guy was right out of central casting. Except—she scanned his outfit again—not quite. He was slightly off... like a few other things. The sky that was a little too strikingly blue, or the white, fluffy clouds that were a little too... cottony.

When she'd gone for her first ride on *The Pirates of the Caribbean* at Disneyland as a schoolgirl, one of the tableaus had had a pirate sitting on top of a mound of gold coins. At the time, she'd been amazed, wondering why no one was jumping out of their slow-moving boat to grab handfuls of the treasure. Years later, she'd returned as a high school student, and her matured eyes clearly noted the coins to be no more than gold-colored foil wrapped over round disks. The loss of her fantasy had left a cold disappointment, and a little bit of anger in her chest.

She squinted up at the too-fuzzy clouds hanging static in the too-perfect sky, and an even colder spot formed at the base of her spine.

"We're only here for a visit." Toni slipped into her regal persona, somehow managing to look down her nose at the man who towered a foot over her. She flashed him an ID card of some sort. "You will let us enter, please."

The stoned cowboy studied the card, then studied Toni from top to bottom before handing it back with a grunt. "You're not what I would've expected. But it checks out."

Bea craned to get a glimpse of the card, but it was gone as quickly as it had appeared.

The man pressed open the gate with the back of his forearm and stepped aside, and Bea had the strangest sensation of his eyes burning actual holes in the back of her neck as she walked away from him. She reached one arm behind herself to swipe at what she could almost swear were embers dusting her shoulder blades, though she found nothing there. As she twisted around, however, she caught him staring and paused in her step.

His lips pulled back in what might have been a smile… if the smile were on a hyena.

He winked, and a bout of nausea rolled through her gut. She spun and trotted to catch up to her guide.

"Toni, that man. There was something about him—"

"Do not trouble yourself about it. He is of no use to us."

They passed a thick stand of oaks and a wide encampment came into view. Rings of tents, yurts, and log cabins circled a public space where artists worked, musicians played, and people practiced yoga. Dotting the hills above were idyllic, whitewashed country churches, open air rows of benches surrounded by prayer flags, a synagogue, and a colorful mosque.

"What is this place?" Bea asked as they wandered deeper into the ranch. They passed a circle of small campers with tiny Christmas lights strung between them. A stack of logs ready to be lit for a fire sat in the middle. Further down the path was a long wooden lodge, the scent of patchouli wafting out the large open windows. She walked a little closer and peered in, stopping briefly to watch the rows of people sitting cross-legged in meditation and humming a mantra.

"Before you ask, no, there are no phones here," Toni said, pre-empting Bea's next thought.

"I get it, I get it. Everyone's off the grid in this camp." She made air quotes with her fingers. "Hashtag unplugged."

Bea watched the chanting a moment longer before hustling to follow Toni, who was already moving further down the path into the ranch. "It's lovely and peaceful, but why are we here if we're not staying?"

"It's a good first stop for you," said Toni. "You might find some information that could be of use on your journey."

"My journey?"

"You must be careful who you seek out for assistance, though. The souls here are kind. They're all seekers and have some hint of the human condition, but they understand only bits and pieces of the spiritual practices they believe will guide them to truth. They all strive for enlightenment, but their information is incomplete, the teachings broken and misinterpreted over time." Toni pointed Bea toward an older woman sitting behind a card table in front of a vintage silver Airstream. "This woman here knows a bit more than most, I think."

With clear blue eyes and a head wrapped in a colorful scarf, the older woman shuffled a deck of tarot cards as they approached, her outfit a dark and dour Victorian frock buttoned to her neck. She nodded at Toni while motioning for them both to take the chairs opposite. "Madame, I see you have a new charge," she said in a thick Russian accent.

Toni flashed a thin smile. "This is Beatrice Allegra."

The Russian reached for Bea's hand and held it a little too long and a lot too firmly, then flipped it over and examined her palm, continuing to hold it even after locking eyes once more. "I am Elena Borovsky." She finally released her iron grip on Bea's hand, but not before giving it a gentle pat. "You will have some work to do before it's done. But I believe you are capable."

Bea pulled her hand back with a grunt. More mystery. She glanced behind the woman through the open door of the Airstream, searching for any sign of whether this was all a real destination or part of a production set.

"You've explained to her?" Elena asked Toni.

"Some of it."

Bea pulled her attention back to the conversation, eyes darting between the two women.

"But she does not yet believe even that much," the older woman said.

Toni shrugged. "It always takes time. She'll come around." She looked to Bea, her blonde brows drawing together as she began her usual scrutiny. "Soon, I hope."

The temperature was mild in this region, but Bea didn't

enjoy it, unable to shake the feeling that everything in the ranch was fake, as if they were on a soundstage. Soft sunlight lit the landscape, but she couldn't find the source, and the same clouds she'd noticed a half-hour ago remained glued in place.

And she still wasn't thirsty.

Evidence to support her hypothesis grew thinner—and her hands clammier in direct proportion.

Elena Borovsky rapped on the table. "Here now, would you like some tea? I know you're not thirsty, but you can drink, and the herbs will calm you."

She poured a fragrant blend in a delicate porcelain teacup and slid it to Bea, who wrapped her hands around it. She brought it to her lips, but it was like she'd forgotten how to drink, and, strangely, didn't care. The warmth of the cup and the herbal scent were indeed calming, though, and she continued to hold it in front of her.

Breathing in the steam, the conversation of the other women faded out as she studied a colorful chart propped on an easel behind the old woman. She recognized the depiction of the chakra system—the outline of the human body, with seven energy center points, each depicted in its own associated color, from the base of the spine to the crown of the head. Bea had played with meditating on the chakras once, imagined "clearing" each potentially blocked point from the root chakra at the tailbone, through the sacral or sex chakra, then the solar plexus, heart, throat, third eye, and, finally, the crown chakra. It had been relaxing and focusing. Whether or not she actually accomplished anything... who the hell knew?

This chart had an odd addition to it, though. Across from each of the energy nodes were words referred to as "sins." But they weren't the famous *Seven Deadlies*, or anything that would have gotten her hand swatted with a ruler by the nuns when she and Dante had been made to attend Sunday church classes as children. Instead, items such as "fear," "shame," and "illusion" rose up one side of the chart. Heck, far from being sins, fear and shame were often the very take-aways she'd brought home after a few hours in catechism.

"You're curious about the diagram," Elena said, her eyes lighting with enthusiasm. "You've not seen it shown this way before."

Bea nodded.

"It's less charming than the usual romantic chakra diagrams and more like a slap in the face, yes?" Elena laughed, displaying even rows of small, tea-stained teeth.

Bea returned her attention to the chart. "I don't understand."

"You cannot achieve awakening simply by crossing your legs like a frog, breathing deeply, and fantasizing about colorful energy swirling through your body. This is a ridiculous notion. Pah! If you want to wake up," she said, patting the top of her head to indicate the crown chakra, "you will have to fight hard for it. You must confront those dark things blocking you at each level, all those distractions that pull you away from the light."

Elena Borovsky sat up straighter as she spoke, her movements becoming faster as the subject matter animated her. She pulled her stool closer to the chart, dragging her finger from bottom to top, then top to bottom. "Look here. With everything you do, every choice you make moment by moment, you are either moving up or down in consciousness. Moving up is hard work, not drum circles and sweet wine. Lucky is the person who faces their demons in life and moves up and out. Bon voyage! For the rest of us, we face them here anyway in a new form."

Elena faced back to the table, her excitement collapsing in on itself as she shoved her tarot deck aside with a sweep of her arm. "Or we continue to be afraid and sit and drink tea without biscuits, rubbing prayer beads or reading tarot cards under an unchanging sky." Her shoulders sank and she looked away.

Toni jerked her head to the side. Time to go, then.

Bea pushed back her chair and stood after Toni did the same.

"You can come with us if you want," Toni said, gentle fingers touching Elena's arm.

Elena waved her off with a swat to the air, never turning toward them while mumbling under her breath, "I'm too old. Too sca—"

"As always, the invitation stands, Madame." Toni ushered Bea away.

They took about fifteen steps before the old woman called out to them, her voice strong and loud once more. "Beatrice Allegra. You're a very pretty young woman."

Bea opened her mouth but paused, sensing something other than a compliment in the statement. "Thank—"

"That won't help you in this place," Elena said. "You must deal with your attachment to the notion right away, in fact. It is the easiest and most basic of traps."

As Bea pondered the specific use of the phrase "*this place*," they continued their tour, which shortly brought them to a complex of buildings. She recognized well the classic façade of a university campus—a smallish one in this case, more like one of the many elite liberal arts colleges dotting New England. At the center of the half-dozen porticoed brick structures rose a marble edifice, ivory in color, looming high over the other buildings in grand fashion.

Bea nearly broke into a trot. Here, she'd find sanity, a bastion of rational thinking, all the answers she needed, and undoubtedly, Wi-Fi.

Toni kept pace as they climbed a series of low, wide steps to a central quad, then onward toward the main structure. More steps led them inside a large rotunda, the domed ceiling soaring several stories above them and topped with stained glass depicting richly colored astronomical bodies floating over a deep blue background.

When Bea finally pulled her eyes away from the magnificent scene, she surveyed the lay of the land. Oak office doors lined the vast round foyer, engraved plaques denoting the occupants. Many had cards taped below their names, listing the office hours and lecture schedules of these academics.

She began to walk to the circle, examining the names on each door: I. Newton, M. Curie, C. Darwin, G. Galilei, N. Copernicus, R. Feynman, L. DaVinci, E. Schrodinger, R. Descartes, A. Rand, and N. Tesla.

When they came to Aristotle's office, she threw up her hands. "What, no Einstein?"

Toni either didn't get—or chose to ignore—her sarcasm. "No, he went straight on ahead."

"Fine. Whatever." Bea stomped off. "I'm going to find a phone even if I have to barge into one of these obviously fake offices to do so."

Three more steps and a door swung open, her toes nearly runover by a wheelchair.

"Hey!" She hopped back.

"Very. Sorry," said the computerized voice of the chair's occupant.

Bea didn't have to be a science expert to recognize this famous physicist and—

Wait. He'd died recently. So, either this was the best body double ever or...

"Pardon. Me. I. Have. A. Meeting. To. Attend."

Once he glided away, Bea turned on Toni, anger the only defense she had left against the dawning horror of the situation. "If this is real, and we're all dead, why is he still disabled? If we're no longer corporeal, he should be walking around straight as an arrow, speaking with his own vocal cords."

"He lived that way for so long, it's part of his identity now. He's unable to let go of his own self-image."

"You're saying he could if he wanted to?"

Toni sighed. "At the moment, no."

"'At the moment,' 'at the moment.' Argh." Bea shoved the heels of her palms to her temples and paced. "Toni, you're so damn—"

"Enough! It's time for you to accept your situation, Beatrice. You're not a fool and the evidence is right before you. You *do* remember falling seven flights to the ground. You watched the *Tour Eiffel* spinning during your descent." Toni stood still and calm while Bea paced, but her thickening accent gave away both its French origin and her growing frustration. "You could *not* have survived a fall from that height, and, therefore, you are not in a coma. This is neither adventure travel nor some television program. You cannot explain your lack of bodily needs, the unchanging time of day, the appearance of people long deceased, or the fact that I know your thoughts. You certainly cannot explain the ferryboat. Admit now what you know to be true."

"Why have you been speaking in riddles the whole time then? If this isn't a game, why act as if it is?"

Toni shrugged. "I told you plainly of your death back at the ruins. You weren't willing to believe. As for the other questions you've asked, some of those answers you are not ready for yet, and I cannot even *begin* to teach you until you accept the truth."

Bea stopped walking and stared at Toni. An uncontrollable tremor started in her knees and spread up through her body until her teeth chattered. She wrapped her arms around her as though she were naked in a blizzard. Acceptance was sinking in, and the facts were bitter cold.

"No, no!" She took off running. Anywhere to get away from the beautiful demanding face looking at her.

To get away from her own truth.

Toni shouted, her voice echoing in the rotunda. "Beatrice, stop acting the child!"

Bea ran across the pale marble floor of the great space to

a wide staircase opposite, then up to the second floor, not caring whether Toni followed or not.

In front of her were double doors to a lecture hall. They were open, revealing a speech in progress. A bald man in a dark monk's robe spoke at the podium, while maybe two dozen people in various wardrobes sat, listening. She caught her breath and tried to silence the blood pounding in her ears as she read the title of the lecture posted outside the door. *"An analysis concerning celestial beings, choreography, and small sewing implements. Speaker: Thomas Aquinas."*

She stared numbly at the sign, until first her body, and then her brain, finally accepted what her gut had known all along. She'd died that night in Paris, on her thirtieth birthday. On the ninth anniversary, in fact, of Dante's death.

Tick.

Tock.

Toni came up behind her and gripped her shoulder.

Bea spun to her, pissed, but relieved now that she'd ceased fighting the truth. "So this is... the Afterlife?"

Toni opened and closed her mouth a couple times, like a fish out of water, finally raising one finger. "Well—"

"Ladies." A man stepped up to them from out of the lecture hall. He was around forty, with rich, brown skin and apple cheeks bracketing a warm smile, giving him a baby-faced appearance. His somewhat rumpled suit was circa nineteen-thirties, and his thick black hair was slightly mussed. His pocket square was askew—absent-minded professor all the way.

Toni smiled and gestured for him to take over where she was struggling.

"It's *an* Afterlife, anyway," he said with an educated British accent. "I presume there are many, but from what I can tell, this seems to be the most common destination." He offered his hand. "Sanjay Patel, professor of mathematics, University of Cambridge. Well, before I died, that is. And thank you for giving me an excuse to take leave of that ridiculous exercise in f-f-futility." He nodded at the lecture hall behind him.

Bea shook his hand, offering a soft smile. Now that she was no longer denying everything, she acknowledged the thrill of meeting two of her brother's biggest idols. She wondered if Dante had also met such amazing people after his death. She began to wonder where exactly Dante was. "A pleasure to meet you. You say this is the most common destination after death. So, it's…"

His boyish face pulled into a shy grin. "Most call it by the traditional name: Hell."

Chapter 5

CAMP SUMMER DAZE
Near Boston

17 Years Ago

Spindly, little ivy plants drooping in their plastic nursery pots graced the camp infirmary's only windowsill, doing little to cheer up the place. The smell of rubbing alcohol overpowered any attempt to bring some rustic campground charm to the whitewash-over-paneling walls.

Ironically, the view from Bea's bed looked right onto the sandy volleyball court where she'd broken her ankle two hours before, her foot now elevated in a purple cast. A few of the kids were out there still, pantomiming the awkward fall, loud crack, and apparently nightmarish howl of pain she'd produced; epic stuff for thirteen-year-old boys. Had it happened to someone other than her, Dante himself would've been out there loving every minute of the gory retelling.

It seemed to Bea that thirteen was a little too old for a sleepaway camp, but her protests earlier that year had fallen on deaf ears. Dante had said their parents probably wanted some time alone so they could "do it." She'd made a gagging face at the thought, and he'd laughed. In truth, it was kind of nice to spend time in a place where not everyone knew they were twins. Some of the counselors and returning campers knew, but, as fraternal twins, most people had no idea—and that anonymity brought a certain type of freedom.

Until it'd gone to shit a few hours ago as they were picking teams for volleyball. One of the kids who knew them from school had let the cat out of the bag when he'd said they should put the twins on opposite teams so they would have to compete against each other. That had started the inevitable excitement and barrage of questions the *twin mystique* always brought: Were they psychically linked? Did they share the same best friends? Had they created their own private language?

People were boring fools. And Dante had stormed off, leaving Bea free to break her foot on whichever side of the net she preferred. She didn't blame him for that, having done her own share of sneaking away over the years for the very same reason.

Her brother's voice now echoed in the hall outside the infirmary room as he gave someone serious attitude.

"How the hell was I supposed to know what happened? I was down at the creek."

"Language, Dante." The junior counselor strode into the room behind him, her slick ponytail bouncing and her ego enjoying a small taste of power, though she had no more than a year or two on them in age. "I only figured you must've sensed it when she broke her foot. Twins are supposed to feel each other's physical pain, right?"

Stopping midway between the annoying little camper cop and Bea, Dante pretended to scratch the bridge of his nose, using his middle finger.

Bea giggled and the counselor shrugged, then walked back out.

He sat on the edge of the bed, being careful not to jostle her raised leg. "She's not wrong though. Stupid, but not completely wrong. I should have been there."

"Nah, I totally get why you needed a break. Besides, it's not like you could have done anything to prevent it. I'm a klutz, we both know that."

He twisted his lips to one side. "Dad won't think so. He'll make a big deal about my not being there when it happened."

"Well, Dad's just wrong. And it's not like I was keeping an eye on you either." A tiny flame of anger warmed her cheeks. It was one thing when they'd been little kids, but they couldn't be joined at the hip forever, even though they *were* usually aware of each other, circling together like binary stars. They'd always have each other's back, which was a gift she never wanted to lose... and never would. "You might've... I don't know... tripped over your big, fat feet and fallen into the creek and washed away all because *I* wasn't there to watch over *you*."

His eyes softened for a brief moment. Then he lifted his chest, his fleeting sweet blush becoming a snort. "Yeah, right."

"Anyway, we'll tell them you were there when it happened. We can even say it would've been worse if you hadn't caught me and slowed my fall."

"You really don't mind telling Dad that?" His posture sagged with relief, but he smiled and peered at her through floppy chestnut bangs. "'Cause it kind of makes you sound like a dork, dork."

"You're welcome." She grabbed his hand. Their fingers flowed through the intricate secret handshake they'd perfected over the years.

"Stronger together," he said, fist bumping at the crescendo of the complex maneuver.

She smiled, her world warm and safe despite her broken foot. "Two halves of a superhero."

Chapter 6

THE FIRST CIRCLE
Le Cirque

"I believe I'll join you at least part of the way, if you don't mind," Sanjay said as the three descended the wide quad stairs and began to backtrack the path Bea and Toni had taken from the camp entrance. "I must admit, I'm more than a *tad* curious to see a little of what lies ahead. I've heard rumors that Le Cirque operates quite the supercomputer."

Bea shook her head, still too amazed at finding herself strolling a scenic path in the afterlife with the likes of Sanjay Patel to wonder much at the notion this was Hell. If it was, boy, did the mythology ever have it wrong. It certainly wasn't an Eden, but neither was she catching any whiff of brimstone. Whatever the hell that smelled like.

They passed beneath the Circle One Ranch sign and back onto the main dirt path. The creepy cowboy was absent, and they turned left to continue along the road their fellow boat passengers had gone down earlier.

"Are you considering joining us, Sanjay?" Toni asked. "Of course, I do not mean simply to Le Cirque."

He glanced at her sharply, his smile falling away, then returned his gaze to the road without answering.

The sky came alive, growing darker with each step away from the ranch. Clouds roiled like snakes as wind lifted dried leaves and dust into swirling eddies. In the distance, a bolt of lightning shot to the ground, backlighting a towering thunderhead.

"I do not know when—or even *if*—you will have another opportunity," she continued.

He still didn't answer, but, instead, tugged his suit jacket tighter, mumbling to himself. "The devil you know or the d-devil you don't."

Bea pulled her hair into a loose knot to keep it from blowing in her face with the increasing warm gusts. "I don't understand—where, exactly, are we going?"

"Our plan is to go all the way down. It's the only way out," Toni said, and though she spoke with her usual unflappable tone, she hooked a stray curl and began twirling it around her finger.

"All the way *down*?" Bea asked.

Toni nodded as their path took a slight climb, raising her voice over the winds now buffeting them straight on. "Each level will present you with the opportunity to conquer those inner demons Madame Borovsky spoke of. Beyond them will be your ultimate freedom."

"Well said, Antonia." Sanjay chuckled. "Of course, you left out the bit about how, here, those inner demons become outwardly manifested."

Toni let go of the ringlet she'd been gripping and straightened her spine. "All the better to fight them off. They're much clearer targets in the so-called flesh."

"And you're my escort through this… journey." Bea smoothed the rising goosebumps on the back of her neck. "Most of the travelers I've seen here are walking alone. Why have I been granted a guide to…"

Her question faded to smoke as they crested the hill and were high enough now for a clear view of what lay ahead. She dropped her hand to her side with a thud. "Whoa."

Toni studied the foreground, her eyes narrowing as she took its measure. "I assume this is more of what you had in mind when you heard Sanjay's use of the word Hell, yes?"

Bea nodded, though neither woman moved their eyes from the scene.

"It is the start of the torments proper," Toni added.

On this side of the rise, the path took a steep slope, down to a flat dirt plain that arced off to either side, as though they were looking at one point on a vast circle. Beyond them, the plain ended at a cliff, which dropped abruptly into a thick gloom, like the edge of a volcano crater, only deeper and darker. The far side of the pit was much too distant to see, obscured even more so by a storm raging over the center of the massive hole, lightning and funnel clouds stirring whatever story lay hidden below.

Even this infernal new landscape, however, couldn't compete for attention with the sight ahead of them—an insane circus tent beneath the pea-green and gunmetal-gray sky.

"Good God," Sanjay breathed, as they picked their way down the rocky trail. "Look at that."

The hideously colored big top could easily fit two warehouses beneath it, more than capable of holding the thousands of souls who, from this height, appeared ant-like as they moved around on the hard-packed pan of dirt. Above the nightmarish black-and-purple-striped tent, Bea could make out the name of the venue. It was lit up in giant, red neon lights arching over the top. *Le Cirque du Tourment*, it read.

"The Circus of Torment." Sanjay apparently knew his French.

The hulking big top appeared menacing yet grotesquely beautiful. Bea would give anything to post a shot of it because,

43

seriously, the view was surreal. #nofilterneeded, #creepyAF, #therealnightcircus. And if she didn't document it for all to see, who would believe her? If there's no photo, it never happened. Experience was meaningless if you couldn't share it with others—preferably *thousands* of others.

She caught Toni giving her major side-eye and wondered if she'd spoken out loud.

As they watched from their hilltop view, clowns slipped out from flaps in the tent, setting up small round risers throughout the crowd, stepping onto them and beginning to perform their mimes. Sad-faced clowns swept their platforms, happy-faced clowns juggled bowling pins. Men in sparkling vests wheeled out carts offering cotton candy as tinny calliope music played from ancient speakers high on the peaks of the big top.

But the recorded music played too slowly and was off pitch, and, instead of caramel corn, the air smelled of rancid oil.

Even if she had a camera, Bea suspected she'd snap that photo and then run straight back to the relative comfort and safety of Borovsky's tea and tarot before posting the shit out of it. Fake clouds or not, the shiver factor of Circle One Ranch had nothing on this place.

"If all of this—everywhere we've been so far—is truly Hell, the ranch and college don't seem too bad by comparison," Bea said as they walked on, joining the back edges of the shuffling crowd. "A little stuck in a plastic moment maybe, but peaceful enough. Why would anyone leave it to come here?" Because she'd take creepy cowboys over creepy clowns every single day of the week.

Sanjay cleared his throat. "We have our own tortures in the First Circle, a place which you might also recognize by the name Limbo. We're without hope, you see, having failed to achieve the enlightenment—the answers to our questions of meaning and the Universe we'd sought in life. Now, unless we choose to venture forth like you, we never will. No matter how many eons we pray or debate or study, we will never achieve what we seek. This is the end of the line for us, and an eternity of regret is its own torment."

"But still, I mean..." Bea gestured toward the monstrous tent and roiling pit before them. "No offense, but, hashtag first circle problems."

"Most don't have the option in any case," said Toni. "You might recall the demon who was hesitant to allow us beyond the gate."

"Demon?" Bea shot a hand over her shoulder, jumping at the sensation of embers burning her skin once more, and, this time, her fingers connected with actual hot ashes. "Shit!" She flicked them from her neck, her heart racing as she spun around, convinced she'd find the demon cowboy staring her down, but too many bodies cut off her view.

For the first time since Sanjay's revelation of what this place was, a deep cold dread moved through her veins. In truth, she'd only now begun to fully believe.

Until this moment, she'd only allowed herself to flirt with the question that now became a growing concern—where was Dante?

"Only those officially assigned to the First Circle may enter it. Anyone who chooses to can go further into Hell to find their escape," Toni cast a meaningful glance at Sanjay, "but it is not possible to go the other direction. One cannot go higher than the circle of suffering they are initially assigned."

"Assigned?" Bea asked.

"By the ringmaster of Le Cirque." As if to punctuate her words, the calliope music wound to a whining stop, and wide panels on the big top pulled open to the sound of trumpets. "Come and see. I believe they're about to begin."

Those people up at the front rushed into the tent, leaving everyone else pushing and shoving their way forward.

As she, Toni, and Sanjay moved along, awaiting their turn

to enter, giant television monitors flickered to life above the crowd.

"Welcome, welcome, dear souls, to the one million, two-hundred-thousand, and twenty-fifth episode of Le Cirque! I am your ever-present ringmaster, your eternally eloquent emcee, your toastmaster of taunts, Master Minos." Canned applause and recorded cheers sounded from the speakers as the screens revealed the master of ceremonies strutting the center ring in red-and-black tails with gold braided accents, brass buttons stretched to within an inch of their life by his round belly. He wore a gleaming, black top hat, a waxed handlebar mustache curled at his rosy cheeks, and light glinted off his septal nose ring. Holding two lion tamer's whips, one in each hand, he cracked them repeatedly as he spoke.

"We've a big crowd to get through today, oh yes, oh yes." He giggled and spun in place, twirling the whips as he circled. "We won't leave anyone out though, we won't, we won't!"

The throngs of people still outside the tent inched their way forward, their heads cranked up to watch the monitors, their feet slowing as a collective murmur spread through the crowd, excitement giving way to trepidation. Behind them, Bea noted the clowns, though still performing their skits, had moved their pedestals closer as if herding everyone inside.

Casting a glance at Sanjay, she caught his eye. She tipped her head toward the nearest monitor as they continued their slow path forward. "The devil you don't?"

He sucked in a lungful of the air and shook his head. "I'm not sure what I expected. N-n-not this."

They were within a few yards of entering when the ringmaster dove into his task. "Keep filing in, everyone, though we've no more time to waste. We haven't, we haven't. And so we begin."

His right hand shot out like a frog's tongue grabbing a fly, his whip coiling around the body of a tall, skinny man sitting front row center on a bleacher. The long braid of leather wrapped the man like a mummy and then spun him right up next to Minos and held him there. The cameras zoomed in tight on his shocked face as the ringmaster's voice boomed from behind him. "Charles Williamson of Chicago, Illinois, Third Circle, Gluttony." His left hand shot out with the second whip, grabbing a woman from a section to the far side and pulling her cocooned body up to his chest. "Ursula Bergdahl, Stockholm, Sweden, Fifth Circle, Wrath. Oh my, oh my!"

The whips extended back out at whirlwind speed, reaching behind Minos on either side through the open flaps at the back of the tent. The cameras followed, somehow still capturing the action as the whips uncoiled and extended far beyond what was physically possible. Straightening a mile or more out over the dark abyss, one uncurled its last few feet to drop a screaming Charles Williamson into the void, the other stretching even further, another mile beyond the first, the horrified face of Ursula Bergdahl filling the monitor as she was let loose before the camera switched back to the center ring.

The small crowd remaining outside gasped, followed by a moment of silence, the tension finally cracking as an older woman beside Bea looked down at her blue cotton candy and screamed, "Cobwebs, they're cobwebs!"

Chaos split the crowd and people started running. A middle-aged man stepped on Bea's foot as he flew past, sending her sprawling into Toni.

But no one got far.

The sweet and baleful clowns on their low pedestals straightened their spines and… grew taller. Limbs and torsos cracking as they lengthened, they rose to a good six-foot-ten inches tall, the pedestals giving them another two feet over the crowd. Their jaws, ears, and eye sockets elongated to an equally exaggerated degree, their clown makeup running and flaking.

Brooms and juggling pins morphed into long stage hooks

47

as the freakishly tall clowns thrust them into the crowd, pulling the runaways back and tossing them into the tent.

Bea put a hand to her mouth, whispering into her palm. "Fuck me."

The nearest of the clowns swung his upper body around and sought her out, his gaze landing on her as his too-big mouth spread into a grin of pure lust. He ran his tongue around his red-painted lips as he waggled a finger at her. "Be careful what you wish for here." His voice was a fork scraping across a plate.

Sanjay stepped in front of her, guarding her with his body. The clown laughed but spun back around, returning his attention to the runners in the crowd, foregoing his hook to grab one woman by the hair, then throwing her toward the tent entrance.

The mass of people shifted again like a flock of starlings, everyone now racing inside the big top, not risking the long arm of the clown law.

The tent filled with the sound of sobs and chattering teeth as Minos flung people left and right into the gaping pit with the speed and efficiency of a teppanyaki chef on a cruise ship. "Sean McIntosh, Dublin, Ireland, Second Circle, The Carnal. Maritza Lopez, Mexico City, Mexico, First Circle, Limbo. Very lucky, yes, yes!"

Taking a seat on the edge of a bleacher, Bea hoped the crush of her two companions sitting on either side of her would calm her trembling limbs. "Toni, where is my brother? Tell me he wasn't dropped like that. Tell me he isn't here at all."

"Sadly, I do not know," Toni said, her eyes soft. "I would tell you if I knew."

The crowd was thinning at a breakneck pace, yet nobody pled mistaken identity even once. And Minos never missed a beat. Never paused to think or wipe the sweat from his brow. No cough or hitch in his voice. No moment to take a breath or to swallow. The man never blinked.

"How is he doing that?" Bea asked, "How can he possibly remember all those details, and so quickly? I don't see any teleprompters. There are thousands of us here, but he's processing almost a person a second. It's impossible."

His eyes, though... Something about them. A strange flicker pattern in the pupils, an occasional flash of something deep within the irises...

He *was* blinking, but the pattern wasn't random.

She leaned into Sanjay. "Do you see that? His eyes?"

Sanjay squinted at the ringmaster. Then he began counting or timing something, his finger tapping out a measurement on his thigh. Finally, Sanjay closed his own eyes a moment as he listened intently. He opened them again and inhaled sharply. "He passes the Turing test." His face pulled into a grin and he almost stood with excitement, his butt lifting off the seat before Bea tugged him back down. "Don't you see? That, my dear, is AI. *He* is our supercomputer. And he's magnificent."

That wasn't necessarily the adjective she'd have chosen, but this was still good news. She looked back and forth between Sanjay and Toni. "So, he would know about Dante, right? I mean, if Dante's here, he would've placed him somewhere. He can call up that information, can't he?"

"Can he? Of course. But he will not," Toni said. "We're going to make a special request of him as it is, and we cannot beg for more."

Bea stiffened. "He's my brother. If that's what it takes, I'm going to beg."

Toni continued watching the ringmaster, not bothering to look at Bea in response. "You will not. But we can try to find him on our own. We'll keep our eyes open as we pass through every level."

Growing angry, Bea poked Toni's shoulder until the infuriating woman turned to her. "Keep our eyes open as we pass through? But how many people are down there? There're thousands here today alone." She rubbed her palm along her jeans as she attempted to do the imponderable math in her head. "If you're saying almost everyone who dies comes here—everyone who's died in the history of the human race—then that's... that's impossible. There's no way we'll find him."

Irritation flickered at the corners of Toni's mouth, but she offered up some helpful facts. "To be fair, this Afterlife location really only covers those born to a western ideology, and then only in the context of the last couple thousand years of spiritual thought. And, don't forget, it's only those who didn't manage to bypass this place altogether."

Bea dropped her jaw, gaping at her. "He's a needle in a *thousand* haystacks."

Toni paused, studying Bea's face before finally relaxing her shoulders and nodding. She took Bea's hand and squeezed, offering a gentle smile, but the reassuring words Bea assumed would come next failed to materialize. "I cannot argue with that. But one always has hope."

It was not enough. Not nearly enough, and Bea snatched her hand back. She looked to Sanjay for support, but he wasn't paying attention to the discussion.

He was sitting straight as a pole, studying the periphery of the room, eyes squinting, body rotating as necessary, his gaze moving with precision from one end of the big canvas to the other.

"What are you looking at?" Bea asked.

He shot his attention to her, then back to a spot near the flap behind them. He stood up. "I'll be right back."

"What? Where are you going?" both women blurted simultaneously.

"Popcorn." His response was a breath, eyes focused on a classic red-and-yellow vendor cart, the fluffy kernels bursting like a fountain under the glowing heat lamp.

He's lost his mind. Or he's leaving us. Not that Bea could blame him. But still, his companionship calmed her in a way Toni's didn't.

"Seriously? After you saw what happened with the cotton candy? And I know you're not hungry," Bea said.

"Huh?" He finally looked back at her in earnest, his expression focusing as he must have noted her concern. He clasped one of her shaking hands in his. "No, no. I have something else in mind. I'll be right b-back, my dear. I promise."

They watched him walk off until he became lost in bodies and shadow. The tent had emptied quite a bit while they'd been arguing about Dante. Bea could never tell how much time passed here, but the seats were far more empty than full now. Maybe a couple hundred quaking bodies remained, those with companions gripping each other's hands tightly.

Bea's mouth went dry as she realized she still had no idea what exactly was supposed to be happening to her now. She'd accepted her circumstances—great—but it was time to pay attention and find out what it all meant from here on out. She wanted the detailed plan. The itinerary and packing list. Preferably a map of the... uh... Underworld.

While studying literature in college, she'd taken a course in creative writing, and she'd learned every good protagonist had a well laid out goal, a deep motivation, and inevitable conflict. Forget all this "forward is the only way down" cryptic bullshit. It was time she knew exactly what was on the other end of this journey, why she wanted to get there, and what problems she could expect to face along the way. Because, if they were *really* going to walk all the way through—she risked another peek at the vast, dark pit beyond the tent—whatever was down there, she needed a freaking good reason and a clear plan before she set one foot—

Her head snapped back as something tight and rigid gripped her body, plastering her arms to her sides and smashing her legs together vise-tight to the ankles. A scream failed her throat for lack of air to her lungs as she flew forward under the heights of the big top, cocooned in a leather leash.

"Toni!" she shouted as she finally found her lungs inflated and her feet back on the ground. Still wrapped in the whip, she stood face-to-face with Minos, who studied her in a way he'd done with no one else.

"I see that your assigned level is…" He paused, eyelids blinking as if he were trying to remove an irritant. His usual enthusiasm waned, and his voice did not project. She'd somehow stumped the computer. "However, your name is marked with an asterisk for possible…" He paused as if processing again. "Very strange, very strange."

Toni, thankfully, appeared at her side and the ringmaster eyed her with a nod of recognition. "Ah, I see now. You come to me with yet another favor to ask, *Madame Déficit?*"

Madame Déficit. A moniker that rang familiar, but Bea was in no head space to start reviewing her French history lessons.

Toni, however, appeared unamused by the nickname, whatever it referred to, and her curling upper lip was the first example Bea had seen of her temper.

It was the only sign of it, though, as Toni's words were gracious, even somewhat fawning. "If you please, Master Minos, I would once more beg your goodwill to grant me and my charge, and possibly one other," she stole a glance over one shoulder, "permission to venture all the way through your resplendent domain."

With Bea still wrapped up like a mouse in a python, the ringmaster blinked, sparks of color flashing within his dark pupils like tiny galaxies. "You have sought this particular favor of me almost one hundred times, Madame, you dauphine of indulgence, you queen of excess."

"I admit I have," she said, hands now fisting at her side, though her speaking tone remained neutral. "This will, in fact, be exactly the one-hundredth time. I shall not ask this favor of you again, as you well know. She is the last one."

Bea ripped her attention from Minos to Toni, surprised to note the flush darkening Toni's face at her own pronouncement. Surprised more to note the slight tremble in Toni's lips as she awaited his answer.

She is the last one.

Minos raised his head and voice. "Very well. But as this will be your last time, let us make this a most memorable finale, shall we?"

Toni's eyes widened, barely perceptible.

"What will it be, what will it be?" The master of ceremonies, now fully himself—*itself*—again, giggled while snapping the one available whip. "I know! How about a little entertainment? You understand entertainment, don't you?" He eyed Bea, his dual star chambers lighting up like the Fourth of July. "Oh, I see you do, you do."

Toni's agitation rushed to the surface. "But you have already made a promise with me to—"

"My agreement with you, Madame, is unrelated to any I choose to make with Ms. Allegra. If anything, you will be doubly motivated now to achieve a successful conclusion to her journey."

Bea's throat went dry. "Agreement with me?"

"I shall give you a choice, Ms. Allegra. I will allow Her Royal... your guide... to lead you down through the Nine Circles and out of here to a far better place, as the euphemism goes. However, in return, your journey will be broadcast for all to view."

Great. So a reality show after all. Fine. She was used to cameras on her in life, why not in death? No biggie.

"Alternatively," Minos continued, "You can remain a fully anonymous citizen of Hell, spending eternity in your assigned circle with no chance for escape. The choice is yours."

The two women spoke at once, their words trampling over each other.

Toni was louder, nearly yelling, her face gone stormy. "She does *not* have a choice! She is rightfully assigned to *me*. I *must* take her through!"

"Silence!" The ringmaster flicked a whip, the very end of it coiling around Toni's mouth like a gag. "I am the only distributor of *musts* around here." He switched his attention back to Bea. "Ms. Allegra, you have a question?"

Pulling her gaze from Toni's trembling, glossy-eyed face, Bea turned to Minos, her voice thin and shaking. "What would my assigned circle be?"

A grin lit his bovine-esque face. "I think I shall decline to tell you that. Makes your gamble much more exciting, it does, it does. However, I will promise that your place is in Upper Hell, and in a fairly peaceful situation as far as it goes here. On the other hand, should you decide to embark on the journey instead and fail anywhere along the way, you will be trapped there, potentially in a far darker level of the pit, for all of time. That is your gamble. Possible escape from Hell should you succeed, probable horrific eternal suffering should you fail. Decide now."

Bea considered the pros and cons. Toni had mentioned there were five circles in Upper Hell, which meant a twenty percent chance of landing in Limbo. Not the worst gambling odds ever. And then there was the risk of getting stuck somewhere in Lower Hell. Bea already knew Toni's vote—she needed to guide her last soul out and was clearly beyond eager to be done with her task. Enough so to face off with Minos. But Bea had already made up her mind. Dante might be out there somewhere, and she had to find out. In fact, there was no option but for her to do just that—at least, not as far as her heart was concerned. "I agree to the cameras and the risk. I want to make the journey."

"Fantastic!" he bellowed, the sudden volume shocking enough to almost make her question her choice. "What fun, what fun!"

He jerked his wrists and the coils both released, spinning Bea the opposite direction until it unwound fully. She stumbled, wheeling her arms to regain her balance. Recovering her footing, she sought Toni's face, now free from her lasso gag. She nodded her support of Bea's choice.

"Ladies and gentlemen, on your feet please, and prepare for a round of applause." The ringmaster spoke to the crowd as he spun Bea around by the shoulders to face them. "Le Cirque is proud to present to you naughty citizens of Hell, a rare entertainment. Beatrice Allegra has chosen... The Game!"

The crowd beneath the big top gave a half-hearted response, seemingly as confused as Bea was, but the monitors that circled the inside of the tent just as they did outside switched their focus away from the center ring onto masses of people located... elsewhere. The screens rotated through sweeping vistas looking down on marshy swamps, charred deserts, and frozen lakes of ice, where those who were able (many, many were not) broke out with shouts and fist pumps, some of them trampling others for a chance to be shown on screen. It was like the kiss cam at Fenway Park, except, here, the excitement was grotesque.

The ringmaster's cheeks glowed a red that appeared almost LED in nature. "Instead of a private journey through our hellaciously glorious Nine Circles, Ms. Allegra's travels will now be televised live for all our entertainment! And she might well find some surprises along the way to increase our viewing pleasure."

The camera zoomed in on one figure and Bea recognized her demon cowboy. He held up an eight-by-ten glossy photo of her. She recognized the image, it was currently her profile pic on all her social accounts—a photo she normally loved, shot by a popular celeb photographer she'd waited a year to get an appointment with. The demon rubbed the print against his crotch while giving the "rock and roll" sign with his other hand.

Acid rose in her throat. This was not exactly what she thought she'd just signed up for. It was... worse.

Toni approached and touched her arm. "We'll be okay."

Considering the unexpected fear Toni had displayed under the grasp of Minos' whip, Bea was no longer so sure.

"It's just spectacle," Toni added.

Spectacle. Entertainment. She thought of Nadi then, the first time she'd thought of her and Mel in hours... or maybe it was days. Who could tell in this place? A tear slipped down her cheek. She wiped it away, pretending she wasn't scared out of her freaking wits.

The ringmaster worked the audience. "Can we get a preliminary vote from our viewers before we send her off on her merry way? Yes? Then tell me, who's in favor of Beatrice Allegra making it all the way through to the Ninth Circle and out, maybe even give her a helping hand along the way?" The monitors shifted to a static image of her profile portrait as hundreds of little blue "thumbs up" symbols floated across the screen.

Bea stared at the big monitor, ignoring the gooseflesh on her arms. Who, exactly, was voting and by what means? Did the Minos artificial intelligence simply "know" the thoughts of the populace in the same way he/it knew every person under the tent or was there a divine entity running the whole process? The devil operating a supercomputer in the Afterlife? When it came right down to it, the technicalities of it hardly mattered. But if a certain number of people were, in effect, "liking" her, then—

"And who of you, my friends, my friends, are *not* in favor of her success, and will not feel so inclined to ease her journey? How many of you might, in fact, be more of a mind to do just the opposite?"

56

As a din of cheers and shouts rose from deep in the pit behind her, a wave of red "thumbs down" icons swarmed the monitors, ten-fold the number of blue, covering her face until the screens were an unbroken sea of red.

Chapter 7

BOSTON

13 Years Ago

Bea leaned forward on the black leather sofa, reaching over her laptop screen to grab another handful of chips from the big ceramic bowl on the coffee table. The cushy basement family room at her next-door neighbor and bestie Ronna's house had hosted most of their high school parties—Ronna's parents were pretty cool and kept a safe but forgiving eye on their fun over the years. This evening was a more serious get-together, though, as she and Dante, Ronna and their girlfriend Karli studied for their upcoming SATs.

The girls kept drifting off their study pages and onto gossip, but Dante regularly steered them back to the task at hand. His sights were set on one of the top physics universities, and though his grades were impeccable, competition was stiff. Bea worried he hadn't done enough extracurricular activities to round out his application, and she blamed herself for this. Sports would never be his thing, but her bro had a great singing voice and he would've been a heartthrob in the lead role of their school's performance of *Beauty and the Beast*. She'd tried her best to convince him it would be worth his time. Tried, and failed. He feared that kind of limelight, not to mention the long hours spent around a big, loud group of people, so he was taking his chances with pure academic prowess. She'd chewed down more than one fingernail at the thought it might not be enough. His heart would break if he didn't get into MIT or Caltech or one of those big brain science schools. It would break hers, too.

Karli sighed, shoving away her laptop and throwing herself backward onto a bright white beanbag chair. "Facebook stopped being fun six months ago when my parents signed up."

"That's not even so bad," said Ronna. "My freaking *grand*mother has an account now. We need to find a new social."

Sitting cross-legged on the floor on one side of the coffee table, Dante sunk down, hiding his face in his work and shrinking away from the loud chit-chat.

"You guys, save it for when we take a break in a little bit," Bea said, hoping to gain him a few more minutes of peace. "Let's make some more progress before Dante gets all growly and threatens to crack the whip."

Her attempt failed as Ronna leaned forward, crossing her arms on the table and squishing her cleavage up. "Ooh, that sounds fun."

The rest of the room groaned and blushed, especially her brother. But Bea caught the way his lips moving into a fleeting bow even as he kept his eyes on his computer. He didn't mind the female attention. Or maybe he was imagining all the physics problems he'd soon be solving in some sterile, gray university lab. One never knew with her handsome, quiet nerd of a bro.

"Fuck it," he said, stretching his arms overhead, back to being oblivious as her friends absorbed the way his shoulder muscles flexed when he cracked his back. "Let's take a break now. I'm hungry."

"Perfect timing." Ronna's mom came down the basement steps carrying a take-out pizza. She placed it on the coffee table. "How's it going down here? Studying hard, I hope." She gave them each a pointed look.

"Dante's studying enough for all of us," Karli said.

"I don't think it works that way, girls. Unless he's actually tutoring you, you're on your own."

Two female pairs of eyes shot Bea's way. *Great, here it comes.*

"What?" She jumped into defense mode, cutting any comments off at the pass. "It's not like we're identical twins. He can't take my tests for me."

"No one said that, Bea." Ronna folded a slice of pepperoni and aimed it at her mouth.

"We know that, sweetheart," Ronna's mom said. "But it is awfully nice that you're both the same age and in the same grade. You can study together. He can help you prepare for the SATs. It's convenient, that's all."

Her cheeks flushed and she avoided looking at her brother, staring at the disappearing pie instead.

"Why can't everyone stop assuming she needs my help? She doesn't." He came to her rescue as he always did, and she knew he truly believed what he said. But his defense was perfunctory and expected at this point, spoken without energy and falling on deaf ears. "She'll get into whatever college she wants to on her own."

"Of course, she will," Ronna said as her mom nipped out of the room, escaping a conversation that had become uncomfortable. "Anyway, it's no big deal, you guys. Everyone thinks it's awesome how you're like two sides of a coin. I mean, hey, I'm sure you help him with all kinds of things, Bea. So, what if he helps you with math-y science-y stuff? If I had a genius twin, I'd use the hell out of him as long as I could."

60

Dante uncurled his long legs and stood. "Just lay off her, okay? She brings more to the table than I *ever* will. You don't understand." He stomped toward the basement bathroom, agitation rolling off him, and Bea's heart twisted with a bruising love. He totally did help with some of her coursework, always had. The moment he'd shown aptitude for academics, it had been expected of him, just as she'd been expected to keep him from withdrawing too far into his imaginative mind and isolating himself from the world. Because they *were* two halves of a whole, he with his intelligence and creativity, always imaging new ways the world could be, and her, with her charm and popularity and... well, she had charm and popularity.

"I guess you'll be going to two different schools?" Karli asked, unphased by his upset. "What happens then? Will you see where he gets in and then choose a college nearby?"

"Jesus, Karli," Ronna said, moving the empty pizza box off the coffee table and settling down to her laptop. "It's not like they're conjoined twins or, like, somehow they'll die without each other. At some point they'll have to go their own ways, get married, have families. You know, like regular people. Maybe Bea should start now. Wherever Dante goes, pick someplace else."

And though she chose not to respond, that was, in fact, *exactly* what Bea had been privately contemplating for months. Pondering the idea that perhaps it was time to find out if she really could be a "regular person." Time to find out if she and Dante were two self-supporting structures, or one fragile lean-to.

And it was time to get a break from conversations like this one.

She gulped down the last couple bites of her pepperoni slice as the blood quickened in her veins. Separating from her twin was either going to be the best decision—or the worst mistake—of her life. *I can't survive on charm and popularity alone.*

61

But no. She brushed away the scared voice inside and made her decision. Wherever he chose to go to school, she'd pick a college far away. If it didn't work out, she could always come home. Dante would forever be there for her one way or the other.

It was time to find out if she really was only one half of a superhero, or a wholly complete, boringly competent, wonderfully mere mortal.

Chapter 8

THE FIRST CIRCLE
The Ledge

"Let The Game begin now! Off with you, off with you." The ringmaster swung his head back to what remained of the crowd in the stands. "I have other work here to finish up."

Two of the grotesquely tall clowns flapped their way over in their even more outsized clown shoes, one taking Bea by the elbow, the other reaching for Toni.

Bea broke away, running back to Minos. "Please, tell me where my brother is first. I beg you."

He cracked his whip, the snap an inch from her face, all trace of the giggling, flamboyant personality gone. "You beg? I've already granted the one and only boon you're likely to get in this place. Maybe if you're very, very good at getting down on your knees and... begging, you'll be able to convince some of the lonelier and, shall we say, aching souls beyond to help you. But I've become bored with this myself, so let me stoop down to your level and speak in a language you understand." He leaned his techno-human face into hers, eyes now dark and still as black holes, and bellowed. "Hashtag get out!"

The clowns were back, nearly throwing Bea and Toni through the rear of the tent, the big flaps closing behind them.

Standing on the ledge of the vast abyss, a cacophony of despair, fear, and anger rose up to greet them, the separation of sounds much clearer and more visceral from this proximity. Deep within the gloomy and frothing weather, the thunder and lightning, glowing spots of ruby red broke through in places.

"It's classic *Inferno*," Bea said, eyes glued to the scene below. "How can it possibly be that, seven hundred years ago, the poet Dante Alighieri, a hardline Catholic writing what was basically a love poem for his dead fiancée, got it right?"

"I beg your pardon?" Toni said, her face a mask of concern as she, too, stared into the pit.

Bea pulled her attention from the darkness. "I was a literature major at USC. I may not be as smart as my brother, but I made the grades, so I recognize that all of this," she spread her arms wide, "is straight out of *The Divine Comedy*, specifically, *Inferno*. The Nine Circles of Hell, the temple of Minos, and… I now realize, the ferryman over the Acheron. I mean, it's a bit of a funky version of it, I'll admit, but all the classic benchmarks are here."

"I realize you are no fool, Beatrice. Indeed, you have far more substance than even you choose to see." She studied Bea's face with a new fierceness that made Bea wonder what she was seeing. "Or perhaps there is some guilt in admitting that you are no less clever than your brother. In any case, a part of you has recognized this landscape since you awoke on top of the monument, preparing to enter the gates. Your instincts were faster than your rational mind, that's all."

"The gates? On the monument?"

"Abandon all hope, ye who enter here."

"You heard that?"

"I did, and it was a clever personal touch if I may say so," Toni continued, not reacting to Bea's world-class eyeroll. "You and everyone here, we're all creating this. Universal subconscious, the agreed-upon vision of a painful Afterlife. Continually updated over time, of course, as the psyche of the population and cultural norms change. It won't look exactly like it did in Alighieri's version. It's malleable."

"If that's the case, can't we just change it?" Bea asked. "Snap my fingers and turn this godforsaken landscape into white-capped mountains, lush green forest. Maybe a few angels holding harps?"

Toni smiled, a big, beautiful hope-filled grin that lifted Bea's mood. "I would love to see that. I truly would. But, unfortunately, no, not yet anyway."

"But you're saying it can be done. That's… that's what you're trying to help me do here, isn't it? To realize I control my own reality or some crap? You help people evolve, achieve some kind of higher consciousness, move into the big white light. That's how you get them out."

Toni's face fell. "Don't get ahead of yourself. There is much work to be done first."

Bea shrugged. "Well, obvs."

Toni spun on her so fast, Bea jumped back. "For starters, stop speaking in shorthand and faddish lingo. It's lazy and lacks communicative intent. There's your first lesson."

So, Bea hadn't been wrong about Toni continually sizing her up. Judging her.

"Not judging," Toni responded to Bea's unspoken thoughts. "Determining who you are, what you're made of, thereby deciding on the best course of action to get you out of here, which, I assume, is what you want."

"Fine. But you don't have to be snobby about it. If you don't know what I mean by something, just ask." They were both growing irritated, their bickering, no doubt, an unconscious stalling tactic as their path forward looked so damn uninviting. And where, exactly, was the path forward?

All Bea could see was the sheer drop off. "How old are you anyway? I mean, when were you born, or when did you die, I guess, such that you don't know my *faddish lingo*?"

"I was thirty-seven when I lost my... life. That was somewhat more than two hundred years ago by your perceived time." She spoke looking down her nose, her royal highness attitude, which she occasionally whipped out, appearing hugely put off by the question. "And I don't need you to explain anything to me. I understand your modern parlance, your pop culture references, as does everyone in this place, no matter when they lived."

"Everyone here knows everything it seems." Bea watched as Minos' whips deposited the remains of the crowd, stretching miles out over the pit to drop the latest two screaming victims into the depths before coiling perfectly back into the tent. "Just another example of the fact that we're not dealing with the known laws of the universe here. The generally accepted principles don't apply."

"The real question is, have they ever?"

Bea snapped her attention to Toni, but before she could query further, they looked back toward the tent as the sound of fast footsteps and hard breathing caught their attention.

"Sanjay," Toni said, relief on her face as he trotted up to join them. "I'd assumed you'd left us."

"No, my dears. Sneak off without a word? Never." He clasped each of their hands in turn as he spoke. "When I realized Master Minos was an artificial intelligence, I knew at once he must be using a database to call up all those people. But a database of that size, well, that's when the p-popcorn machines caught my attention—interspersed at regular intervals around the tent, and the decorative lights flashing, like the ringmaster's eyes, at predictable frequencies. I suspected at once they were servers. It took some doing to keep out from under the eye of the demons, but..."

He pulled a slip of paper from his pocket and handed it to Bea. "Once I figured out the interface, I hoped it would release the data I needed. We were quite lucky. It spit this out."

She glanced down at the dot matrix printing on the receipt-sized paper. It read:

DANTE ALLEGRA – FIFTH CIRCLE – THE SULLEN

"Oh. Oh my God. You found him, Sanjay." She flung her arms around the professor, crushing his already rumpled suit. "Thank you so much."

He smiled with a blush as they stepped apart. "I haven't *quite* f-found him. I imagine he'll still be one among a vast number, but it narrows down the search quite a bit, I hope."

"Definitely. I'll hold onto—"

Toni snatched the paper from his hand before Bea could do the same, shoving it into her pocket with an expression closer to irritation than gratitude. Then her gaze landed on the two surprised faces looking back at her and she relaxed her shoulders, offering the brush of a smile. "Thank you," she said to Sanjay with a nod. "That was very kind," she added as her eyes refocused on their surroundings, shifting from one spot to another as her brows drew together. "I really think we should get moving now."

Bea and Sanjay followed her gaze. Ten or more clowns had slipped around to their side of the giant tent, some swinging their long hooks, others holding video cameras up to their eyes—video cameras pointed at the three of them. The clowns stood in place, keeping their distance, but watching… and filming.

"Yes, I agree it's best to get a move on," Sanjay said, "but I'm ashamed to admit I've decided not to join you. I'll return now to the ranch."

"Oh, Sanjay." Toni snapped her focus back to her friend, returning the full force of her attention to him as she placed a hand on his shoulder. "Are you sure? You already understand so much. You're halfway there, I think, and like I said, I won't be—"

She won't be coming back. I am the last one.

"I'm probably a coward, I know, but even though it's an endless, limited life in the First Circle, it's nevertheless far freer than the one I had while alive." He turned to Bea. "I chose to love the wrong person, you see, according to the apparent rules of such matters. I fell in love with a man. We were not allowed to... I could not be my true..."

Bea touched his hand. "I know. It's different nowadays. A little bit better anyway, but still not perfect. Not yet."

"Ironically, here in Hell I can be myself." He offered a smile. "I've decided to go with the devil I know."

He leaned into Toni, trading European double-cheek kisses, but she seemed hesitant to let go, her hands clinging to his shoulders. Tears slid from her eyes, causing Bea to take a step back at the unexpected intimacy. She was fast coming to notice the way Toni appeared so confident one moment, then so utterly vulnerable the next.

Sanjay wiped a tear away, and the two spoke quietly, but not so much that Bea couldn't hear.

"Ah, Antonia. You're almost free," he said.

Toni shook her head, maybe to shake away the tears, maybe in doubt of his words. "I'll never see you again. And I've had so few true friends."

"You'll soon be awash with your loves. I wish I could see it." He hugged her once more before addressing Bea.

"And you," he said, clasping her shoulders. "You've been granted a profound and incredibly rare opportunity, which won't be easy. Remember, for every action there is an equal and opposite reaction, and you're going to have to fight very hard for what you want—finding your brother, then finding your way out of Hell. And the harder you fight..."

She offered a thin smile. "Gee, thanks for the pep talk."

His own smile was broad and relaxed. "I'm just saying, be prepared and don't let up. I know you're capable of this."

"*How* do you know? I'm just a bullshit social media influencer. I'm not brave at all."

"Beatrice, as a brilliant colleague of mine once said, sometimes it is the people no one can imagine anything of who do the things no one can imagine."

A monstrous howl of pain sounded from deep within the murk to destroy the moment.

"Right. That'll be my cue to go." Sanjay nodded and headed back toward the tent.

The clowns kept their stares and cameras fixed on the women, who returned to the dizzying drop-off.

"How do we get off this ledge?" Bea asked as a loud grunt, rather like a baboon, echoed from beneath the gloom.

"I'm afraid we jump."

"Jump?" The shock of Toni's response made Bea's legs so weak she almost went over the edge without any effort.

"I know you can't see it through the mist, but the Second Circle is not so far below. A hundred feet perhaps."

"Uh, I'd like to remind you that I've made that kind of descent before. It didn't go so well last time."

Toni faced Bea in earnest, her voice calm even though the stains of her tears were still fresh on her cheeks, glowing with each snap of lightning. "You can't die twice. Besides, the physics are different here, remember?"

"You're saying we're going to fly off the ledge?"

Taking Bea's hands in her own, Toni squeezed.

This time, there was a genuine connection between them as Bea noted the lines of pain around Toni's eyes or, rather, Toni allowed them to be revealed. Emotional war wounds, soul-deep battle scars. On such a young face. A map of her strength, and her vulnerability.

"The pain we'll experience here is nothing compared to what we both lived through on Earth. They can't take from us what we've already lost. We have only to gain."

Bea swallowed a lump before talking. "You lost someone, too, before you died, didn't you? A child? A partner?"

"I lost all of them."

"All of them," Bea whispered in response.

Who was this woman with so much of her own pain? She had to have loved well to hurt so deeply. Yet, here she was, in this place, guiding others like some sort of penance.

Toni held her gaze, her expression sad but serene. She seemed to be waiting, as though she wanted Bea to figure it out, figure Toni out, and to do it *now*, before they went farther.

French. From over two hundred years ago, so the late eighteenth century. Bea stared at the soft strawberry blonde curls, the classical oval face. The regal air Toni adorned so easily. She breathed in the scent of powder that continually encircled Toni. *Madame Deficit.* The queen of excess.

And this beauty would have died in France during the...

Bea mouthed the unbelievable words she couldn't voice out loud. "Marie? *Antoinette?*"

Her partner dipped her chin in a slow nod, and curtseyed low as only a royal could. As she rose back up, her clothing morphed from jeans and t-shirt into a courtly gown of robin's egg blue silk, fanning wide at the hips and studded with gleaming white pearls along every seam. The bodice cinched tight at the waist, and the neckline, framed in delicate white lace, dipped low to show a hint of bosom. Her ponytail was now a high, white-powdered pompadour, a spectacular birdcage headpiece crowning the top.

She was exquisite, radiating beauty, love, and sorrow.

Before Bea could speak a word, the image dissolved once more into the "Toni" she'd been traveling with, generic jeans and all, though still standing straight, tall, and proud.

The clowny production crew moved in, red recording lights flashing on their professional-grade digital recorders. The audience—if she could call it that—grew restless and rowdy down below as catcalls, obscenities, and a few scattered shouts of encouragement floated up from the blackness.

The clowns pressed forward.

The women turned toward the ledge and scooted their feet to the precipice, their toes hanging in open air. Bea took Marie's hand and squeezed, and Her Royal Highness, Lady of Versailles, Queen of France—Toni—squeezed back.

Together, they jumped.

CAMBRIDGE, MASSACHUSETTS

9 years ago

McDuffy's pub had all the earmarks of a college town dive bar: sticky floors, an odor of cheap, stale beer, and hormones filling the air in an almost visible mist. With Cambridge being home to both MIT and Harvard, McDuffy's clientele might have a higher-than-average median IQ, but their brain cells died off with every shot of Jager at the same rate as any other shitfaced coed, regardless of SAT scores.

Bea estimated she'd already lost about one percent of her higher thinking ability in the last hour or so, but who cared? It was their goddamned twenty-first birthday, which was *the* perfect day to get a little bit dumber.

Dante, being the smarter twin, had a few more neurons to spare, but he was currently nursing the same bottle of Sam Adams he'd started with. He was no teetotaler, but the way he kept checking on her drinking progress meant he'd gone into their "keep an eye on each other" mode.

Which really irked her.

He'd relinquished that responsibility the moment she'd

gone off to USC and he'd turned down Caltech to stay local with MIT. Not that she would've expected—or wanted—him to have followed her to California; they had their own lives to live and she didn't need him strapped to her side anymore. But he wore his guilt over the long-distance-twin situation like a martyr, and whenever she returned home for a visit, he donned his cape and played the role.

Screw it. If he still wanted to play at their "twin responsibilities", then, right now, hers was to keep him from crawling too far into his introvert shell and get him to enjoy the celebration.

"Nadiyah, order a round of shots. We're getting my brother drunk tonight if it kills us."

"Oh, hell yeah." Nadi leaned into the bar, flashing cleavage and her signature glorious smile. The bartender nearly dropped the beer he was serving someone else in his haste to get over to her. Thrown together as roommates three years ago in the freshman dorm, she and Bea had rapidly become an inseparable pair. This was Nadi's third visit to Bea's home in Boston, and Bea's family adored her.

Nadi held up three fingers. "Shots of Patron, please."

"Make that four." Ronna slid in out of nowhere, pouring her perfect curves onto Dante's lap. "If we're getting him drunk, I'm so in. Are we getting him laid, too?"

Dante flashed his best put-upon look, but he slipped his arm around Ronna's tiny waist, pulling her in that much tighter against him.

Ronna beamed. She'd had an obvious crush on him since junior high, but the twins always tried not to date within their circle. Bea and Dante had enough of an overlapping social life as it was without complicating things further by turning their friendships into a Venn diagram.

It'd become much easier when they'd gone off to live on opposite coasts, and Bea assumed he had an active dating life

73

whenever he tore his eyes away from his books—or his feet out of the physics labs. Her brother was gorgeous, with a messy flop of dark curls, big thoughtful eyes, and a strong jawline. But she doubted he ever thought about it for more than two seconds, his mind usually occupied with the latest groundbreaking discovery instead.

Tonight, though, the messy relationship boundaries didn't bother her as Ronna giggled into Dante's ear and his fingers brushed the edge of her breast. Maybe it was the alcohol warming Bea's veins or the joy of being home and surrounded by old friends and new, or maybe even the fact that it was damn good to be an Allegra twin on their twenty-first birthday, where everything was warm and golden and soft around the corners.

Nadi continued to flirt up the bartender as he poured their drinks, though more eyes than his tracked her willowy move-ments and contagious laughter. She was the most self-confident person Bea had ever known, and that in itself drew both men and women to her like moths to a flame. At one time, Bea thought perhaps she'd been interested in Nadi as more than a friend—it hadn't been the first time Bea was attracted to another woman. But, in this case—and thankfully before any-thing developed that would irreparably alter their relation-ship—Bea realized it wasn't so much a physical attraction that produced such strong feelings toward Nadi, but rather, the powerful experience of having a friendship *all to herself.*

Nadi lifted her glass as the shots were passed around. "Happy birthday to the finest pair of siblings now on both sides of the Mississippi."

"To the Allegra twins," Dante added without irony as they clinked glasses.

The tequila—Bea's third such shot—burned its way down as it fired up her moxie, and she slid off her stool to dance in place, sometimes undulating around Nadi or Ronna, sometimes lost in her own world.

Dante soon had a matching fire brightening his eyes. Whether from the same booze running through his blood, or from Ronna's languid attention, Bea didn't know, but he'd grown loose and relaxed and Bea laughed as he now ordered a round of Sex on the Beach shots.

"Oh, hell no," Nadi said. "Mixing that sugary shit with Patron...? I'll pass, thanks."

"Same. Nothing for me," Bea added.

"I, on the other hand, am totally game." Ronna slipped her arms around him from behind as he sat on his stool, rubbing her chest to his back and breathing into his neck. "Which reminds me, *is* there a beach nearby?"

Dante blushed and Nadi groaned.

Bea stood. "On that note, I think I'm going to skedaddle on home before I'm too drunk to face the folks—who, you know, are waiting up even at our age." She tossed her purse over her shoulder. "Ready, Nadi?"

Her brother placed money on the counter. "Give me your keys, Bea. You're not driving Dad's car home in your condition."

"Of course I'm not. That's what Uber is for, dork." She wobbled a bit as her heel skidded on a spill, and he grabbed her elbow. "And you're not driving anywhere either, bro."

"I don't need to drive anywhere. My apartment is down the street. Give me the keys, anyway, and I'll drive the car back tomorrow."

She shrugged and pulled the house key off the ring before handing the rest to him.

As Dante ordered the ride, Ronna pulled Bea to the side, the two of them bobbing equally for balance like a couple of buoys on the water. "Bea, I want to ask you first... I mean, I would never have... but tonight he's... I wasn't sure if you'd mind and I'd never, *ever* want to hurt your feelings or... would it be weird if Dante and I..."

Bea grabbed her friend's waist, both for stability and reassurance. "Yes, it's weird. Everything's weird when you're a twin." Emotions welled in her chest, fueled by booze, and she poured them out with all the drama alcohol could provide. "But, also, it's totally *not* weird. I can't imagine anything cooler than my best friend getting together with my best friend. It's freaking perfect, in fact."

Arm-in-arm, head tipped to head, they followed Dante and Nadiyah out the door. When the ride pulled up, Nadi hopped in. Ronna hugged Bea goodbye and went back inside to wait for Dante.

"Happy birthday, sis." He hugged Bea tight enough to lift her off the ground, then swung her around.

Score one for alcohol, Ronna, and Bea's party instigations for bringing him an evening of fun out of the lab. The smile on his face when he put her down was all the birthday present she wanted. "Happy birthday, bro."

They performed their precisely tuned secret handshake, ending on the fist bump.

"Two halves," was all Dante said.

"Stronger together," she finished.

When she was settled in the car, he leaned through the window. "Tell Dad I'll bring the car back tomorrow morning in time for breakfast. I'll hang with you guys all day and we'll do family dinner together, too. I know you're heading home Monday."

"Sounds good."

He tapped the window and the driver pulled out.

***

The sun had barely risen, a pink glow backlighting the sheer curtains of her childhood bedroom, when she blinked her scratchy eyes open, a sound pulling her from sleep.

A *wrong* sound.

A *bad* sound.

"Beatrice. Bea." Her father's voice came from the door of her room.

But that wasn't the bad sound. It was the sobbing.

She rolled over toward the door and the noise, attempting to work her groggy voice. "Whaa…?"

Her dad stood there wearing gray sweatpants and an old rugby shirt with holes at the shoulders, his hair smashed to the side of his head from sleep. From somewhere down the hall, her mother's cries rang out, and he swiveled his head toward the sound, then back to Bea, his face pinched as if triaging who to attend to first—his wife or his daughter. He gripped the doorframe as if he were a hundred years old.

A glance at the clock showed it was not quite six in the morning.

Bea pushed up onto her palms, swung her bare legs over the side of the bed and pulled the edge of her girls' boxers a little further down on her thighs, adjusted her t-shirt. "Dad? What's going on?"

Somehow, God-knew-why, when Nadi walked into the room on the other side of her father, her model-long bare legs trembling below her oversized USC Trojans t-shirt, Bea *knew*.

She stared at that logo of the Roman head and helmet half showing beneath Nadi's shaking crossed arms, and asked anyway, "What… what's going on?"

Only now did she notice the sound of men talking outside, followed by car doors shutting, and one single *whoop-whoop* of a police siren as their engines started up and they pulled away from the curb.

Her dad stepped toward her. "It's…" He cleared his throat and tried again, but his voice was all broken and strange. "It's Dante. There was a car accident. A few hours ago, they told us. He didn't make it. He was drunk and he—"

"No!" She flew from the bed and pushed on her father's chest. "That's not right. He *wasn't* driving anywhere tonight. He left the car at the bar and walked to his apartment. He'll be here in a few hours for breakfast." She craned over his shoulder. "Mom?" she shouted into the hall. "Mom, go make breakfast!"

"Honey." He tried pulling her into a hug but lacked any strength in his usually solid, reliable arms, which he then dropped to his side. "The police were just here, and they said—"

"Tell him, Nadi." She turned to her best friend, who now leaned against the wall, wracked with sobs. "He was walking back to his apartment with Ronna."

"He was driving Ronna home in the wee hours." Her dad's voice was like a gnat buzzing in her ear that wouldn't go away. "They must've kept drinking and... Ronna's gone, too, sweetheart. They went over the side of an onramp. The car rolled."

She was slapping him now. *Slapping, slapping.* She couldn't breathe. From somewhere in the distance, her mom was wailing. Nadi and her dad both grasped her flailing arms. She fought them off.

Slapping, slapping.

Suffocating.

"He's *not* dead because I'm *alive.* I'm proof." The room spun around her as she grew lightheaded. "We're twins. We're *twins*! He can't die without me. That's not how this works. He can't, I can't..."

Her dad scooped her up and placed her back on the bed as he mumbled a to-do list for himself. "I'll call Stacy. She should pack a bag. We'll need her here for a while. I'll ask her to bring Xanax or whatever she's got."

Bea rolled into a fetal position on her side and her dad pulled the covers back over her. She rocked and mumbled, her fingers curling at her mouth. "He can't be dead, he can't be dead. Not without me. He *needs* me." A strangled sound escaped her mouth. "I should've kept an eye on him!"

"No, sweetheart. It's not your fault. It's…" Her father choked on a sob as he straightened, then paused, his face gone slack, until Nadi took his hand.

"You were going to call somebody, Mr. A?" Nadi steered him into the hall. "Let's find your phone."

Bea soon heard the start of a muted phone conversation, then Nadi returned by herself, kneeling at the side of the bed. With half-focused eyes, Bea stared at that damn Trojan logo at eye level. *Rocking and staring. Rocking and staring.* After this, she'd never be able to look at that logo again. Couldn't even *think* about returning to that school where she'd see it everywhere.

Nadi put a hand on her shoulder as Bea kept rocking and whispering—willing, praying for this imbalance, this screw-up in the natural order of things, to be fixed.

"I have to die, too. I have to die, too. There's been a mistake. I have to die, too."

Chapter 10

THE SECOND CIRCLE

Lying at the base of the cliff, cold, damp air wrapped Bea's broken body like a heavy shroud. Her fractured back saved her from feeling any pain, but the trade-off was paralysis. Her head lay to one side, her left ear to the ground, like some ancient Grecian statuary. She appreciated the irony as she watched Toni/Marie walking back and forth, her tennis-shoed feet the only thing visible from this ground-level perspective.

"Marie?" Thank God her vocal cords were still mobile. Must've broken her neck at a lower C-spine level.

"I've come to prefer Toni, please."

"What are you doing?"

"Pacing."

"Why?"

The tennis shoes came to a halt, toes pointed at Bea's face. "There's nothing else to do while I wait for you to get up."

"No, I mean…" She swallowed with the effort of speaking, and the strange sensation of moving nothing but her throat and facial muscles as she did so. "Why aren't you hurt, too?"

Toni squatted down so Bea could see her face. "Because I learned long ago what you have yet to understand. We are deceased, *chérie*. There is no body to break. But you, like the wheelchair-bound scientist, cannot yet wrap your head around that idea. Your mind insists you must be hurt, and so you are." Now that she'd revealed her identity, a French accent painted every word.

"So, until I learn mind over non-corporeal matter, what do I do?"

Toni rose from her squat. "You have been lying there for quite a long time now, prior to regaining consciousness. You should be healed and able to move shortly, if not already."

Bea tried to wiggle her toes and fingers and found they now worked. Next, her wrists and ankles flexed as normal. Gingerly, she rolled her neck, discovering a squid ink sky stretching from horizon to horizon. She pushed up on her elbows and finally stood. "Was I actually healed right this moment or was it the power of your suggestion?"

"What you expect is what you project." Toni walked toward a marked trailhead. "Though mastering that concept is far easier said than done, of course."

Bea followed a few paces behind as she regained a steadier gait. "I get it. You're talking about the law of attraction. I've always believed that, if you display happiness and emulate the lifestyle you want to live, it will happen. Eventually, you'll feel it; you'll live it." By now, she'd caught up to Toni, who rolled her eyes in response. "Okay, I admit fixing a broken body is a little more specific—and harder. But I get the concept." *#fakeittillyoumakeit.* Lord knew, she'd faked a majority of those internet smiles over the years.

As they arrived at the trailhead—the trail itself nothing more than a flatter, more trodden section of dirt—a wooden sign topping a simple post greeted them. Painted a dull shade of brown with yellow lettering, it resembled a U.S. National

Park Service sign, and announced a "scenic view" a mile up the trail, a little yellow arrow pointing the way. Exactly who the sign was intended for—assuming it unlikely that many souls arrived at the Second Circle in the same manner they had—was unclear.

"How many people are given the same opportunity as me? And tell me again—*why* me?" Bea moved with a slight limp down the path, some of her bones having healed imperfectly. An extra angle now jutted from her right ankle, and her left shoulder hung a bit lower than the right. All her joints throbbed.

"My understanding on this matter is limited as the rules here are complex and many. I'm unsure how many are given the opportunity. I assume I am not the only guide here. But it's true that, considering the overall number of deceased, relatively few are offered this journey. The majority are sent straight to their circle of pain."

As she spoke, they continued along the path, an uncurving line through a featureless landscape. No more than a few small boulders broke the flat plane of dirt, and, as they got closer to their destination... a fair amount of trash. They chose their steps carefully around discarded used condoms and "morning after" pill boxes.

"As for why you're one of the lucky ones?" Toni shrugged. "My concern is not to question *why*. It is simply to guide you out and complete the task assigned to me as part of my own journey."

"And I'm your last one. The hundredth person you've taken through this place. What happens to you after you get me out of here?"

"I will be reunited with my children, joining them in whatever wonderful place they've been sent. That will be my reward." She turned to Bea, a smile on her lips and a lighter step in her pace. "Marie Therese, Louis Joseph, Louis Charles, and my sweet little baby, Sophie. Little children, of course, don't come here. They're all immediately sent forward at their death."

As they passed another sign—this one telling them they had a quarter mile to go before the scenic overlook—she felt the weight of a new burden. Besides finding Dante and getting them both the hell out of Hell, Toni, too, was counting on her success. The future of not one, but seven, souls rested on Bea's uneven shoulders.

"And if, for some reason, I fail and don't make it? You'll just get another charge, right? You'll keep trying until you get that hundredth person out."

Toni halted abruptly, placing a hand on Bea's shoulder to stop her, too. The gaze she leveled on Bea was nearly pleading. "No. I had not planned to lay this additional concern at your feet, but you have asked, and, now, with your desire to find your brother, you should understand this. If we do not succeed in getting you through the Ninth Circle and out of this place, the opportunity will be over for me. I, too, will be trapped here for eternity. Do you understand? I will never see my children again."

Bea coughed. This... this was not good. She wasn't the right person for this responsibility. She certainly wasn't clever or brave—so *absolutely* the wrong choice to be the final leg in a hundred-person relay through Hell. "Okay, so what do I need to do exactly? What happens at each level—some kind of puzzle I need to solve, a moral lesson I have to learn? Please don't tell me I'll have to vanquish a demon in every circle because I've never studied up on sword fighting or spellcasting." Her attempt at humor fell flat and failed to calm her nerves.

"Nothing like that. We simply need to get you down through the Nine Circles and out as expediently as we can. Point A to Point B. Survival, nothing more."

"And find my brother."

Toni grabbed Bea's wrist, her grip tight enough to hurt. "I

need you to commit to this, to getting out of here. No matter what it takes. I need *this* to be your priority." And by that she meant *not* Dante.

A triple chime of bells interrupted the conversation, and television monitors rose up from the ground, one on either side of the path. They flickered to life as the women stopped to watch.

"Welcome back to The Game," a male voiceover announced, a little reverb added in like they were introducing a football team at a stadium. Animated fireworks burst across the screens, dissolving into a bright red Halloween-esque devil's face with black horns and goatee, apparently the logo of the official television network of the Underworld—Brimstone TV. "Tonight, let's learn more about our contestant, Beatrice Allegra, who is currently making her way through Circle Two, The Carnal. Or, as we here in the pit like to call it, Luussssst."

A roar erupted from the depths, whoops and hollers—and the occasional shout of "Show us your boobs!" A particularly energetic response came from straight ahead on the trail, and Bea now identified the acrid smell she'd been noting—the mingling of sweat and sex.

The monitors began scrolling through the photos on her Instagram feed, one image after the next, each filling the screen for a couple seconds as the voiceover continued, "Born into upper-class, White, American privilege, Beatrice had a fairytale upbringing. Side-by-side with her twin brother Dante, the two Allegra children had everything they could ask for growing up. Yet rumor has it that Beatrice was often resentful and jealous of her brother, who everyone knew was smarter and more popular, and who often covered for her missteps and recklessness."

Jaw-dropped and fists curling at her sides, Bea turned to Toni. "What? That's not true. I mean, exaggerated at best, outright lies at the worst."

They'd had a privileged childhood; she couldn't argue that. But being a twin was neither a fairytale nor a burden. There'd been issues to navigate, sure, but their "sources" had her relationship with Dante painfully wrong.

And, dear God, was her brother somewhere down in the Fifth Circle watching this broadcast right now, thinking it was the truth?

The narrator continued as her pulse quickened with this new worry. "When Dante died, Beatrice snatched the opportunity to crawl out from beneath his shadow and grab the limelight for herself, launching into the world of social media influencing. Spring-boarding off her familial tragedy, she used the particular sympathy garnered from being cast as a tragic figure who'd lost her twin, to pimp for travel and fashion companies."

The images on screen now zoomed in on not just the photos in her social feed, but the comments she'd posted with them—tagging all of her sponsors and the locations she'd visited around the world, hash-tagging every possible keyword even if they made only a tangential connection to the product or service she was being paid to promote.

They scrolled years back into her profile, showing posts where she'd still been offering up saccharin-sweet humblebrags. At the time, she'd simply been naïve. Now, she knew better, and absorbed the embarrassment of every single one.

There was so much more to her story than the broadcast was giving. Their redacted version of her life made everything appear so totally shitty. But though her mind argued with the picture they drew of her, she burned with fear that maybe they'd captured a tiny piece of truth—perhaps she really *was* an asshole.

Tears collected in her eyes as the narrator continued, "Soon the sympathetic, grieving sister took a back seat to the shallow, materialistic, follower-collecting, free-ride-seeking,

85

glorified door-to-door salesperson with no real value beyond her tits and teeth."

Limbs trembling, she dropped her chin and let the tears fall as the narrator moved on to talk about her great fall from fame—and the balcony—but Toni wrapped an arm around her and moved her forward down the trail.

"Welcome to the downside of being in the public eye, *mon amie*. You must learn to ignore it because you will never convince the public of the truth. They make of you what they want—and especially what they *need*."

Bea remembered enough of her history to know that much more than a quote about eating cake had been erroneously assigned to Marie Antoinette. She'd been wrongly accused of everything from participating in pornography, to a great scandal involving extortion and a diamond necklace. Most of the untruths were either concocted specifically for, or used advantageously in, turning the masses against the monarchy during the initial stirrings of the French Revolution.

"The public is very adept at compartmentalizing facts to suit their purpose," Toni continued. "They railed against the cost of my lavish wardrobe. Yet, between the silk farmers, textile weavers, designers, and seamstresses, I employed nearly a third of the country, and, for the first time, elevated the status of these craftsmen to the level of renowned artisans."

Her back, long and straight, and her cheeks flushing with the color of excitement, a flash of the regal Marie ghosted over the milder Toni. Bea sensed—almost saw—the swish of full skirts from the corner of her eye.

"They weren't even my choice, really." Toni glanced at Bea as they walked. "The ridiculous dresses, I mean. It was expected of a queen to wear them, a display of the country's wealth and power. But they were cumbersome and hot, and inappropriate for my days in the countryside with my children. I had the court designers make me a simple white peasant dress for regular use, and the public loved the idea and adopted the look. Wearing the light shift made life easier for them as well, and they were far more affordable for the masses. Everyone could wear them without shame."

Toni paused. Their feet crunching on dirt and the gusts of wind brushing past their ears were temporarily the only sound. "None of that mattered in the end, though. None of it was remembered. Most of the angry women gathered that day in the *Place de la Révolution* wore them, my white cotton dresses... as they took my head."

The *Place de la Révolution;* later renamed the *Place de la Concorde*—Toni and Bea had died at the exact same spot.

The trail ended abruptly at a cliff's edge, the drop-off to the next level of the pit below. Yet another National Park Service sign announced the attraction as "The Winds," which was playing out in nearly identical fashion to the original *Inferno.*

Beyond the edge of the cliff, thousands upon thousands of bodies blew in a vertical cyclone of cold air that moved in a clockwise motion, the twelve o'clock position so high above her that they disappeared into dark weather. The six o'clock position appeared to nearly reach down to the Third Circle below them— a five-hundred-foot drop. So vast was the radius of the human storm that the three o'clock and nine o'clock spots were far out of view to the left and right. The sounds from this vantagepoint had grown so loud she had an urge to cover her ears, because it wasn't merely the freight train roar of the winds themselves, but the pitiful moans and sobs of the souls tossing within it.

The riders of the storm were all naked, skin goose bumped and nipples hard from the cold, or possibly from yearning, the men with hard-ons, the women's thighs glossy and wet, everyone reaching desperately to one another as they were thrown about like ragdolls on an angry sea.

Occasionally, almost as if on purpose (*probably* on purpose), the winds would blow two or more people together and hold them there, creating a small spot of calm, a time-out from the ceaseless movement. But just as their hands—or someone else's—moved to their genitals, they were, once again, torn apart, cries of pain and desperation ripping the air.

"They are forever at the peak of their libido. They'll spend eternity in the moment just before orgasm, never achieving release," Toni said, gazing out at the kaleidoscope of bodies that were painted every beautiful color of flesh. "They are The Carnal. In life, they gave short shrift to true emotional connection, instead, attempting to fill a void inside themselves with empty physical sensation. Over and over, they instinctively craved something real, but, whether out of fear or ignorance they inevitably got stuck at—"

"The second chakra."

Toni shot a glance at Bea. "Yes. Exactly."

The faces of the wind-tossed souls, when some slowed down enough that Bea could examine them, were far more expressive of grief than lust.

"And for this they're punished? The Universe, or whatever runs this place, thinks teasing them forever is the answer? Promiscuity shouldn't be a sin as long as everything is consensual and honest."

"You misunderstand." Toni stepped back from the edge, rubbing her arms against the chill gusts. "There is no actual *punishment* in this place. But without the daily distractions of being alive—jobs, family, household tasks, survival—people here are forced to stare at the particular shadow, the crutch, the so-called *sin* on Madame Borovsky's chart, that most greatly pulled them away from the light while they lived. The choice they made over and over in a misguided attempt to feel something, but which, inevitably, led to greater and greater disconnect. Here, they are forced to see it, to study it, because there is nothing left to distract them from it."

"The road to Hell is paved with good intentions," Bea muttered.

"*Pardon?*"

She pulled her gaze from the view. "If I understand what you're saying, we all did things in life we hoped would ease our human pain, but, rather than helping, it pulled us further from what would truly salve it—connection. So, now it's our task, after death, to face this and study it. Perhaps... eventually to move on?"

Toni nodded. "A fine way to put it, yes. Unfortunately, the vast majority do not, as you say, move on."

"Then the system is broken. The education methods here are poor."

"Perhaps," said Toni after a pause.

"And Lower Hell—that's different?"

"*Oui.* The sins of Upper Hell caused pain mainly to the individuals themselves. They were sins against their own growth, their own joy. Those residing in Lower Hell, though, their pain in life was so great they tried to cast it off onto others, spreading it all around them like a rat with the plague. The souls in those circles face true torment. Because they are so deeply entrenched in their own shit, much more prodding is required for them to see it."

"Who doles out their method of suffering? The demons?"

"They are some of the actors in this tragic play, yes. But you must try to remember, *chérie,* that it is *we* who are collectively creating this reality, including the very people in Lower Hell themselves. In the deepest recesses of their souls, they know what they need to face. A part of them begs for it. Yet, the torment itself will never free them, because it is not some morbid justice that needs to be satisfied, but under-standing that must be achieved, and most have no hope for that."

In the story of *Inferno*, Dante Alighieri divided the Underworld in the same way. The circles of Upper Hell were passive sins, sins of overindulgence. The sins of Lower Hell were active sins, those of violence to others, and those lower circles were all contained in what he called The City of Dis, a vast, putrid and decaying place of crumbling towers and moats, thronging with demons. The classic depiction of Hell.

Mordor.

A stinging chill rolled up Bea's spine, past her neck, and tingling her scalp as she realized that, eventually, The City of Dis—however it would manifest in this updated version of the landscape—would be her latest, and possibly last, great travel adventure.

As she ruminated over the possible scenarios awaiting her beyond the Second Circle, as she rehearsed her denials of the tabloid TV coverage to her brother, one body morphed out of the cyclone and came to a stop in front of her. Held still in the winds, he floated upright in the air only inches from the ledge. Only inches from Bea herself.

Fuck, was he beautiful.

Tan skin over rippling muscles, long, bronze hair blowing around his shoulders, chiseled jaw line covered in a bit of scruff... He was every romance novel hero she'd ever imagined. Every golden god come down from Asgard with a hammer. He was Thor. He was Loki.

He was *nude*, his erection slick and rigid.

And all of that paled under the dark sun of grief painting his face, which rendered him breathtaking.

He lifted his hand to her, palm up, beseeching.

Her body responded—pulsing with both desire and empathy—and she shifted her weight to her front foot.

"Beatrice, you must not."

Toni's voice broke her from the near trance, though the man silently held his spot, awaiting her response with outstretched arm.

But she pulled her gaze away as a familiar tingling sensation on her back caused her to turn around. The demon video crew was back, moving closer, with their cameras covering half their faces. At a height of seven-and-a-half feet, they wore nothing but long, buttoned trench coats, one demon bald, the other sporting a thin, greasy ponytail. They stopped ten feet away, recording.

"I'd prefer not to find out what is under those coats." Toni spun Bea away from them with a hand on her shoulder. "We need to move on."

But the tortured man still floated, and she felt pulled by his pain, even as large monitors rose up once again, beginning their broadcast anew.

She and the handsome man filled the screen as the announcer narrated over their image. "Let's see a show of thumbs! Should she… *ahem*… give him a hand?"

A roar of cheers rose from the abyss, and the screens filled with blue thumbs.

"Where are those votes coming from?" she asked. "Who, exactly, is liking me, and how?"

"It is my impression that much of the population has use of communication devices whenever Hell desires their input. Phones appear in hands as needed to cast votes or make comments. Disappear just as quickly, too, to maintain control. Given your challenge in The Game, I doubt we will be granted such access. Nevertheless, the monitors keep everyone informed, including us."

A scroll along the bottom of the broadcast now displayed a count of Bea's "friends"—presumably, friends here in the circles—and as she stood there, inches from a hard-on, the count rose, the numbers leaping by ten thousand per second. This, now, was familiar territory. It felt good. She understood it. And, ability to make her own posts or not, she could use it.

She took a step toward the man, her own hand rising.

"Beatrice." Toni's mouth became a pale, flat line, her eyes narrowed.

"They want this." She tipped her head toward the screens. "And we need all those friends on our side to make it through. It couldn't hurt."

"It could, actually. You think they're really friends? You mistake attention for affection."

Bea watched the numbers rising on the screens, then looked back to the man still hovering inches away. His full lips mouthed the word "Please" even while she felt the heat of Toni's silent anger. But that word—and his pain—convinced her more than any follower count.

She reached to grasp his erection, but he grabbed her wrist, bringing her palm to his chest and placing it over his heart instead. Tears slid down his cheeks as he held her gaze, his hand clutching tightly over hers, fighting to hold the precious connection.

"He begins to understand." Toni slid to her side, speaking softly. "You feel his pain, and you give comfort. But you must let go now, *chérie*. Any moment the winds will pull him back and you cannot risk being pulled out with him."

Bea's own eyes were wet, but she couldn't let go. Couldn't abandon him to despair.

The winds, however, could, and they yanked him away.

He released her hand—a gift, a *Thank You*, of his own.

The television screens went blank.

Toni and Bea turned at the sound of a double thud as the demons dropped their video cameras, hands moving to the buttons on their trench coats, though they remained in place, eyes half-lidded with lust as they towered a good two feet over the women.

"We must go. Now." Toni scanned the edge of the cliff, left and right.

"How? You said it's a five-hundred foot drop this time."

"That is correct. And you are not yet ready to survive the jump undamaged. I suspect you will be unconscious far longer than we safely have. There will be more demons down there."

Bea rubbed her misshapen shoulder. "How long was I out last time?"

"I have no way of knowing for sure, but I estimate a month or more by Earth time."

"What? Did you experience it that way while you waited?"

"It does not matter now. You must hurry and decide how to go down from here. We can follow the circle around. There is a place where the cliff has crumbled, and we could pick our way down the rubble to the Third Circle. It will be steep and slow-going, yet manageable. But the rubble is quite far, on the other side of the pit." She tossed a look over her shoulder at the trench coats. "So whatever you decide, we must get started."

"The other side of the pit? That'll take too long. I need to find Dante. I'm worried about him; now that people might be aware he's my brother, I've put him on the radar."

Toni nodded, her brows drawing in. "That may be true."

Bea studied the winds, stepped to the edge, then looked down. "I have an idea. We can ride the winds down to the bottom."

"Ride the…" Toni lifted a brow.

"Hop on someone as they're rotating to the bottom of the spin, then hop off when we get close, before they rise back up. Like grabbing the hour hand on a clock and jumping off when it gets to six." She smiled with confidence at her idea, tapping her foot with proud impatience as she watched Toni work through the idea.

"It is too risky. We do not know what your assigned circle would have been. If The Winds are your place, you might not be able to jump out of them. You could be trapped here."

Bea put no more than a moment's thought into it. While she hadn't yet spent any real time pondering which circle was properly hers, she knew herself well enough to know which it wasn't. "This isn't my place."

Ignoring further protests from Toni, Bea watched for the perfect human carriage to float past. Her eyes narrowed, hawk-like, her muscles taut and ready as she waited… and when a linebacker of a man drifted close to the cliff edge, she jumped onto his back, her arms circling his meaty neck, her legs wrapping his torso.

They fell, the gusts so strong they whipped her hair and dried out her eyes. But she refrained from closing them as she watched for the ground below to reveal itself through a low-lying fog that obscured the landing zone.

As she looked down, waiting, she smiled, giving herself a mental pat on the back as she remembered Sanjay's words about people doing things they could never have imagined. Her bullshit social-media-influencer self was indeed becoming pretty damn brave after all, and, as he'd predicted, here she was doing things she'd never have imagined before. Maybe she *was* half of a freaking superhero after all.

Her smile was huge as they broke through the fog, then melted away as she saw what lay below. A sea of dark water, dotted with ice, and ghostly white objects bobbing on the surface. The sight was bizarre, and she had a moment of doubt until the linebacker gripped both her arms and she realized she might've made a huge miscalculation. This giant of a man seemed disinclined to let her go. She'd been a fool to not factor that in.

She struggled against his hold as they reached the bottom of the rotation only to begin the climb up the other side. She yelled into his ear, but the force of the winds blew her words away, and she wasn't nearly strong enough to yank herself free.

They were approaching the nine o'clock position when she managed to slam the heel of one foot into his groin.

He howled and let her go, but the fall was much farther than she'd planned.

Bea closed her eyes as she belly-slammed into the freezing water, her cry of pain choked off as her body—and her pride—sank into the frigid black depths.

Chapter 11

THE THIRD CIRCLE

Shock and panic ignited her blood like a match to gasoline. Bea kicked and flailed upward through the murky water, breaking the surface with a sputtering cough. Bicycling her feet to stay afloat, she rotated, getting her bearings while ripples tossed her about, and her skin burned with the pain of her body slamming onto water. What she'd seen as white objects during the fall, were pale, shivering human bodies, each one sitting on a cramped white plastic chair with no armrests. Each chair balanced atop a long pole sticking several feet out of the water. The whole effect was like a forest grove of precarious lifeguard stations.

She craned up at the nearest person, a pallid, zit-faced, twenty-something young man wearing white cotton clothing and balancing a laptop on his thighs. His teeth chattered in the frigid air, the sound mimicking the clack of the computer keys as he frantically worked the keyboard. A quick survey of others showed the identical situation—same clothes, same laptops balanced on their legs, some rapidly typing, others motionless, eyes glued to the screen.

Still dog paddling, Bea returned her attention to the man closest. "Um, hello?"

Though he was clearly within easy earshot, he didn't respond in any way, his fingers still pounding the keys.

"Little help?"

He finally tilted his head in her direction, eyes not moving from the screen. "I don't take voice calls. Text only."

"What? I'm right here."

"No talk. Text only."

Her legs were tiring, and her muscles had begun cramping in the freezing temps. As she looked for the closest shoreline, a burst of movement grabbed her attention and she squinted for a better look. A woman jumped up and down, arms waving, from atop what looked like a low-sitting bridge crossing the water. Toni.

Bea kicked and swam toward her, then scrambled up broken, sharp chunks of concrete while Toni reached out to help her up the final steps.

"How long have you been waiting for me this time?" Bea wrapped her arms around her torso, bending in on herself as the chill wind on her wet skin and clothes caused knife-slicing pain. Her shoes sloshed and her jeans had become long and heavy, sticking to her legs as she stood there with her teeth chattering. Wasn't Hell supposed to be hot? She stomped her feet, trying to get the blood moving. "You're not even wet. Of course."

"You, too, will be able to control your physical state when you truly believe you can." Toni surveyed the landscape. "We should keep moving."

They strode down the concrete path, which was one branch of a network of such walkways snaking over the dark sea to the opposite shore of the Third Circle. There, strange pale foothills rose up under a sky so gray and cold she could imagine reaching a hand into the low-hung clouds and getting sliced on ice shards.

As they walked, Bea paused now and again to study the nearest pole-chair occupants. Some played video games, hands racing to complete level after level as they grunted curse words on foggy breath when their avatars died. Others sat glued to Netflix or any number of other streaming services, shivering in their insufficient clothing as they gawked sightlessly.

Bea stopped by one such viewer, a woman who must have died in her sixties, her complexion sallow with deep, gray bags hanging heavy under her eyes. Bea was close enough to watch as the woman clicked to begin the next episode of *Stranger Things*. The listing said, "Season 54, Episode 2." The show began, and the starring kids now looked to be in their thirties.

Bea looked to Toni, her mouth opening in question, but she got her answer before needing to ask.

"They will never finish the series they are watching or complete the game they are playing. There is always another level, another season, without end. If they drift asleep, they will fall into the water and sink into the icy depths. If they simply give up and stop playing or watching," Toni again scanned the environment, searching for something that caused her jaws to twitch, "then Cerberus itself will knock them into the sea."

Cerberus. The three-headed dog holding dominion over the souls stuck in the Third Circle. Bea searched through her memories of *Inferno*, recalling the sin of the Third Circle as she surveyed the scene before her, and it suddenly made sense—Gluttony.

"Let's go." Toni touched Bea's elbow, encouraging her onward and pointing to the foothills ahead of them. "We've got a long road ahead and still need to pass through The Gorge."

They came to a fork in the snaking path, the left branch seeming a more direct route to the opposite shore, the right taking a longer, meandering course. Bea stepped onto the left branch, but jerked back when Toni grabbed her wrist.

Still damp, cold, and growing irritated, Bea snatched her arm back. "What? This way is obviously shorter. I thought you were in a big hurry to keep moving."

"I am, but..." Toni squinted down the bridgeway ahead, fingertips pressing to her lips. She may have been checking for signs of Cerberus, but her slumped shoulders and hesitant steps backward spoke more of a personal demon; remorse, not vigilance. "It is best we go the other way."

Bea picked up the pace to keep up with Toni, who'd practically bolted off in the other direction. This branch took a serpentine route across the waters, the bodies more congested here in the confined pools formed within the switchbacks. A lot of the souls in this circle were young, twenties to early thirties at most, especially the gamer contingent.

The cluster she and Toni were now approaching looked to be packed with kids in their late teens, which gave Bea a queasy feeling as she remembered their actual mortality status.

The kids worked their keyboards like pros and interacted with each other more than elsewhere in the Third Circle, sharing information about whatever game they were playing, perhaps some Hell-set MMOG.

"What happened here?" Bea asked. "A school bus crash or something? They're all... they died so young."

"Not necessarily an accident, no. I find that, particularly with the people in this circle, there was a lot of... *elective* withdrawal from the world. First into their world of digital fantasy. Then later..." Toni paused and watched the gameplay, the desperate movements of the participants' shaky hands, the constant scrubbing of their sleepy eyes. "The average age has gotten increasingly younger over the years."

Only then did Bea notice scars on some of their wrists. Far too many and far, far too young. Were they here *because* they were suicides? That was one of the biggest issues she had with Alighieri's *Inferno*, the thought that souls in enough pain to want to exit their lives would be sent to Hell for their choice. It had pissed her off, quite frankly. That and the fact that the old poet had seen fit to place the LGBTQ community here, too. In fact—

"Oh my God. Sanjay isn't in Hell because he's gay, is he? Please tell me that, at least in this more modern version of the Underworld, people aren't sent here because they chose to take their own life or because they're not…" She flailed her hands around in rapidly growing frustration. "I don't know… cis hetero?"

"The manner in which someone exits their life has become irrelevant here," Toni assured her. "Nor does it matter *who* or *how* someone loves."

"Then why—"

Toni stepped closer, her gaze intense. "What matters is only in the ways they did *not* love. Just like everyone else here."

Bea took that in for a moment before following her guide, soon catching up as their path skirted the perimeter of the young group of gamers. Her gaze drew again and again to a flicker of red bobbing against a canvas of ghostly pale skin and monotonous white wardrobe.

Proximity finally revealed the spot of color to be a homemade t-shirt graphic, the words "Okay, Boomer" hand-scrawled across the chest, though brick red smudges and drips marred the attempt. The aesthetic was familiar—reminiscent of the banks of the river Acheron and the coin vendor's signage.

"Is that blood?" Bea gaped at the writing before lifting her focus to the wearer's face, an older teen with a high, dark mohawk and an intense energy that stuck out amid the rampant apathy of the place.

The girl's attention snapped to Bea and Toni, returning their observation with equal interest, unlike the other souls they'd passed on this level, most of whom had gone numb with disinterest.

"Got to do something to break the monotony once in a while; something to help, you know, remember." Her fingers kept working the keyboard though her eyes drank their fill of the strangers, then she went back to the game with a shrug. "Especially when the dog's off somewhere else."

Bea studied the bloody writing again, holding her expression neutral though her stomach began to turn over. "But how do you...?"

"Fingernails work. Teeth, if necessary."

When Bea gasped, the teen shot her another look. "You *do* realize we don't have bodies here, right? No real body, no pain. Or haven't you figured that out yet?" She slid a glance to Bea's misaligned shoulder and still damp clothes before turning back to the game. "Guess not."

Toni smirked as she tipped her head, indicating they should continue, and the two women stepped off.

"What?" Bea said, flinging a hand toward the teen. "She's been here longer than me. She's had more time to figure it out."

"It's not just that. The child is restless and senses there's still a chance. She's fighting to keep that little flame still burning within; a flame, it seems, that was never fully doused to begin with. Which, I might add, is both lucky and horrific for her at the same time."

The pair had not gone far when a shout from the group of gamers halted their step.

"Ha! I found out where it is," a young man called out. "I knew it existed."

"Seriously?" called an adolescent girl. "Dude, where?"

"Wait. It's *real?*" This from the teen they'd been talking to, who now glanced back at Toni and Bea, brow drawing in.

"Oh, it's real all right," said the first voice. "Guarded like a motherfucker, though. Of course."

The anomaly of that much social interaction in this place had Toni trotting back to check out the activity, and her expression grew pinched. "What's going on?" she asked the mohawked teen as they approached her once more.

"He says he found *The Book of the Dead*. But he's full of shit. He just wants attention."

"What's *The Book of the Dead?*" Bea asked, realizing with

a passing thought that her own clothes were now thoroughly dry and unsure of exactly when that had happened in the last few moments.

"It's the most highly sought-after treasure in *Hellscape*." The mohawked teen fixed on Bea's blank expression. "The video game we're all playing. The only game we *ever* play. For fucking *years*. The goal is to get out of Hell, but most of us can't even get past level three." She rolled her eyes. "And, yes, I get the irony."

"I'm in level five now, losers, and I know the book's fucking here. But the demons on this level—well, shit." The guy bragging about his success flung his head back with a groan. "I just bit it again. Back to the goddamned ferry."

"Why do you want to find it so badly?" Bea asked.

"Because it's *The Book*, idiot!" the guy shouted without bothering to even look at her. "It gets you out."

"It's a myth to keep us playing, that's all," said their teenage friend.

"It's *not* a myth. It's the phone book for Hell," said the adolescent girl who'd spoken earlier. "It can tell you exactly where your deceased loved ones are located."

Bea shot a glance at Toni, who was focused on the conversation playing out in front of them.

"Or your enemies," snorted an older man.

"It's more than that."

Bea startled at a soft voice behind her on the other side of the path.

A skinny kid with a dark complexion and big, liquid-brown eyes worked his laptop as he spoke. "Some say it tells you how to get out of here. I mean *really* get out of here, not just finish the game. But finding it virtually is just the first step. You have to find the real physical book, too, here in actual Hell, and only then can it help you." He finally stopped clickity-clacking and looked up at them. "They say it's the key."

Bea took the few steps to the other side of the path and leaned toward him. "The key to what?"

His brows lifted. "To everything."

She straightened and shifted her attention back to Toni. "We've got to find that book."

"What? No." The regal chin lifted as Toni crossed her arms in front of her chest. "That is *not* part of our plan. And, besides, I've never heard of this book before, *or* needed it. Its existence is doubtful."

"But what if it does exist? If this gamer is correct, it's located somewhere in Dante's circle anyway. It won't be out of our way and could make our search for him easier." She crossed her own arms, mirroring Toni's stubborn stance. "We have nothing to lose. Who knows what other information it might offer as well? It's a *key*."

"Why, because some gaming rumor says so?" Toni rolled her eyes. "The Fifth Circle is enormous. You want to waste time finding this mythical book before looking for your brother?"

Bea stomped back to the other side of the path, shouting to the gamer who'd boasted his discovery of the book. "Hey, do you know where in the Fifth Circle it is?"

"Gameplay indicated it's considered a reliquary. That's as far as I got." He shrugged.

"Reliquaries are usually in churches or tombs," their original friend said, watching them with renewed intensity, a sudden energy as if she'd just struck upon an idea.

"Beatrice, that whole level is one giant tomb. They're all..." Toni bit off her words when she noted Bea's wounded expression.

Her brother lay in a fucking tomb. Bea's hand went to her stomach as if someone had just gut-punched her.

Toni gave her a moment before continuing. "Nevertheless, there are priorities. We discussed this. First, you asked to find your brother, and now you want to add *another* errand to our list? That is *not* our deal."

"He's my brother, *not* an errand. And you and I never made a deal." Bea ignored the rising color on Toni's cheeks. "This book *could* make reaching our goal easier."

"More likely it will make it *harder*."

Their matching stubbornness was getting them nowhere.

"Look, we actually have the same priority, and that's family," Bea said. "Let's help each other out here, okay? Help me find the book and my brother, and, as soon as we've got him, I'll focus everything I have on getting out of here, and getting *you* to your children. One thousand percent effort. No straying from the path. I promise. How 'bout that for a deal?"

Toni chewed on her lip for several seconds. "Fine. Deal. But, come on now. We've got a long way to go before it's even an issue."

Before they could step off, something cold and clammy grabbed Bea's wrist like a vise. Dark brown, feminine eyes, round with urgency, looked up from beneath the mohawked hair. Their young friend had abandoned her post and leapt off her chair onto the concrete abutment. "You're the girl on TV everyone's watching. Aren't you going down through the levels to get out of here?" Her grip tightened. "Take me with you."

Bea gaped at the hand clenching her wrist, then back to the face, which suddenly looked less the hardened punk-wannabe and every bit the vulnerable kid.

The girl tugged harder on Bea's wrist while scrambling the last steps onto the path. "Please!"

Toni stepped up to intervene. "No, I'm sorry. We do not have permission."

The teenager refused to release Bea's wrist.

Now that the kid was standing next to them, she was smaller than she'd originally seemed—short with a petite bone structure—but a strong upright posture, and Toni's eyes softened as she studied the girl.

"Why not?" Bea asked. "You were ready to bring along Madame Borovsky and Sanjay. What's the difference?"

"The difference is, I know them. I know their level of understanding, the amount of insight they already possess. But this one..." Toni gestured to their applicant.

"Jesse," the kid said. "My name is Jesse Chen."

Bea slipped her wrist from Jesse's grasp and took hold of her hand instead. "I'd say Jesse has enough insight—not to mention balls. She's making the choice Borovsky and Sanjay weren't able to. She wants to move forward. Let her."

Toni reached out and cupped Jesse's chin, lifting the young face, and staring hard into the teen's eyes. "You realize you may well not make it out. Worse, you could end up stuck further down the pit, where there are far worse ways to suffer than eternal game play."

The kid nodded and returned a fearless gaze, back ramrod straight, jaw firm.

Toni relaxed her shoulders with a sigh. "Very well, *mon chou*, you may join us—though I make no guarantees and can offer little to no protection."

She released Jesse's chin, but Bea caught how the back of her hand slid gently against the teen's jawline before moving away.

She noted, too, how Jesse let her.

The moment ended, and the teen took the first step forward. "Let's do this thing, then."

"Lead the way, kid," said Bea, gesturing toward the path.

Jesse shot her a fierce look. "*Not* a kid."

"Got it." Bea chuckled, already drawn to the girl.

They turned to move off, taking a step or two before she noticed it—silence. The ever-present background noise of multitudinous fingers on keyboards had ceased, leaving an acoustic void heavier than the quiet after a storm.

Slowing, they took a couple more steps, then stopped all together.

Bea scanned the water on both sides of the path, discovering a sea of little lifeguards holding their laptops up, webcam eyes pointed at the party of three standing on the breezeway. A thousand cameras were broadcasting Jesse's escape, their conspiracy of rebellion. She'd never even seen anyone move.

A gust of wind broke the moment, Jesse's spiked hair bending against the sharp breeze. "Time to go. Right now." The teen was the first of the three to bolt.

Toni and Bea joined fast behind, their six feet pounding the concrete, their breath heaving as they raced around switchbacks and flew down straightaways, the mountains on the other side fast growing closer.

But their sounds of flight soon faded against something bigger… stronger. A pounding that vibrated the ground beneath them, sending jolts through Bea's bones. Rhythmic in nature, its tempo in four-four time. *One, two, three, four. One, two, three, four.* A horrifying tango, growing louder by the heartbeat.

"Keep going, we're almost there!" Bea shouted, pointing at the strange mountains now looming above them. What she'd originally thought were brush-covered foothills, scrubby and brown like the Malibu canyons in high summer, now showed themselves to be… something else.

Weirdly angular and monochrome in color, like towering piles of huge brown sugar cubes.

"No. We're not as close as you think!" Toni shouted back. "Those mountains… It's not a straight shot there." She stopped running, hands on knees as she gulped for air her dead body didn't really need. "We're too late."

Bea and Jesse joined her, scanning the path from where they'd just come and seeing nothing, as they, too, caught their breath. Their lungs worked at the same speed as the pounding of the unknown thing marching closer.

"What is that sound, anyway?" Bea ran the back of her hand across her sweaty forehead.

Jesse stepped toward it one pace, shoulders dropping in resignation. "It's the dog."

Cerberus.

It stepped into view as it rounded a corner. It was a canine only in the way one might draw a stick figure of a dog. Towering above them, a mechanical beast with four hydraulic legs, a metal tube of a torso, and a finely articulated tail, infinitely long like Minos' whips had been. With a cluster of razor barbs on the end, the tail wagged and stretched, flexing and threatening over the sea of people.

The heads, though. Three of them, of course, twenty feet above the ground atop long necks—bearing not eyes, noses, or mouths, but rather, *monitors*, each broadcasting one faction of the social media triumvirate: Facebook, Instagram, Twitter.

On one of the three heads, Cerberus was currently streaming a Facebook Live feed, the stunned faces of the three members of Team Beatrice front and center of the screen. The comment thread raced beneath the image, showing support and hate in equal measure:

"Looks like a triple serving of dog chow to me." 536 likes.

"Somebody please make Mohawk Girl the next Marvel superhero." 7,201 likes.

"Mark my words, Beatrice Allegra is an antifa false flag operative." 10.9k likes.

Unlike when the cameras had broadcast Bea's interaction with the naked man in the winds, where her follower count had gone through the roof and blue thumbs had rallied in support, this time, the consensus was decidedly mixed. And far less friendly.

On the second head, the Instagram feed suddenly produced a brand-new account for Jesse Chen, the tiny profile image showing the same scared shot of her face currently showing on the Facebook Live stream.

"Instagram?" Jesse asked. "How could I possibly have an

Instagram account? I have no fucking phone. I haven't done anything except sit in a chair for ages. I'd have nothing to post."

"Well, you do now," Bea said.

Jesse's photo feed began filling, first, with shot after shot of the girl's previous gameplay screencaps, and now, images of her standing with her new friends, toe-to-toe with the dog. Jesse's follower count moved from zero to over a million in seconds.

"Holy shit," said Jesse as the monitor zoomed in on the comments, again a mix of supportive and hateful, each commenter talking as if they had some kind of personal knowledge of Jesse.

Bea knew well the strange discomfort of that, but at least she'd had years to slowly get used to it. The teen was going from anonymity to infamy in a matter of seconds. Poor kid.

The Twitter screen was more static, quietly showing a list of the trending hashtags: #whoisjessechen, #thebookofthedead, and by far the most disturbing, at least to Bea, the number one trending hashtag of #finddantefirst.

A fist gripped the back of her t-shirt. Toni had one hand each on her and Jesse and was slowly tugging them away from the monstrous dog.

"What do we do now?" Bea said as they all slunk quietly backward.

"*Mes amies*, although I doubt it likely, right now would be an excellent time for you both to realize you simply do not need to be here."

"Huh?" Bea placed her own hand on Jesse's shoulder, a protective move that was far more an instinctive gesture than actual assistance.

"She's telling us to wake up. You know, turn all *Enlightened Being* on the spot. Create your own reality and all that," Jesse said.

The dog kept pace as they crept back.

"Click our heels three times and disappear?" Bea added.

"Right," said Jesse.

A subtle rushing sound caught Bea's attention, a soft, white noise coming from somewhere behind them in the direction they were inching.

Toni cocked her head for a moment, listening, but still moving back. "Jesse has already conquered her fear of pain, the illusion of bodily permanence. The next step is—"

"Kind of hard to think about the next step right now when my imaginary heart is somehow pounding through my ears." The girl clamped a death-grip onto Bea's arm. And still they backed up. "I mean, ol' Bea here hasn't even managed to straighten her damned shoulder and you want us to—"

The dog's tail whipped forward, curling around Jesse's waist and flinging the teen away from Bea's grasp and high into the air. As her slight body arced above the water, the tail flung out again, this time, the barbed end glinting even in the murky light before slicing through her torso. Non-corporeal or not, bright red guts spilled from the gash that now lay straight through the words "Okay, Boomer," and Jesse's mind-killing shrieks evidenced the fact that this time, at least, the kid felt something.

As she dropped from the sky, the tail made a second pass, finishing the job and separating her tiny body into two halves— that crashed into the icy water, first one splash, then a second.

Bea's limbs became concrete; her breath failed in her lungs. She could only stare as the water closed in over the ripples, eventually smoothing away all evidence of the dual splashdowns.

The world quieted.

The dog went inert.

The heads of the gamers turned away from the sight and back to gameplay.

Toni had gone equally still, a pallor on her face that even a good eighteenth-century powdering couldn't match.

Bea managed to mobilize first, then Toni straightened beside her.

The dog no longer seemed interested in them, and, instead,

the Facebook head began a scroll of random personal pages, all with posts offering thoughts and prayers to Jesse.

Someone started a GoFundMe on the teen's behalf.

Someone else began an online petition to limit the dog's reach. The fine citizens of Hell had a lot to say—virtually, anyway—and held strong feelings about the tragic event, but no one moved from their lifeguard chairs to search the waters for Jesse, who was likely drifting helpless and scared in pieces below. No one moved to collect one of Jesse's shoes that had floated up from the depths and now bobbed horrifyingly on the surface. No one moved so much as their mouth to call out Jesse's name.

No one, it seemed, cared enough to bother moving at all. They were willing to tap a finger on the kid's behalf, but not actually lift one.

Bea and Toni turned, and with vision warped by tears, began their run forward again, toward the mountains and the ever-increasing volume of the rushing white noise.

The sound revealed itself in moments.

Had she not been so occupied with the tragedy they'd just witnessed, the source of it would have been obvious much sooner.

A raging waterfall, high as the Empire State Building, but narrow and powerful like the stream from a garden hose when a thumb is held half over the end, falling into a steep gorge that separated the Third Circle from the base of the mountains rising up out of the Fourth. Chunks of ice swept to the cliff's edge and then screamed over the side.

Bea knew the drill by now, and she didn't care, didn't pause. Already hovering at the edge of self-loathing, she refused to grant herself the luxury of fear. Stepping straight into the rushing waters, her body was instantly yanked forward and under as if pulled by a freight train. She relished every slam to her head, every gouge to her ribs, every tearing laceration as her thoughts grew liquid and her tears became one with the flow.

USC MEDICAL CENTER
Los Angeles, California

9 years ago

Her feet were freezing. The thin hospital blanket had been tossed over her legs haphazardly, leaving her bare toes exposed. Bea kicked at the soft cotton, trying to move it down to cover them, but her agitation only messed the sheets up more, so she sat up and threw the linen into place, ignoring the fear screaming in her skull.

Blue curtains printed with tiny white daisies ringed her bed on a track, pulled shut for privacy. The emergency room doctor stood next to her bed, speaking to her parents on her cell phone, and she listened to his side of the conversation over the beeping of the vitals machine to which she was currently hooked up.

Her mom had been hysterical when Bea had called after arriving at the hospital, and she'd handed the phone over to the doctor, hoping he'd convince her parents they didn't need to hop the next flight to L.A. Maybe they were ready to be convinced. Her family couldn't handle any more trauma. Not now. Not a mere month after Dante's death. And, besides, she *was* going to be okay.

Even if the weird pull on the left side of her face and her half-closed eyelid suggested otherwise.

She laid a palm against her paralyzed cheek, a fresh round of adrenalin shooting through her limbs. The night before, she'd crawled into bed feeling what she'd assumed were the first signs of an oncoming cold—an itching eye, a slight headache on one side. But she'd gotten the second biggest shock of her life (so unfairly back-to-back with the first one) when she'd woken up this morning to half a drooping face and a trail of drool from one side of her mouth—what she now knew was Bell's palsy.

Her panicked shouts had brought Mel flying into the bedroom, and the look of horror on her roommate's face mirrored in full what Bea could only express on half of her own. Minutes later, she'd been tucked into Mel's beat-up old Mini, well on her way to the hospital and a backless paper gown.

At least she lived with Mel in an off-campus apartment rather than in a dormitory. After Dante's death the previous month, Bea had gotten permission to finish her classes remotely and she rarely set foot on the actual university grounds anymore. Thank god for *that* because she didn't have to cross the school grounds this morning and face anyone with her… face.

Bea glanced around for a mirror while she waited for the doctor to wrap up the phone call. Maybe her symptoms had improved in the last couple hours and the doctor wasn't downplaying things to her folks quite as much as she thought.

But there was no mirror in the small, curtained space. Thankfully she spied something just as good—Mel's purse. Her roommate had slipped off in search of a restroom, leaving her giant bag, and the budding makeup artist had to have at least two or three mirrors in there.

Bea rummaged through the sack and found what she'd sought.

It *was* as bad as she remembered.

The left side of her mouth dipped a half-inch lower than her right and didn't move. Her attempt at a smile rendered her a female Tommy Two-Face, so she stopped trying. Her left eye was mostly closed, though it still dropped a tear in perfect synchronization with the right eye. The right half of her lips began to quiver in fear while the left remained rudely stoic.

She dropped the mirror onto the bed.

The curtains drew back with a zipping sound and Melanie stepped through just as the doctor ended the call with her folks.

"All's well on the parental front." The resident tried to sound chill and more hip than he was as he handed back her phone. "They've promised not to fly out, but I'm guessing they'll be calling every hour for a while."

Bea kept her expression neutral—it was the least gruesome thing to do. "Thanks. I appreciate it."

"I think we can go ahead and send you home. Remember, it'll get a little worse over the next couple days, so don't panic. But then you'll begin to heal. Just rest and relax and try to not to worry. We don't know exactly what causes Bell's palsy. Our best guess is a virus, but stress can trigger it," he said. "I know it must've been frightening to wake up this morning, feeling like you're missing half of yourself, but I promise, over the next few weeks it'll resolve, and you'll soon be whole again."

She thanked him for his help, and though the last thing this guy deserved was any sarcasm, she couldn't help herself. With great effort to enunciate, she pointed out that it wasn't this morning when she'd lost half of herself, but rather, four weeks ago. And she was pretty damn sure she'd never be getting it back.

***

Three days later, the resident was proven right on both counts. Bea's symptoms had peaked, her left face drooping further, and her parents called on the hour. But she'd done her internet research and everything the doc had told her checked out. Her Bell's would likely resolve over the next few weeks, but her grief—which had no doubt been a factor in triggering the illness—would take far longer to heal.

Her web searches had also given her ideas to help in that process, and journaling was an oft-suggested tool. She'd resolved to start a video blog, putting her Dali-like melting visage right out into the world, maybe connecting with others facing similar issues. Maybe helping them see they weren't alone. Helping herself see that, too, because loneliness and fear were breaking her.

She pulled a chair up to the dining room table and popped open her laptop, adjusting the fancy little webcam Nadi had brought her the night before. Logging into YouTube for the first time, Bea stared at the account creation page.

"Hey, what's up?" Mel's voice and the sound of her heavy bag landing on the coffee table announced her return from class. She breezed into the small dining room and leaned over Bea's shoulder to look at the screen. "You're starting a YouTube channel? Why?"

"I'm going to try documenting my healing journey. They say it helps to open up and share. Vulnerability and all that crap."

Mel's gaze zig-zagged between the laptop screen and Bea's face. "Is this about your brother or the Bell's?"

Bea shrugged. "Same thing."

"Huh."

There was silence except for Bea's fingernails drumming the tabletop. She glanced up at Melanie who seemed to be studying the web page, repeatedly starting to chew her bottom lip, but remembering her lipstick and stopping, as was her habit whenever she was stressed.

She straightened and turned to Bea. "How 'bout I do your makeup for you? Doll you up for your first broadcast. I can use highlighting to minimize the droop and to give the illusion of opening up your left eye a bit. It'll be super easy."

Her roomie was missing the point entirely. Or just couldn't stand the thought of "ugly" being recorded for all internet eternity. "Thanks, babe, I appreciate the offer. I do. But this is about sharing my real-life circumstances. It's about honesty and acceptance. Makeup would be counter to that. So, no glamour, no façade. Just truth. That's all I ever want to put out there."

Mel blew out a resigned breath, but nodded. "At least let me do your hair. Add some volume and shine. That has nothing to do with the Bell's, and there's no reason to shun a little self-care where you can get it."

Self-care. Bea could concede that point, and she half-smiled. "Okay. Just some curl."

"Great." Mel clapped her hands before running off to grab her toolkit.

As her roommate worked, tugging strands of Bea's hair through the curling iron and creating a fine cloud of sweet-smelling product spray throughout the room, Bea sat before the laptop and set up her YouTube account. She paused as she stared at the box asking her to enter the title of her first broadcast. She rolled some choices around in her mind, finally deciding on the perfect one, and typed it in:

"Life After Death: Getting Through Hell, One Step at a Time."

She pressed Enter.

Chapter 13

THE FOURTH CIRCLE
The Foothills

Something skittered past her head.

Bea rolled halfway over, her right arm flopping open to land with a slap in warm, slippery liquid. The sound of the falls still rang in her ears as she sneezed and opened her eyes.

Petroleum.

The smell assaulted her senses and threatened to invite an instant headache.

She pushed up onto her hip—oily brown rivulets running down her arms, dripping off her hair—and realized she'd been lying in a shallow pool not far from the base of the waterfall. It was much warmer down here at the bottom of the gorge, all signs of ice long evaporated. The sky above burned sickly yellow, shrouded in a greasy mist.

She rose and moved away from the puddled area, her tennis shoes squishing as she walked along the bank of a shallow, dark creek that flowed through the canyon, its surface ribboned with oily prisms. Her skin had already begun to scar from the hundreds of wounds received in the fall.

L.M. Strauss

As she ran a hand through her hair, it brushed past a bald spot where she'd been partially scalped, stubble already growing back in, but she barely gave her body and its rapid healing a second thought, her mind consumed with other things.

Dante. Toni. Jesse.

She wrung out her hair and scanned the scene. Even with the movement of all the water, the air down here was heavy and still.

There was the skittering sound again. And movement at the base of the cliff, seen in her peripheral vision.

"Toni?"

With no response after several calls, she began to pick her way across the slippery creek. Forward was the only way down, after all, and Toni knew where they were headed. She'd catch up.

Bea slipped now and again, losing purchase on the slimy river rocks, but she made her way across, choosing to focus on the opposite shore rather than the discomfort of her body. Her clothes had only dried earlier when she hadn't been focused on the freezing wet pain. Her body healed when she wasn't watching. So, for now, she'd simply ignore herself clean.

The ground on this side of the creek was dry and crusty, brown and devoid of any life, though trash began to make an appearance. Bubble wrap and Styrofoam peanuts broke the landscape, masquerading, at casual glance, as odd vegetation.

She soon came upon another brown National Park Service sign, this one welcoming visitors to the Fourth Circle and displaying a simple trail map painted in yellow. The bottom of the map had a little squiggly line apparently representing the oily creek she'd just crossed, noted as "The Gorge." A yellow "X" was placed there with the words "You Are Here."

From there, a winding path led up the mountain, with a spot marked as "The Forest" about two-thirds of the way up, and, at the very top, the trail ended at—not surprisingly—a spot called "The Summit."

She set off at the trailhead, her route leading up through a passage between two peaks in the mountain range—a mountain range whose formation was now obvious. Not granite or sandstone, not concrete. The big brown squares forming the peaks were a massive pile of cardboard boxes, some the size of refrigerators, others no more than a few inches per side. They were tattered and torn, stained and weather-beaten, empty of contents with ripped corrugated edges and flaps hanging by threads. There had to be millions—no, *billions*—of them. Maybe more. Enough to form peaks the height of, if not the Himalayas, at least a local ski resort.

And every one of those brown boxes, big and small, firm or smashed, was smiling at her. An eternity of two-day deliveries.

As Bea moved up the path, something else began to take shape. She jogged up the trail to what had, at first, seemed to be a mini white boulder—an anomaly among the brown cardboard and other trash—but what she now recognized was a shaking, sobbing, French queen, huddled over in a fetal position.

Bea fell to her knees beside Toni, placing a hand on her quaking back. "Toni, my God." Seeing her stoic companion in a state of such vulnerability sent a chill through her blood.

Toni only shook her head, mumbling something in French that sounded like *l'enfant* and *mort*.

Bea sat with her, rubbing her back while keeping an eye on their surroundings. They weren't alone, though whether their company was of the human or creature variety remained unknown. "Toni, I'm sorry, but we can't stay here," Bea said, in a reversal of their usual roles. "Something... something's out there."

Her partner sat back on her heels, wiping her face of tears, though a streak of dirt across her cheek and oil stains on her pant legs were unsettling for the lack of control they represented.

Again, something Bea had yet to witness in her guide. Something that did not provide reassurance. And she saw one other thing on Toni's face which rattled her far more than the oil and mud—she saw doubt.

Toni was still rambling on in French as Bea helped her to stand. "My French isn't that good, Toni."

"It's okay, everything is all right, *ma chérie*." Toni patted Bea's arms as if Bea were the one who needed calming. "She will be fine, of course, the young *mademoiselle*. She is already dead, after all, and cannot die twice."

Toni regained her posture, nodding as she set out on the path toward the crest. "She will heal. Become whole again. Find herself right back in her chair, playing that infernal game."

"I know this. But it doesn't make what happened any easier." Bea had to hurry to keep in step now, as Toni had taken up a swift pace ahead of her. "We should talk about what happened. Shouldn't we have stayed and helped her? Could we have done anything? We're the adults. God, I can't believe we just ran away and—"

Toni whirled on her. "I warned her that we offered no protection. And *of course* we could not have stayed. You would have frozen yourself in those waters had you gone searching for her. You can barely imagine yourself dry." She strode forward again, her fists balling at her sides even as her arms swung stiffly. She tossed words back over her shoulder. "We have other priorities. You *insist* on finding your brother. I *insist* on getting you out of here and seeing my children." Her non-corporeal breath came furiously, her porcelain face turning red. The path was growing steeper, and their feet had begun slipping on cardboard as they started the ascent into the mountains proper, but that wasn't the reason Toni strained.

Toni halted suddenly and Bea slammed into her

companion's back. If Bea hadn't been that close to her, she wouldn't have caught Toni's whispered words.

"Children. She was just a child herself." She tossed a look back at Bea. "A child!" She relaxed a fraction, then continued the forward climb, this time not looking back as she said, "The Third Circle. I *hate* the fucking Third Circle."

Apparently, that hadn't been Toni's first go-round with Gluttony, and Bea remembered the way she'd balked at going down one particular path. But they were making good progress up the passage now, so Bea chose to withhold her questions. Or maybe she couldn't bear to reopen whatever wounds Toni was silently trying to stitch back together.

The climb to the top was steady, the switchbacks numerous and only moderately steep. But their progress was slowed by the fact that other feet had walked this path before, and the cardboard beneath their steps was mashed and decomposed, trampled to a slimy paste. For every three steps they took, they slid back one.

Smaller valleys branched off from the sides of their trail, and they kept a particularly sharp eye on them. Inevitably, there were more of the mysterious shuffling sounds coming from those recesses, occasional soft moans or quick shrieks. Often, a box would shake as if something moved within. Once, Bea could have sworn she saw light glinting off a pair of eyes peeking out from between brown flaps, but she averted her own rather than study them further, hustling up the path instead. The Fourth Circle was, so far, the most subdued of any of the previous levels, with no truly obvious threats. Which made it the most uncomfortable one yet. Though still in Upper Hell, they were, nevertheless, almost halfway down the pit, and Bea knew enough to be restless and disquieted. Obvious or not, a threat was out there. And the *population* had to be somewhere.

At one point, they paused, and Bea looked back from where they'd come. Having done her fair share of hiking during life, she estimated they'd climbed about a thousand feet from the creek at the base. Her misshapen ankle had never healed, the sight of it too glaring to easily dismiss, and it was protesting the hike with every one of its imaginary nerve endings. She begged Toni for a break, and they sat down on the most intact boxes they could find.

Bea stared at her red, swollen right foot, now resting on the opposite knee. Touching it, she winced, then yanked her hand away, cursing at her inability to see the truth—that her foot was just fine. There was, in fact, no actual foot. She'd never make it through if she couldn't control at least that much of her reality.

Closing her eyes, she inhaled deeply, trying to find some kind of Zen-like calm. She pictured her ankle in her mind's eye, "seeing" it well-formed and pain free.

"We must talk about your brother." Toni startled her from the visualization. At some point, Toni had risen from her own seat and was now pacing. "You could be putting him in the same danger as the teen. Placing him in the public eye and the demons' crosshairs." She stepped directly in front of Bea. "Reconsider your plan to find him."

Bea gingerly set her foot on the ground, then leaned back onto her palms. "Nuh uh. No way am I leaving him behind. That wouldn't be fair."

"Fair? I have no idea why, but *you* were the one granted this opportunity, not him. Maybe you deserve it; maybe he doesn't. You are not some package deal. Fair has nothing to do with it."

"For all you know, I was given this chance in order to get him out. You literally just said you have no idea why I was chosen. Maybe Dante is *exactly* my job." Bea circled her foot at the ankle. The damn thing was no better, and she'd just have to keep going with the pain. She stood and tested her weight on it.

"I've never seen it work that way." Toni thrust her head forward an inch, pushing her face a bit too far into Bea's personal space, studying her. "And I think there is more behind your desire to find him than a sense of heroics."

Bea took a step back. "What do you—"

"Do not lie to me. More importantly, do not lie to yourself, Beatrice, or you'll never make it out of here."

"What do you mean? I'm not lying." But she was, of course. At least a little. Her need to retrieve Dante wasn't *purely* out of love for her brother. Well, it was that, definitely. One hundred percent that. But also, "It's right that I find him. I have to. I'm supposed to." Her shoulders dropped and she averted her gaze, half-seeing a ravine just off the main trail. "I owe him that. And, anyway, I can't do this without him. Whoever is in control here, whatever cosmic force gave me this chance, obviously had to know that. I'm not brave enough. I'm not *smart* enough to make it without Dante."

Toni pulled Bea's attention back with a finger under her chin. Her pale eyes held sympathy, but, thankfully, no pity. She shook her head. "Beatrice."

"It's true, though, isn't it?" Bea blinked back into her guide's concerned gaze. "I'm only half."

Toni took a long beat before responding, something softening in her expression. "I don't know about that."

Which was a better response than nothing. "Anyway, we had a deal."

"Very well," Toni shook her head. "First, your brother, then my children. We will find them." She lifted her chin, the angles of her face reforming into the harder, sharper queen. "But no more offers of guidance to others. It will only hinder us, and family is the most important thing. In fact, it is the *only* thing." She glanced back down the trail in the direction of the Third Circle. "No one else matters."

Bea remembered Toni's interactions with Madame

Borovsky, Sanjay, Jesse. Her gentle touches and moments of sorrow. She shook her head. "Except you don't believe that last bit. Not really." She pointed at the dirt still caked on Toni's knees from when she'd been weeping on the trail. "I think you do care about *others*," she made air quotes around the word, "sometimes even people you've known only minutes." She tipped her head back toward the waterfall. "And, perhaps, far more deeply than you care to admit because you're afraid of potential pain. Just like the rest of us."

Toni looked like she wanted to argue, her gaze roaming from Bea to the hills, then back again. But then she muttered something under her breath, pointedly waving away the dirt on her jeans before turning to the path, and Bea let the conversation drop as they walked on in silence.

Soon, something shifted in the ravine. Bubble wrap popped and crackled, followed by a crisp sound as a jumble of foam peanuts spilled onto the path. Toni's steps grew more hesitant with each new bend in the trail. Whoever would have imagined that packing materials could be so darn creepy?

"What is this place? I can't remember much about the Fourth Circle. I read *Inferno* so long ago, and it wasn't something I tucked away in my memory for repurposing in the future as a travel guide. Some of the scenes tend to stick in one's memory, but all I remember of this level is something about rich people pushing a boulder around."

The path grew steeper here, and Toni placed a hand on a box to help steady herself, but only managed to dislodge it, causing her to stumble. She grunted and righted herself. "The poet referred to this level as the Hoarders and Wasters. It is Overconsumption. Materialism and Excess. The throwing away of wealth, and, with it, possibility." Now halfway to the top, the switchbacks were tighter, and it was hard to see what was up ahead around each curve. "Alighieri failed to look deeper, of course. His descriptions showed no interest in understanding that the people here are like those in every circle, they attempted to fill the emptiness inside themselves, in this case with objects, often for luxury and vanity. Rather than spending their wealth based on empathy and connection, many were fueled by pride and envy. Others simply fortified their isolation and salved their wounds with a mountain of junk."

Bea knew there'd been many times when she'd "one-clicked" away an emotional pain. But how much shopping did it take to land you here?

"When it becomes a way to hide and disconnect." As had happened before, Toni seemed to read her mind and offered an unprompted answer. "When you disregard the harm it causes yourself, others, or the planet. When it puts you to sleep. When you weaponize it."

"Weaponize it?"

"Like I said, pride and envy."

An image of her own Insta feed scrolled through her mind, the wardrobe, the exotic travel locations. The thousands of comments on each post by followers dreaming of experiencing the same thing. *Praying* they'd one day have the opportunity. She'd always known most of them never would, and there was as much pain as joy for them in viewing her posts. Her relationship with her followers was, in all honesty, rather sado-masochistic.

She pushed aside the passing thought that, perhaps, *this* was her circle—

No, no way. She'd only ever meant to *help* people. For years, she'd used her platform to promote young designers from underrepresented communities, and she couldn't do that without the following she'd built up from her lifestyle posts. Every philanthropist knew they couldn't help those in need without the money or power earned elsewhere.

Wait. Was that what she thought she was—a philan-thropist?

Rounding a steep corner brought them to a long plateau, where they stopped for a breather. It was different here, on this broad landing. Something besides boxes and packing material rose from the ground like an unusually colorful forest, which Bea assumed must be the spot she'd seen marked on the trail map sign. She took a moment to enjoy the change in scenery after the miles of monotonous brown, though her eyes struggled to define what she was looking at.

She began to approach one of the softly textured, multi-colored pillars, but Toni tugged her away. "They cannot hurt you, *chérie*, but it's best to leave them be. They are already... confused enough as it is."

They? With Toni still pulling her away, Bea looked more closely, her eyes widening. The short-statured forest stretching out before her was not made of trees or even a colonnade of pillars as she'd previously thought.

These were... people. Women mostly.

But they were round and solid, no taller than the usual five- to six-foot average human height, but with diameters more like ancient sequoia trees than human beings.

As she took a moment to study them, the reason for their shape became clear, as did the reason for their lack of movement. They were clothed in layer upon layer upon vast layer of luxury garments, one sartorial couture item draped over another. Gowns, furs, leather coats... cashmere and vicuna. Yards-long bridal veils and ropes of silk scarves. Piles of designer shoes spread out at the base of each, like thick, twisted tree roots.

Bea had no sense of what the weight of each wardrobe must be, but it was clear the wearers could barely move. They attempted—and were occasionally successful—in sliding a foot in front of the other, so they must, eventually, accomplish some forward movement. But one would need to watch a time-lapse video to witness the progress.

Their arms were far too weighted down to do anything but dangle at their sides.

They could speak, though, and the soft murmur Bea had first thought to be a gentle wind now took shape to her ears. They were talking to themselves. Some were lucid enough to converse, but those souls who could were too few and far between to communicate with one another. Fewer still even *faced* another person, and their necks were too laden with collars and hoods to rotate and seek each other out. Nevertheless, with the arrival of Bea and Toni, some were roused to attention at the rare movement in the surroundings and they could be heard calling out.

"Hello?" came a voice from the distance.

"Who's there?" shouted one closer by.

Bea hastened her steps, needing to be free of this place— a place she had begun to sense did not necessarily want to be free of her.

"Ah, here we are," Toni said, pointing to the spot where they could rejoin the uphill path. "This is the last leg. It is the steepest part of the climb, but there are handrails at least."

Handrails in Hell? Was this an OSHA requirement?

Her thoughts were getting loopy. Maybe it was the elevation, though, more likely, panic. She needed out of this grove while she was still able because an idea was forming in her mind about this place. About whether it might be *her* place.

Voices seemed to call her name from somewhere in the sartorial forest, or maybe it was just in her mind. *Bea. I bought the gown.* Flashes of crimson caught the edges of her vision. *I thought it would make me happier.* A Tokyo designer's sheath dress stretched to an imponderable girth. *It didn't.*

She bolted past Toni, launching herself up the last leg of the Fourth Circle. Whether she used the rail, whether her feet even touched the ground, she couldn't say.

Eventually, she put enough distance between herself and

the forest of fabric and flesh that she could slow down and allow herself to become aware of her surroundings again.

Wordlessly, Toni reappeared behind her and they continued, the summit now visible just a hundred feet above them.

The hidden denizens of the Fourth were more abundant at this elevation. Or, perhaps, she'd merely become adept at sighting them, picking them out of the background. She now recognized that the twitch of a box meant a person was moving around within it. Over and over, she spotted pale, emaciated heads poke out, shyly reaching a hand to pluck an item from a collection of things piled up against their box, quickly pulling the treasure inside, then disappearing back into its tiny depth. This one surrounded by jewelry and baubles, that one by tall stacks of trading cards, another buried under a mound of sweets and savories.

Bea understood almost immediately that none of these souls was grasping in any sort of vulgar way. They were in pain—as they had been in life—and these objects, whether cheap or expensive, enduring or ephemeral, were nothing more than largely unsuccessful attempts at feeling safe. They were bejeweled painkillers, collectable security blankets, edible hugs.

They passed another trembling package, and she paused, her attention caught by extra movement and mewling sounds. Kittens. A large litter, maybe three months old, rollicking and napping at the base of someone's cardboard home. A small, brown hand, weathered and well creased, reached out of the box—someone old. Bea never saw the face, didn't know if it was a man or woman. The occupant felt around the soft pile just outside the flap, finally collecting one small feline body, then sliding it inside with all the precious care of someone handling a Faberge egg.

Bea's tears came hard and fast then, but she refused to drop to her knees. Her jaw set, she pressed ahead, because every minute more in this place was a searing pain to her heart. Toni had issues with the Third Circle, but the Fourth was Bea's kryptonite. It was insidious. It was unforgiving. It was a hot blade through tender mortal butter.

It was unfair.

Toni strode up beside her, not puffing for breath like Bea was from both exertion and distress. "You will suffer less when you realize there is no great being on high dishing out punishments. No secret council sitting in cruel and unreasonable judgement. It is only us—all of us—trying to learn the truth. Trying to master by brute force what we failed to understand in life."

"And yet you were on the ground yourself only a short while ago," said Bea.

"As you recently pointed out, I am not perfect either, Beatrice, or else I would not be here with you, still learning my own lessons."

"Then consider me ever so fucking grateful you haven't graduated yet." Bea turned her back on the patronizing princess and resumed the steep, slippery, bullshit climb to the summit and whatever new fuckery awaited them there. She didn't even care what it was. She had to get out of these mountains before the sentience of the place realized she was one of their own—a fellow collector—and decided not to let her leave.

127

THE FOURTH CIRCLE
The Summit

The final stretch to the summit was more scramble than hike, but the change in atmosphere urged her on. The sky darkened in what hinted at dusk. But time stood still in the pit, with no rise or fall of the sun, and the current purpling atmosphere brought to mind threatening storms backlit by a heat lamp. It was louder up here, too. The soft scrabbles and moans grew piercing and loud, and, as they finally crested the top, the voices and shouts became a riotous assault.

If the foothills below were a forest of sorrow and regret, the summit was where the party was. Like a scene from a post-apocalyptic blockbuster, the theme of this shindig was muscle-steel and petroleum.

The attendees, Toni explained, had been masters of capitalism—corporate giants whose entire focus had been progress and production at all costs. Together, they'd ripped out the rainforests, drilled the oceans, cemented over paradise without regard to who or what they destroyed in the process. If the collectors at the bottom of the mountain were consumers, those at the top were more than happy to produce what they wanted. To shove it down their throats, if necessary.

Populated mainly by men, the top of cardboard mountain was yet another broad plateau, in this case strewn with the evidence of a combustion engine-loving world—rusted out hubcaps, blown tires, empty gas cans, upended vehicles glowing in flame. It smelled of sweat, oil, and rubber, like a mechanic's shop crossed with a boxing gym.

Heavy metal blared from giant concert speakers rigged to scaffolding around the main event, which was going down right in front of them.

Toni and Bea skirted the perimeter, keeping to the edges as they sought an unobtrusive path to the opposite side.

Torches flared to life around a large circle of SUVs and ATVs, muscle cars and motorcycles, watercraft and monster trucks. The brighter light in the place now revealed its horrors. Lashed to the front of each revving vehicle was a tortured soul who'd, presumably, had numerous gas-guzzling toys in life, and had now become merely a fancy, wriggling hood ornament. It was now *they* who were guzzling gas, petrol nozzles crammed down their throats, drowning them in fuel. The overflow from the choked and sputtering bodies poured to the ground, forming the rivulets she'd been spotting as they'd climbed the mountain. Rivulets that eventually joined up to create the greasy creek at the base.

Darting from one hunk of debris to another, Bea followed her guide's lead while keeping a careful eye on what was the most directly aggressive scenario she'd seen yet. As they moved, she found herself grabbing handfuls of the mud created by a combination of heavily trodden paper, oil, and gasoline, and rubbing it onto her cheeks as camouflage. Anything to avoid detection by the testosterone-laden crowd. More precisely, the gas-pumping, testosterone-laden demons meting out pain and enjoying the eponymous hell out of it.

Standing nearly eight feet high, these party hosts wore harnesses and straps worthy of a leather bar or BDSM club, but their riggings were created of plastic. Specifically, six-pack rings, looped and tied to stretch and crisscross over their bodies, weaving them to create arm braces, chest plates, collars and cod pieces. Most had erections bulging against the plastic. Bea noticed. She couldn't help but notice. She noticed the hard-ons, and the high fives, and the cruel laughter as they began their literal version of Burning Man.

The demons tossed lit matches as if they were handfuls of confetti, the omnipresent petroleum flaming to life and teasing the miserable souls with a display of fire that burned their toes and singed their hair, but never quite set them ablaze.

"They will not actually light them on fire. We are still in Upper Hell and will not see true burning until further down the pit," Toni whispered in her usual way of explaining, which always sounded like *It's not a big deal*, while her rigid muscles and narrowed eyes shouted *It's a huge fucking deal!*

The chained men seemed to agree with the latter assessment. They screamed and shook, living in a constant state of teasing painful burns and perpetual fear at being turned into a human torch. The shrieks and cries mixed with the heavy metal blaring from the speakers.

Crouching behind an overturned speed boat, Bea puked, and, for the first time since she'd begun her journey, questioned her ability to go on.

She *couldn't* go on.

She scooted back the way they'd just come, hyperventilating, and managing to stumble even on hands and knees, one elbow collapsing into the paste.

"Beatrice." Toni grabbed the waist of her jeans, but Bea whimpered in response and swatted her hand away. "There is nowhere to go except forward. Tell me, what will you do, climb back up the waterfall?"

"Maybe I will."

"Oh yes, and then what? There is no chair for you in the Third Circle. Will you try and leap into the winds? Perhaps find your beautiful, bronzed man? You are not welcome in any of those places. You have made your choice. You can only go onward."

She ignored the damn mouthy queen and kept moving, hopping behind a pile of busted leaf blowers. At least the obnoxious things were silent.

"And what of your brother?"

Bea spun on her, eyes bugging and mouth working on silent pain.

But something rough and hot grabbed the back of her neck, pulling her upright in one effortless grab. Her toes dangled a couple feet above the ground as she looked into the pock-marked face of a demon who held her by the scruff. His breath reeked of burning rubber.

"What do we have here?" her demon asked, his voice like grinding gears. "Looks like we get to play with the rare female. I'm thinking spread eagle on the '78 Camaro. Agreed?"

"Ah, now that'd be a fine sight," said another who stepped up to Toni, keeping her away from Bea. "Which hole do you wanna pump first?"

Bea kicked and struggled, but he clutched her that much harder, forcing her head to tilt back as he responded to his friend's comment with an oily laugh. She fought to hear Toni somewhere behind her, arguing with her own demon captor, but he slapped Bea's flailing arms with his free hand and yanked her closer to him.

A crowd was beginning to form around the spectacle they were creating. "Hey, that's the one, man. The one Master Minos placed in the game," said a newcomer, draping a thick rope of chain link over his shoulders as he stepped up.

The one holding Bea spared him a glance over his

shoulder. "What are we supposed to do? Stop them or let them through?"

Bea curled into herself as a fourth approached, his face hidden beneath a welder's mask, his voice muffled and rusty from underneath. "Fuck that shit. I say keep 'em." He flicked on the blow torch in his hand. "I'd *really* like to keep 'em."

Her stomach turned over again, and she wondered if it would help or hurt her cause if she upchucked on her captors. She gagged it down as a row of monitors rose up, granting her a temporary reprieve from their decision.

The hellish mechanic set her back on the ground but tightened his grip as they looked to the screens. "I'm thinking we're about to get instructions."

The familiar logo of Brimstone TV's red devil filled the screen, and the demons gathered in front of the monitors closest to them, leaving the penitent souls struggling in their straps but at least free to breathe for a moment.

A voiceover narrated the local newscast as footage of her time in the Third Circle played on the screens, culminating with Jesse's demise. The events were spun to imply that Bea and Toni had lured the kid out of her "safe" Third Circle chair to help them on their journey, promising safety and success they quite clearly couldn't deliver. Witnesses to the event were interviewed.

"I don't know what they were after exactly," said one of the gamer kids, speaking from his chair nearest the concrete pathway. "They heard about *The Book of the Dead*, and I guess they thought Jesse knew where it was. The brunette lady jumped down and grabbed Jesse by the wrist. Pulled her right out of her chair."

"They made Jesse go with them!" shouted the guy who'd first announced his discovery of the Book. "It's totally their fault Jesse got ripped by the dog. Totally."

The camera now displayed the pit from a drone's

viewpoint far above the circles before zooming down to a woman standing outside the big tent at Le Cirque, a microphone shoved in her face. "Well, I don't know," she said. "When I watch the footage, I think it looks like that one with the mohawk… what's her name?"

"Jesse Chen."

"Oh yeah. Well, I think it looked like she climbed out on her own and wanted to go with them."

The camera switched to a man perched up on a tree branch, his clothes tattered and filthy, his skin sunburnt and weathered.

Bea didn't recognize the location. It had to be further down the pit.

The guy shouted down to the camera from his high perch. "If you ask me, I think Bea is a hero! Like a… What do you call it? A pied piper. She's trying to lead people out of here."

The announcer spoke over an image of her Instagram profile. "Not surprisingly, Ms. Allegra's follower count continues to rise. Whether her intentions are for good or evil, she certainly knows how to keep the public eye trained on her every move. But is that to her advantage in this game?"

Close-up shots of random comments on her various social pages showed a fifty-fifty mix of support and hate, the tone turning nearly tribal on both sides, with doxing and *ad hominem* attacks.

"Jesus," she whispered, the amount of unintentional impact she was having on this place only adding to her nausea.

"He ain't here, sweetheart," her demon laughed.

"In related news," the broadcast continued, "the demons have their hands full lately with more than the usual number of citizens attempting to escape, many fueled by Beatrice Allegra and her quest for *The Book of the Dead*. Others, once inevitably caught, confess to being motivated by curiosity regarding her twin brother, Dante Allegra, though knowledge of his whereabouts is only rumored at this point. And now, onto the weather. Eternity's forecast looks…"

Bea craned her neck as much as she could to catch Toni eyeing her back. The new urgency their quest had now taken on passed between them unspoken.

"We interrupt this broadcast to bring you a special announcement." The demon twisted Bea's head back toward the monitor.

"Welcome back to The Game." A deeper voice took over narration. Fireworks filled the screen as the tinny circus music from Minos' tent worked up the audience before changing to a live shot of Bea held in the grip of her demon. He shouted, bragging of his success in capturing Bea, as his free hand began stroking his hard-on for the camera.

She cringed away.

"In light of our fine population's sudden interest in our contestant's brother, Dante Allegra, the producers have decided on a little change-up to the rules. A fantastic opportunity for our viewers. Beginning immediately, any citizen soul who finds Dante before his sister does and presents him to the Administrative Center of Dis will trade places with Beatrice and be allowed the chance to try to make their way through and out of Hell with the assistance of her French guide. Ms. Allegra, on the other hand, will replace that citizen in their assigned circle, stepping into their place of pain for the rest of time. What say you, people of Hell, to this unique opportunity?"

A tsunami of shouts and applause went up from every direction, sounding above and below. The human men on her current level banged their metal bonds against the machines they were strapped to and roared with excitement.

Her knees went weak, her head flopping forward, and the demon let her fall to the ground as he whooped and hollered, now pumping both fists in the air.

The television announcer continued, "The producers hereby leave it to the demons to decide which citizens they want to help or hinder. They are free to choose whether to allow someone free rein to take on the quest, or whether to catch and restrain them. We do hope, of course, that their decisions will always aid, first and foremost, in providing us all with good television entertainment. And, with these new rules, people of the pit, let The Game continue!"

The summit turned riotous, the men twisting and shouting for release, the demons scanning the scene with a new fire in their eyes, licking their lips at the buffet of choices before them. They'd momentarily forgotten the two women, and Toni skittered over in a hunched position to Bea's side.

"We must find a way down, and now."

Bea nodded, fear for herself outweighed by her fear for Dante. "Let's just get to the edge fast and jump."

"That is not an option this time." They moved like they had before, ducking behind vehicles and keeping to the periphery. "The fall to the next level is several thousand feet. By the time you regain consciousness from such a fall, it will be too late."

"I doubt anybody knows where Dante is yet except maybe a couple people in the Third Circle," said Bea. "We have time."

They stopped behind a mid-sized private jet. The pilot— or perhaps he was the owner—was roped to the fuselage, eyeing them as the engines roared and the blades rotated.

Toni shouted over the noise, "You don't understand, *chérie!* A fall from that height, with your inability to control your reality, could mean the Afterlife equivalent of years!"

Bea hadn't yet seen the drop or discovered what waited below and decided perhaps it was best she didn't at this point, honestly doubting she'd be able to make herself jump from such a height. She looked around, considering their options while continually brushing her hair out of her eyes as the plane's engines created a strong wind of their own.

The plane…

Complete with a possible pilot who was currently

L.M. Strauss

struggling against his bindings, shouting to be heard over the roar of the engine, "Get me the fuck out of here!"

Yeah, not the pilot. The owner. Platinum blond hair cut long in front, fading to close-cropped on the sides. Ice blue eyes and a German accent. His slate gray European suit was soaked in oil, twice as shiny. Even in his vulnerable position, he looked down his nose at the two of them, years of practice, no doubt, making it second nature regardless of how long he'd been forced to fellate a gas nozzle.

Still, Toni's nose was higher. "We will release your bonds, and you will fly us in the plane down to the Fifth Circle."

He squinted at the rope lashed to his wrist. "Fly you? I'm the owner of this *jet*, not its fucking pilot."

Toni—no, this was *definitely* Marie—backhanded him across the cheek. "Then you will burn." She turned her back and strode away like she hadn't a care.

But even as his cheeks and temper blazed, Bea recognized the aircraft as a Cessna luxury personal jet. A model friend of hers had done a photo shoot in one for a travel magazine and spoke endlessly of the leather and hardwood seating and dining areas that were nicer than the interior of her New York condo. She'd also snarked about the annoying owner, sitting in the cockpit and acting as if he were Chuck Yeager himself, ready to take the controls if need be... though the damn thing was so advanced it could practically fly itself, requiring far less human feedback than the man's fragile ego.

"Something tells me you made it your business to know this baby inside and out." Bea slid up next to him, testing the knots at his hands, all the while letting her fingers drift over his as she did so. "I'm sure you have more important things to do during a flight than stare out the big front window, but I bet you've made it a point to understand this beauty's most important workings."

His eyes burned with eagerness as she teased his possible

136

escape—as well as his ego—though they snapped away when a pair of demons strode up, video cameras raised.

"Motherfuck. You two cunts are going to place me in the crosshairs."

Bea shrugged and stepped back, feigning loss of interest in his bonds. The demons seemed more inclined to film the entertainment than to recommence their other duties, at least for the moment. "I'm already making you famous. I'm quite good at that. The question is, do you want to be viewed as a villain or a hero?" She lifted her chin toward the cameras, smiling at the unseen millions while letting one hand sweep along the German's outstretched arm toward the rope at his wrist. "Your audience is waiting for a decision. Tick tock."

While the demon cameramen may have been willing to take a wait-and-film attitude, the rest of the summit participants were not. As other demons began releasing some of the souls, a tide of movement started rolling its way toward them. Bea and Toni weren't the only ones who thought the plane a good idea.

"One way or another, somebody's taking this plane to go after my brother. You might as well be in the cockpit, making the choices." Bea didn't wait any longer. She began searching the debris for something to slice the ropes with.

"And why should I throw my lot in with you when you're such a bright and shiny target to begin with?"

"Because, unlike everyone else here, I know where he is."

Toni reappeared from behind the craft, handing Bea a piece of metal with a jagged edge. She held a similar tool of her own. They each stepped to one of the German's hands, poised to begin cutting his binds.

He licked his lips, casting a glance at the crowd slowly boiling their way over. "I don't trust you. It's not like you're going to hand your brother over to me if we find him together."

Toni muttered something in French that sounded urgent.

Bea shrugged. "I don't trust you either. Let's fight over him when the times comes. Yes?"

Toni was already cutting when the German agreed, forcing out a rapid "*Ja, ja,*" and the first of the crowd began clamoring over the vehicles adjacent to the jet.

With both wrists freed, he used one of the dangling ropes, the other end of which was still attached to the fuselage, to shimmy up to the door and yank it open, hauling himself inside. He stared down at Bea, square jaws grinding as he seemed to consider leaving them.

When he disappeared into the cabin, her blood pressure plummeted—until he reappeared and dropped a ladder down for them to climb.

The moment Toni followed Bea inside, he pulled the door shut just as the sounds of people jumping onto the wings rattled the craft.

"I'm Bea and this is Toni," she offered, more out of habit than courtesy.

He rolled his eyes as he swung into the pilot's seat. "Wolfgang," he said, taking longer than a trained pilot to assess the situation, all the while fists pounded the hull and faces screamed into the windshield. The engine was already burning, though it must have been running on some paranormal power because the gas gauge was at empty. He flicked it with a finger.

"I mean, however the engine's running, it's running. Will it get us out of here?" Bea sank into the co-pilot's chair, Toni standing up between them.

"Who the fuck knows? My bigger concern right now is that." He pointed to the length of mountain top between the nose of the plane and the edge of the cliff. On the plus side, there was a clear path. On the downside, there wasn't much of it. Even to Bea's untrained eye it wasn't nearly enough runway for a safe takeoff.

"Will we make it?" she asked.

He shrugged. "I doubt it."

"It's several thousand feet down. Can't we do that thing

like in the movies where we go over the edge and then pull up at the last minute?"

He doused her with a silent, icy blue stare in response. Then he turned back to the controls, flicked some switches here and there, and began to drive the jet forward along the crest, jaw set and knuckles white as he plowed over anyone in the path. Bea squinted against the sight of flattening bodies, praying instead for the continued sound of an engine powered on unseen fuel.

Toni remained stoic, pointing ahead at their path as their de facto pilot accelerated, bringing them exponentially closer to the edge. Bea had flown enough to know what a jet should feel like just before lift-off, and this wasn't it. "We're not going to make it."

"Do not stop," Toni ordered, even as it became obvious they were well past the point of safely stopping.

"Shut the fuck up, both of you." He accelerated harder, their heads pressing back against the force, the sound of the engines drowning out their voices.

The abyss opened up before them. Her stomach dropped along with the jet as they launched off the edge, the nose immediately turning downward. "Pull up, pull up, pull up!" she shouted like an idiot after all, because, really, what else would one shout? Her eyes clenched shut and her fingers punched holes through the leather seat, but she felt the plane level out, and risked a peek.

The base of this circle was uncomfortably far below—it was clear now that she never would have been able to bring herself to jump—and the radius across was equally far. Directly below was another river, this one as wide as the Mississippi, and dark and choppy. From a level below the opposite shore, barely visible from their distance, spires and towers rose up, black silhouettes against the red glow of what, at first, appeared to be fireworks, but, on further study, were explosives of a more sinister type. Molotov cocktails and surface-to-air missiles.

Toni glanced at both Wolfgang and Bea as they were fixated on the view. "It is known as Dis. It contains the Administrative Center of the Underworld. It separates Upper from Lower Hell and is home to the Sixth Circle of pain." She pushed further between the pilot seats to get a better view, searching for something along the river's nearer shore. "But for-get about that. For now, our only concern is landing safely in the Fifth Circle, and we are searching for something specific."

"Which is?" Bea asked.

"One of several entrances that will lead us below the River Styx."

The River Styx? Bea had always thought of that as the mythical gateway *into* Hell. She didn't realize it was halfway through the place. Then again, as she glanced across at the glowing city in the distance, maybe it wasn't all that inaccurate a description.

"And why are we planning to go *under* the river?" She wasn't claustrophobic, but the idea of traveling beneath water made her twitchy. "Why don't we just fly straight across?"

Toni shook her head. "The Fifth Circle is divided into two parts—half above ground, on the river, and half underneath it. Underneath is where the catacombs lie. Where your *Book of the Dead* is supposedly hidden. Where your brother sleeps."

Her brows tightened. "Sleeps?"

As they descended lower, she could make out that the river was thickly dotted with tiny boats, each with one useless small sail flying, tattered, on the wind. Each boat also carried one passenger. The crafts were tossed on the angry water as the single human soul on each gripped what amounted to a toy mast bearing a flimsy white canvas, each person appearing to be… shouting.

Bea leaned closer to the window, squinting to see better, and though the weather down here was turbulent and dark, she could make out hands cupping around angry mouths, fists raging into the air.

The plane jolted and she bumped her head on the windshield. "Ow. The fuck?" Their ride stuttered and lurched.

"Now we really *are* out of gas." Wolfgang gripped the steering column like he could keep the plane going on force of will alone. "They've pulled the plug on our magic fuel."

Toni huffed. "When will you realize it was fuel either one or both of you created in the first place. You can…" She waved her hand around "…believe it right back in the tank if want. We're halfway down the pit now. You should be fifty percent better in your understanding by this point."

Bea snapped around. Toni's face was blotchy with red, her lips pressed in frustration or worry. But what did *she* have to worry about even if the plane went down in a fiery ball? Unless she'd begun to fear Bea's failure and, therefore, her own lost prize and doomed future.

Bea spun forward again, gripping the console as the plane—and her stomach—dropped a few feet. "Well, I'm sorry I'm not sharp enough. That's why we need my brother." She waited for an argument from her royal mentor, but none came, which was the worst thing. Tears pricked the corners of her eyes. "Why don't you just fix the damn fuel for us then? Change the reality of our situation for us."

"As I told you before, I can guide you, but I cannot do things for you. Nor can I make your choices. All I can do is—"

The plane jolted. It was dropping fast, and the German was spewing foreign curses.

"Can you land us?" Bea asked.

"I'm just trying to get us there in one piece."

Toni leaned in and pointed. "I see a door to the catacombs. There."

Bea and Wolfgang squinted in the general vicinity of her target.

"At the base of the cliff?" Bea asked.

"*Oui*. There is a torch on either side of it. Do you see the two spots of light?"

"I see them," Wolfgang said, "but we're going down on the water. I'll get as close as I can."

The nose of the jet was angled low, the river rushing up to meet them—the river, and a whole shit ton of tiny boats and bodies. Bea felt like she was strapped to the front of a meteorite plummeting straight into a crowd.

"Hold on!" he shouted as the craft hit the water hard, their heads slamming first to the roof of the cockpit and then flung back and forward. They were down in one piece, floating atop the water. Their shouts from inside the cabin joined with those from outside, merging into a white noise of chaotic sound, while her body vibrated from impact. It was like being inside a giant metal bell.

After reeling for a moment, the three looked to each other for the next move. Bea grabbed the German's wrist. "You did it. Thank you. Thank you for all of it."

He nodded. "You're welcome."

Toni had already moved to the back and was fiddling with the door, but the echoing sound kept coming long after the screams from the crash had stopped. It reminded her of the rolling sound of Buddhist monks chanting, but, instead of being soothing, it was painful, as if thousands of them were chanting at the top of their lungs inside an enormous tin can.

"What the hell is that?"

Wolfgang joined Toni as they flung open the door, and all three jumped back at the wall of noise that hit them, hands flying to cover their ears.

The thrumming sound shot through her head like an icepick, the pain stirring nausea and a migraine.

Toni ran back to the hatch, shouting and pointing to something outside, but no way could her words be heard above the din.

Bea sank to the floor though Toni clearly wanted them to deplane, and Wolfgang was moving around the cabin, looking through one window after another. She didn't care what was going on with either of them. She wanted to curl up in a ball and eyed the luxury seat cushions of the passenger cabin, wishing she could cut one open and shove her head into it.

With her eyes shut against the pain, she felt a tug on her shoulder, and assumed Toni was urging her on. She swatted it away, but the touch came back, and she opened her eyes to see Wolfgang encouraging her to stand.

His own face had no color in it, and sweat beaded on his forehead, but he held out a hand to help her up, letting her know through pantomime that the aircraft was sinking. They needed to get out.

With his hand clutching her upper arm, they joined Toni at the exit. About seven feet above the water, spray from the river and a brewing storm misted their faces, the chill actually easing her pain somewhat.

As her head cleared a little in the fresh air, she began to understand the source of the sound. It was the people on the boats, all yelling at one another, millions of them filling the breadth of the entire Fifth Circle, all vying to be heard, to have their say, to prove themselves right, to take down their detractors, expose their enemies, get their vengeance, receive their due.

The Wrathful.

Toni leaned close to their ears. "Jump in and make for the shore near the door! We'll meet up there!"

Bea was a strong swimmer, but the river was frothing, and the storm had arrived, sheets of rain lashing her face and drowning her confidence. Occasionally, a bolt of lightning would catch a sail and fry the tiny boat and its captain. She glanced at Wolfgang, who nodded and pointed to their feet. The plane was sinking fast, their shoes already soaked.

They jumped, the cold hitting her like a slap, but not nearly as bad as the icy lake in the Third Circle. She righted herself, got her bearings relative to the shore, and swam, catching snippets of anger as she navigated around the small watercraft in her path.

"Suck it up, snowflake!"

"Can everyone who's older than a Millennial just die already, please?"

"Let me sip at those sweet liberal tears."

"Does anyone know where K-Mart Karen works so we can get her fired?"

"Am I the asshole?"

"SAD!"

"Bot!"

"Blocked!"

The echo chamber of trolls and reactionaries, combined with physical exertion and mouthfuls of cold water, acted on her like a psychedelic. She grew disoriented, reaching for the only solid thing in front of her, the bow of a boat.

A foot came down on her head along with accusations of privilege and elitism. She swallowed too much water and coughed, arms slapping and feet bicycling as the rain lashed her skin and limited her vision.

An elbow came around her neck from behind and she struggled to push it away, but her strength was waning.

"Hang on. Stop fighting me." The German's accent broke through her confusion and she calmed as he kicked them both to the shore, laying her on the black gravel at the base of the towering cliff. Strangely, the rain seemed limited to the river itself, the shore granting her a reprieve from that assault at least.

Once she coughed up the water she'd inhaled and caught her breath, she rolled over and eyed the entrance, still too weak to move more than lift up on her elbows. The black-as-midnight door stole her attention, though, so she pushed through the pain and accompanying nausea to join Toni and Wolfgang there.

Carved of the same shiny obsidian as the cliff it was set into, it appeared, at first glance, to be a classic Underworld architectural element, covered in sculptural relief. Something Rodin might have seen in a dream. But each lightning strike behind her revealed a poignant beauty in the carvings, the imagery far more celestial than infernal. Stars and moons, galaxies and—shockingly—angels cradling limp bodies.

Bea stepped up and touched it, her fingers tracing the carving of a winged woman, her visage staring lovingly into the face of the man she watched over. The ache of the pounding voices around Bea was replaced with the ache of remorse and a burning need to see Dante. She pushed the door, but it didn't budge. "How do we get in?"

Toni lifted her voice over the noise, which, though lessened here off the water, was still intense, "I have not had reason to come down here in many ages. My companions usually moved straight across the river into Dis. The last time I entered the catacombs it was under different circumstances."

Bea had no time for the game of mystery. She needed to escape the aural pounding threatening to destroy her sanity and get to her brother before, well, everyone else. She searched for any kind of hidden handle on the door's face, while Wolfgang felt around the edges, his intensity matching her own.

"So, um, Wolfie…" She put a little flirt into her voice.

He stopped his pursuit and glared. "No. No Wolfie."

"You saved my life again. In the water. Thank you for that."

He grunted and moved to the other side of the door, continuing his exploration.

"So, I'm guessing that means you're not totally averse to helping us? I suppose what I'm asking is… are you?"

He stopped and considered the entryway, then turned to consider her with equal scrutiny. "You are asking if, once we find a way in, I will be friend or foe?"

Toni interrupted. "I see no need for a foe." She waved a hand at the foolish thought. "The Game can create whatever perceived competition it wants, but there is no reason I cannot guide you out of here right alongside *Mademoiselle* Allegra. I have made this offer to others before."

He smirked. "We all witnessed your success with the teenager."

Toni's shoulder blades drew in, her hands curling, even as she forced the words he needed to hear. "Jesse was weak. You are not."

He played his own game in return, withholding his response and staring out over the water just long enough to make Toni shift her weight. "Very well." He flashed his veneered teeth in more warning than smile. "I expect nothing less than success from my business partners."

Bea returned to their first objective. "So, our plan is...?"

"We will enter, find where the reliquaries are kept, then seek out *The Book of the Dead*. It shouldn't be too hard—it will be where the majority of the demons are stationed," Toni said. "Then we collect your brother and move as quickly through Dis as possible. Beyond that is Lower Hell, and it will be far harder for anyone else to compete with us at that point."

"Pretty simple then. Got it." Bea rolled her eyes. "So how do we get this door open?"

Her guide's response was no more than a shrug, her own eyes scanning the elaborate door for answers.

Forcing herself to maintain enough patience to think, Bea stepped back and studied the large dark slab, once again appreciating the way the carvings almost glowed with the lightning. There was fantasy in the imagery, yes, but science as well. She recognized the symbols of sacred geometry, the Golden Mean, and Pi, as well as the astronomical symbols for each of the planets in the solar system. Her brother had once had a poster of those planetary symbols tacked to his bedroom wall and Bea used to find it mesmerizing, and the symbols were still familiar to her.

Stepping up to the door, she touched the glyph representing the sun—a dot inside a perfect circle. As soon as her fingers met the carving on the slick black stone, the icon lit with a silvery glow.

Toni sucked in a breath. "What did you do?"

"I don't know," Bea said as the trio all leaned in to examine the glowing symbol. "I just touched it."

"Try another one," said Wolfgang.

Another one. But which? Bea shrugged. Why not try the next symbol in order? She searched until she found the icon looking like the sign for a female—a circle with a cross on one end—except, in addition, it had two little hooks on top, appearing almost like horns. The symbol for Mercury. She found it, touched it, and it, too, lit up.

"What are they?" Toni asked.

"The symbols of the planets. I started with the sun and moved outward. Next is Venus." She searched the door for that symbol. It glowed brightly as soon as she placed her fingers on it, and she kept going, moving further out into the solar system, each planetary icon lighting in sequence. She was almost done. "So, does Hell consider Pluto a planet or not?"

Nobody answered, but, as her fingers moved close enough to almost warm the symbol of a little "P" with a tail, the door swung open. She glanced to her companions with a query on her face.

"Unclear." Wolfgang shrugged.

Either way, the door was open, and Bea took a tentative step across the threshold, her two companions right behind. The corridor before them was pitch black, but just as the noise of the door swinging shut nearly sparked terror in her gut, a row of sconces set into the walls ignited in bright blue light, one after the other down a tunnel stretching before them out of sight. She blinked, her eyes adjusting to the dim light as she caught the familiar scent of talcum coming up behind her followed by a *thump, squeak,* and *thud* in rapid succession.

She spun back, catching a flash of strawberry blonde on the ground before looking up, her face making contact with a big German fist. The back of her head slammed into the wall behind her, and the world finally became silent as she slid down the cool obsidian into sleep.

Chapter 15

BOSTON

One Month Ago

"Oh my God. Are… are you breaking up with me?" Bea turned away from Angel's pained expression and began pacing the living room of the apartment they shared in the Allston neighborhood. The matte-black walls they had painted side-by-side in paint-splattered t-shirts when they'd moved in together the previous year now threatened to mock her. One afternoon they'd even painted while nude, the trendy color splattering their skin and, soon thereafter, had created a body-sized Jackson Pollock on their crisp white bedsheets.

The room began to blur.

"No. Bea, that's not what I'm saying." His warm hands on her shoulders, his sweet breath on the back of her neck, eased her sudden chill. "Not yet, anyway."

She spun back around. "Not *yet*?" Her fingers gripped the sides of his silk shirt, her disbelieving gaze darting over his chest, his arms, the beautiful dip between his collarbones. Anywhere but to his eyes.

She'd actually had the gall to think he'd planned on

proposing to her tonight. He'd been avoidant the last week or so, ducking away when he took a call, or running an unannounced errand. Not his habit at all. But their relationship was on a Pinterest-perfect track, and when he'd made reservations for tonight, a week before she'd be leaving for Paris with the girls—a trip he couldn't join due to business—she'd assumed all his sneaking around had been to plan the... to buy the...

What a fool she was.

She'd made a pompous, stupid joke as they were walking out the door, telling him to check and make sure he'd brought the ring. And, oh God, the look on his face...

The painfully long pause before he told her he'd only wanted to have a good talk before she left.

A *talk*.

"I don't know why you thought that, Bea. I'm so, so sorry, baby." He took her hand, easing them both onto the sofa. "Please don't be embarrassed. Of course I've thought about it, too. I love you. It's just that... I don't know... Do you really think you're ready for that kind of commitment?"

"Do I think I'm *ready*?"

Now his gaze was the one ping-ponging around the room. "I wanted to talk tonight before your trip, because I thought... I thought you might take some time to really think while you're there. You know, hours on the plane, walking around museums, that kind of thing."

"To *think*?" She was reduced to parroting fragments of his sentences.

"About us. About what you want from us. From life, really. Because, honestly, Bea, I'm no longer sure I can give you what you need."

"I need *you*, Angel." Her hand on his cheek brought his eyes back to hers. Their rich, dark depths and his infuriatingly long black lashes made her want to lean up and kiss his eyelids. Because the pain on his face seemed no less than what she felt.

150

"Maybe. But I'm not enough. I'm not sure any one person will ever be enough." He took her hand and flipped it palm up, planting a kiss in the center. "You think there is a hole in you that Dante left. And that hole you imagine has become far bigger than Dante himself ever was. You think if enough people see you, your hundreds of thousands of followers, that, eventually, you'll be able to fill it. But there is no actual hole there, babe, and so you can never fill it."

Pain flipped to anger. A non-twin could never understand. The hole was a real, tangible, living, breathing thing. And it was immense.

She sprang from the couch in one fluid movement and ran to the windows, looking down on the city. She breathed in and out, forcing herself to calm down before she bit out words she'd regret.

Angel gave her silent space while she relaxed her limbs, practicing her meditation exercises and imagining her root chakra grounding her, visualizing healing color move through her body and out the crown chakra at the top of her head.

She turned back around and leaned against the window. "I'm not giving you enough time and attention. I'm sorry, Angel. I know you hate it when I put our life on the camera for all to see. Turning us into some kind of… Insta-couple. You're absolutely justified in being upset about that." Her shoulders relaxed as she noted his open body position, his serious attention to her words. "When I get back from Paris, I promise I'll do it differently. I'll better manage my time, and I'll keep our personal life private."

He leaned forward on the couch, elbows resting on his widespread knees, and looked up at her. "I appreciate that, I do, but it's more than that. I'm not jealous of your half-million followers. I'm happy your career is thriving. And I'm not exactly camera shy either."

She snorted and he laughed, his perfect smile fluttering her stomach into knots.

"Well, okay, those selfies of us entangled in bedsheets with my chest on exhibit for all the world may be a bit much for my taste."

"Your bare chest deserves to be fully on display for all the world."

He laughed and shook his head. "All right, but listen. You and I both know it's more than that." He patted the couch and she came over, snuggling against him. He wrapped an arm around her and rubbed her shoulder. "Somehow, you got it in that beautiful, clever little head of yours that, without Dante, you no longer know who you are. And you expect those five-hundred-thousand followers to tell you."

"*Seven*-hundred-thousand."

He paused. "I'm really worried that your self-worth hinges on them. It scares me."

She had no response because part of her recognized the truth. Every new person who followed her or left a comment or told her she was amazing or smart or creative or lucky, every one of them was another grain of sand filling up a spot that had once been Dante, but was now a crater the size of the Grand Canyon. It would take so, so many of them.

With a lump in her throat, she acknowledged his words with a nod against his shoulder.

He continued to stroke her arm. "You still up for dinner?"

She snuffled. "How about we stay home and order Chinese? We can binge-watch something."

"Perfect." He didn't move. "I don't want to break up."

"Me neither."

"Will you think about all this while in you're in Paris, though? Maybe..." He hooked a finger under her chin, lifting her face to him. "Maybe even consider giving therapy a try when you get back? Just to see."

She flopped back against the sofa, relief rushing her like a wave. He wasn't leaving her. But she did have work to do.

"Oh, boy. Me on the couch with good old Freud." They

laughed and she hooked a hand behind his neck, pulling his face close. "I'll do it. You're right. It's time. As soon as I'm back from Paris, I'll make the appointment. We'll do this thing."

"After Paris, it is." His lips moved onto hers and the world righted itself again.

Moments later, he disentangled their limbs and stood. "Let me go change out of these clothes,"

Bea made a pouty face. "But you look so damn sexy all dressed up."

His smile almost did her in as he performed a mini runway walk for her before heading into the bedroom. She wanted to go change into something comfier, too, but she picked up her phone first and held the camera a little above her head. Damn, she'd done a good job with her hair tonight. And her makeup was on point, too. *Why waste the look?*

She lounged back on the white leather sofa, which contrasted perfectly with her brunette waves, and snapped a selfie. Bea cropped the image, added only minimal filter, decided on some hashtags, and posted it.

The comments were already coming in when Angel stepped back into the room, holding up his own phone. "Seriously? You can't let it go for one fucking evening? After everything we just talked about?"

"What's the big deal? I didn't post anything personal. Just a fast shot of my face. You have to admit I look hot tonight." She tried batting her lashes, pouting her lips.

He wasn't buying any of it. "You lied, Bea. To them and to me. *That's* the big deal."

"Lied?" She sat up, a renewed combo of fear and defensiveness raising her heart rate.

Angel read her post out loud, using a snide imitation of a female voice. "The man and I decided to skip the night out on the town in favor of some stay-at-home snuggle-time. He looked too damn delicious for me to keep my hands off him long enough to go out to eat. #eatingin #youknowwhatimeanbythat."

Her face burned with heat. "It's just—"

"It's promo. And I guess you didn't hear a word I said tonight." He grabbed his wallet off the coffee table and shoved it into the back pocket of his jeans. "It's clear their opinion of you is more important than mine. Even if it's built on nothing but illusion."

He threw on a jacket and opened the front door. "You know, I'd actually have been less upset if you'd posted the whole story of what happened tonight. The *real* story. Let people know that *real* couples have *real* issues and have to talk things out. But the truth, including all its ugly bits, isn't exactly your *brand*, is it?"

Bea was already standing. "Where are you going?"

"To get some air. And to think," he said with his back to her. And then he left, slamming the door behind him.

Chapter 16

THE FIFTH CIRCLE
The Catacombs

Her eyes fluttered open, her skin exchanging the heat of Angel's words for the chill of black stone, both sensations unpleasant. It was the first dream she'd remembered upon waking from her various knockouts since she'd begun her journey in the Netherworld, and one she was reluctant to let go of, upsetting though it was. It was also the first real time she'd even thought about Angel since she'd woken up from her death. In fact, she'd had only brief moments where she'd thought about her friends or her parents. Perhaps it had been some sort of buffer she'd built as she did her best to keep putting one foot in front of the other here. Especially in regard to Angel, from whom she'd been ripped away most painfully, their relationship left tilting on a knife's edge. And good God, her parents had lost both their children now. She couldn't begin to fathom the pain they must be in, and her limbs nearly ached to reach out to them, to tell them she was okay—sort of—and that she was on her way to Dante.

A wave of grief—the first real one she'd felt since arriving

155

here—shot up from her gut and out her throat in a gag. She had followers here, just as she had followers there. More so even. A million more. Yet she'd never felt more alone. She wanted Angel; she wanted her family and friends. The touch of a real human being. Human beings who spoke truth to her, as Angel had, not just flattered her or wanted something from her. She wanted back every minute she'd spent swiping and tapping instead of hugging and laughing.

She let loose a torrent of tears for all she had lost. For her pain then and now. For the shared grief of her family and friends. For her foolish actions that had led to it all.

After some time, she forced herself to sit up, one hand sliding over her jaw to test the German's impact zone. No pain whatsoever, and, come to think of it, her ankle had stopped throbbing some time back. She ran her palm along the side of her foot, finding no malformed edges. Her shoulder, too, now lined up with the other side.

As she stood, a pale shape moved up beside her, eventually forming into Toni's light skin and white t-shirt as Bea's eyes adjusted to the blue-black glow of the tunnel. In silence, they began their journey forward, the path brightening with a sapphire luminescence from orb-shaped sconces placed regularly along the walls. White twinkling stars, like tiny floating Christmas lights, swirled around their feet as they walked, and eddied about their hands when they gestured.

The path they took was at a decline, and, as they rounded corners, it became clear they were making their way beneath the river, yet there was no dampness on the walls or ground. Neither did the place feel stuffy or muggy. In fact, a clean scent of minerals tinged the cool air. Remarkably, the whole effect was peaceful, not at all claustrophobic as she'd feared earlier.

"Wolfgang will be headed for my brother." Bea picked up the pace, the newly opened emotional wounds now adding to her urgency. Though she had no idea where they were heading, there appeared only one path forward, and the German was that much farther down it. That much closer to Dante.

Fuck! She was failing her brother already. Just like she'd failed him the night he'd died, when she'd encouraged him to drink then go home with Ronna. Getting him to socialize and participate in the lighter side of life was the only goddamn thing she'd brought to their twinship and it had gotten him killed. Now, she was doing it all over again in death. "How long was I out this time? How much lead did I give that asshole?"

"Actually, this time you were out no longer than I was. He caught me off guard and even I went black for a moment. It happens. I do not believe he has more than a few minutes on us."

Toni kept pace by her side as they descended a long flight of stone stairs, the tunnel widening at the base to nearly ten feet in width. A soft hum, barely audible, met their ears on this level. They kept moving forward.

"Do not worry about the German. He does not know where either the book or your brother are, and I do not think he is so special that he'll find him before we do. I admit, for a moment there, I thought maybe he had possibility, but it turns out he is no more than an average man."

Bea cast her some serious side-eye. "You under-estimated the average man before, and, from what I know of history, that mistake did not turn out well for you."

Toni kept her eyes on the tunnel though her nostrils flared and she lifted one hand to her throat.

Bea almost regretted her words until she remembered her brother and envisioned Wolfgang coming upon him first.

The tunnel took them down another long flight of stairs, and, this time, when it flattened out, their route dead-ended at a perpendicular path, with a choice of turning left or right. A sign on the wall directed them to groups of numbers that lay in either direction. The number ranges here were astronomical. To the right, the sign indicated "Chambers" numbering from 1 to 2,000,000. To the left was 2,000,001 to "and upward."

"We go to the right," said Bea without hesitation.

Toni lifted her brows. "How do you know?"

"Because we're looking for the reliquaries, and they'll be in the oldest of the chambers."

They chose the right-hand path and began to run—because Wolfgang would've been able to figure out at least that much, too. They took the first left, continuing the plan of moving toward the oldest numbered chambers.

Around the next turn, The Sullen revealed itself.

The hall opened onto a series of chambers, each with four walls of human-sized alcoves, from floor to ceiling. And they were human-sized because they contained humans.

Bea felt as though she'd seen something like this before, maybe in movies or photos of ancient crypts with skeletons or caskets in each. But these were not filled with bones or boxes, they contained the sleeping bodies of the Sullen souls. The women dressed in gowns of ivory linen, the men in loose pants of the same cloth, they were each in their own nook, lying on their backs or stomachs, looking peaceful in their slumber.

The place wasn't decrepit or putrid. In fact, the earth-and-mineral scent of the tunnels was even sweeter here, with a floral hint teasing her nose. The white pinpoints of light moving through the air on this level clustered around the bodies, creating a warm glow. And the humming sound that had been growing louder as they'd gotten nearer the sleepers was the collective sound of their soft breathing.

No one in this place would be aware of the game that Bea and the rest of Hell were engaged in. No demons seemed interested in disturbing the sleepers to let them know. And, no one in this place would probably want to leave even if given the opportunity. Which was, Bea feared, the point of this circle. It was beautiful, and safe, and the worst kind of trap.

They left the chamber and continued through the tunnel halls, running and turning at each junction. Running and turning, running and turning. The numbered signs zipped past in a blur. Still, Bea felt no lack of breath as she asked Toni about something that had bothered her since discovering the sleepers. "Do they dream?"

"The Sullen? No, one cannot dream in Hell. Dreams are nothing but a function of the body during its nightly renewal. As they have no actual body, there is no need to dream."

In light of all the other things Bea experienced in a very physical sense even without a body, she was not at all convinced this was true. After all, the sleepers were all breathing. Some were snoring. Muscles tensed in her non-corporeal neck as they seemed to do whenever she noted possible cracks in Toni's logic.

"But I just *had* a dream back at the entrance when Wolfgang knocked me out." Bea shoved down her grief over Angel, which now threatened to rise up her throat in a scream every second.

Toni shot her a look. "I do not trust that what you experienced was a mere dream. We are getting deeper into the pit now, no more than a short distance from the precipice to Lower Hell. This place might be starting to play games with your thoughts—showing you what it wants to in order to scare and weaken you."

Except that her memory of that night with Angel was an accurate one. She didn't need any hellish manipulations to feel scared and bereft. Only now, far beneath the River Styx in this place of relative calm and quiet, was she truly experiencing the loss of her family, her friends, her lover. She could easily imagine crawling into one of the coves and crying herself to sleep alongside her brother.

She came to a halt at the next junction of tunnels, collecting her thoughts to refocus on their goal. But, as her body ceased to move, it almost seemed as though the walls caught up a fraction of a second later, sliding into place in front of the two women with the numbered signage popping into focus only as her eyes sought it out. And the sign told her that, not only were they quite close to the oldest of the chambers, but that they'd passed tens of thousands of halls, which meant they'd been running a far longer time than she'd been aware.

Or moving at an astronomical speed.

"How is this happening?" Bea asked.

Toni only shrugged. "It could be either, or both, *mon amie.* It does not matter. What *does* matter is that you're figuring it out and taking control. I had prayed you would finally do so, as it is the only way we will ever find your brother without spending an eternity down here. It is the only way we will make it through the levels at all."

"*Me? I'm* doing this?"

"Of course. I've explained to you numerous times that I can only guide you, not do it for you."

"But I didn't even try—"

"Part of you is beginning to believe that you control your reality. *This* reality. And the more you believe, the more you will be able to do. Right now, it is only your subconscious mind that understands, though, and we will not get much further until you believe it on every level. Until you are no longer afraid."

Toni gestured for Bea to continue leading the way, but Bea stumbled with her first step, unsure how to purposely move in that preternatural manner.

Toni startled her into action. "Don't think, just *go!*"

And she did. They took off running again, and, as Bea imagined the halls flying past her, they simply did, faster than even before. She stopped pretending to move her legs. Rather, she simply leaned into the desired direction and watched as the tunnels and signs blew past—but even that wasn't an accurate description. At that speed, there was no actual reading of the signs. She simply knew, from moment to moment, what they said and which way to turn. She was motion. She was energy. For a moment, she was purely focused knowledge.

Then, suddenly, they were still. They were at their destination. An enormous mahogany door, flanked by twin torches shooting five-foot-high blue flames, guarded the entrance to the reliquary chamber.

Well, the door *and* one ancient, putrefying, giant of a man seated in a chair to the side. Dressed in chainmail and a helmet layered with symbols and crests and medals, the glint of the armor stood in stark contrast to the decaying flesh that sloughed from his face and arms onto the metal. A spear stood by his side, leaning against his shoulder. Hell's version of a Knight Templar.

But instead of raging over them, instead of halting their approach, he slept. Spittle ran from the edge of his half-open mouth, his rancid breath forcing the women to retreat as much as anything else. Silently, they slid back around a corner.

Bea lifted her brows, silently asking the obvious question.

Toni responded with an equally confused shrug of the shoulders, her words no more than a soft breath. "A trap?"

"It must be." Bea leaned into the Queen's ear. "And where are the cameramen? Where are the monitors? Our competitors? All the demons the gamer kid said guarded the reliquaries? It's far too silent."

"Agreed. We should turn back and continue on to Dis. If Wolfgang has already reached your brother, we can seek them out there."

Bea stepped back and shook her head, mouthing her words. "We still need the book. It's the key."

"*Merde.*" Toni threw up her hands, the two women arguing like actors in a silent movie. "We don't even know what that means."

"Exactly."

161

They faced off, mirroring each other with fists on hips, until Toni relented. "Perhaps he is truly sleeping. The knight's a thousand years old if he's a day."

Bea offered a half smile. "Probably naps a lot."

They tiptoed back, skirting like mice past the knight, whose chin had fallen to his chest and he'd begun to snore. She gave the smooth mahogany door a push and it opened on silent hinges. Stepping through, they closed it behind them again, its thick depth sealing off all sound, and they took in the chamber.

More blue-flame sconces lit the round walls of the grotto, the stone lining the chamber here black and shiny. Probably onyx.

They separated to stroll the circumference from opposite directions. Here, too, were rows of nooks in the walls, only, unlike in the sleeper chambers, these varied in size depending on what reliquaries they held. Each honored item was lit with a small spot of light, a placard of gold placed above, identifying it.

Bea let her gaze roam across the room, half-looking for a book, half-puzzling out what significance these objects held since they were kept with reverence in this hellish holy place.

She circled the chamber, her hand grazing across the objects as she passed them: an enormous variety of weapons, vintage political propaganda pamphlets—including an embarrassing one depicting Marie Antoinette, which Bea did not point out—the earliest model of a black-and white-television set, yellow felt stars, placards announcing "whites only," an early gaming console, a smart phone.

All objects that led to greater and greater human disconnect.

Toni's voice punched into her thoughts. "I see no books here save this one." She crossed the room to Bea, carrying a slim hardback pinched between her fingers at one corner and holding it out in front of her as if it might bite.

Bea relieved her royal highness of the apparently distasteful thing and read the gold embossed cover. *Mein Kampf.*

"I have heard of this manifesto in my travels here. Met the man himself once. Both are rubbish." She turned her back with a shiver and kept exploring. "That is not the book we are looking for."

"No. Definitely not." Bea replaced the book on its ledge and kept looking. She'd imagined a big leather-bound tome with locks and buckles, but Toni was right, apparently no other book had been deemed worthy to rest in Hell's place of pride.

Disappointment had begun to set in when a familiar, flat white object caught her eye. She snickered at the irony. She'd had the exact same laptop with her in Paris—

Wait. No. It couldn't be that twisted.

In three quick steps, she grabbed the slim computer up and flipped open the cover. The monitor booted up immediately, the home screen a black background with red lettering. At least the cheesy, gothic font gave a nod to its occult essence.

She failed to suppress a snort.

"What is it?" Toni crossed the room as Bea slid down the wall, placing the computer on top of her bent knees. "What did you find? Is it *The Book of the Dead*?"

Bea lifted the laptop an inch. *"The* Mac*Book of the Dead,* to be more precise."

A quick scan of the table of contents confirmed what the gamers had predicted—it was an address book of sorts, listing the exact location of every person in Hell, including, of course, the chamber and alcove number of every slumbering soul in the lower Fifth Circle. "There are also a good twenty appendices at the back of this thing. What look to be esoteric writings and treatises at first glance."

Perhaps the *key* the brown-eyed gamer boy had mentioned was hidden somewhere in those writings.

"Later," Toni said. "We'll read it once we've retrieved your brother. I'm growing ever more suspicious over the lack of cameramen and competitors."

"Good point."

Except how, exactly, to find her brother even with the book? The directory was alphabetical, but the listings numbered in the billions. He was a needle in a thousand haystacks after all. "If only there were a—"

But of course—there was the search feature.

She found Dante's location in seconds. "Oh my God, Toni. He's really here."

His chamber was a thousand halls away but so what? They would reach him in seconds. After nine years, he was within a supernatural arm's reach.

Bea was already standing and moving toward the exit as Toni took the slim computer, closing it into the cradle of her arm. They made for the door and pushed through it, stopping short at the towering knight blocking their way.

No longer the oblivious, drooling Methuselah, the dark templar stood over them like an oak, laughing even as a tooth fell out of his decaying gums.

The women backed against the wall, inching their way around him toward the open hall. This elicited more laughter, and he held his arms wide, his reach broad enough that they had to duck under, though he never attempted to touch them.

"You do not need to inch your way past me. If I had wanted to stop you, I would have done so on your way in, not your way out." His voice was loud and deep, but dusty and rattling, like the bass keys on a pipe organ being played for the first time in a century. "You see, I did not need to stop you, as I had already given your brother's location to the German. I only pretended to sleep upon your arrival to give you a false sense of security, and him a greater lead." His smile dropped, creating the impression that his face had lengthened by inches. "I slowed you down."

A hand on the small of her back and Toni's shout of "Go!" was all Bea needed to start the sprint. She took the lead as they flew, again, down halls and around corners at inhuman speed, seeing only the numbered signs they needed to see, guiding them to Dante.

Only, this time, they weren't alone in the tunnels.

Footsteps other than their own echoed through the corridors. Laughter and shouting both mocked them and spurred them faster. The glint off camera lenses caught the edges of Bea's vision periodically, and none of it slowed her, until one particular hall number rose up in front of her as if in greeting.

Dante's chamber.

She stepped into the cool glowing quiet of the space, breathless, but not from running. Nobody else was present, though the sounds of footfalls and yelling continued from halls all around them. Either no one had yet found this spot, or they'd already come and gone.

Bea knew the numbered location of her brother's alcove from the book's listing. Moreover, each was adorned with a golden name plaque in alphabetical order around the room. But she didn't really need to look because she'd already spotted her answer, though she averted her eyes a moment longer from the single empty alcove she'd caught in her periphery, pretending she hadn't yet discovered the truth. Pretending she still had hope for a reunion.

"*Chérie*. Over here." Toni waved her over. "I am sorry. He is gone."

"I know. I know, okay? I saw." Fists curled at her sides, Bea stomped across the chamber to the waist-high nook that had held her twin only minutes before. She shoved Toni back, needing space, then sank to her knees.

A bed of silky white sand still held the imprint of his sleeping body. Tiny, floating white lights danced over the spot as if searching for its former occupant.

"I already saw," she whispered before resting her cheek on the edge of the alcove.

She slid her fingers and palm into the impression Dante's own hand had left behind in the soft sand. Had he woken and walked out with whomever had found him, thinking he was being rescued, or was he taken while still asleep? Did the handprint mean he'd pushed off the sand on his own, or was it merely where his palm had been resting for nine long years? Perhaps he was slumbering even now as someone carried his body into the horror of Dis.

It hardly mattered. Whoever had taken him was now well on their way, following who-knew-what route. She'd lost her twin. Again.

It was worse than that, though. If she'd left him alone and not gone searching for him, at least he'd be sleeping, unaware, in this peaceful place. Instead, she'd doomed him to an unknown fate in Lower Hell.

She now knew the despair of The Sullen. For nearly a decade, she'd thought she'd known pain, but she hadn't scratched the surface. This depth of remorse must have been what Dante had felt, choosing eternal sleep to avoid the memories. He'd lost a twin, too. And he'd lost Ronna. No doubt blamed himself for both.

Bea understood. This might not have been her proper assigned circle of Hell, but it was her circle now.

She slid her upper body into the alcove, inhaling her brother's lingering scent, and brought one knee up as she began melting into the fluffy white powder. Sleep was what she needed. Deep, deep, sleep. Her other foot lifted from the floor—

Two hands gripped her arm, fingernails biting deep into skin and muscle. "Beatrice. Stop."

Bea yanked her arm back, the intruding nails leaving scratch marks in their wake. "Leave me alone. I failed. There's no point now." She turned her head away, closed her eyes.

166

"*Excuse* me?" Toni grabbed the arm again, pulling it backward in its socket and dragging a squealing Bea half out of the alcove. She gripped Bea's head, which now hung toward the ground with half her body flopped out of the nook, and flipped it up to look at her. "You may feel you have no more reason, but *I* still have four very good ones and I intend to see them again. I have been indulgent enough with your special requests and look where it has gotten us. Media attention. A drastic change in The Game. There is no more time for delay. You *owe* me. You will *not* fail me."

Bea listened to the rant, as she hung half in/half out of the alcove, her head propped up on Toni's fist in a stupidly awkward position, her mouth agape. She blinked once or twice in silence before her guide finally released her to let gravity take her the rest of the way to the floor.

Like a beaten dog, she slowly righted herself, crawling into a sitting position on the chamber ground, body crunched in on itself. "I *will* fail you. I'm sorry. Without Dante, I'll never be able to make it the rest of the way. He's the smart one. He's the solid rock. All I am is… All I *was* is… popular. I'm not even that anymore because I can't control the narrative down here. I can't pretend to be someone I'm not. And what I'm not is smart or brave or anybody's rescuer."

Toni wove a stream of angry French under her breath before finally squatting down at her side. "I will not suffer this pity party any further. I am going to point some things out to you once and only once. You will hear me, and then you will stand up, harden your resolve, and we will continue our journey."

Bea angled her head just enough to give her companion one ear and some serious side-eye.

"You've created this idea that you are not smart. Yet you figured out a way down from the Second Circle to the Third, you solved the puzzle of the catacombs entrance, determined where the reliquaries would be located, identified *The Book of the Dead*, and are beginning to control your reality with the way you now move through these halls. You say you are not brave, yet you've put yourself and your own journey at risk to save Jesse and Dante. That is a choice—and you've made it over and over since arriving in Hell. As you once said to me, how do you know that you are not, in fact, supposed to save your brother from this place?"

"But I failed them both. I've made things worse."

Toni stood. "Then do better. Fight harder. Having courage and taking the necessary action even when it's frightening— *that's* what makes you a heroine. Actually succeeding in the quest, well, that often comes down to luck. And *not* giving up."

She held out a hand to help Bea stand, and as she did so, her shoulders relaxed and her expression softened. Letting go of her own urgency for a moment, Toni placed a patient hand on Bea's shoulder and looked her in the eyes. "You are not half a person, Beatrice. Perhaps you are twice the force when paired with your brother. Many relationships are like that, more powerful together. Parents and children, lovers, friends. But you are fully formed, and more than capable on your own. It's time to finally believe that." She gestured toward the exit. "Now, would you care to resume rescuing the prince?"

"It's not too late?"

They moved back into the hall, which had now gone totally quiet. "It will be quite the journey for whoever took him to get through the gates of Dis and across the city to the Administrative Center. They won't get there easily or quickly. And we're going that direction anyway."

They raced through the remainder of the halls, Bea letting her desire manifest their way through the labyrinth. They emerged through an exit, which landed them below the river on the opposite side. It seemed their travels through the catacomb maze had brought them down to the next, and lower, circle of

Hell. They exited through a solid iron door set into a concrete abutment sticking up like a thumb against the rocky edge of the tall cliff behind them. Stenciled yellow spray paint on the concrete wall announced their arrival into the Sixth Circle.

The sound of the rushing river and its loud sailors was now no more than a soft wash of white noise above them. As they stood within the shadow of the abutment, they had time to survey their next obstacle.

Before them, and as far as the eye could see in either direction, were the high walls of the City of Dis. Like the doorway they now stood in, all was Cold War décor: concrete and iron, barbed wire at the top with guard towers set along the ramparts, and everything was covered in a frenzy of graffiti. Like the shore on the opposite side of the river, no rain fell here, but the stormy sky raged dark and threatening above, and the spray-painted letters occasionally flashed brightly under the bursting glow of a lightning strike or a skyward cherry bomb, the words screaming momentary obscenities or cries for help before fading into the gloom once more.

Their path out of the catacombs had landed them directly across from the entrance to Hell's center city at the heart of the Sixth Circle. Twelve-foot-high wrought iron gates blocked the way in, but the bars were wide enough that Bea could see some of what lay beyond, and it bore no resemblance to the administrative complex she'd been told to expect. Instead, a combination of dim flickering bulbs and the constant flash of exploding missiles overhead lit the ruined main street of an amusement park from a post-apocalyptic nightmare. A radioactive meltdown of childhood fantasy. A theme park of decrepitude.

A long-abandoned ticket booth marked the entry point, and though no one appeared to be manning it, a few souls wandered up, forming the beginnings of a line as a pair of guards paced back and forth before it like evil Beefeaters.

Smoke and ash filled Bea's nostrils as she ducked behind her bunker to study them. Nearly nine feet tall, these demons wore orange hazmat suits, full-face gas masks, and held shotguns cocked and ready at their shoulders and pointed at the growing crowd. And on their heads... well... Bea squinted to make sure she was seeing what she thought she was seeing— little black hats with round rodent ears.

A chill ran across her skin and she shivered even as her gaze lifted higher to the marquee hanging high above the gates. Once painted in bright gay colors, the signage was now long faded and scratched, dozens of bullet holes breaking up the lettering. But she could still read it well enough. It announced: "Welcome to Dis Land."

Chapter 17

HOFBURG PALACE
Vienna, Austria

258 years ago (1762)

"Maria Antonia Josepha Johanna!" Her music teacher's voice echoed from the grand hall beyond the door and his boots clicked on the marble tiles. Oh boy, he was angry. The use of her full name was never a good sign, no matter who uttered it.

Still, she giggled as she tucked herself beside a large armoire. She'd successfully avoided the maestro for the better part of an hour, and even though she was only seven, the fact that any members of court within earshot weren't chastising him—a staff member—for addressing her that way and ignoring her title meant they sympathized with his frustration. She was, after all, famously good at hide-and-seek. Though admittedly, Master Gluck probably did not consider himself to be playing a game.

The teacher's hard-soled steps ended just outside her family's private quarters, and there was a pause before the maestro rapped thrice on the door. The staff always hesitated before intruding on this space. Maybe he'd think better of it and move off.

The knock sounded again.

Uh oh! Caught! She laughed and skipped across the warm study, sliding beneath her father's work desk and tucking herself behind his legs, sharing the space with a big wolfhound.

Her father chuckled, too, as he bent down and peeked at her, extending his hand to guide her back out. "My dear little Antoine," he said, using her private family nickname. "You've given good chase thus far, but now it is time to attend to your harpsichord lessons before your poor maestro simply drops dead of frustration."

She took his hand and let him guide her back out, hopping onto his lap as he called for the teacher to enter. She snuggled in tight, enjoying the warmth of the fire in the big hearth and the bright colors of the pillows thrown without care around the soft, well-used chairs and chaises. Antoine much preferred her family's private chambers over the rest of the palace. She could be relaxed in these rooms, comfortable and safe.

The rest of the palace was hard and cold, filled with furniture and art she was not allowed to touch. Filled, too, with a steady flow of strangers, always new faces attached to long names she was expected to memorize. Everyone said that Hofburg palace, the Habsburg family home, was especially beautiful, and she assumed it must be, though she'd rarely been off the grounds her whole life and, so, had no idea what everyone else's palace looked like. She'd heard the one in Versailles was even more lovely—"Like a fairy tale" someone once described it—but it seemed her country was always at war with France, so she was unlikely to ever visit there.

Her teacher entered and her father handed her off with a sympathetic smile.

"Do I have to?" She put what she thought was *just* the right amount of whine into her voice for a chance at mercy. She'd already practiced her music five times this week and still had plenty of time to perfect her skill with the harpsichord. There were fifteen other siblings that her mother, the Empress, could marry off before Antoine had to worry about impressing anyone. Couldn't she just spend the afternoon playing with Papa and the dogs out in the fields?

"Yes, my little featherhead, you do have to. You already play like an angel and you'll only get better and better." Her father gave her a last quick kiss on the cheek as he waved her out. "And don't give me that pout, you. If the worst thing that ever happens to you in life is harpsichord lessons with Maestro Gluck, you will be blessed indeed."

Antoine surrendered with a dramatic shrug of her shoulders. She was a Habsburg princess after all, and her father was not wrong. Truthfully, the thing she worried about most was the idea she might one day be forced to marry someone old or ugly. God forbid both! Now *that* would be the worst thing that could ever happen to her. But it would be a long way off in any case—not for another whole six or seven years at least— so she decided not to worry, and, instead, daydreamed about summer picnics and pony rides as she skipped ahead of her teacher into the music parlor.

Chapter 18

THE SIXTH CIRCLE
The Gates of Dis

The crowd forming before the park entrance had tripled in size during the last few minutes, and more of the demonic vermin walked the ramparts above, guns pointed and ready. Given that there was enough of an audience, a pair of monitors rose up, one on each side of the iron gates, high above the crowd.

Strangely, Bea hadn't spotted a cameraman following them since back at the plane. She'd caught glimpses of them running with the crowd at the end of their catacomb journey, but their cameras hadn't been focused on her.

"Dante is the more interesting news story now. He is the goal and the prize, not you. You were merely the competition, and now that someone has captured him, the focus is on that story, not yours." Toni pointed at the monitors. "This is good news because the attention is off of us for now. Meanwhile, we get an update on your brother."

With a voiceover narrating, the screen played back footage of what must have gone down only moments before she and Toni had surfaced from the catacombs. It clearly depicted a rushed and sweaty Wolfgang pulling a groggy Dante by the wrists. The

German approached the entry gates even as several men and women—some covered in mud or blood, others shivering in wet linen or soiled jeans—stormed in on them. A guard considered for only a second before swinging the gates wide and choosing to let them all enter, the horde climbing over each other to get at Wolfgang and his prize.

The image tightened as Dante looked back over his shoulder, and his round, searching eyes caught the camera. The broadcast froze on that image, zooming in until her brother's wide-eyed confusion filled the screen. He might as well have been looking right at her, pleading for help.

Bea clapped a hand over her mouth and ducked back into their concrete hidey hole, holding back the barrage of emotions threatening to exit her mouth in a wail. Seeing his face, his living, breathing—in a manner of speaking—self was a joy she'd never thought to experience again. But the lost look in his eyes ripped that joy away as quickly as it had arrived.

The two women faced each other, blocked from the guards' view. "They let everyone in," Bea said. "Let's just follow them in, too. They're only a few minutes ahead and if I can get close enough to get Dante's attention—"

Loud, rapid-fire percussion made them jump, and they risked a peek around the wall. Guards on the ramparts above the entrance sprayed automatic weapon fire into the sea of people clamoring to get in. The crowd had ballooned in size even in the last few moments, and soon fifty percent of them lay sprawled and bloody on the ground.

"It appears they've reached maximum capacity," Toni said as the huge monitors broadcast the massacre.

"Shit." Every minute they lost sent her brother's captors that much closer to delivering him to the Administrative Center. "What about that pass you used to get us into the First Circle? The one you showed the creepy cowboy demon. Can't we just get in with that?"

"That only provided access to the Ranch. Besides, you forget, *mon amie*, that was *before* we agreed to play The Game. We no longer have any of the special privileges that may have otherwise been granted to me as your guide."

"Ugh. Fuck!" Bea slid down the wall into a squat. "Let me just... I need to think for a second."

Toni crouched down to mirror her position on the opposite wall, her hands caressing the smooth cover of the MacBook as it rested on her knees, and, for the first time, her eyes displayed a longing Bea hadn't yet seen on the young-but-also-old queen's face. Her pale hands fiddled with the edges of the laptop lid, searching for the release.

Bea leaned across the distance separating them and opened the monitor for her. "Who do you want to look up in there? I know your children aren't in this place. Is it... the King?"

Toni stared at the screen—through the screen, really—her gaze distant. "Hm? Oh, pardon, no. The King was not my... No, not the King."

Bea's memories of what she'd known about Marie Antoinette's love life weren't exactly crystal at this point. She remembered they'd been young teens when they'd been forced into marriage for political reasons, and there was something embarrassing too... something about the young dauphin not making any moves toward producing an heir. He'd been reticent and had needed... instruction. But the princess—later queen—had been young, beautiful, and the toast of Paris. Surely, she'd had lovers, maybe one in particular.

"Axel," Toni whispered, recapturing Bea's attention.

Toni's fingers hovered above the keyboard, and Bea had the silly thought, even in the midst of this insanity, whether an eighteenth-century queen would know how to type or if she would have to hunt-and-peck the letters.

Toni's expression turned sharp. "I have been in this place for over two hundred earth years, and I constantly learn of the ever-changing ways and tools of the corporeal world from the continuous flood of new souls. I am not some naïve bumpkin. I could have opened this laptop myself if my hands weren't..." She trailed off.

Shaking, Bea finished the thought as she shrugged off the unnerving telepathy. "Do you want to go find him? Your Axel?" She asked because, well, she *did* care. At the same time, perhaps selfishly, she prayed the answer would be *No*. If they went off on a side quest, her brother would be lost—just as Bea's requests had repeatedly put Toni's own family reunion at risk. What a pair they made.

"I admit I am tempted. After all this time, to have this information at my fingertips... To find him, see him, to... possibly... touch him." She shook her head. "It is best I do not know. It will be a distraction from the goal."

Empathy coursed through Bea's veins, and she touched Toni's hand with a smile. "Hey, I understand the loss." And, once again, she forced back tears as she thought of Angel. "But soon I'll be reunited with my brother, and you with your children. I call that a win-win situation."

Toni returned a brief smile as another volley of gunfire ripped the two of them out of their sentimental bubble. They got back to their feet. A glance at the monitor showed her brother being lifted high on the hands of the crowd inside the rotting park like a rock star crowd-surfing off the stage—only, his expression had gone from confused to panicked, and his German captor was no longer in sight.

"They're gonna pull him to pieces." She sounded shrill and didn't care. She eyed the tall iron gates. Enough of the crowd was now in piles on the ground that she had a clear shot to them, and the bars looked wide enough to slip through. "We've got to go now while we have a chance. Let's just move super-fast like we did in the catacombs. We can slide between those bars into the park and disappear into the mob before they can shoot us."

"Beatrice, no, that iron gate is—"

Toni's words dissipated on the stormy wind as Bea shot forward, moving with that preternatural speed she'd begun mastering. Her guide would follow, and she was at the ticket booth in what seemed like one step, her arm already reaching to grab at the bars but *bam!*

Something punched her shoulder, agony ripping through her like red-hot evil itself.

She fell onto her butt, her left hand going to the bullseye of pain on the right shoulder and coming away bloody. A scream sounded in her ears, but she soon realized it wasn't her own—a middle-aged man next to her lay on his side, hands groping at the gaping hole in his gut.

Her breath came in spastic coughs as Toni pulled her to her feet and dragged her back to the abutment. The shoulder burned like a hot poker had been inserted into the joint. "How did he hit me? The speed I was moving... How did he even see me?"

"He didn't. He shot at the crowd and it was coincidence that a bullet ricocheted and grazed you." She examined Bea's shoulder. "That's all this is, just a shallow tear."

Bea grumbled. She wasn't even shot outright and she still felt as though she was about to lose her last lunch. However long ago her last lunch had been. "It still hurts like a son of a bitch."

"Are you *sure* it hurts?" asked Toni. "Are you sure the wound is even there at all?"

As Bea looked down at her slimy red shoulder, the stabbing heat faded to a dull throb, then quickly disappeared altogether. She wiped away the mess and found no wound at all. Nice, but she knew it was more of a Jedi mind trick from Toni than her own will.

"It is time for another leap in your understanding." Toni pierced her with a look of pure intensity.

Bea checked around the concrete corner of their little bunker and saw the man who'd been shot still squirming on the dirt. A guard caught sight of her and raised his gun, so she bolted back behind the wall, her heart thundering so hard in her chest she figured the demon could hear it.

Another leap in my understanding.

"I know the gore isn't real. I can watch myself heal, but still I—" A new round of gunfire sent Bea cowering into the back corner of their bunker.

"Moving through space the way you've learned to do, that's a good first step," said Toni. "But it's easy because it's fun and you sense there's no real risk. What you must learn now is infinitely harder. Your fear of pain will stop you. The only way to get around the fear is to truly know with every part of your mind and heart that there is no bullet. You have no body. There is no way to wound you."

"But…how long will it take to learn that? I've only got minutes to spare. Toni, how did the other souls you guided get through these gates?"

She looked away. "This is always the hardest part."

That wasn't exactly an answer, and something odd clanged deep within the non-verbal part of Bea's brain.

The voiceover began again, and, this time, the narrator was laughing as he spoke—but this wasn't a news broadcaster; it was the faceless host of The Game. "The crowd inside is trampling itself as they fight for the twin-turned-trophy. Do they really think they'll all fit through the castle portcullis? It's likely to come down on some of them. Slice and dice," he said with a greasy giggle. "Have you viewers picked out your favorite competitors yet? Placed any bets?"

"The castle?" Bea asked.

Toni shrugged. "It's where the administrative offices are located."

"Of course it is," she said as she considered the string of

tags she would've used to define the current situation if she could've posted something. #literalroyalshitshow #ratastic #bizarrodisne—

Wait. Stop.

This wasn't a game, and it was nobody's entertainment, much as whoever was in charge here liked to present it as such. This was, in fact, a far more real real-life than the one she'd previously lived. The one where she'd couched her world in hashtags and memes and where she'd measured her success in followers. What had Toni said to her earlier in this journey? That her language lacked communicative intent and strength? She saw that now. In this world—in this *death*—she needed strength and intent in order to *live*. What she needed—what her *brother* needed—was for her to... lean into it.

Bea rubbed her palms down her thighs, sucked in a lungful of air. "Whatever happens, don't let me fall asleep."

Those pale blonde brows drew together. "Pardon?"

"Immersion therapy. There's no other way for me to learn this fast enough to save Dante. I don't have time to pass out for eons. Do you understand?"

Toni stared in response, her knuckles turning white as she clutched the computer against her stomach.

"I don't have hours, Toni, I have *minutes* to learn this. Wake me up, every time. Tell me you understand."

The Queen licked her dry lips, nodding in response. "*Oui.* Yes." After a moment's pause, she touched Bea's shoulder. "Remember what I said to you once. What you expect, is what you project. You write the story."

Okay, good. Got it. She could do this.

With possibly the biggest breath she'd ever taken, and perhaps a word or two of prayer to whomever or whatever had placed her here, Bea walked out of her concrete protection. Not running, but walking, her arms wide out to the sides and her chin lifted as she dared the demon rodentia to... "Ugh!" A spear of liquid heat ripped through her right knee and she fell face down onto the hard pan of dirt, vomiting up the pain. The screaming in her ears this time was her own as her hands flailed at her leg and the world began graying out. Her eyes fluttered shut into...

"No, Beatrice, don't pass out!" Cool hands turned her face-up and she looked into pale blue eyes. "You are fine. Stand up. Now."

Bea groaned, a deep chill cramping her muscles. "No, I can't. It hurts so bad."

"Why are you lying there when there is nothing wrong and we have things to do? Move, damnit!"

She looked down at her blue-jeaned leg, no rips or blood at all. And, suddenly no... pain.

A decided success on round one. But she had to know for sure she could do this without Toni's mental persuasion. Maybe she already was, but she had to *know*, had to trust in herself.

She rose up, her movements awkward and trembling with the memory of pain still in her limbs. A glance over her shoulder proved Toni had retreated, awaiting her next intervention, and Bea continued to the gates.

The guards swiveled their heads toward her, their weapons at the ready, and they might have had bemused expressions under those gas masks. Were probably laughing at the tears of panic streaking down her cheeks, at the obvious fear animating her jerky limbs. Who knew? But her brother was being carried off by an angry mob in Hell, so fuck those rat bastards.

She lifted both hands and gave them double middle fingers.

Bang! All the breath in her lungs evacuated like someone had opened an airlock into space, her chest going painfully concave, and, right behind it, came a mist of bright red from her mouth, painting the ground in a sea of crimson splatter as, once again, she face-planted. This time, though, the pain fled quickly, and she soon felt nothing except the flight of all language and meaning from her mind as her brain thought it starved for oxygen.

She... Something... What...?

A hard, open-hand slap to the cheek stopped her fall into the void. "Ouch! The hell?"

Toni kept silent, but jerked a thumb for her to get up.

Bea wiped the wetness from her cheeks, but her hand came back clear and dry. No blood.

She filled her lungs deeply with the welcome taste of smoke and storm. Letting out one short cough, she got back up. "Geez, your highness, I appreciate your help, but you don't have to be so brutal about it."

Toni raised a brow at that, but quickly hopped back to avoid something and... a chunk of concrete the size of a washing machine body slammed into Bea, driving her lower body into the dirt. She swore she heard sniggering from atop the ramparts as she rotated her upper body to take a look, but only her upper body—she felt nothing from the waist down and puked again into the trampled earth. Fear was becoming a much weaker enemy at this point after repeatedly witnessing her rapid healings, but exhaustion rolled over her like a heavy blanket, and she let her head rest on her outstretched arm.

"Bea."

"I just need a minute. Just...a couple minutes."

"There is no time. And you wanted this."

She closed her eyes, but the inevitable slap came. This time a graceful, regal backhand. "Ow. Stop!"

"Time is wasting. You must finish your lessons *tout de suite.*"

Bea resisted the urge to spew all kinds of snarky responses and twisted, again, to look at her lower half, realizing she could, indeed, move her legs beneath the heavy block. And maybe... not so heavy after all.

She dug and kicked, creating a little groove in the earth, and finally slid out from under it.

Standing up, she rolled her shoulders and cracked her neck, looking at the ramparts above. She curled her lip at the nearest rat. *Let's finish this, asshole.*

Time slowed in her vision as his finger tightened on the trigger and *pop*! Her head snapped back on a fractured cervical spine, smoke drifting down into her vision from the hole in her forehead. Images of a cartoon coyote crossed her mind and she chuckled as she stumbled backward a step or two.

Toni's hand braced the small of her back to steady her, but Bea brushed it off. "Nope, I'm… actually, I'm good," she said as she flipped her head up with a loud crack, resettling it properly on top of her spinal column. Wiping a hand across her forehead, both the hole and the smoke dissolved into nothing.

Something felt odd, light, empty. It took her a moment to understand it was a lack of fear—at least, fear for her physical body anyway. How insane that the mind held onto that fear even in death. Held onto it when she could so easily just be… free.

Toni was watching her with a look of astonishment, as if she hadn't really expected her to pull this off, which irked her somehow, and yet maybe was okay because Bea really hadn't been too sure about it either. But she'd pulled it off and *hell yeah*!

She let loose a full body laugh, and God*damn* if the stoic queen didn't break her disbelieving stare and do the exact same, her strawberry curls bouncing as she jumped up and down. Her royal-freaking-highness was actually jumping and squealing with laughter.

Bea couldn't help it, she wrapped her arms around Toni and squeezed her tight, nearly crushing the laptop between them before she let go.

The guards lowered their guns, nodding in acknowledgement.

Take that, rat boys!

"Almost done," Toni said as the women stepped the rest of the way up to the rusty ironwork. The remainder of the crowd parted for them, and the guards did not stop her, but neither did they open the gates.

"Slipping through the bars it is," said Bea.

Toni placed a hand on Bea's arm. "I started to warn you before, but you should know those gates are red hot metal. Your skin will—"

"Be fine," Bea said as she turned sideways and crammed her body between the bars. Her flesh smoked and sizzled, slid off and then reformed, leaving a trail of ash on the ground behind her as she stepped through without pain. Without fear. She failed to suppress a grin.

Once inside, the women stood in the center of the park's dingy village square. Candy shops, magic stores, tourist information booths and the like circled the entrance plaza, all with broken windows, huge flakes of peeling paint, mold on the faded awnings, and blinking green fluorescent lights glowing from within. A miniature train puffed greasy black smoke as it circled a dried-up fountain in the center.

She and Toni were watched by the dozens milling around, but left alone as they made their way to the far side of the square where it opened up to a main street of shops, at the end of which lay the expanse of attractions, and the towering castle in the distance. They stared up at the clock tower marking the spot. The minute hand must have fallen off at some point, and was lying on the ground at the base of it. The hour hand, though, was pointed straight up at the number twelve, and, hanging from it, the arrowed point of the hand jutting out from a bloody chest, was a male body, head limp and very, very dead.

Again.

Wolfgang.

Chapter 19

VERSAILLES, FRANCE

248 years ago (1772)

"Aha! I win again!" Antoine leaned across the mirrored parlor table, dragging her winnings into her already mountainous pile of success. The two noblemen sitting opposite sank back against delicate embroidered cushions and groaned, while the rest of *la noblesse* who'd watched the game play applauded her victory. Polite little claps. Quick and soft.

Fraudulent.

Same as their fraudulent response to her arrival at Versailles when she was fourteen, her marriage to Louis at fifteen, and, now, at her seventeenth birthday festivities.

"The Dauphine is *truly* skilled," a garish beet-red silk tittered, champagne spilling from the fluted crystal in her hand as she leaned toward her companion.

"*Truly* I'd be honored to play against her," the young peacock-blue damask concurred, long blonde ringlets failing to cover an intentionally far-too-overflowing bosom. The woman shifted her gaze to the older marquis standing to her other side,

185

and those bosoms pressed into his arm as she wound up a giggle. "But I *truly* have no idea of the rules!"

Truly, they were full of shit.

The falsity began to suffocate her, so Antoine rose from her chair. The tight cluster of nobles stepped back, still fawning and feigning. Soon, they'd slip off without her to tuck behind some tall croquembouche or, perhaps, the harpist's broad curtain of strings, where their whispers would be drowned in the music and their adulation would turn to denigration.

Antoine swept back her skirts and ignored the pile of cash on the table, instead collecting a single playing die carved from garnet, the dots on each of the six sides formed of opal, and tucking it into her palm. She rolled it in her hand as she moved through the room. The die was solid and comforting, warming at her touch. It was something to focus on and grip tightly when eyes invariably went to her flat, empty, heirless womb. When her young husband, the future king, turned away from her genuine smile and ducked out of the party to sleep alone.

When everyone witnessed his rebuff.

The palace musicians stood for a break, and the empty bench before the harpsichord beckoned her to play. Members of the court would, once again, gather round and play-act their fondness for her, pronounce her musical talents even greater than her card play, slather her in sycophancy. With her hands on the keys, she *might* be able to tune them out. Might.

Antoine rolled the die in her palm.

Or… she might retire from the festivities herself. Slip off to her bedchamber—or the Dauphin's. After all, she had a bit more hope tonight in that regard. Her dressmaker and wig designer had outdone themselves for the party. Her gown was a buttery yellow, a sartorial miracle that was somehow both innocent and flirty, and her hairpiece was piled two-feet tall with tiny faux birthday cakes pinned throughout. People said she was particularly glowing.

Perhaps, if she tried her very hardest, her husband might find her attractive enough to—

"Royal Highness." A court messenger interrupted her thoughts, out of breath and flustered from disturbing her. "Your brother, Joseph II, the Crown Prince, has arrived at Versailles."

Antoine lifted onto her tiptoes, tossing the die aside and clapping with exuberance, causing the messenger to blush and other heads to turn. She didn't care a whit. "Please have rooms readied for him at once." She clapped again, adding a squeal this time, for the joy she felt at her brother's surprise appearance could not be held back by the tightest of corsets. "Find out if he'd like to see me tonight or tomorrow morning. We can have breakfast and, afterward, take a walk in the—"

"Forgive me, Highness." The messenger lowered his voice. "He desires to meet with you immediately. He is already waiting in your audience chamber."

"Of course. He wishes to greet me before midnight while it is still my birthday." She lifted her wide skirts and rushed off, soon bursting through the doors to the more intimate parlor adjoining her personal rooms. Unlike the larger game hall she'd just left, with its ivory white walls and two-story, floor-to-ceiling mirrors, her private greeting room—though elegant— invited warm embraces and softer discussion. Walls of the palest moss green and silk curtains stitched in silver and gold were reflected in round, gilt-framed mirrors, dozens of candles warming even the quietest corners.

In the center stood her eldest brother. Joseph looked grand in his red-and-gold waistcoat, dark breeches, and white silk stockings, even after hours of cross-country travel. He carried the air of one who'd someday become Holy Roman Emperor, yet opened his arms in welcome to his baby sister. "Ah, how lovely you are, my little Antoine."

She raced to him, nearly diving into a full embrace before remembering the demands of both court decorum and the logistics of her hairstyle and wardrobe. Instead, she settled for some pecks on the cheek and being content to merely hold his hands as they took each other in. "You have come to celebrate with me. I am so thrilled."

He released her hands, and she saw at once from the change in his expression that her birthday was not the cause of his visit.

He took a seat on a cream-colored chaise, crossing his legs and draping his arms over the back. Flickering candlelight from a side table dappled half his face as he nodded once. "Happy birthday, dear sister."

She moved toward the fireplace mantle, not far from where he sat, and ran a finger along the cool marble. No fire was currently lit, and a draft of cold air floated down from the chimney. "That is not why you have come, is it?"

"It was a fortunate coincidence, but… no. I have come because our mother has sent me to make sure things are well with you."

She stepped from the cold hearth and began pacing the room. "To make sure things are well with my marriage bed, you mean."

"I come here not in judgment, but to see how I may assist. There are fine doctors in the court whose wisdom may be of value in this matter. An heir is of utmost urgency for the continued peace of both our countries, as you know." He uncrossed and then recrossed his legs. "However, even in the short time since I arrived at Versailles, I am reminded there are additional things we should discuss as well. Appearances, as you are aware, are important. The constant expenditures on excessive feasting and gambling…" He trailed off, but his eyes were not as tentative as his words after glancing back to the party.

"We are in the Palace of Versailles, my dear brother, where appearance is indeed important. *Including* the appearance of success and power." Which was true. But it was not *her* truth. Not the reason for her love of cards, sparkling gems, lush fabrics or double-cream cakes. They gave her pleasure—warm, sensual, tactile pleasure—that she couldn't seem to get from anything animate since coming to France. And they did it without wanting something from her in return. They did it, in fact, these objects, without *seeing* her. They did not talk behind her back or spot her numerous failings. If she could not find a way to satisfy the human ache inside her—the need to be touched and comforted—with friendships or romance, then, at least, she was in a position where she could satisfy it with the slide of diamonds against her cleavage or the slip of custard over her tongue.

Her brother stood, his expression hardening now to somewhere between bossy older brother and demanding head of state. "You are the Dauphine of France. Your behavior is unbecoming, Marie Antoinette."

Air rushed from her lungs, and she dove toward him, throwing herself to sit on the very edge of a stool near his feet, craning her neck like a supplicant. A tiny cake came loose from her wig and fell to the floor. "Please do not call me that. I cannot bear to hear that foreign French name from your lips, my brother. I am Maria Antonia Josepha Johanna, if you must be formal, but do not forget I am your Antoine first and foremost."

His lips thinned and his cheeks darkened, though a note of empathy still glimmered in his familiar eyes. It was clear for a moment that he was battling feelings of duty versus those of family.

Duty, however, won.

As she'd known it would.

As it must.

"That is not your name anymore, *ma sœur*. You will one day be Queen of France. Versailles is your family now. Know who you are."

His image began to blur as her eyes grew wet, and her fingers searched for the die she'd regrettably tossed aside when she'd thought comfort would be coming from elsewhere. "You tell me to know who I am, but who am I if not a child of Austria? Who am I if not my parents' daughter, if not my siblings' sister?" She slid off the stool onto her knees before him, humiliating herself further. But this was her *brother*. She needed to see herself reflected in *his* eyes at the very least. She could make her way through this theater that was the French Court, she could perform her duty, but only if she recognized herself behind the powdered mask, the very one now streaked with tears. "Tell me, please, brother. If I am no longer your Antoine, who am I?"

Chapter 20

THE SIXTH CIRCLE
The City of Dis – Main Street

Bea averted her eyes from Wolfgang's body hanging from the clocktower at the end of the square. At least it wasn't Dante, but the sight was still chilling for the macabre possibilities it threatened for him.

As the two women moved down the Main Street concourse, the crowd of people grew thicker around them. A populace of sullen and sickly faces stepped out of shops and poured closer to the park entrance, their stares focused on Toni and Bea.

"What's going on?" Bea asked while taking in the growing throng on each side of the broken asphalt street. The crowd followed her and Toni at a distance but made no threatening gestures toward them. "Why are they watching us?"

A middle-aged woman, salt-and-pepper curly hair topping a sallow face, silently pointed a finger toward a shop window a few doors down on their right.

Bea and Toni followed that direction to see a cluster of people gathered before the large window display beneath the sign. *Ye Olde Wager Shoppe.*

"Wager Shoppe?" Bea asked as they moved toward the crowd staring excitedly through the glass at something inside.

"A bookie," Toni responded as if it were the most normal thing in the world to see at an amusement park.

Bodies parted for them as they approached the window, but eyes continued to watch the two women as they, in turn, studied what was beyond the glass. A display of old-time-y black-and-white TVs filled two shelves, all with rabbit ear antennas and a "Dis CCTV" icon in the upper left corner of the broadcast. Each of the television sets was running the same news footage of Bea: Bea getting gunned down, Bea getting flattened by concrete, Bea losing her skin on red-hot iron. And Bea, recovering like a god every single time.

"You're back on the map now," Toni whispered beside her.

A sharp whistle from inside brought her attention to a short, stout man behind the counter. One of several attendants working the shop, his head was mostly bald but for a horseshoe fringe of silvered brown, and he seemed to be in charge of the place as he waved her in.

The group out front moved to let them enter, but, inside, a throng of busy people crammed the L-shaped counter, voices shouting as they vied to get a vendor's attention while the two women pushed through to the front. On the wall behind the counter were a couple chalkboards. One had team names with current betting odds for each hastily scribbled, and two young men stood on ladders with chalk and erasers, constantly changing the numbers. The teams included such groups as the "The Hot Heads," "The Big Chill," "The Barons," and "The Hammer." The last team on the board was listed simply as "Two Cunts," and Bea had an uncomfortable suspicion as to who *that* referred to. Even as she stood there, the odds on that last team changed from one-in-twenty-five to one-in-twelve.

The title on another board read "Dante's Data," and it contained his current location, the group presently in control of him, their distance from the Administrative Center, and the general situational status.

At the moment, he was apparently on the loose (*Good for you, bro!*) but was unknowingly running straight toward the haunted house attraction and a team called "The Sickos." *Lovely.*

Still, a glance at the other board showed that even with Dante rushing straight toward them, The Sickos were only favored to win—a win still being defined as successfully bringing Dante to the Administrative Center, though whether that meant the entire group would win the prize was unclear—at one-in-fifty, which seemed strange to Bea, but left her hopeful.

As she stepped up to the front, the little sausage of a man slid over a stepstool in order to gain enough height to lean on the counter conspiratorially. "I'm Benny." He didn't bother to offer his hand.

"Apparently, I'm a cunt. What do you want, Benny?" Bea said.

At least he had enough grace to blush. "Since you happened to cross my path, I thought I'd take a closer look at you. See if I've got my current line on you correct."

"Do you want to check my teeth? Kick my tires?" She started to turn away and Toni with her.

Benny grabbed her hand. "Wait, wait. I'm sorry. Let's talk."

"Okay. Start with why my odds are still so high, considering what people now know I'm capable of." She tilted her head in the direction of the television display.

He shrugged. "Eh. That's only closed-circuit TV. Broadcasting within the bounds of Dis to anyone with a feed, which might only be me now that I think about it. Most of the other players don't yet know you're back in The Game, let alone inside Dis *and* with a new set of skills. Which means they won't yet hold back when they come upon you. We'll see how the odds shift as the match-ups start happening in real time."

Match-ups. She didn't particularly love the spark of light that popped into his eyes as he said those last words.

Benny leaned so far over his chin nearly touched the counter. "Look. Tell me something. Rumor has it the book is real, and you guys have it. That true?"

"You think I'm going to tell you that kind of information just so you can adjust your odds?" The press of bodies suddenly felt tight and hot, and awareness of the laptop's vulnerability hit her for the first time.

Benny straightened up, leaving Bea with more breathing room.

"Truth is, I'm more of an information broker than a bookie. What are these guys going to pay me with, after all? Rancid desserts from one of these shops or a boon some demon granted them? I make my way in this Underworld by what I know, and I protect my sources." His eyes darted to the flat tablet clutched in Toni's hands, then he nodded toward a door to a back room of the shop. "Come through here and follow me. We can talk away from all these eyes."

He flipped up a panel on the countertop to let them through, but Bea paused, leaning into Toni. "Can we trust him to go back there? Is he a demon?"

Toni shrugged. "No. More like a... staff member. He probably made his own deal of some sort to work this place rather than sit in pure torment. That's probably true for much of the populace that runs Dis and its administrative processes."

Bureaucracy even in Hell. Bea followed the bookie into the back room. In fact, Hell's pencil-pushers probably suffered the worst.

Benny sat behind a wooden desk, piled high with paperwork and otherwise covered in scratches smoothed over with age, and long dried splashes of dark maroon that left Bea with questions she didn't allow to form in her mind.

"I see you've got something there, and I'm going to go

ahead and presume it's the book." He cast a pointed glance at the Mac. "Not what I'd imagined, but, nevertheless, in a show of good faith, I'll go ahead and offer you some information first. A bit of useful advice, let's call it."

Bea glanced at Toni who lifted a brow but gestured for him to continue.

"Let's assume you find your brother and succeed in keeping him out of anyone else's hands. Don't take him to the Administrative Center. You already have your guide. You'll have your brother. You don't need anything from the castle, and I wouldn't trust any promises they make you. Instead, get out of Dis Land and down to the Seventh Circle. Once there, if you can make it past The Hammer and drop down to the Eighth, you'll be home free."

Bea settled onto a cold metal folding chair opposite the stubby little dealmaker. "Home free?"

"They'll call off the competition over your brother. The challenge to take your place on the journey out of Hell will be over."

"Without actually arriving at the Castle?"

He nodded. "Correct. Get down to the Eighth Circle, and I guarantee they'll end this new twist in The Game. See, nobody will follow you further down into Hell at that level without already having achieved the prize and reward. It's far too risky that they'd never make it back up here and they'll be stuck in the lowest circles. Not worth the risk at all. And the people down in the Eighth and Ninth? They're way too trapped to be able to climb up higher or to challenge you as you pass through. Too trapped to do much of anything really."

She and Toni shared a look. It made some sense.

"The show producers will know it's over. They'll revert The Game back to its original goal—entertainment for the Underworld populace as they watch your journey. Who you choose to take with you at that point will have nothing to do with it, and the masses, at least, will be off your back for the rest of your travels. I can't say the same, of course, for the demons or the producers of the game show itself, entertainment being their highest priority."

Bea slowly nodded. "Okay, thank you."

Benny sat forward and rested his thick elbows on the wood. "Now, tell me what's in the book? Is it true that it's a directory of the populace?"

"It is," Bea ventured.

His voice quieted by half. "And more?"

Toni jumped in. "Possibly. We've not yet had time to peruse it any further than to find her brother."

He studied the two women, and Bea's patience began to wane as she remembered her brother's headlong run toward The Sickos.

Benny finally leaned back in his chair. "Will you... would you mind terribly looking up my wife for me? In the book?"

His demeanor appeared genuine. Bea knew the shape of grief and loss on a body: the rounded shoulders, the concaved solar plexus, the downturned edges of the eyelids. She'd seen herself in a mirror often enough. Still... "That's a new ask. I want another thing in return."

"Name it," he said.

She tipped her head in the direction of the busy shop they'd just come from. "Change the name of our team."

He chuckled but rose from his seat in an instant. "You got it."

Toni handed the laptop to Bea before following him to the door as he called out to one of his men, and soon thereafter she nodded in confirmation. "It now simply says 'Beatrice.'"

Bea popped open the lid. "What's your wife's name?"

"Lorelei Petrosyan." He leaned over her shoulder and stared at the screen.

A few clicks and Bea found her.

196

"Limbo," Benny said as he sank into a second folding chair beside her. "Thank God." He paused for a moment, his thoughts somewhere else, and his lips relaxed, verging on a smile. "I may never see her again, of course, but just to know she's okay... Well, it's a gift."

A knock on the door jamb ended the moment. One of Benny's young workers stood there. "Boss, I think they're beginning to suspect who's in here with you. They're getting a little twitchy."

"Got it, thanks." Benny gestured toward the Mac as he stood. "Look, you get internet on that thing?"

Internet? Oh my God. It hadn't occurred to her that this might be a fully functioning laptop. She switched back to the home screen and hunted around—

Sure enough, she found Hell's browser. Okay, it was an ancient version of Internet Explorer, but at least she had a freaking connection. Now, she'd just have to see if she could log on to her Underworld socials. Would they have the same username and passwords as her Earth-based socials had used? Doubtful. But the crowd beyond the threshold was growing louder, so that answer would have to wait.

Benny was already writing something down. "Here's all my @ info."

"You have regular access to communication?" Toni asked.

He grinned and pulled a phone from his pocket. "I managed to procure this. Permanently. I'll keep you updated on the information I can see from here on the CCTV if you'll keep me posted with boots-on-the-ground info. You'll help me make some profit and I'll help you get your brother out of Dis. Deal?"

Bea spared a glance at Toni who didn't have anything negative to add, which she took as about as much of a yes as she would get. "Deal."

Benny went behind his desk again and grabbed a couple

things. "Here, take this map of the park." He found a pen and drew a route. "This is the fastest way to the haunted house attraction. And you," he looked up to Toni, "can put the book in here." He handed over a satchel with straps, into which Toni slipped the Mac before securing it around her torso. "It's waterproof, which won't hurt with the rides here in Dis."

"Thank you," Bea said as he hustled them through the crowd in the front part of the shop. People now greedily watched her before clamoring even harder to place their bets. She spared a last glance at the chalkboard and found her odds now listed at one-to-eight.

As they stepped out onto the main drag, the crowd was even more hushed as Benny pointed them in the general direction of their destination before slipping back inside and leaving them to their own strategy. A few people nodded at her in acknowledgement. Others offered helpful tips and pointed them in the direction of the castle or toward Suburban Square, the location of the haunted attraction. Their new confidence in her equated to their assistance, or at least meant they'd think twice before trying to hinder her. However, the further they walked down the main road, going deeper into the park, the fewer people had seen her gate footage, and here most ignored her and Toni. Some, though, eyed them up with suspicion, or gazed with a covetous eye at the pack strapped to Toni's chest.

"We should find a way to let everyone see what you've learned," said Toni. "If most of the populace responds to you with respect the way those who viewed the footage have, regaining your brother and completing our journey will be far easier."

Toni was right. Bea was on her way to becoming a proper influencer again, possibly with more cachet than even Toni now, and her mind began to chew over thoughts of how to best utilize their internet access.

Still… another idea had begun jangling around in her head

since her lessons at the gate. She'd learned a set of skills that were changing her entire reality in this place, and she couldn't be the only soul to whom that opportunity was available. And if, like Toni had said, it required a mass effect of the populace to change the nature of the Afterlife, a group-subconscious all on the same page, then at least a majority of the souls here would have to learn those skills, too. They had to see that there were no bullets, no icebergs, no blowtorches.

"Yes, we need to get our hands on that footage," Bea said, suddenly thinking less about her own journey than this collective concern. "We need them to see."

They came to a circle where a huge dead tree stood surrounded by rusted and broken park benches. A quartet of musicians stood beneath it, dressed in faded and dirty tuxedos. They played a song that wanted to be upbeat, but the trumpet player lacked one arm and, therefore, played only one note, which sputtered out between breaths. Thunder rolled softly overhead in the perpetually dark sky, punctuating the end of the tune like a sad *waah-waah* the trumpeter failed to produce.

Paths led off from the circle in different directions, and Bea checked the map they'd been given before pointing to the left, toward Suburban Square. As they walked down the middle of the hot asphalt road into this quadrant of Dis, the façades of the shops and eateries changed from a small-town Main Street vibe, albeit a dilapidated one, to a world of monochromatic beige stucco. All here was cookie-cutter and bland, an unbroken sea of boring with nothing to draw the eye except the numerous patches of gray mold crawling the plaster and hiding in the crevices of the too-green patches of Astroturf. Backlit plastic signs announced the store names, though a chain of the same shop seemed to be on every corner. The place gave her the willies in a way even the decrepitude of Main Street had failed to do. It felt the most… dead… of all the places she'd seen in the Underworld thus far. The suburbs sucked.

There were fewer souls in this section of the park. In fact, she now realized that as they'd been walking, the few people she'd seen had been ducking out of sight or peeking cautiously through faded mini blinds from inside buildings. Their steps now echoed loudly on the path. A little too loudly, come to think of it. The echo of too many steps. And, now, too many voices.

They paused at the sudden wall of sound coming from around a corner ahead of them. Bea recognized this sound, and she fought back the urge to press her palms over her ears to cover the hate-filled shouts.

An angry mob came into sight as they rounded the bend about a hundred yards away. As they drew closer, it became clear the mob's clothes were tattered and dripping, and in their fists they gripped weapons—ragged planks of wood and boat masts sharpened to wicked points.

Bea and Toni took a few steps backward while monitors rose up on either side of the street, showing images of the wrathful gang as they screamed their challenges from raw throats. The scroll across the bottom of the broadcast stated, "The Hotheads move into Suburban Square."

"Looks like The Hotheads are people from the boats in the Fifth Circle. The demons must have let a ton of them into Dis," Bea said as she and Toni headed toward the sidewalk, out of the path of the oncoming wave of weaponized snark. "The other teams must be from other levels. The Big Chill team?"

"I'm guessing the Third Circle," Toni said as the image on the monitors changed. Now the video focused on Bea and Toni on the side of the road, and the scroll gave away their identity. "*Merde.*"

The gang turned their heads almost in unison their way, and, a heartbeat later, loosed a shriek of fury as they bolted down the road toward them.

Bea didn't waste a moment to check with Toni. She took off at supernatural speed straight toward the gang in the direction of the haunted house, knowing the Queen would be hot on her heels.

They were at the mob in what seemed a heartbeat, the crowd size great enough to fill the breadth of the road. Bea was bounced and jostled among them as she tried to maneuver past without slowing too much.

At their speed, she and Toni would've seemed to disappear into thin air, and people swung blindly with their makeshift weapons.

Fast as she was, Bea caught her share of injuries, though she caused many of the baffled boaters to trip and fall as she blew past them. Her wounds were incidental, of course, because they healed as fast as they occurred.

One lucky hand managed to grab hold of the satchel wrapped around Toni's torso, and Toni fell to the ground, shocking those around her as she miraculously reappeared. She managed to kick the person away, then raced to catch up to Bea.

They soon ditched the crowd, running beyond the bend in the road and arriving, just as they'd experienced in the catacombs, suddenly before their destination as if it had rushed up to greet them.

Some of Bea's skills were now public knowledge, and who knew if and when the broadcasters would relay her current location in the park, but, for now, they took a beat to study the place where Dante had last been headed.

A lone house stood with empty lots on either side, like a fully finished model home in a development that had yet to be built. A cheaply constructed monstrosity with two single-story wings on either side of a soaring three-story center, the décor couldn't seem to decide if it was Colonial, Victorian, or wannabe stately mountain house. The façade moved from red brick to river stone to whitewashed wood, though the edges hinted that all three fronts had been sloppily stuck over cheap siding. White columns flanked the steps leading to the front door, but an intricate gingerbread porch fronted each of the wings. Dormer windows had been stuck randomly here and there, and a single turret shot up from one side of the roof.

The awkward silhouette loomed dark against the flashing thunderheads in the charcoal sky above as lights stuttered on and off, on and off, from inside the numerous windows. The line of souls waiting to take a ride through the Ghostly McMansion wove like a snake in loops around the building, but had been at a standstill for so long that most people were sleeping on their feet, covered in bits of dirt and leaves that had blown into their clothes and hair over time. None of them noticed Bea and Toni as they approached the steps.

"How do we even know your brother is in there? We could be embarking on a colossal waste of time," Toni said as they watched for any movement at the entrance, some indication that anyone would be allowed to enter soon.

There was nothing except the flickering porch light swinging on the breeze.

Bea looked up at the house, at the inert souls waiting in line. She called out, "Dante?"

No person stirred, no answering shout responded, but the front door swung open on a squeaky hinge, inviting them in.

They climbed the steps alone to enter a dark, unfinished foyer. Caged electric work lights hung on nails against paint-splattered sheets of drywall, flickering just enough to illuminate a plywood floor with a rail track running through it. They stopped here and waited as there was no real room to walk.

From out of the gloom on one side, a small open carriage slid to a stop on the tracks in front of them. With seemingly no other way to explore the premises in search of Dante, they hopped in.

"Keep your arms and legs inside the ride at all times," a recording advised, as if Bea had any intention of flailing about in the pitch black of a haunted house in Hell.

The car pulled forward and headed toward a set of double doors, which swung open at the last moment, thrusting them down a track that twisted into the gloomy depths below the house. A smell like a hospital sick room assaulted their nostrils, and Bea covered her nose and mouth with a hand. At the same time, the speakers began playing a children's song—high-pitched young voices singing an instructional lesson about washing one's hands and covering a sneeze.

"That's not creepy at all," she said, feeling a little nauseated herself by the whole vibe.

They passed rows of closed doors that breathed in and out—some of them coughed—and the floor was littered with unused face masks. The track straightened and continued forward through a dank hallway that looked institutional, with pitted concrete walls painted a sickening pea green. In odd contrast, large framed portraits were spaced evenly on both sides of the hall, ornate gilt frames surrounding incredibly life-like oils. A little *too* life-like. The subjects' eyes seemed to follow them as their vehicle moved slowly past. The people depicted in them were... hideous. They'd all been painted covered in oozing pustules and open sores.

One of the subjects shot a hand right out of its frame and reached for her.

"Jesus!" She cringed, scooting into Toni.

A long moan escaped from the soul who'd failed to touch her.

"Okay, so not paintings. People. Sick people. Hung on the freaking wall."

"The Sixth Circle is not just the bureaucratic center of the Underworld, *chérie*. It is also home to its own population and their torments."

Bea searched her memory of Alighieri's story. "The Sixth Circle contained the heretics, if I'm recalling correctly."

"Indeed, you are," Toni said as they kept their eyes peeled

for any sign of Dante. So far, there didn't seem to be any place to hide. If he were here, they'd see him. "But this version of Hell reflects your modern world and its current idea of heretics. The souls on display in this particular house were…"

Bea needed no further explanation. She saw it immediately. "Anti-vaxxers."

Toni nodded as their car continued its journey. They passed above a ghostly scene where transparent apparitions of nurses in masks and protective gear attended to pale spirits on ventilators in row upon row of hospital beds.

Bea now understood something else—the souls inhabiting this house were The Sickos, and it was clear why Benny's odds on them were so bad. They were too ill—or, at least, *believed* they were too ill—to accomplish anything. If her brother had, indeed, been here, he would have moved through unharmed.

As they rounded another corner, a new sound began to compete in both volume and annoyance with the creepy little children's ditty. Over the shouting of voices, it took Bea a minute to recognize the sound of metal banging and wheels screeching.

"They found us." She could see them now. Flashes of bodies moving in the gloom, makeshift weapons tipped in ragged pieces of metal, glinting under the flickering lights. Familiar rage echoed from the walls. Not that any of those things could hurt her anymore, but she didn't have the time to stop and fight. She didn't have the time for any of this BS.

Toni was unfazed. "We can be faster. Let's move."

Bea was already angling to stand up in their tiny car even as Toni was adjusting the satchel to her back for a more streamlined position.

Bea jumped first, leaping in front of their carriage to race along the rail track, far outpacing the cars themselves as she ran in their reality-bending way. She caught up to the preceding car and leapt onto the shell-shaped back of it, balancing on top to reach back for Toni who followed her up.

The voices grew a tad more distant, but still persistent and even angrier; there was no option to slow down or stop. The women jumped forward off of the latest car and outran it again, catching the next and continuing the leapfrog until their pursuers had fallen far behind. Standing on the seat of another car, they rode through a graveyard where decomposing heads sang of their regrets while skinny dogs gnawed on their corpses. There were more places where her brother could hide in this tableau than anywhere else on the ride, and Bea had to check before they lost the chance.

"Come on." Bea grabbed Toni's hand and they hopped off the track, darting behind a fake mausoleum, one leprous hand reaching through its crumbling door. They sank down behind it, waiting silently as the throng of wrathful pursuers rode past on their cars, cursing in frustration at their lost prize.

When it quieted, Bea searched behind headstones and peered into open graves, quietly calling for her brother, but to no avail. She returned to the tomb, finding Toni had perched the laptop on her knees and had already opened the crappy browser.

"I was hoping to check for messages from Mr. Petrosyan, but I'm not sure how to—"

Bea took the computer. "Here, let me. I want to see if I can log into my socials." As she'd hoped earlier, her old passwords from when she was alive worked for all her Hell-based socials. "Fuck yeah." And Benny had already dinged her on her favorite message app.

"He says my odds are now worse. Back up to one-in-fifty."

"How is that? Surely, they broadcasted your fantastical run through The Hotheads."

Bea shook her head as she clacked on the keyboard. "He says nobody really understood what they were seeing when we did that. Although, he did say someone started a TikTok challenge to try to recreate our magical-looking run." She giggled. Maybe the kids would actually figure it out in the process. TikTok could be far more of a subversive tool than many people gave the song-and-dance app credit for. But Bea's excitement fell again. "Shit. He says it was revealed that Dante is now headed for something called the Island Adventure, and a group known as The Barons are headed there fast.

"They've taken all available water vehicles to reach the island, so Benny says we should ride the sky-tram over." Bea snapped shut the lid, slid the book into Toni's pack, then consulted the park map. "Let's go."

They tore out of the house, racing over cars on the remainder of the track, then ran onto a moving walkway leading up an incline to the exit. In no more than a moment, they covered massive ground, manifesting their arrival at the other side of the park and coming to a halt at the entrance to the sky-tram.

One of the suspended carriages swung from its overhead rigging as a demon in the form of a park character—an uncomfortable mash-up of pirate and parrot that did not actually appear to be a costume—studied Bea from his seven-foot height. His demonic eyes should've sizzled her skin like his cohorts' had in the past, but she was no longer affected by the illusion.

He nodded for them to climb in and, with a pathetic *auck* sound that was part pirate *aargh* and part parrot *squawk*, he pulled a lever to start their ascent.

As they climbed, Bea wasted only a moment to grab a view of the park below, the dark castle still off in the distance and a murky slime-covered body of water—more moat than river—surrounding the jungle island where they'd soon be landing. Long, dark shadows moved in the water, which was now thirty feet beneath them.

"Horrible, mutated things live there," Toni said as she

noted the direction of Bea's interest. "Radioactive waste has altered those creatures, as well as those on the island. There is a population of souls living within those trees, though most hide in the branches or burrow underground in the mud to stay safe from the beasts and the elements. The temperature is scorching half the time, freezing the rest." She then answered Bea's unvoiced question. "Climate deniers."

Bea almost snorted, but stopped short, her ability to express snark not coming as easily as it once had. Instead, she took the few minutes they had to hit the internet. She popped a message to Benny, keeping her end of the bargain by telling him their situation.

"I appreciate your updates," he typed back. "And I'm still hoping you'll eventually share more secrets of the book with me. In expectation of that, I have left you a gift."

When he finished his message, Bea turned to Toni. "He says to check the inside zippered pocket of the satchel."

Toni fished out a thumb drive, which Bea promptly plugged into the Mac. "Oh my God. It's the gate footage."

They bounced in excitement for only a second before the carriage's wild swinging they'd created reminded them to calm down. Toni was nearly as animated as she'd been over Bea's success at the Gates of Dis, and Bea suppressed a smile as she logged on to the platform that seemed best for getting fast viewership.

She fluffed her hair—the spots that'd been scalped during her fall down the waterfall having long since grown back—but decided to leave it a tangled mess to let them all see her current unglamorous truth. She looked into the webcam eye. God, it felt like eons since she'd done this. *Like riding a bicycle though, right?* She attempted a smile and it held. "Hey baes, it's Bea. I'm baaaack! And I've got something to show you."

She posted the video and the old familiar adrenaline rush was immediate as the likes and comments blew in so fast she could swear she felt a breeze. Yeah, they were impressed as heck, and she was definitely gaining massive support, which was fast confirmed by a message from Benny stating her odds had now dropped to one in three. *Holy crap!* Yet, along with their admiration came a mountain of questions. How did she do that? Who taught her? Was there something special about her or could they learn to do it as well?

She wanted to tell them everything, but, right now, the tram was descending toward the green canopy and her brother was somewhere down there. Sure, she'd love to help the masses, but her twin was her priority. Her reason for it all.

She popped a few comments in the thread, letting people know that anyone could do it. It was mind over matter, blah blah blah, that's all. They clamored for more answers, but she'd have to deal with that later. A pang of guilt heated her cheeks. She'd made a deal with Toni—first, they get her brother, then they get the hell out of Hell. No more diversions. She couldn't afford to help these people.

Before closing the laptop, she sent Benny another update to say they were landing. She almost didn't wait for his response, but the three little repeating dots kept spinning and spinning, and something about that made her pause.

His message finally popped in. "You must be fast, Beatrice. You've only got thirty minutes to get your brother out of there."

"What's he mean?" Bea asked.

Toni's brows drew, then a word burst from her like an exploded balloon. "Fuck."

Okay, that's not a good sign. Not a good sign at all.

"Why, Benny?" Bea typed. "What happens in thirty minutes?"

"The same thing that happens exactly every twelve hours down there. A tsunami is going to wipe out the island and everything on it."

Chapter 21

VERSAILLES, FRANCE

237 years ago (1783)

Her cheeks burned red hot, showcasing her embarrassment. The damn traitors.

Antoine kept up a pace several steps in front of her long-time personal advisor, the Comte de Mercy-Argenteau. He would only see the unbending length of her spine and relaxed set of her shoulders—feigned though her posture was—as they strolled across the wide expanse of lawn toward her private residence at Le Petit Trianon. Her husband, upon his ascension to the throne eight years prior, had gifted her with the idyllic little chateau located in a distant corner of the Versailles property. A lovely hideaway all her own from which to escape the formalities of court life. Yet, here was Mercy, still dogging her every step with ugly news as she tried to enjoy the beautiful spring day with her children.

"Highness, we must talk about this," he buzzed like a gnat ruining a picnic. "These pamphlets are now everywhere. Plaster-ed in windows or for sale in shops from Paris to Marseille."

Oh, how she longed to pick up the pace. The sooner she was back at the chateau, the sooner she'd be able to retreat to her rooms and shut the door on Mercy. The sooner she'd be able to toss the papers she now clutched in one hand, the papers Mercy had shoved at her a few minutes earlier, into a hearth fire. But her other hand currently held the tiny fingers of Louis Joseph, whose two-year-old legs were struggling to keep up with her steps as it was.

Her first child, five-year-old Marie-Thérèse, skipped along ahead of them, blonde ringlets glowing in the sunshine. She twirled around, trotting back to them and reaching up for the papers in Antoine's hand. "I want to see the pretty drawings, *maman*."

"No, my little featherhead, these are not for you." Antoine forced a smile. "This afternoon, after your nap, we can paint some pictures of our own. Would you like that?"

Her daughter, the first half of her heart, nodded with glee, and, apparently satisfied, darted off back toward the house.

Antoine found herself clutching the papers closer to her chest as she released the horror that had momentarily clogged her lungs, though her young daughter would not have understood the images had she seen them. The pornographic, misogynistic scenes depicting her, the Queen of France, opening her legs and mouth to every court noble, foreign dignitary, military general, or palace housemaid available. Men and women. Sometimes incestuous. Often in groups. Always depicting her as either ravenously lascivious or ashamedly submissive.

The most hurtful part, of course, was the rampant insinuation that her children were illegitimate. Most hinted they had been fathered not by the King, but by Count Axel von Fersen of Sweden. This was untrue, of course. Marie-Thérèse and Louis Joseph were the King's natural children, not Axel's or any other man's. In fact, other than her duty to her husband, there had been no other men *but* Axel. And though they were careful to make sure he did not father her children, her love for Axel was second only to that of her love for her children.

Mercy was still prodding as they reached the top of the golden stone steps leading to the chateau, a trio of tall French doors rising above them, beckoning her to enter. And hide.

"Your Majesty, you cannot simply ignore this problem."

The children were escorted inside by their governess, then Antoine turned to the Comte, shoving the pamphlets back into his hands. "These are nothing. Lustful fantasies for a bored citizenry. They need not concern me and, in the future, I prefer to *not* know about them."

"With all due respect, *madame*, these do not arise from prurient interest, but, rather, anger and desperation." He began to unfold one of the sheafs, flipping to a particular image. "Note the choice of participants in this one. It is a political statement. It is *not* random."

Antoine shoved the papers away with a gasp. As if she could possibly bear to look at them again, let alone side-by-side with the Comte. "Nothing in these depictions is true. If they knew me at all they would realize how far from truth it is."

"But, to the people, these images *are* truth. And that is precisely *because* they do not know you."

She ignored him and strode to the heavy marble banister overlooking the acres of her pastoral paradise.

But Mercy followed, stepping up next to her as they viewed the vista of manicured gardens ringed by parkland and wild forest. His tone softened. "You must change their perception of you."

"Since when did public opinion rule the world?" she asked, honestly confused by the urgency of his concern. "I am a monarch. I do not need their approval."

He cleared his throat. "Things are changing. If you were out in the world, you would understand better. Do not let the people decide how you will be portrayed. *You* must write the story yourself. Find a way to win them over once more."

Win them over? It made no sense that this was even necessary. She'd long since stopped her lavish partying and gambling. She'd produced an heir to the throne, and, more than that, she had taken to motherhood like a honeybee to a poppy. She was enamored of her son and daughter and gave them a loving childhood and gentle guidance. Louis Joseph would grow to be a fine ruler one day. Was that not all they wanted from her?

At this point, Antoine wanted only for the Comte to go away, so she acquiesced on this one issue. "Fine. There are plenty of proper portraits of our family. Perhaps we can commission a new one, in fact. One of me and the children here in the countryside, wearing simple rustic attire, maybe include a couple of our goats and some of the chickens. The peasants will see we are not so unlike them." She fluttered her hands in dismissal. "Make arrangements as soon as possible. Then have it printed and distributed in place of these others." She turned from the view and headed inside the chateau.

Mercy refused to let up, still picking at her as they moved into the soaring entrance hall with its black-and-white checkered marble floor and towering spiral staircase leading to an open gallery on the second floor. Sunshine flooded the airy space from the rows of windows on both floors. "That will not be enough. Majesty, I urge you to take some time and travel out into France. Meet your people, see their needs and hear their stories."

Antoine walked away from him, idly stepping to a side table where someone had left a small sewing thimble, white porcelain painted with tiny green leaves. She picked it up and began to roll it in her palm. Smooth to her touch. Warming in her fingers. Calming.

"Forgive me, Highness, but you have never visited any part of France save Versailles and Paris. You've never even seen the French coast."

Louis Joseph must have broken away from his governess because he toddled into the hall on wobbly legs, a giggle bursting forth from his rosebud mouth as he opened his arms for her. She raced to scoop him up with a matching laugh of her own.

She turned back to Mercy, her son's chubby arms wrapped around her neck. "It is the King's job to answer to his people."

Her advisor's face was now as red as hers had felt minutes before, but she knew Mercy's color was born of frustration. She didn't care. Axel would be arriving later that evening, and she'd not seen him in six months. After years of loneliness, she'd finally found love in both her children and her lover. She deserved this time.

Antoine nodded at the Comte de Mercy-Argenteau, knowing her demeanor was probably more dismissive in nature than the man really deserved. "Arrange for the portrait. It is enough." She moved to go.

He called after her, speaking to her back. "The people of France are in pain. Sentiment is turning against the Crown. The king has his responsibilities to them, yes, but the queen should be the sensitive one. You are the Mother of France."

She swung back around. "My duty was to produce an heir. I was a womb and a peace treaty. That is what the people demanded of me, and that is what I have done for them. And, as it turns out, I am grateful for that as my children have become my biggest blessing. But raising them is my only duty now, and until they come of age, they belong to me. So, as apparently I am the Mother of France, I ask you to leave me be so I may put its future king down for his nap."

She turned away from the Comte, still standing in the middle of the hall with a clutch of papers in one fist, while she nuzzled the little dauphin, singing a lullaby into his curls as she carried him to his crib.

Chapter 22

THE SIXTH CIRCLE
The City of Dis – The Island

A greeting party awaited them as they stepped off the sky-tram. A semi-circle composed mainly of twenty or so men, wearing the last shreds of what had once been fine suits or expensive sporting wear. Some were bare-chested or bare everything. All were covered in great smears of oil, burned patches of skin, and an obvious desire to inflict on someone else the same pain they'd endured back on the Fourth Circle summit. These Barons, former captains of industry, oil magnates, corporate and banking giants, now wielded a baser form of power in their greasy hands—wrenches and hammers, barbed wire and flame throwers—and they raised them in warning at Bea and Toni, accompanied by a varied chorus of grunts, threats, and catcalls. But three or four minutes had passed since Benny's last message, and it was an increasing wind that raised goosebumps on Bea's flesh more than the weaponry.

The least likely candidate for leader of this armed group stepped forward. Skinny, pale, and of middling height, the forty-something with a baby face and bad haircut tugged his t-shirt with a children's bubbly television character on it down over the top of his threadbare skinny jeans. His chin lifted at the sound of his men stomping their feet behind him and he pushed his thick glasses higher on his nose.

The asshole tech genius finally spoke. "We've seen your video and realize our weapons will be of no use against you." The line behind him offered a few creative suggestions anyway, and he let them continue their taunts for a few seconds before waving them quiet. "On the other hand, we're fairly certain they'll be effective enough on your brother. From what we've seen of him thus far, he has nothing of your skillset."

"You have my brother already?" Bea risked a step forward.

He nodded once, turning partially and lifting an arm to gesture her and Toni forward. "Come. Let us discuss." The men behind him parted as he led them deeper into the jungle, the gang then closing rank and following behind. The land smelled of green plant and brown rot, mosquitos and gnats the only wildlife visible.

As she trailed him down a narrow path beneath a thick jungle canopy, the crowd surrounding them lighting torches in the ever-darkening gloom, Toni took her hand. The ancient French queen in modern jeans pulled closer as they continued walking, and the trembling in her limbs as their shoulders brushed threw Bea for a loop until she realized that mobs with torches were probably disconcerting for Toni even now. *We all have our triggers.*

Bea ran a hand down Toni's arm in comfort, and a glance at her companion's face showed a lifting chin and refusal to return the gaze even as she gripped Bea's hand tighter. She looked the same physical mess at this point that Bea did, with a big hank of blonde hair having come loose from a skewed ponytail. The woman was human, yes, but her royal pride ran deep, and Toni gave and received only as much comfort as was needed and no more.

Nevertheless, Bea squeezed her hand again anyway, letting her know the need for comfort didn't diminish her in her eyes. Toni may have had centuries of experience guiding people through Hell; she may have known the height of power when alive, but, in the end, she was still just a person. She'd been a woman and a mother. She'd been a child once, with strawberry curls bouncing as she'd run through a palace, playing hide-and-seek and chasing after pups in a field. What must it have felt like having then grown up to be so personally rejected, so thoroughly hated, by an entire country?

Toni released her hand, and Bea caught her wiping a loose tear. Crap, she'd heard Bea's thoughts again... or... wait. Had Bea heard Toni's? The sensation was muddy, and Bea ran a hand through her hair, considering it just as their trail opened onto a cleared space. She stopped short at the sight before her.

"Sis?"

Her brother stood ringed by people from the Fourth Circle summit, his wrists in front of him bound with chain link and secured with a padlock. He still wore his white linens from the catacombs, and his face... God, his face. So familiar and beautiful to her yet captured in time at twenty-one years of age compared to her thirty. No longer the exact male mirror of herself. He seemed equally surprised by the disparity though he soon brightened with relief, a smile forming.

"Dante!" Nobody stopped her as she ran to him, wrapping him in a hug he was currently unable to return. She leaned the side of her head to his, her mouth whispering near his ear. "I've been trying so hard to find you. I'm sorry it took me so long."

"Where are we? I don't understand." His voice began to rise. "Bea, I think I died. I'm pretty sure I died!"

She pulled back and cupped the sides of his face, speaking softly. "Shhh. I'll explain everything soon, but, right now, I need to get you out of here. We have to get off this island immediately."

216

The wind turned angry and the trees began to sway at steep angles. Her brother's eyes grew huge and round.

She didn't yet know what her plan was, but he was going to have to cooperate even in his fear and confusion. "Whatever happens now, I want you to think of this as a dream. The normal rules of physics don't apply in a dream, right? Follow my lead and we'll run as fast as we want."

His brow creased at her words as a soft shower began falling on them. It had to have been nearly fifteen minutes since they'd landed on the island. The situation was crap.

"Just trust me, dork, okay? We've got no time."

She slid one hand down to his, and, with the little movement he had available, they moved through their intricate, private handshake. A warm pulse of love and a fierce feeling of protection blossomed in her solar plexus as they landed the final fist bump. "Stronger together, remember?"

His nod was hesitant, but he voiced his trust in her. "Two halves of a superhero."

Mr. Silicon Valley pulled her away. "Well, that was lovely. And now, here's what's going to happen." The shower opened into a deluge, flattening his hair to his head. He pulled off his drenched glasses and struggled to dry them on his equally soaked shirt.

Idiot.

He had to raise his voice to be heard over the downpour. "We're going to take your brother to the castle now. You're going to stay here on the island or, heck, go wherever you want, but you're not going to stop us."

The crowd around them grew anxious under the pummeling storm and didn't bother waiting for word from their master. Many hands reached to grab Dante, weapons of all manner of destruction poking into his body or held in threat inches from his face. There was no move she could make fast enough before they'd destroy him in any number of ways.

The tech mogul thrust out his hand, pointing vaguely in the direction of Toni's chest. "Oh, and we'll take the book, too. Thank you very much."

But Toni only clenched the satchel more tightly—unusually tight for someone who'd led ninety-nine other people through this place without the book. Perhaps Toni was coming to believe it might help further even her own education. Or perhaps she was thinking of Axel.

Bea grew aware of the demon camera crew filming at the edge of the clearing. Six-foot-two at most and dressed in safari guide costumes, pith helmets and video cams covering their faces. Their little scene was being broadcast, but even with her increased popularity and hordes of new adoring followers, she knew the drill. There were probably a thousand comments on her socials sending little caring hugs of hope, but nobody would be coming to her aid. If there'd been popcorn in Hell, they'd all be glued to their screens and munching it. Worse, the appearance of the film crew had both The Barons and her brother growing agitated.

Dante's eyes zig-zagged between Bea and the cameras as his obvious confusion increased.

This might not work.

She wiped wet hair out of her face. Interesting, though, was that, even in the deluge, her clothes were merely damp. Also interesting was that it made the mob act as if she were part demon herself. They stepped back from her a fraction.

"Take me instead. Let him go and one of you can take my place with my guide." She slid a glance at Toni who evidenced her dislike of the option with wide eyes and an exaggerated shake of the head.

"The hosts of The Game demand otherwise. We can't simply take your spot; we must present the prize to the Administrative Center." The tech dude shrugged. "Them's the rules, baby. Sorry."

He was most clearly *not* sorry. Even standing there like a drowned rat, he was loving this, and Bea was out of ideas.

The Baron looked even dorkier as he suddenly pinched his nose and puffed out his cheeks, the classic maneuver to clear one's ears, and Bea realized that she, too, suddenly felt an inner ear pressure—a low rumble that was more vibration than actual sound followed next, and Toni leaned into her, whispering, "I believe we have only moments, *chérie*. Let them go with your twin so they can get him off the island. They need him and will not harm him. We will catch up again once we are all to safety. Better to live and fight another day."

Bea pulled away, shaking her head. "No. I won't leave him again. I won't risk it."

"What's that?"

The wannabe Zuckerberg was not, as Bea had first assumed, asking about Toni's comments. He was looking beyond the two of them toward the ground.

He shouted to be heard now above the rain and the strange white noise. "What's happening?"

She spun around to see the threat—

The tsunami was landing.

Water rushed up from the river surrounding the island, racing into the jungle interior and now sloshing around their calves.

The men's confusion meant The Barons had not been expecting it. She prayed to God they'd tied their boats to something, or else all of them—including her brother—were about to be royally screwed.

"Let's go! Let's go!" the tech dude shouted at his people. He pointed to her brother as he fought to be heard above the pounding surf, which was now at waist level and yanking them all to and fro like ragdolls. "Grab him and get to the boats!"

Toni grasped Bea's arm and shouted, struggling to stay on her feet. "If this tsunami takes us all, I do not know where your

219

brother will end up when we awaken! I do not know how the rules of The Game will apply to him and the others when this island resets. We must try to reach him and hold on."

Bea fought her way forward through the dark waters now at her chest. Dante was straight ahead of her, and he'd been abandoned as everyone else fought to keep their own head above water. "Hang on, Dante!"

"I can't see—" Dante disappeared beneath the surface, then bobbed back up, coughing out a lungful of water.

Toni had one hand gripping tight to Bea's shirt as they dipped and slid.

"Dante!" Bea swatted Toni's hand and kept pushing ahead.

Toni held on. "We must stay together!"

"I have to get my brother!" Bea narrowed her gaze and tried to make the magical fast-walking thing happen again—to no avail.

"Bea!" He slipped under again, and this time did not come back up.

Fuck!

She flailed against the deluge, reaching around below the surface as if she could still grab him, but came up empty. "No, no, no!"

A wave crashed against her back, kicking her legs out from under her and spinning her upside down in the water. For a moment, her feet felt cool air as they broke the surface, her head banging something hard on the jungle floor. She fought to right herself, but the speed of the tide was now too fast and her limbs were no longer responding to her brain as she was tossed about in a violent ballet.

The lack of air wasn't a problem—she understood the reality of that well enough now—but the chaos of the flood and the knowledge that her brother was weighted down by chains closed off any opportunity for preternatural control. She was powerless, she was scared, she was lost. And she had failed him.

Again.

No part of her had cracked the surface for many moments as she'd tumbled. Who knew how deep the waters had become or how much longer before it reached the treetops and wiped everything away?

A pair of thick glasses brushed her face and caught in her hair. Something slimy slid against her cheek and she cringed away. A hand grabbed her ankle, but she kicked it off. It grabbed her shoulder, but lost its grip. When it yanked a handful of her hair, she screamed out a mouthful of bubbles, but followed her captor up rather than fight against it and scalp herself. She broke the surface on a gasp, looking into the face of the person holding her by the hair as if she were a prize shrunken head.

"Got her!" said a soaked gray-haired man with a victorious grin.

She let him haul her onto the back of his jet ski, which bounced furiously on the whitecaps, because—friend or foe—this was her only option for escape since the tops of the palm trees were the only thing still visible above the waves.

Hundreds of souls—the island's regular inhabitants—perched precariously in the highest leaves, holding on and screaming down for help that wouldn't come.

She wrapped her hands around the stranger and held on fast as she witnessed another person on a similar craft yank Toni from the depths.

"Did we get them all?" Bea's driver shouted across the turbulence to Toni's, a thick-muscled woman with long black hair and dark weathered skin.

Whichever gang they were now dealing with, whatever circle these people were from, they were about as clear-headed and sure of themselves as she'd yet seen. Which, although Bea was glad for the save from the tsunami, did not bode well for her on the back end.

In response, the other driver pointed in a direction and they spun their water craft toward the interior. A third vehicle bounced riderless on the chop, until a flash of motion and a frenzy of limbs erupted from the waters beside it.

Her brother gulped for air as he struggled to keep upright, his chained wrists jerking above his head. A much smaller body than his fought to hold onto him while climbing aboard the craft and then leaning to try to pull Dante's larger frame on. This mad scramble of flailing attempts was not working until a fourth craft pulled up beside them and the driver jumped in, swimming to Dante and pushing him from behind onto it.

This newest arrival, the one who'd just saved her brother, was thrown aside by a new surge, the back of this person's head slamming hard into his craft before both he and his loose vehicle were tossed under and out of sight.

"No!" Dante's tiny driver shrieked before turning their craft, and attention, toward Bea.

Bea recognized the face instantly. The dark eyes never blinked as rain rolled down sharp cheeks to a currently hard-set jaw in an otherwise soft, beautiful face. Even with soaked hair flattened against her skull, the cut of the teen's jet-black mohawk was obvious. Whether for rescue or revenge, Jesse Chen had come for her.

The moment broke, and Jesse shifted attention to the rest of her team. "To the sky-trams, now!" She spun her jet ski toward the dangling gondolas and the rest of the gang—maybe a half-dozen other watercraft—followed.

The flood level now covered the treetops, leaving nothing but roiling water as far as the eye could see, giving the illusion—which it was—that that the rest of the hellish amusement park no longer existed. She saw only the colorful sky buckets now hanging a few feet above the water, which had risen to meet them at their highest point. The far end of the tramway down in the park arced out of view below the horizon.

They reached the nearest gondola and the door swung open. Several of Jesse's team abandoned their watercraft and leapt onto the swaying rig as a couple other gang members already onboard reached down to help pull them up. Those still bouncing on their jet skis watched as that carriage moved away and the next one rose from beneath the flood, water pouring out of it in a rush as it surfaced.

Once it cleared, two of the people from the previous carriage jumped for the cables, going hand-over-hand like a pair of acrobats to the newly risen bucket and jumping in. They swung open the door, reaching out and pulling up first Dante, then Toni and her driver, then, finally, Bea.

As Bea's carriage began its ride back down to the park, the same hand-over-hand athletes again moved down the cable to the next carriage rising from the waters, leaning down to help up Jesse, Bea's driver, and the last few members of the rescue team still waiting on the waves. They shouted with victory as they pulled the last of the gang up to safety. Some of their matching white t-shirts sported familiar hand-painted brick red lettering, now wet and smudged, identifying them as The Big Chill.

Bea turned back to the group in their bucket. Toni's driver was digging through a plastic pack strapped to her waist and bearing the Dis Land logo, and pulled out a paperclip. She picked Dante's handcuff lock like a pro.

When his hands were released, he embraced Bea in a proper hug. Hell and everyone in it slipped away and, for a moment, there was only her brother. Her twin. Her best friend.

Then time rushed back up on itself as reality barged in.

"Dante, this is Toni," Bea said, using only her guide's nickname for now, because her brother was about to be overwhelmed enough without adding an historical legend to the fantastical story.

223

Bea looked to the woman who'd freed Dante from his locks. "Thank you."

Their rescuer responded only with a nod, remaining aloof and keeping her eyes pinned on Jesse in the car behind them. Though the release of the chains was a good sign, the question of *friend* or *foe* remained unclear.

"This doesn't feel much like a dream." Dante said. "And you're different somehow. Not to mention, *older* than you should be. But I remember the car crash. I remember a crazy circus and being assigned..." He shook his head. "That's all I remember. But if I really am dead, and you're here, too... Bea, this can't be real. I refuse to believe that you also—"

"But I did. It was a stupid accident, but it's okay." *It's okay?* She realized then that she wasn't just calming him down; that, in fact, she was—at least at this moment—okay. And not merely because she was finally reunited with her brother after nine years—which was no less than a joyous miracle—but something else was going on. Something she couldn't yet put her finger on, making her feel a strong sense of, well... okay-ness.

"What about Ronna?"

Those big brown eyes held a hope Bea hated to squash, but she took his hand as she shook her head.

Without having to ask, Toni flipped open the Mac and typed while the flood waters slowly receded.

As their silent rescuer stared at the carriage behind them, Bea explained as much as she could to her brother in the few minutes they had. She explained her death, the opportunity she'd been given, The Game they'd been forced to play. She explained the things she'd learned to do.

He listened with an intense gaze and a furrowed brow, but he had a scientific mind and a readiness for big ideas, and so he took it in with little resistance, nodding and considering, a light sparking his eyes as she explained.

God how she'd missed his gigantic, creative brain and, even more, his enormous heart.

"Your lady Ronna is sleeping in the catacombs," Toni said as their gondola approached the ground where a small crowd was gathered in the park just below—spectators, opponents, demon cameramen.

Dante paced from one side to the other, his jaw visibly tightening as he took it all in while Toni continued, "Like you had been, she is sleeping, not suffering."

He let out a deep breath at that news as the carriage came to a stop and they filed out.

Bea had worried about an immediate attack by other teams, and though most of the crowd seemed more interested in lobbing questions at Bea than grabbing her brother, a line of white t-shirts had already formed a barrier, beating the crowd back from the disembarking gondolas. Whether to protect Bea and her companions or to keep hold of their prize—her brother—was still the question.

The last of the gondolas disembarked behind them, and her view of the crowd was cut off when a sopping wet rail of a body stepped in front of her.

From a foot away, Jesse's piercing gaze threatened to rip the same jagged slice through Bea's body that Jesse had been dealt. Though Bea deserved every bit of that agony, if Jesse were now planning to take Dante to the castle, Bea would be forced to... well, she'd...

Jesse lunged toward Bea, wrapping her in a hug so tight they together stumbled back a few steps. Bea returned the embrace as they both fought to cover sobs with laughter.

"I'm sorry it took me so long to catch up to you." Jesse pulled back and nodded to Toni, who stood solidly at Bea's side. "And you."

Only now did it sink in that, except for the few moments when Toni had been searching the directory for Ronna, she'd spent most of the tram ride staring at the car behind them. Staring back at Jesse.

The teen ran into Toni's arms, snuggling in like a child to a mother, and Toni's hand went gently to the back of the girl's head, pulling her in closer.

"Why did you come for us, *mon chou*? You have risked so much by going lower into Hell," Toni asked when they separated. "You *and* your friends from the Third." She scanned the white shirts as if looking for someone specific, and Bea remembered the path over the cold lake that Toni had refused to go down. "Have you come to claim Dante?"

"Well, yeah. But not to hand him over to the castle. Give us some credit." The teen looked affronted in the way only a teen could. "We came to help you win The Game. All three of you." Jesse stepped up to Dante and shook his hand. "I'm Jesse. Nice to meet you, Bea's bro."

"Thank you for saving us," Dante said, returning Jesse's handshake with his most glorious smile.

Jesse blushed before turning back to Bea. "Like I said back at the Third, I'm coming with you."

Bea tipped her head. "You don't...? Doesn't everyone hate me for what happened to you?"

"Nah. I've got some pretty popular social pages of my own now, and I told everyone not to hate you. It wasn't your fault the dog got me." Jesse looked down, scuffing the toe of her shoe before a little bravado bloomed again. "So, what's the plan from here?"

As Bea pulled out the park map, she related what Benny had said about ignoring the castle and dropping to the Seventh Circle instead. One option for getting down there was a mile-long rock fall, which, even on the cartoon-like map drawing, looked jagged and nearly impassable and could easily be hiding enemy teams within the crevices.

"The log ride," Jesse said as she scanned the layout of Dis.

"It'll plunge us straight down to the Seventh, bypassing the cliff face altogether."

"It's on the far end of the park. Past even the castle," Bea said. "And The Barons and The Hotheads will be desperate and aggressive."

"I can run as fast as you and Toni now." Jesse gestured to the others from the Third Circle. "A bunch of us can."

"Really?

The teen shrugged with perfect nonchalance. "We took off following you right after they announced the new game rules, and, shortly after, there were rumors of your run through the catacombs. We began experimenting right away as we moved through the gorge and up the mountain. Then we saw the broadcast of your mysterious dash through Suburban Square, and, later, your video from the Gates. As soon as we saw it, we understood immediately what you were doing. We practiced on our way through the Fourth and Fifth."

Seeing really *was* believing, apparently, Bea thought as they took off in the direction of the water ride. That, and wanting something badly enough. Maybe Bea just happened to land in the Underworld with her adventures put on display at exactly the right time. A tipping point.

"Dante just woke up, though. He won't yet be able to move like us," said Bea.

Her brother jogged up in front of them, trotting backward a few steps as he spoke. "Then teach me. You know, I kind of a have reputation for being a fast learner." He winked at Jesse.

"I can show him how to do it." Jesse said, a blush flaring in her cheeks.

Bea glanced at Toni who returned a subtle smile. Great, they were about to be dealing with a teenage crush while escaping Hell. It was either going to add levity or horror; it was too soon to tell.

Bea picked up the pace, though still at regular human speed, and the others moved with her. They'd soon be passing on the far side of the castle where they'd give it a wide berth, but the crowd following them was growing in size and aggression.

"My team will provide cover. They've all got mad skills," said Jesse.

Bea glanced behind her as they ran. The Big Chill were, indeed, holding back the frenzied mob with a combination of martial arts, archery, and swordsmanship—both with makeshift weapons—and darting with invisible speed.

"How do your Third Circle people have all these skills?" Bea asked as they circumvented the dark, lifeless-appearing towers of what was more medieval fortress than fairytale castle. A firework display of surface-to-air missiles and cherry bombs lit the sky in crimson and pink over the tops of the ramparts, filling the air with acrid smoke.

"Dude, think about it. We've been in those lifeguard chairs for ages, some people for decades. When we weren't playing Hellscape or watching TV shows, we were streaming Twitch, watching people do everything from knitting to jiu-jitsu. Plus, all that game play. We might not have realized it then, but we were *learning*. And it's finally paid off. That's how we jacked The Barons' watercraft, too—we swam across the rising tide and scored them when they broke loose. We lost a few people to those mutant sea creatures first." Jesse's demeanor dulled at some memory. "Lost most of our laptops in the water, too." She pointed at the waterproof satchel Toni wore. "Someone got smart there."

As the towering log ride came into view straight ahead, the crowd chasing them was beginning to overtake Jesse's team. More than one white shirt fell under a trample of feet or was picked off by a demon deciding to change the odds.

Bea stopped her run, the implication—the price—of the rescue suddenly hitting her. "Jesse, even if they all make it out of Dis, which they won't, we can't take everyone with us. It's just not possible for Toni to guide us all. The demons will never allow that, not to mention the logistics."

"They know that," Jesse said. "It was never their intention to go all the way through with us. They're doing this to support you. And me."

"I don't understand." They were sacrificing themselves? For her?

"The ones we lost, Bea, they'll be back. You know this by now. They want to learn. They want to see us get out so they'll know it's possible. Plus, they know you have the book which will reveal more secrets. By your actions, you'll teach them. They want you to give them *hope*. Helping you is the same as helping ourselves."

As Bea was about to suffocate under the weight of that responsibility, Dante touched her shoulder. "Come on, sis. Teach me that supernatural running thing."

Her face slid into a grin. Her *brother* needed *her* to teach him something.

So she did. She may not have the academic explanations for it, but she had an intuitive knowing, an emotional understanding, and, with her help, he caught on fast. They ran together a little before rejoining Toni and Jesse.

Dante smiled at her. "It's like, wormhole stuff. Bending space."

Leave it to him to find the scientific words she didn't have. She returned the smile. "I thought you might get a kick out of that."

"It's more than that, actually," Toni added. "You're manifesting. Creating."

Her brother's lips parted as he considered the notion, the wheels in that big brain spinning.

But Bea had to redirect everyone because The Big Chill was tiring against the growing mob. "Time to put to it to good use. Let's go."

They turned in the direction of the water ride and moved with unreal speed, past the castle and into another section of the park. Bea sensed her three companions moving with her as a blur of color and sound sped past her vision. In the small space of the time it took for her to appreciate her brother's presence moving side-by-side with her in their pocket of reality, they arrived in front of the log ride, the four of them stopping right at the entrance platform. No particular crowd awaited them there, just a steady stream of four-person log-shaped cars floating in a half-tube track, continuously departing and arriving.

This particular attraction appeared fairly un-creepy. Built to resemble a snow-capped mountain covered in pine trees ripe for logging, nothing would have made it out of place in any real, earth-based theme park—well, with the possible exception of the riders in each car, who never actually got on or off. Their expressions ranged from nausea to despair, which made sense given they were trapped on a very damp rollercoaster for eternity.

Still, it seemed pretty harmless, and Bea and her companions weren't going to be stuck on it forever. In fact, she had a little twinge of excitement as an empty car finally pulled up and the four of them stepped into the rocking boat, Bea and Dante in front, and Toni and Jesse in the back. It might even be the rejuvenating break they needed before descending into the secrets of Lower Hell.

The car rocked forward through the half-pipe water track, entering the dark mountain interior where a welcome cool breeze hit Bea's face. They inched slowly up a ramp to reach the mountain's height, and she held on tight as it began to race back down, curling around corners and dipping into little valleys where spray drenched them. They burst into laughter. Damn, this was a refreshing treat she needed about now.

"Hey, Toni!" she shouted over her shoulder as the vehicle raced forward on a straightaway. "What group of heretics is this ride meant for? I can't figure it out."

The car entered a spiraling descent, making tight circles that forced them to lean way over to the side. Jesse shrieked with excitement.

"Flat-earthers," came Toni's response, shouted above the rushing froth.

Flat-earthers? What the heck did a twisting, turning, ride through a steep mountain have to do with them?

"Huh."

Her brother's reaction to Toni's answer caught her ear. He, too, must've been trying to make the connection.

But, no matter. Team Beatrice was now four people strong, and they had The Big Chill at their back. All they had to do now was get past The Hammer, whatever that was, and they'd soon be seeing the light at the end of the infernal tunnel.

The car clicked up one last ramp. Bea had ridden enough coasters in her life to know what to expect here. Anticipation washed through her as she prepared herself for the big finale, the long slide down the last drop and the inevitable giant splash of water drenching them all. And this was going to be the splash of a lifetime as they rode it all the way down to the next level of the pit, where, unlike the other riders, they'd be able to disembark without finding themselves at the beginning again.

But a frighteningly long drop it was going to be, and her non-breath sped up as they inched toward the top. Her hands gripped the sides of the car as a surprising circle of bright crimson sky opened up before them on the back side of the fake mountain. The car crested the apex, tipped down, and—

"Holy shit!" Her words, and similar ones from her companions, echoed in her ears as the track abruptly ended and they shot out into empty space, decelerating, and hanging in air for a heartbeat before dropping like a stone one full mile above the glowing red, liquid fire of Lower Hell.

Chapter 23

MEUDON, FRANCE

231 years ago (1789)

Antoine rocked the lifeless body of little Louis Joseph, tears landing on his golden locks, his seashell ears now deaf to her wailing. Her seven-year-old child, first-born son, heir to the throne had passed in her arms only moments before, his tiny soul having given up the fight against the fevers that had plagued most of his life.

Now, members of court paraded in and out of the bedchamber to witness the death, following an elaborate ritual granting access in a prescribed order of favor, *la noblesse* stroking their own egos even as her child turned cold in her lap.

This was all too familiar. Her hands still remembered the weight of her infant daughter Sophie, her youngest child, who'd also died in Antoine's arms less than one year ago.

She was becoming far too adept at burying her children.

Antoine glanced across the dimly lit room that had seemed to shrink to the size of a closet during the last painful hours, lacking in air to breathe or space to move.

Marie-Thérèse, now eleven, sat on a straight-backed chair, folded in on herself with grief.

Cowering on the floor at her feet, arms wrapped around her ankles, was her remaining brother, Louis Charles. Four years old and, as of minutes ago, the new dauphin.

But Antoine was not the only person in the room looking at her second son. Unlike when Sophie died, this time, France had lost its heir. Few had paid any notice at all to the corpse of a baby girl in her crib, but Louis Charles was already being sized up, speculated on, likely bet against. And young though he was, Louis Charles seemed aware that, not only had he lost his big brother, but he'd also lost something equally significant, though it was doubtful he could name it.

Antoine's heart bled for him because she knew too well the life he'd been accidentally born into. She hated herself for the road that now lay before this little man, her baby boy, all because she, herself accidentally born a queen, had birthed him.

The hushed words around her were like nettles in her ears, and she was on the cusp of screaming when her husband blew into the room. The King's face, already puffy and red from his race across the grounds upon receiving the news, now broke with sorrow. He dropped to his knees next to Antoine as he hovered over their eldest son, so still and silent. The audience in the room tried but failed to suppress a gasp at their monarch's display of fragility, and her husband's face reddened even more in shame. It was so very cruel.

Antoine had enough.

"Get out," she said, her voice soft and monotone, and the whispers ceased—but nobody moved.

She lifted her head, her deceased child cradled against her, her husband bent by her side, and looked toward the crowded room. Her volume rose to a screech. "Get out!"

With expressions of offense or empty whispered apologies, they fled the room just in time to miss another round

233

of Antoine's sobs as the surgeon stepped in and removed Louis Joseph's body from her arms.

The doctor shuttled her son, cocooned from sight in blankets, out of the room.

In a rare moment of shared affection, she fell into her husband's arms and they held each other in their pain. It did help... a bit.

Until the King destroyed what little pocket of solace they'd created when he spoke against her ear. "I understand your outburst. The need for privacy in moments such as these. However, you must be careful not to insult the court. We need the nobility and the clergy to remain on our side. During this precarious time more than ever."

Antoine lifted her head from his neck. "Politics? *That's* what you're thinking about right now?" She shoved his chest and he let her.

He stepped back from her rage, but continued to press. "Politics does not pause to let us grieve. Even now, this very evening, the Third Estate is massing at the Bastille, demanding release of all weapons stored there."

Marie-Thérèse stood from her chair in the corner, taking her brother's hand. *"Père, qu'est-ce que ça veut dire?"*

The King startled, as if he'd forgotten the children were still in the room. But Antoine hadn't forgotten. She never forgot them, not for a second—unlike her husband... and the rest of France.

She answered for her husband. "It means, my daughter, that the commoners are no different than the nobility. They do not care about our family. They demand everything from us and give back nothing. They do not love us. Your brother is dead and France does not even notice." This made her two remaining children rush to her side and cling to her skirts.

Her husband gritted his teeth, a study in pain and frustration. His chest rose and fell as he paused. "Nevertheless, we must decide what to do immediately. Grant them the equal representation they seek or hold them back?"

"Are you asking my opinion?"

He dipped his chin ever so slightly—a nod that would be missed if she didn't know him so well. Of late, he'd become more and more lost amid the discord ripping their country apart, and he'd begun to seek out her opinion regularly.

As if she had any ability or knowledge to lead in such matters. She did, however, have one thing her husband had always lacked—the balls to decide.

"Send in our troops," she said. "Break up the mob in front of the Bastille."

He fumbled for words. "But to send our own troops? Against our people?"

If the people demanded her attention right now—as she was busy burying her child—then she would give it to them. "Send in the troops."

"Very well. It shall be done," he said and began to sulk toward the door. But he paused, his gaze moving from her to the kids, then to the dip in the bed sheets where Louis Joseph had taken his last breath. He took a half-step toward her and the children, opening his arms. "Or should I... Do you want me to..."

So typical. "Just go."

He exited, and for the first time in many long hours, she was blessedly left alone with Marie-Thérèse, Louis Charles, and that horrifying dip in the bed sheets.

Bending a little to kiss the tops of the kids' heads, she took a deep breath—but, still, she felt suffocated. The crumpled sheets called to her, so she pulled the two children along to the bed where she ran her hands over the place he had lain. She breathed in his scent as she climbed onto the downy bed covering.

Head on the pillow, she pulled her remaining daughter and

son up against her, and the three snuggled into a tight ball, quiet sniffles and tiny sobs the only sounds as she plotted out her next steps.

France had at last given up on her, defeated her, and now she planned to give up on France. She'd already been corresponding with her brother, and it appeared Austria would soon bring war against her kingdom. She planned to help her brother win.

Yes, this would make her a traitor. But, when Austria won, they would provide her and the children with sanctuary. Austria would save her. Save her last two babies.

And she would finally be home again.

Chapter 24

THE SEVENTH CIRCLE

Fucking flat-earthers.

Under a blood orange sky, their plastic log plummeted toward a cracked, white plain crisscrossed in bright red ribbons. The screams of her little company battled in her ears with the almost painful rush of wind as they nose-dived to Earth. *There is no Earth, there is no Earth. It's a fluffy mattress. It's a giant bouncy house.*

Nope. The ground rose to meet them and Bea caught the explosive sound of their crash before she blacked out.

She woke instantly, hot gravel against her cheek and her body surrounded by plastic and metal debris. She coughed and rolled over just in time to see a sledgehammer with a head the size of a microwave arcing straight for her. Bea flung herself the opposite direction and *bam!* The hammer missed her, coming down hard on the packed ground, leaving a cleft where her face would have been. She would've healed instantly had it hit her, but still, who needs it?

In a second, she was on her feet and dodging the next arc of the weapon. It took her a good moment to understand that this was The Hammer.

As she ducked under another furious swing, she cursed Benny's name. *Just get past The Hammer and you'll be home free.* Uh huh. The Hammer, it turned out, was twenty feet tall, with the head of a massive bull and a human body built like a brick fortress, all standing on a pair of enormous hooved feet. Long curling horns twisted from above each bovine ear.

A minotaur.

The whoosh of the sledgehammer was enough to blow her hair back each time he swung it. A fast glance behind her—all she could afford to spare—showed Dante unconscious amid the debris. She doubted he'd be waking for quite a while. She didn't spot the other two women.

"Toni? Jesse?" she called while leaping over a blow intended to take out her feet.

One answering shout in the distance pulled her attention further down the baking ground. A blur of strawberry blonde and blue jeans darted in and out a dozen or so people, each of whom were attached by long trailing chains to a sturdy metal belt around the minotaur's waist. These Hammer team members were dressed in scraps of white rags used as loincloths or tied around breasts. Their bodies dripped in red, some from the knees or ankles down, others almost totally coated in crimson liquid. They appeared as savages, each grunting and swinging their own smaller hammers in futility at the blur that was Toni.

Bea continued her own dance of defense against the raging bull, though moving slow enough to be able to survey her surroundings. A lump with black hair lay groaning not far from where she fought. "Jesse. Jesse, get up!" she called as she slid beneath the monster's legs, avoiding the latest thrash but momentarily coming up tangled in chains. "Jesse!"

The beast bellowed when her maneuvering caused him to stumble and the very earth answered back with a quake.

The sound woke the teen though, who flew to her feet in

a fighting stance, eyes narrowed as she surveyed the scene. A half-dozen of the chained fighters had shot past Toni and were now rushing up behind the minotaur, heading for Bea's end of the fight.

"Pull Dante out of the way. Get him to safety. Hurry!"

The kid nodded and took off to drag Dante closer to the base of the cliff where she covered him with pieces of the wreckage. Jesse soon rushed back to join Bea in the fight, but it was clear that speed and regeneration were their only weapons. They could avoid the hammer falls easily enough and were invisible as they moved, but they had no means to go on the offense. Until Dante woke up, the most the three of them could do was keep the enemy occupied and away from his sleeping body.

Dante might be asleep for an annoyingly long time.

Even in the fight, Bea was aware of their surroundings. Demons stood on the outskirts of the action, dressed in reflective silver suits and dark glass-fronted helmets, looking very much like spacemen as they either watched or held video cameras. Curiosity caused her to lose attention for a moment, and she tripped over one of the long chains, becoming entangled and going to the ground. This created a domino effect as several of the attached savages were pulled down with her, and the collective weight caused the monster to fall down.

The minotaur roared as he wiggled like a beetle on its back before finally righting himself. In doing so, he yanked several of the chains free, swung them in the air like a lasso, then flung the attached souls away.

Huge fountains of red erupted where some of them landed in the crimson rivulets, accompanied by bile-rising screams. Bea had no time to figure out what had caused their pain before Toni pulled her up from the ground.

"You've given me an idea. This is what we do, *mes amies*."

"Huh?" Bea said, but she saw the implication immediately

as Toni intentionally repeated what Bea had just accidentally done. The Queen moved like a ghost among the chained fighters, pulling the links and wrapping them around limbs faster than they could see it happening. Bodies fell to the ground and the minotaur was yanked this way and that.

Bea and Jesse flew into the fray and joined in, creating a mass of confusion and fallen bodies.

The minotaur lost his mind.

The angry bull-man lifted his wide arms and roared over the scene, no longer paying heed to any particular target. He swung his massive hammer at whoever lay in his path, smashing people to the ground or knocking them to far-flung areas.

Bea, Toni, and Jesse continued to create confusion, pulling on chains and shouting at the beast from constantly changing locations as he chased their ever-relocating sounds.

His roars became shrieks until all the bodies were either laid low or thrown far away. When they started laughing at him, the minotaur abandoned the crash site completely and ran, raving and screaming, into the distance.

In his absence, the landscape became eerily quiet. A few silver spacemen remained filming. Others had gone to collect the fallen populace, presumably to return them to their regular spot in the Seventh.

Bea took her first long look at the Seventh Circle. In the far distance to the left and right, a pair of volcanoes stood like sentries, smoke and fire rising from their cones and trails of bright lava flowing down onto the plain. It was hot on this level. Fiercely hot, as though she was standing in a furnace. The bright sky reflecting off the demons' metallic suits and the white baked dirt added to the heat, which burned her skin. Here, then, was the first real depiction of the classic Hellish landscape. At least she'd be able to heal herself from any blistering, unlike…

Bea ran to Dante, pulling the scraps of log ride off of him.

His skin was frying already, and God knew how many broken bones shaped his twisted body. "Dante, can you hear me? Please wake up."

Jesse knelt next to them, doing her own fussing over him.

Toni paced nearby, her footsteps fast and hard. "We do not have time to wait for him."

Bea shot her a look. "What are you talking about? You waited long periods for me several times. Why not him?"

"He is not my charge, *you* are. And, besides, we are so near the goal now. To be this close and risk something going wrong?" Toni stopped pacing, her eyes darting between Dante and Bea. She brought one hand to her mouth, fingers curled as if she were about to start biting her nails.

Then she dropped her hand, crossing her arms over her chest instead. "*Non.*"

"He's my *brother*, Toni. And we had a deal."

"Our deal was to retrieve your brother and then make our way out of Hell expediently. We retrieved him, and now our task is to get out. We did not agree to a delay like this."

It was Bea's turn to grow frustrated. She understood Toni was anxious to be with her children, but this selfish sort of panic seemed to come out of nowhere. "But we've risked this much already to get him. Why abandon him now? There's only a few more circles to go before you'll be rewarded. Can you not summon just a bit more patience? What are you so afraid of?"

Toni's face grew red, and it was not from a sunburn. "I am not afraid of anything. But, yes, after all this time I have grown impatient and am not inclined to wait weeks or months for him to wake up, all the while risking our success with every passing minute. He can follow after us on his own. You do not need your brother's help to get out of Hell."

"Of course I don't *need* him."

Toni's eyebrows shot up, and Bea realized what she'd just said.

241

They stared at each other in silence as she examined her own words. Part of her fought to take them back, part of her wondered at their truth. She would need to sit with this for a bit, so she let the words hang.

Bea returned her attention to her brother as Jesse tapped her on the arm. "You're his twin, right? Maybe you can wake him more quickly. Maybe he'll hear you. You know, aren't you supposed to have some kind of psychic link or something?"

This time, the ridiculous *twin mystique* question didn't bother her. Because, in this place, maybe it was true. Heck, maybe it had always been true and she and Dante had just not considered it might be so. Maybe twins really could connect like that.

"Maybe we all can," said Jesse.

Bea shot her attention to the teen. "What?"

The kid's knitted brows reflected Bea's own astonishment at the notion.

Bea touched an uninjured part of his arm. "Dante, it's Bea. Wake up now. We need to go."

His eyelids twitched as if he were dreaming. Or, perhaps, on some level, he was responding.

She placed the back of her hand on his forehead, imagining her cooler, unburned skin soothing the angry red there. Remembering what she always thought of as Toni's mind tricks, Bea gave that tactic a go as well, and not just attempting to convince a sleeping Dante, but *knowing* in her own gut that he was about to wake. If she could create herself healed, she could create him healed, too. "Dante, you are healthy and awake. Open your eyes and look at me."

His lips worked and his eyelids fluttered open. He cleared his throat and rolled his head toward her. "Bea?"

"Welcome back, bro." Her smile expressed her relief, and, perhaps, some small portion of pride at her success. "We had a little bit of an accident, but you're fine now."

Dante dipped his chin to study the length of his body, his expression one of skepticism.

"You have no actual body to break, remember?" Bea said.

He lifted a brow, and a moment later his crooked legs flexed straight.

A fast learner, her brother. Or a powerful Jedi, she. Maybe both.

Jesse jumped up, hopping from foot to foot in renewed excitement. "Dude, you totally missed it. The three of us kicked serious minotaur butt." The teen skipped away, then skipped back, full of confidence and energy. "Argh, I can't believe you didn't see it!"

As he slowly got moving, testing every limb at first, he mouthed silently to Bea, "Minotaur?"

Bea helped him stand. "Yup. But we've got to get moving. Someone's getting grouchy." She tipped her head toward Toni, who had already begun walking in presumably the direction of the next drop down, though this circle was so vast the edge of the pit could not yet be seen.

Dante had healed reasonably well, but he still walked with a limp and rubbed his darkening sunburns. The confidence and excitement her brother had displayed back in Dis had waned somewhat since the crash had dropped them into this frightening landscape, so she hesitated to push him, but he pressed on, moving more fluidly with each step.

When they caught up to Toni, the four of them headed across the baking desert beneath its distant twin volcanos. The cracked, white plain was flat and unbroken except for outcrops of black volcanic rock and the rivulets of red, which soon joined together to form small creeks, and, later, minor rivers. The crimson liquid bubbled and steamed, and though Bea had at first assumed it was lava, the metallic smell and degree of viscosity soon reminded her of what she knew about the Seventh Circle—these were rivers of not lava, but boiling blood.

"These are The Violent," Toni said as the first of the sufferers came into view, along with the new sounds of moaning and screaming.

Bea originally thought she was seeing gnarled and leafless trees thrusting up from the bloody creeks, but these turned out to be the people of the Seventh, their sun-blackened bodies tied to stakes. Some were bound within shallow rivulets, their feet and ankles the only parts covered by the boiling blood. As the four of them proceeded further, many were staked within the center of deeper rivers, up to their necks in agonizing pain.

"These souls, like all those found in Lower Hell, had so much emptiness and pain in life that they attempted to displace it onto others. Unlike those souls in Upper Hell, though, this group's acts of violence were intentional, even if they lacked understanding of the deeper cause. Some were schoolyard bullies, or bigots who beat up strangers not matching their skin color, religious, or political beliefs. Others were rapists, murderers, mass shooters. The degree of their crime decides the depth to which they are sunk in the blood."

"Jesus," said Dante as they picked their way around the veins of red, their progress slow as they occasionally had to double back for a safer route.

Although Bea, Toni, and Jesse could move through the boiling liquid without any effect, Dante was not that advanced yet. And moving across this landscape at speed, which he could do, would have been nearly impossible unless they knew their intended goal and the path to get there. This time, there was no map or numbered halls, so they walked.

"But who are all these other people?" Jesse asked. "The ones who are helping the sufferers."

Bea had been about to pose the same question, for along with the demon guards who kept watch throughout (and whose non-flammable suits now made sense), each of the Violent souls was being attended to in their misery by one or more people who attempted to ease their pain with gentle words, a sip of water from a flask, or a cool towel to the forehead.

"They are their victims. Well, not the actual souls of the victims, but an illusion of them," Toni said.

"NPCs," Jesse said.

"NPCs?" asked Bea.

"Non-Player Characters," said the teen. "In gaming, NPCs are characters not operated by actual players or, in this case, real souls. They're just created and run by the software to interact with real players and move the game along."

Toni nodded at the assessment. "This sounds correct. Though I don't imagine the suffering realize they are not actually the souls of their victims."

Dante crinkled his nose in disgust. "Why on earth would that be part of their lesson here?"

Bea understood immediately. "They're demonstrating compassion, even in the face of what has been inflicted upon them. These souls are forced to see what connection would have brought rather than the extreme disconnect they perpetrated instead. Look, some are already feeling the remorse." She pointed to a man up to his waist in the boiling liquid, his head tucked into the neck of his victim as he cried onto her shoulder.

"I can't imagine the likes of a Jeffrey Dahmer or Ted Bundy ever becoming *that* aware," her brother said.

Toni shook her head. "You are correct. Some people are broken beyond repair. No more than damaged machines. And they are not here."

"Where are they?" Jesse asked.

"Recycled," was her response.

They walked on, and the heat pounded through them. The ground became cakey and crusted like an ancient salt flat. Eventually, Jesse and Toni drifted ahead, leaving the twins to walk alone.

"So, you got old," Dante teased, his boyish smile luminous and his eyes twinkling. His limp had long since disappeared after Bea had explained to him how that worked.

"Yeah, well, you took the old joke about dying young and leaving a good-looking corpse a little too seriously," she responded, giving him a punch in the arm. The morbid joke was easy to make now that he was alive again—well, as it were. She filled him in on the nine years he'd missed, both the good and the bad. Together, they worried about and grieved for their parents. Most of all, she reveled in his company, slowly realizing it was exactly that—his company—that she'd loved and missed. She'd missed their understanding of each other, their shared experiences, their mutual support. That meant everything in the world to her, but, she now realized with more than a little shock, it hadn't been her *whole* world.

"Wow, Bea. Nearly a million followers you said?"

He likely didn't understand the concept of social media-influencing. Insta had barely even started before he'd passed. But his pride was no less genuine.

"I'm not surprised. You've always been a magnet. Everyone always loves you, and for good reason."

She took his hand and stopped him. They had a moment of quiet and privacy, with no anguished souls or cameras in the immediate vicinity. "That's the thing, Dante. They don't love *me*. I'm just an idea to them, a fantasy. Without you, I thought... I thought I needed them to define me." She studied a black chunk of rock at her feet, kicking it away before looking back at him. "It's stupid now, looking back. I *had* people—*real* loves, *real* connection. But, somehow, without you, I was convinced I wasn't whole and had little value on my own. I really believed all those followers would build me back up, like a plaster cast, to replace you. To recreate all the working parts and make me strong again."

He stared at her, his jaw dropping open. "My God, sis. I

can't believe you lived with that pain all those years." He wrapped her in a hug and she melted into the familiarity. "I know you missed me, but you never *needed* me. Not like that. Since we were little, you were *always* fearless in the face of the world when I never was. I hid in labs and behind books. They're easy; people are hard." He pulled back, his hands still on her shoulders. "It was always obvious to me that you were the stronger twin. I didn't realize it wasn't obvious to you."

Bea dissolved into tears.

All. This. Time.

Would it have helped had she known much earlier what he'd thought about her? She doubted it. Doubted she'd ever have believed in her own strength...until now, that is. Now, she was beginning to suspect.

No, not just suspect. She was coming to *believe...* in herself.

She wiped away the remaining tears and tipped her head in the direction the other two had gone. "I guess we'd better catch up."

Her steps were lighter now as they moved off.

"So, do you want to know who Toni really is?" she asked.

"Who?"

She giggled as she told him about Toni, and eventually they neared the edge of the pit, which Bea could determine by the different colored sky now visible in the distance. It was a soft, soul-relieving blue. Toni marched onward with determination, and Dante shared a glance with Bea, chuckling as they watched Toni stomp across the land.

Jesse had the MacBook open as she walked. "I've been messaging with Benny. He says our fight against the minotaur was broadcast live, but they cut it off right after the monster fell to the ground the first time. There's been no new updates since."

"Why would they do that?" Bea asked. "They lost out on some damn exciting footage after that."

Toni paused long enough for the rest to catch up. "Because they did not anticipate your continued wins, and it is becoming a threat to them."

"I thought this was just about entertainment and ratings," Dante said.

"It was, at the start. But, now, your sister has caused a tangible shift in the citizenry." Toni tossed a pointed look at Jesse. "People are learning too much. Perhaps becoming a bit less compliant."

"Which I'd say is a good thing," Bea countered.

Toni lifted her chin. "Perhaps. But not necessarily for us."

"What else does Benny say, Jesse?" Dante asked.

"He says that, based on what they did see before the broadcast was cut off, consensus on the street is that we beat The Hammer. There's a lot of confusion and talk, but, for the most part, people are saying Bea's won the competitor challenge." The girl stopped walking, and the others waited while she finished typing. "Benny says there's a mob forming outside the Administrative Center. They're calling for updates on The Game and demanding the producers declare Bea the victor. Bea, he says they're trying to break into the castle."

"Holy shit," said Bea.

Toni lifted her chin, her eyes narrowing. "This could be problematic for us. I've not been in this situation before."

"The Big Chill will get inside. I'm positive." The kid stood toe-to-toe with the Queen. "They've got our back."

"I'm not even sure what that means at this point, child. In any case, we must hurry forward." Toni continued on while the others followed.

The smaller creeks and streams had merged into one river, maybe twenty feet wide and four or five feet deep. The anguished were lined up along the center of the liquid, one after the other like a row of toy soldiers, all up to their chins. Bea didn't want to know what these people had done in life to be standing here now, and, at this point, she barely even noticed their cries anymore.

But the line of sight to the edge of the Seventh Circle was now clear, and they took Toni's suggestion and kicked into their hyper-speed movement. They were at the drop-off to the Eighth Circle in the blink of an eye. Boulders of black igneous rock bunched up at the edge as if they, too, had been running forward and all came to a halt just before falling, and the red boiling river found a path between them to fall over the edge in one hot, crimson cascade.

The group slipped between the rocks to stand on the ledge and survey the situation. The gentle blue sky Bea had spotted earlier was, indeed, the crown over this level. Soft wisps of cirrus clouds floated overhead, realistic and changing, unlike in the First Circle. Far, far below them, the pit was obscured by pale fog, which was lit from below with warm patches of light as if the mist were hiding a happy cityscape beneath its soft folds. The whole effect of this penultimate circle of Hell was utterly... pleasant.

"Do not be fooled," said Toni. "Remember what sin the Eighth Circle represents."

Jesse and Dante turned to Bea for an explanation.

She shrugged. "Fraud."

"Damn," said Jesse. "How do we get down there anyway? This looks like the longest drop yet."

They paced the edge, looking for any way down, but all they saw was a sheer cliff face, whose bottom disappeared into the fog.

"Toni?" Bea pressed. "How have other people gotten down?"

Toni didn't answer.

Bea stepped in front of her, crossed her arms and raised an eyebrow.

Toni lifted her arms, dropped them again. Her mouth

moved as if she were about to say something, but she changed her mind and shook her head. "It's different every time."

Bea was losing it with her. They were losing it with each other. Maybe it was the damn heat. "Well, pick one of the—"

"Hey, you guys." Jesse had settled on the ground, crossed-legged and leaning against a rock. "Benny was asking again about the findings in the book. I've been looking through the appendices, but they're like freaking gibberish. Most of them are full of obscure ancient history or demographic data. There's even a glossary. What the fuck?"

"Here, let me take a look." Dante reached for the tablet, then sat down next to Jesse. He searched through the document while Bea and Toni paced. "Yeah... See... I think..."

"What?" Bea stopped in front of him, her body helping to block the glare and Dante's brow relaxed a little in the shade.

"Jesse's right. The appendices themselves are worthless. The interesting part is the footnotes. There're tons of them. Thousands of them. Nearly every damn page throughout the appendices is footnoted."

"And that's interesting why?" Bea asked. "To me it sounds like a college student's worst nightmare."

"It's interesting because... Well... Look." He waved for her to sit down, too. Even Toni joined the huddle. "Not only do they seem completely unrelated to the sentences they're notating, but every last one of them says the exact same thing. Every. Single. One."

"Which is?" Bea leaned closer to see what his finger pointed to. It was a list of three statements, and Dante was right; the same list was repeated in every footnote. She read it out loud. "Number one: Nobody is forced to suffer in Hell. Anyone may be free at any time. Number two: There is no exit. Please see yourself out. Number three: Time is irrelevant."

Their mouths gaped. Even Toni seemed struck enough by the cryptic message to stand still.

Jesse broke the silence. "What the hell does all that mean?"

Dante handed the laptop back to her, then stood, bouncing on his toes as he began walking in circles.

Bea recognized the nearly manic look in his eyes as his hands moved through unseen calculations and his mouth worked silently. She'd seen it once before when she'd popped in on him at his lab at MIT while he'd been in the middle of working on a project and hadn't seen her come in. Right now, he was working up to something juicy.

"Part two… That sounds like a riddle. I'm not sure what it means yet." He paced in a tight circle, repeating the line. "There is no exit. Please see yourself out."

"Wait," Jesse said, legs bouncing. "You skipped right over the first footnote, which is the best one. You know, the one that basically said everyone is free to just up and leave Hell. Can we talk more about that, please?"

Her brother ignored the comment, still laser focused on his thoughts. "I'm guessing whatever the riddle means is related to part three—time is irrelevant—which sounds like they're referring to seeing things in multiple dimensions—aware of all possibilities or timelines at once." He ran his hands through his hair, leaving little sprigs sticking up in his best Einstein impression. "Choosing how and where to manifest— My God! This is all science based!"

"And utterly meaningless to us mere laymen," Toni said, though the look on her face said she hung on his every word. It said she wanted to understand. She was *hoping* for something.

"No, you're wrong," he said. "It's like when we move from Point A to Point B at supernatural speed. Or when you heal yourselves and feel no pain—which, by the way, I'd really like to learn that trick soon, please. That's part of it. It's a first step, you see? If I understand what the book is saying, though, we can manifest ourselves right out of here. Or we can change the nature of this place altogether." He smiled at Jesse. "That's the *anybody may be free at any time* part."

"I think they sort of put the cart before the horse on that one, though," said Bea. "Remember, it also said there is no exit."

"I agree," he said. "I'm guessing it requires a serious level of consciousness. And probably would require a mass effect. Most of the souls here would have to understand and see it."

"And most never will." Toni returned to the ledge, a hint of defeat in her dropped shoulders. She paced the lip, searching for a way down, but spoke over her shoulder, "They are all too blocked by pain and fear."

"They're too identified with the idea of individuality, of a personal timeline. Personal desires," Bea added.

"But I think being deceased, and, therefore, no longer incarnate, makes it easier to understand," he continued. "Death removes the boundary of the physical form. It's possible... winding up in Hell might actually give us an advantage."

Toni moved back to their little cluster. "Do *you* even know what all that really means, Dante? In a literal sense. Can you use the knowledge in any helpful way?"

The spinning wheels behind her brother's forehead were obvious. He even lifted his hands once or twice as if attempting to maneuver something. Finally, he deflated. "It will take some time."

Undaunted by the exchange, Jesse was setting fire to the keyboard, and Toni raced to stop her. "What are you doing?"

"I'm telling Benny what we found. What's the point of having the opportunity to advance if nobody except the four of us even knows it's a possibility? We need to get the word out."

"*Non!*" Toni snatched the tablet out of Jesse's hands. "Not yet."

The kid stood, her cheeks flushed. "Why not?"

"Nobody will understand it yet. You heard what Dante just said. It will be of no value right now."

"No *value*?" Jesse tried to grab the laptop back. "The footnotes say nobody is stuck in this hellhole. That everyone can leave. At the very least, it will give them hope. A reason to learn more. Don't keep this from them, *please*."

Toni softened in the face of the girl's emotion. "I understand your frustration, *mon chou*. But if we put the word out now, I am afraid Hell will come down on the citizens and ruin everything in an effort to stop a potential sea change. You see how they are already hesitant now to broadcast Beatrice's success."

"But if the word is out, they won't be able to stop us. Not all of us," Jesse argued.

"People cannot achieve this level of consciousness that fast. And if Hell brings more pain, they won't be able to learn at all. They will be suffering too deeply."

Jesse grabbed the laptop back and flipped it open, but Bea closed it with a gentle hand. "I'm inclined to agree with Toni. I'm sorry, Jesse. I think it's better if we wait until we're all about to exit the Ninth Circle and *then* present the findings to everyone. The populace will see us succeed with their own eyes, and it will be harder for Hell to quash them once they've witnessed it."

Dante stepped to Jesse's side, battlelines drawn. He spoke directly to Bea. "You're both acting out of fear even now. Which is not the way to succeed here."

Bea stepped closer to him. My God, was she having to plead with her brother now? She was thrilled to see how he'd become so willing to step into the public eye and possible line of fire, but she wasn't used to being on the opposite side of a debate. "Dante, please. Let's get the four of us out of here. This is *us*, remember? We'll help everyone, I promise. But let's make sure we're all safe first."

He placed a hand on Jesse's shoulder and shook his head. "We should tell them now. We don't know what might happen to us before the end."

Bea worked to formulate a response to her brother's chilling comment, but before one came to mind, a shadow stretched across the searing sky and a welcome rush of wind blew over the group.

They stepped back from the ledge as the round globe of a brightly colored hot air balloon rose from the depths of the Eighth Circle below. Cheery hues decorated the canvas, and the empty bucket hanging below was adorned in ribbons and garlands. A large monitor hung from inside the basket, scrolling a silent announcement in bright, white letters. "Congratulations, Beatrice. You have beaten your competitors. Please accept this gift from the producers of an easy ride down to the next circle where you may continue your journey." The broadcast then began playing unedited footage of their complete victory against The Hammer.

"Fuck, yeah! Look at us kick ass!" Jesse pumped both fists in the air and ran toward the rope ladder now being lowered.

But Bea was more hesitant. She looked at Toni. "Do we trust this? It's coming to us from the fraud level."

Toni hesitated, zigzagging her gaze between the pit and the balloon. She rolled a black pebble between her fingers as she considered. "I don't know what other choice we have. But we must stay vigilant."

Toni began to step toward their ride, but Bea pulled her back. "I asked you before how you've previously gotten down to the Eighth, but you didn't exactly answer me."

"Those ways are not available at the moment. Let us take the option presented to us," she said and moved off before Bea could stop her again.

Fair enough. And anyway, Benny had told them this would happen. Bea made sure someone had the laptop—Jesse did—so, with Dante at her side, they followed the others up the rope ladder into the basket.

She'd never been in a hot air balloon before and enjoyed

the swaying motion and cool breezes as they moved over the pit, then slowly descended.

The raging blood river waterfall went over the edge then disappeared into thin air, no longer existing on this level.

Below them, the view resembled an Impressionist painting of Paris as the twinkling lights from beneath the thin fog put on a magical show. For a few moments, the four of them were quiet. They might even have appeared relaxed to an onlooker, but Bea was already worrying about what awaited them below, and she assumed the others were thinking the same.

As they lowered further into the Eighth, the monitor flickered on again. The silly Brimstone TV logo came on, and the familiar announcer's voice began his narration.

"Welcome back to The Game! We are proud to congratulate Beatrice Allegra and her team on their many accomplishments thus far. They've been a little lax with the rules though, she and her French guide, as the producers never gave permission for them to bring additional guests on their journey."

A hot, queasy feeling rose up from Bea's gut, and her three companions went still as stone.

The broadcaster continued. "In light of her amazing feats, however, we will honor Ms. Allegra with one other favor in addition to the balloon ride she is now enjoying. To wit, she is welcome to bring one extra soul with her on the remainder of the journey out of Hell. But only one. And she is free to decide who it will be: Her brother, Dante Allegra, or the teenager, Jesse Chen. The one not chosen will be returned, gently and without supplemental punitive measures, to their initial place of pain where they will remain for eternity. We await your choice now, Beatrice. Decide before you touch down or both will be returned. Who do you choose?"

Chapter 25

THE HOT AIR BALLOON

The balloon still descended at the same gentle pace it had been, though Bea swore it was plummeting. Her heart definitely was.

Jesse and Dante rushed to her simultaneously, speaking over each other to volunteer their sacrifice.

Bea put up her hands as though she might slow down time, but only succeeded in quieting their voices for a breath.

The basket sank lower.

"Send me back, Bea," Jesse said, strength in her young voice, though defeat shadowed her eyes. "It's an easy choice. Dante's your brother. I'll understand; everyone will."

Dante pushed the girl gently back with his arm. "That's not enough of a reason and you both know it. You have to send me back, sis. Jesse deserves this. She saved us both back on the island. She fought the minotaur while my unaware ass was still asleep. She rallied an entire team to support us. For fuck's sake, the kid earned this."

"Not a kid." Jesse pushed forward, the flash of a wounded expression across her delicate face there and gone. "Anyway, I can fight again another time. Once the attention is back off me and the rest of The Big Chill, we'll do it again. We know how."

"No." Dante tightened the gap, inserting himself between Bea and the teen. The look of conviction on his face told her the discussion was over, and a lump formed in her throat. "I want this."

She shook her head. "You can't want it. No one would. And I can't lose you again." *I can't lose Jesse again either.* She shot a fast glance at Toni, and the soft, sad expression the old queen wore said she understood the pain Bea suffered, but could not help with the choice.

"I think you know it's different this time," he said. "You'll be okay. Besides, I want to find Ronna. It's been bothering me that I left her behind, and we know her location in the catacombs thanks to that book."

"But you'll be asleep again. You won't be able to—"

He cut off her words with a hug, whispering privately into her ear. "I won't sleep again, because now I feel hope, not despair. They can send me back to the tombs, but I am no longer one of The Sullen. I'll fake sleep until the attention dies down and then I'll find her and bring her out of here."

They pulled apart and he placed his hands on her shoulders. "We'll learn and follow in your footsteps. I'll make you proud. And if the book is right, we'll meet up again somewhere in space and time. I'm sure of it."

She took a breath, but had no argument left to her.

"I love you, Dante," she said as one end of an impossibly long lion tamer's whip unfurled in the air beside the basket. It undulated on the breeze, waiting for them to finish their good-byes.

She choked back a sob as they hugged one last time, but, strangely, the hole she expected to reopen in her gut didn't quite materialize. Instead, what she felt was a vast overflowing ocean of love and connection, which she experienced as an actual wave of warmth from her solar plexus.

Dante must have felt it, too, because they both glanced

quickly down at their bodies to see a golden glow flowing like a gentle river between their torsos, there for only an instant and then gone again, as if a trick of the mind. Or the heart.

"I love you too, sis," he said as the leather coil wrapped carefully, almost seductively, around his waist.

At the last moment he grabbed her hand, their fingers moving through their secret handshake. "Stronger together."

They finished on the fist bump. "Two full-on superheroes," she said as he was lifted out of the bucket and pulled away. But not before she caught the confident, radiant smile he flashed her. Through tears, she smiled back.

Then... he was gone.

And now she was pissed.

Maybe there really *was* someone sitting on high, forcing her to play this horrible game, to lose her brother a second time, to cause the pitiful tears now streaming down a brave teenager's face. Maybe, as Toni kept saying, there was no one sitting on high at all and this was no more than a painful corner of mass human subconscious. Whatever the case, she'd had enough.

Bea gestured to the satchel the teen now wore on her chest. "Jesse, flip open the laptop."

Jesse slid it out and booted it up, swiping away her tears and regrouping for battle. "Ready. What are we doing?"

Toni stepped forward and put up a hand, halting the conversation. Her attention moved between the TV monitor now showing the silent logo of Brimstone TV, then to Bea, and finally, her gaze lingered on Jesse's face. She released a deep breath and finally spoke. "We must broadcast what you found in the book," she said, as Bea and Jesse gawked at her. "Show them the footnotes. Tell them what Dante explained to us."

"Yes!" Jesse shouted as she punched one fist into the air.

Bea raised an eyebrow as she studied Toni's firm expression. "But our deal? Your children?"

Toni lifted her chin. "Hell has played enough games with us already. It's time to take back some goddamn control. It is time to help the people," she said. "I see who you've become, Beatrice, and what you're capable of. I'm sure I will be with my children soon enough."

Bea grinned at the Queen's response, and the kid's fingers flew, working the new plan as the balloon continued to lower.

"Dudes, they're going crazy!" Jesse's eyes opened wide enough to reflect the flying images on the screen. "There're hundreds of comments already. Our post has been shared a thousand times."

Bea leaned over to watch the feed.

Jesse clicked around, viewing the posts of others in the population, and photos showed people were already testing their bonds, crawling out of their boxes, abandoning their tiny boats. "Holy shit."

Toni rubbed her arms as if chilled, pacing the confined space. "I did not think they would react this quickly and decidedly. I merely sought to open their eyes to the possibilities. To give them hope. They are not yet ready to act, and I fear that—"

"Wait. Something's not right." Bea took the MacBook. She clicked all over the internet, checking. "No. No, no, no. This can't happen."

"Fuckers!" Jesse stood, raging at the sky. "They can't do this."

"What is it? What is happening?" Toni asked.

"They've blocked me from posting anything else on my socials and removed our video not just from our feed but all the re-posts, too." Bea kept surfing, but it was no luck. "They replaced it with a worded warning, saying the information on our page is disputed. Some people are already calling it fake news."

Toni shook her head, hands gripping the rim of the basket. "We are about to land in the Eighth."

Bea looked over the edge just as they slipped into the mist. Their world became gray and opaque. It seemed nothing existed but the three of them. "Jesse, message Benny before we lose all internet access. Ask if they breached the Administrative Center yet, and if so, tell him to find the broadcast center in there, commandeer it, and get out the message. Tell everyone it's all true—the book, the footnotes, all of it."

The thick atmosphere inside the clouds muffled the sound of the teen's fingers hitting the keys. When Jesse finally spoke, her voice was subdued and lacking its normal energy. "Bea, he says they easily took the castle as there was little to no resistance, and they've already scoured the whole building. He says…" She looked up from the laptop and closed the lid. "He says he's in there now and there's nothing inside the place at all. It's an empty shell, and it appears it always has been. Dusty and covered in cobwebs." She slid the laptop back into the satchel, and goosebumps rose on her skin. "I'm not sure there actually *is* an Administrative Center, you guys. So, where's the broadcast been coming from?"

The fog began to dissipate, and soon they could see their landing spot now fifty feet below them, and it was exactly as Bea had imagined it. A shiny, cobbled road lined with warm glowing streetlamps arced out of view in each direction, with the base of the impossibly tall cliff up to the Seventh on one side. On the other side were what looked to be a descending series of shallow mini circles, as though the Eighth Circle itself were terraced.

Their balloon paused its descent, hanging twenty feet above the road, waiting, perhaps, for someone to come grab the dangling ropes that would tie the basket to the ground. Even from this height, the smell of freshly baked croissants wafted on the breeze, and from somewhere in the distance, a street musician played a sweet song on a violin. Above them, the fog cleared to reveal a rose-gold sky lightly dusted in wisps of cloud.

"Why does this scare me more than anyplace we've been yet?" asked Jesse.

"Because it is a trick," said Toni.

As they waited to anchor, the monitor flickered on again and the screen filled with news footage showing exactly what Toni had originally feared—people struck down by demons. Tossed, sliced, burned, buried. All returned to their places of suffering.

"This is all my fault," Bea said, her knuckles white as she gripped the basket, temporarily stuck between levels and helpless to do anything but watch the chaos she'd brought.

Toni placed a hand on her shoulder. "No, it is not."

Bea scoffed. "You were correct back in the Seventh when you said we should withhold the information. I know you wanted to support us when Dante was taken and you took our side, but we should have listened to your first words."

"What I said back in the Seventh was wrong. It was right to have tried." Toni appeared genuinely tired for the first time. Defeated, maybe. "Perhaps. I... I don't know."

Nothing unnerved Bea more than when Toni appeared uncertain. She'd take the Queen's lifted nose and toe-to-toe arguing over her current deflated posture every time.

It was the kid who pulled them back from doubt. "No, it was def the right thing to do." Jesse stood tall even as she watched the carnage on the monitor. "Sure, the demons tossed them back. But now the people know. They *know*."

A graphic suddenly reported more breaking news, and, from a distance as if teasing the viewer, the camera slowly zoomed in on what at first was a tiny smudge on a white cracked landscape crisscrossed with red ribbons. The smudge grew bigger as the camera got closer, and Bea gagged when the image finally filled the monitor, revealing the broken body of a man, a pulpy mass of flesh where the head had been before the minotaur's hammer had pulverized it.

She didn't really need the text crawler at the bottom of the screen for an explanation. Already she was turning her head to vomit over the side, her face red from both the heat and guilt.

Nevertheless, the crawler told the story: "Benjamin Petrosyan, traitorous citizen of Hell who organized an insurrection against the castle, has been silenced."

Chapter 26

LE CIRQUE

227 years ago (1793)

Antoine plodded down the dirt path, as alone as she'd ever been in her thirty-seven years, even surrounded by other people. Strangers. A mix of languages and clothing styles, ages and attitudes. All of them moving as if compelled toward an unknown destination under an odd and unchanging blue sky. The clouds overhead were a little too perfect, the sky a little too blue. Rolling hills and low bushes dotted an unfamiliar grassy landscape, but more than being foreign to her eyes, the scenery appeared every bit as phony as a Versailles smile.

Still, she walked on. They all did. It seemed a human response to follow the flow of other humans when no specific directive was forthcoming. A "stick together" instinct, a "somebody must know what they're doing; they're all going that way for a reason" rationalization. Antoine knew better than to assume anyone else knew what they were doing. Nevertheless, she also followed. Because she was equally lost. And she was human.

Besides, nobody looked to her for leadership. Nobody recognized her in this place. She wore no powder or rouge, her hair lay loose and drab on her shoulders, and her body was draped in unadorned cotton and simple canvas shoes. Most of her fellow travelers were not her countrymen in any case. But Antoine remembered enough to know she had been a queen not so long ago.

Her recall had slowly filtered back from the moment she'd woken in the center of a crumbling Greek ruin. Memories had then trickled in, step-by-step as she crossed the hot, ancient landscape. She remembered the sounds of shattering glass, the bright torches of a mob, her family being chased from the palace in the dark of night.

As she boarded a curious ferry, she recollected the years spent in prison with her family, the crowds taunting them by hanging the decapitated heads of their royal friends in the windows of their moldy cell.

And, later, as she disembarked the strange boat and began the hike down the dirt road she now trod, passing some kind of encampment they were not allowed to enter, she recalled being separated from her children, her husband's execution, and, most painful of all, the cruel treatment of her youngest son, Louis Charles, as he was forced to lie on a witness stand against her. Horrible, perverted lies that had left him trembling and sick, and she'd been unable to offer him any comfort beyond what she could express with her eyes as she held his gaze and prayed he would understand that she did not blame him.

Antoine slid a hand to her collarbone, fingers splaying along her neck as she regained the last of her memories. She could still hear the masses shouting, could feel the wooden steps to the platform creaking beneath her feet, the cold wet October air slap her face, though a hot wind now kicked up in the present time, yanking her out of the reverie.

She crested a rise, and, like many of her fellow travelers,

stopped there, staring down at the vista before her. The hill where they stood ran steeply down to a hard pan of dirt. Not far in the distance lay a dark pit, wide as the eye could see, with smoke and flame rising from the depths.

In between, under a pea green and charcoal sky, lay a scene that gave rise to the same chill she'd had upon approaching the guillotine. It was a circus, but, as with the landscape she'd just been walking through, it was wrong. Antoine had visited such a performance once, set on grounds not far from the palace. Like that one, this circus was an outdoor ring backed by an open-air half-shell constructed of wood, creating a back-drop for the performances in front. But unlike the one in Versailles, this venue was ramshackle and decrepit. The wooden amphitheater was blackened and charred, and had been patched together as if it were repeatedly burned down and repaired.

There were clowns wandering the ring in front, and they began to beckon the travelers.

Antoine kicked up a pebble, rolling it in her palm as the crowd began moving again, and she picked her way down the slope. Off-putting as the scene was, perhaps, here, she would find some answers. Perhaps learn what this place was. She had died, that much was clear, but where was her family? Where was her husband? Her first-born son, Louis Joseph, and her infant baby Sophie, both of whom she'd lost to illness long before *la revolution*.

Unless this was Hell... She glanced again at the dark pit beyond. Perhaps she had earned that outcome, but she dare not believe that option yet. She dare not consider an eternity without her children.

An organ began playing, the music growing louder as she approached the venue. The pipes were rusted and rickety, the instrument out of tune, and an odor of uncleanliness filled her nostrils—animal feces and rotten food.

The crowd around her grew agitated, but the clowns had

them seated on benches before they could change their minds. Before they noticed the master of ceremonies enter the ring with his lavish costume and waxy, curling mustache and the ghastly metal ring through his septum. The whips he snapped in each hand.

By the time those whips had started their horrifying dance, grabbing souls and tossing them into the pit, by the time the screaming and crying had begun, the clowns had grown monstrous and there was no escape.

Hours later when the lash came for her it was a shock. Surely, *she* was not to be included with the rest of the masses.

But the whip told her otherwise as she found herself confined in its leather and staring into the bright eyes of the ringleader.

"Ah, I recognize this one. Your reputation precedes you, Marie Antoinette—or should I call you Maria Antonia? Perhaps Antoine? Little featherhead? You have so many names, you do, you do!" He giggled.

It was too much, this manhandling, this use of her most private names.

Antoine spat in his face. "How dare you? I am the Queen of France and require your respect even in my death." She wriggled against her bindings. "You will release me at once."

If anything, the bonds drew tighter and his smile wider. "Oh, believe me, I will, I will!" He turned to his assistant, who stood next to him with the huge book they'd been referring to. "To which level is her royal highness assigned so that I may release her to the pit *tout de suite*?"

Antoine didn't wait to find out. Her feet were just loose enough that she could lift one foot and bring it down hard on the ring master's toes.

This merely brought a louder laugh. "Oh my, oh my! I haven't been this entertained in ages." He brought one hand to fiddle with the tip of his shiny mustache as he considered the prize wriggling in front of him. "In fact, perhaps a little diversion is just what I need, *Madame Déficit*. To break up the tedium, you understand."

In the face of his cryptic and vaguely threatening response, Antoine reconsidered her tactics. "I do not care what you do with me, *monsieur,* but my children have been punished by the mere fact of their birth. In the short time I've been sitting in the stands, it has become clear what this place is. Is there no chance for redemption? Not just for myself, but so that my son and daughter may be reunited with their mother?"

The man considered, still twirling his mustache. "You make a fair point. The children of royals are often so pathetic."

Antoine kept her expression pleasant though she wanted to rip the mustache right off his face.

"Perhaps there is a way to satisfy *both* our needs. A little diversion for me, a little chance at redemption and reunion for you."

Her heart skipped into a higher pace as the possibility dangled before her. If there was ever a time for her to be the one faking respect, it was now. "*Oui, s'il vous plaît.* I would be forever grateful for the opportunity. In your wisdom, sir, what do you recommend?"

The ringmaster unfurled his whip, releasing her from its coils. She shook out her arms as she awaited his verdict, partly to keep herself from slapping him.

"I will set you a challenge, and if you are successful, you will be released from this place and sent onward to be with your children."

Antoine let out a sigh, her shoulders relaxing. She'd faced numerous challenges in her life, why not one more? Especially when the prize meant everything—*mais non*, the *only* thing to her.

"But this will be an extremely difficult challenge, as I want to take pleasure in watching your adventures and struggles. And I do not want you to succeed—or fail—too quickly. In fact, what

I have in mind could keep me entertained for centuries." His surreal gaze burned into her as he considered. "Here's what we'll do… First, how do you feel about the number one hundred?"

THE EIGHTH CIRCLE
Part I

Their balloon finally touched down with the help of a half dozen French mimes clad in black and white, who took the ropes and anchored them to the ground. The mimes were, of course, demons, and their eyes still flashed red as they handed Bea down from the basket, though she felt no burn of embers on her skin. In fact, ever since the Gates of Dis, the demons had been successively diminishing in both height and threat. Likely because Hell knew they could no longer hurt her. In fact, they'd become almost comical in her eyes, with their ridiculous level-themed costumes.

The trio disembarked onto the shining, cobbled street. With each stride they took, more of the Parisian fantasy appeared before them, as if they were moving through a complex video game or hologram, the environment building around them as they walked, outdoor cafes, quaint shops, watercolor painters set up with easels on the sidewalks. Yet a pall hung over the scene, the romantic façade colored by the residual mental image of Benny's punishment. Like someone had spray-painted graffiti across a Renoir.

As if in a trance, Jesse veered toward a patisserie, perfect rows of *pain au chocolat* displayed in the windows.

Toni took the girl's elbow and gently pulled her back. "Remember, we are in the Eighth Circle—fraud. Believe nothing you see."

"Where do we go now?" Bea asked, eyeing the dark espresso a waiter was currently placing before a café patron—probably NPCs. How long had it been since she'd tasted coffee? Since she'd enjoyed the sensual and physical pleasure of *any* food or drink? She didn't require such things anymore, but now that they were before her eyes and nose, *damn* she wanted them. It would be so easy to get lost in the illusion.

"We must now descend through the Malebolge," Toni said, ruining the fantasy.

"Through the *what*?" Jesse asked.

"Beatrice, you remember your *Inferno*. Fill our young friend in."

Bea had to dig deep into the recesses of her literary memory for this one, but the imagery soon came to mind. The Malebolge was a concentric series of ten "evil ditches"—the bolgias—each containing its own collection of anguished souls, and each a little bit lower into the pit. At the very bottom of the Malebolge funnel lay their final destination, the Ninth Circle.

Their way out.

Bea explained all this to Jesse as Toni pointed them toward the entrance to a wide stone bridge, which descended at a gentle angle across the ten bolgias, down to the center of the pit. A Park Service sign marked the way, welcoming them to the "Malebolge Scenic Walkway to the Ninth Circle," and noting the length of the bridge over the ditches to be approximately 2.5 miles, but giving an estimated time to cross of "an eternity."

"If I recall correctly, each ditch contains people representing different types of fraud," Bea said as they stepped onto the bridge and began their journey across, mimes with cameras following at a comfortable distance behind them. "I can't remember what each of them were in Alighieri's poem, but I'm sure it's changed over time anyway, same as the rest of Hell."

"This is true, in a manner of speaking. Though much remains the same," said Toni. "Here, you will find your ministers; the ones who preach out of crystal cathedrals in front of cameras, collecting tithings from their worldwide congregants and amassing a personal fortune."

"You mean televangelists," Jesse said, and Bea couldn't help but feel a slight guilty pleasure in hearing of these showmen's home in the Eighth.

"Correct," Toni confirmed.

"Who else?" the teen asked.

"Flatterers and sycophants. Hypocrites. Practitioners of corruption or extortion. False prophets and cult leaders. All of them spouting lies for personal or egoic gain, of course." Toni stopped. "It's strange that there are quite a lot of your so-called newscasters down here. I thought their job was to truthfully inform the public, but it seems that has changed in recent times."

Bea and Jesse shared a look, and the teen shrugged with a giggle. "Alternative facts."

Toni continued, "You'll find many down here who sell products, supposed medicines, diet aids, or glamour enhancers of one sort of another, none of which do anything more than divest the hopeful of their money. Or worse, pull them away from the proper treatments they could otherwise be receiving. Treatments that might have saved their lives."

"Snake oil salesmen," Bea offered.

"Yes, that is what they used to be called," Toni said. "All of these people, the rank and file of fraud perpetrators, have always existed no matter the time period. Only their resources have changed, their ability to reach more and more people. In my time, they might harm an individual or a family. Maybe even deceive an entire town. Now, their reach can harm thousands. Millions. Their duplicity can and does kill."

Midway across the first bolgia, curiosity got the best of Jesse and Bea, and they moved to the side of the bridge. Looking over a short stone wall into the ditch no more than fifteen feet below, there was no longer a vista of Parisian streets, though the sight was equally beautiful.

Pristine, white-sand beaches edged calm, turquoise waters. Lush palms and bright pink bougainvillea framed a smattering of empty beach chairs and vacant cabanas, their canvases flapping on a gentle breeze. A scent of gardenia and the song of busy finches reached Bea's senses.

"Where is everybody?" she asked.

Toni pointed a few yards further down the bridge to an ornate, copper-plated viewing device like the ones Bea had looked through at the top of the Empire State Building and the Eiffel Tower. It seemed a silly thing to use when they were a mere story-and-a-half above the scenery, but she gripped the handles anyway, pressing her eyes to the two lenses. She swiveled the viewing scope left and right as she tried to make out what the viewers now revealed.

"What… What the hell am I looking at it?" she asked.

But she soon realized. The horror was clear enough.

Pulling away from the device she looked over the bridge with her bare eyes again, seeing, as before, only empty pristine beaches. The people only became visible through the scopes.

She glanced through it again only briefly, a chill moving up her spine because, scattered everywhere on this luscious landscape, lay human bodies. They were piled deep in gold coins, the sun burning down and heating the metal blanketing them. Only their faces were exposed, their mouths clamped open as demonic cabana boys poured molten gold down their throats. The cool turquoise waters flowed soothingly past, only inches from some of them, yet forever out of reach.

Bea backed away from the viewer, too weak with shock to stop Jesse from stepping up to take her own look.

"Who are they?" she managed to ask before bending over, hands on knees, to stop the bile from rising.

"Grifters and blackmailers. Finally getting all the riches they ever hoped for as they lounge amid the landscape of their dreams," said Toni.

Bea was aware of the teen bolting from the viewer and heaving over the side of the bridge, and she waited as the three of them caught their breath before moving quickly away. She no longer felt even the tiniest bit of humor at the irony of these people's current situation.

Each bolgia seemed roughly a quarter-mile in length, and the women continued down the sloping ramp past the second one before moving close to the side again to venture another look down.

Bea realized that, as long as she didn't peer through the viewers scattered along the way, she could fool herself into thinking she was merely on a worldwide scenic tour. Every ditch revealed a new wondrous landscape, and she ignored Toni's constant warning and allowed herself to revel in the visual fraud for a while.

Pausing over the third bolgia, Bea appreciated the view of an alpine meadow. The pastoral setting might have been Switzerland or Austria, with rolling hills, tiny, thatch-roofed cottages, and wooly, grazing sheep. She purposely ignored the available viewing scope. "It's hard to believe we're in Hell, let alone this close to the bottom of the pit when you're looking down on a scene that seems straight out of *The Sound of Music*, isn't it?" she said to Jesse who stood next to her, gazing into the same ditch.

"*The Sound of Music*? I've seen that movie and I don't know what you're talking about." The teen's scrunched expression revealed her confusion. "That..." She pointed down to the ground. "That's Times Square. How can you miss the giant video screens?"

Now it was Bea's turn to crinkle her face. "What?" She looked over the rail again. Nope. Definitely the Alps. Maybe the Dolomites. Most certainly not Manhattan.

Toni looked into the third bolgia. "We are seeing different things. The Eighth Circle is showing us our own personal heart's desires." A glow of serenity settled over her face. "I see the grounds of Hofburg palace. My childhood home in Austria."

Had they been witnessing different things all along? What had Jesse and Toni observed back at the first bolgia when Bea had seen a Mediterranean coast? It seemed clear, however, that they'd all witnessed the same torments, because that was the only truth in this place.

They set off walking again as Jesse shrugged. "Toni's not wrong. I've never been to New York City, but I always wanted to see it. Maybe even move there one day. Life in the small town where we lived wasn't right for me."

Not for the first time, Bea glanced at Jesse's wrists. Matching vertical scars marked each one. This kid had not been messing around with her intent.

"I needed to be some place where I could get lost in a sea of neon lights and a blazing palette of people," Jesse continued, her chin lifting and eyes brightening. "Somewhere I could figure out my own color of weird, my own flavor of freak, my fluidity and identity, without having to hide while I explored."

"So, growing up you were…?" asked Bea.

"Bullied? No shit." Jesse said.

A wave of images swamped Bea's mind.

"What's with the mohawk? You some punk-rocker now?" The football jock sneered as he passed in the school hall. "What's it gonna be tomorrow? Goth? Drag?" His friends laughed.

A cheerleader and her entourage, sickly sweet smiles as they surrounded Jesse at a cafeteria table. "So, we've all placed bets and we're dying to know, because we just can't tell—are you into boys or girls?"

Jesse rubbed at the scars as they continued across the bridge. "Even at home everything was a battle."

Her mother arguing during dinner. "You'll never make friends if you hide behind that stupid computer all day. What's the point, living in those fantasy worlds?"

"The point is my future, mom. I want to be a game designer."

"Oh no you won't. All that violence! That's a job for men, not women."

4Chan and Reddit agreed, and more disturbingly so. "Just shut up and play, cunt! Unless you want to get #swatted. We know where you live."

Bea felt every molecule of fear and anger and loneliness in the teen's body, noted the temporary soothing balm of virtual fantasy realms as the girl locked her door and settled in behind the monitor. Epic battles with warriors and mages, endless hours of gameplay until the real-world sounds of fighting and taunting were drowned by the soaring soundtrack of the video. Until the drab white walls of the bedroom were morphed into luminous rainbows over floating mountains. Until the shining dagger blades gripped in characters' hands on the computer screen called to her more loudly than the sharp razor blades in the dresser drawer.

For now.

Memories, but not Bea's own.

"You took back a sense of control by playing a Norse shield maiden, a lizard warrior, and an ancient vampire king," Bea said, her gaze focused inward. "But your favorite character to play was a quiet, dark elf. A bard who sang their magic and moved with stealth."

Her focus snapped back to the present and she locked eyes with the girl, who confirmed the story with a creased brow and a single nod.

"The video games helped for a while," Jesse said. "I could choose my avatars, like you just bizarrely but accurately pointed out. Be whoever and whatever I wanted. Nobody knew the real person behind my screen character; nobody could see me. But eventually, it only compounded the problem. In the game, in real life—it made no difference. Nobody saw me."

The threesome walked on, silent for so many reasons. Time alternately stretched and collapsed as they went, the journey over the ditches seeming at one moment swift, as if they'd only been on the bridge for minutes, but, other times, it felt as if they'd been crossing for years.

They made their way over the fourth bolgia without looking down before Jesse broke the silence. "How did you know my memories, Bea? Why are we sliding into each other's minds? Finishing each other's sentences?"

"Toni's been reading my mind since we began our journey." Bea glanced at her older companion. "At first, I thought it was just a tool she was granted as a guide, but the longer we're all together, the more it seems we're all…"

"Connected?" Jesse said.

"I have often seen it happen once the souls I guide get far enough along their journey in this place," said Toni. "Once their subconscious minds begin to truly grasp that they are non-corporeal and that there are far fewer limits here. Do you understand?"

Bea chewed her bottom lip a moment. "Without a body, where does one person end and another begin—is that what you're saying?" A flicker of something warm and, at the same time, chilling moved across her non-existent skin. Chilling only because the idea was so foreign. "What is the boundary condition of a soul?"

"What indeed?" Toni lifted a brow.

"Whoa," said Jesse.

Bea slid the teen a half-grin. "Eloquent."

Jesse snorted and playfully slapped against Bea's arm, but, for a fragment of a moment, it almost seemed as though the kid's hand passed right through Bea's flesh, along with the same pulse of golden light she'd seen when Dante had hugged her, gone so fast it might've been imagination, except that Jesse's eyes had grown wider, too.

The novel concept, followed immediately by an unintentional demonstration, had made everything suddenly a bit disconcerting. She and Jesse moved slightly apart as they continued down the sloping bridge, though Bea soon became aware of a sound coming from beneath them in the fifth bolgia, and she moved to the edge to look down.

This time, the vista below was made of warm, reddish stone. Buildings crowned with tall, ramparted towers or soaring, round cupolas circled a grand square. Phantom crowds of busy locals and excited tourists moved about, stopping at vendor carts, or lunching on fountain steps.

"Florence," Bea said.

Jesse shook her head. "African savannah." She pointed to the distance. "Herd of zebra."

Even Toni stepped up. "Prague. The Vitava river running through."

The wonder of each of them seeing something different was fleeting, though, as the sound which had initially drawn their attention grew louder—a whining, pleading, cacophony punctuated by a shout here and there.

She moved a few steps to the nearest viewing scope and risked a look through the lenses. This part of the population was standing, some walking, wandering in circles or pacing to and fro. Though their bodies moved freely, their heads were encased in old television sets with rabbit-ear antennae just like the ones Benny's shop had displayed in the window, their faces trapped behind the rounded glass front.

From inside their personal TV, the souls shouted and lectured, trying desperately to be heard, though none of their fellow fifth bolgia neighbors responded. Each was stuck in their own programming even as they passed side-by-side, often bumping into one another with their lack of peripheral vision. Occasionally, a person would fall down, then struggle to get up because of their awkward heads. Others would trip over them and the result would be a temporary pile that looked a lot like an appliance junk heap.

"Who are they?" asked Jesse.

Toni took in the scene through the viewer. "Those are your broadcasters. The newsmen and television preachers."

"Why aren't they helping each other? At least stopping to talk to one another or organize themselves in some way to avoid these accidental clusterfucks?" Bea asked.

Their guide shrugged. "They cannot hear each other, cannot see each other. They see only their imagination. Most likely, they're witnessing a huge audience around them, crowds filling an amphitheater or a studio audience, but they are frustrated because their words are falling on imaginary ears and they are no longer heard or seen."

"Well, I can certainly hear them." And it didn't take the viewing device for her to bear witness to their frustration and pain. "In fact..." Bea stepped away from the scope and looked directly over the bridge, and, this time, she was able to view the anguished inhabitants with her naked eyes. "I see them now. Right there. Without the viewer."

Jesse looked over the edge. "Me, too."

Toni tipped her head. "Your understanding is growing by the minute. You're more able to see past the illusion to the truth," she said as she continued down the path.

Bea didn't move. "We have to do something. I... I can't

278

just keep skipping my way toward the exit, ignoring all this suffering."

"We tried to get the word out and look what happened." The weariness on Toni's face grew evident in creases Bea hadn't seen before. "Our only remaining option is to be an example to them when we get out. That does not mean you shouldn't be proud with how far you've come."

Fists clenching, Bea pushed away from the wall and continued the descent. She understood Toni's renewed fears, and it was clear her guide's shoulders now carried more pain than they had before their actions had unintentionally set demons upon the residents.

Bea understood her friend's desire to now be done with this quickly, anticipating the sweet joy of reuniting with her children. But, right now, Bea struggled with the ache she felt for her brother, for Benny, for the masses of people in pain all around her, and had a hard time imagining any happiness at merely crossing her own finish line out of Hell. If anything, her travels here had only further agitated the populace, and she owed them. Who knew if the citizens would even witness the trio's exit, or if the event would soon pass into useless legend?

Bea turned to see Jesse, who trailed behind her.

Jesse raked her hair across her face and sighed. "My friends in the Third will definitely follow. They've already seen enough to know it's possible. But these people down here in the Eighth? They're so trapped in fantasy... I don't know, Bea."

The bridge took a sudden sharper decline toward the sixth bolgia, where Jesse and Toni soon caught up to Bea who had come to a dead stop. At some point, the bridge had crumbled. It no longer crossed over the sixth ditch, but, instead, left a rockfall down to the bottom and back up the other side. The climbs down and up wouldn't be too difficult, as the cascade of stone left a veritable ladder each direction, but it meant their little trio was going to have to walk straight through the ditch itself to cross to the other side.

"If we try to ignore the miserable souls, it might not be too bad," Jesse said. "Let's just focus on the fake beauty and get to the other side as quickly as we can."

And beautiful it was—if they didn't look too carefully.

"What do you see, Jesse?" Bea asked, stalling a little as she braced herself to walk among the suffering.

"A desert. The pretty kind. Like Joshua Tree."

"Interesting," Bea said as she led the way down the rockfall, because what she saw was a Japanese Zen Garden lushly filled with cherry blossoms in full bloom. She caught the pagoda-like tops of tea houses scattered throughout the arcing circle as she picked her way down the jumble of stone bricks.

The noise, though. That was becoming a problem. As if surrounded by a sea of carnival barkers, a million voices assaulted her ears, each hawking their bogus products or services with slick promises supported by flimsy anecdotes and accompanied by the pressure to commit to auto-ship. She chose not to see the struggling souls of this level until she scrambled down the last chunk of stone, where curiosity got the better of her.

When she stifled her fear and allowed herself to see the people, she gasped, backing away from someone standing right in front of her.

She moved around the man as he turned to continue facing her, immediately pitching his click-funnel scheme for obtaining more followers.

Every step Bea took away from him, her feet landed on soft white-and-pink petals over smooth, gray flagstones. Every step the man took to follow plunged his feet, ankle-deep, into human excrement. His legs worked like plungers, churning the shit and sending the fecal stink up through her nose.

"Full of it in life, living in it in death," Jesse said as she moved quickly past. "I'm out of here. Come on, Bea."

Bea didn't argue. She broke into a trot, going slow enough to avoid bumping into any souls and making sure her footfalls stayed on a clean path as she followed Jesse across the bolgia.

Toni brought up the rear, mumbling various references to *merde*. They were twenty feet from the far end of the ditch and the mirroring rockfall that would lead them back up to the bridge when someone called her name.

"Bea? Beatrice Allegra?"

Bea stopped so fast Toni bumped into her from behind.

"*Ooph*. Why did you stop?" Toni said, stepping back and checking her shoes for cleanliness.

"Did you hear that?"

The shout came again. "Bea, I'm over here!"

She spun toward the voice and soon spotted a woman moving to meet her, arms waving to get her attention.

With careful steps, Bea went to meet the woman halfway while trying to place the vaguely familiar person with long, blonde hair and a tight, tanned body. The name finally came to her as they got closer—Kaitlyn McKenna, an internet fitness guru who'd become a minor celebrity, appearing on a reality show and eventually selling her own line of reportedly dangerous diet teas and fat-burning supplements. Whether or not she used them herself became unclear when she'd died on the operating table while getting cheap liposuction at a strip mall body-sculpting chain.

She reached for Bea's hands, but Bea stepped back. Kaitlyn was splashed from the knees down in feces. "Kaitlyn, oh my god."

The celebrity didn't seem to notice her filthy state or, more likely, had grown used to it. "Girl, I've been watching you on the broadcast. You're so lucky! How did you get this gig? I would die to be in your shoes."

Bea didn't bother pointing out each of the ridiculous things the woman had just said. Instead, she looked down at their feet—Bea's on a literal garden path, Kaitlyn's sinking into a trench of poop. She took a breath, ignoring the stench and looked the woman deep in the eyes. "You don't have to be here either, you know."

Kaitlyn shook her head. "I can't go with you. The Game said you can only take one other person."

"That's not what I mean. You can get yourself out, Kaitlyn. I'm sure you heard what the book said before they cut us off. It's true we're not exactly sure how yet, but there's hope." Bea took the woman's hands and squeezed, then gestured down to their feet. "Just look."

With the connection of their hands, the trail of cherry blossoms spread from beneath Bea's feet to Kaitlyn's, the crap clearing away and leaving both pairs of shoes standing on clean ground. She returned her gaze to Kaitlyn's. "You don't need to be standing in this. It's not real."

Kaitlyn blinked twice, her mouth partway open in wonder. She looked down at her clean feet, then back to Bea. And then the open window on her face closed once more as her mind refused to believe. Lips firmed and jaw tightened as fear set back in and she pulled up her defenses. She dropped Bea's hands and plastered on an Insta smile. "Listen, I know you picked the teenager to go with you. I mean, I still don't understand why you didn't take your brother. Twins getting all the way out of Hell together—there's, like, so many ways you could work that story for money. But… whatever. You picked the kid. It's done. It's just that… you're a savvy influencer. You've got to know you'll get a ton more viewers if you team up with me instead of the kid. I legit understand you feel obligated to her for rescuing you and all, but—"

"She's not a kid, or an obligation," Bea said.

Kaitlyn rolled her eyes. "Whatever. I'm just saying that choice is not going to pay off with any major sponsors."

Bea glanced down. Kaitlyn was up to her ankles in crap again.

"I mean, I guess it *could* land you some guest spots on talk shows or something, if that's the direction you really want to go," Kaitlyn rolled her eyes. "But wouldn't you rather be doing ultra-glam photo shoots in Morocco or Budapest? With my name attached, we can get you those gigs."

The shit under Kaitlyn's feet began spreading beneath Bea's shoes. Bea stepped back, each step sloshing in the fecal flow. Kaitlyn's identification with crap was infecting Bea's world. Bea had to retake control.

"Photo shoots in Budapest? Kaitlyn, you're dead. *We're* dead. There are no more photo shoots. The only gigs to aim for now are... I don't even know. But something far beyond that. Something much more important than freaking Budapest."

She continued to back up as Kaitlyn continued to spew, the shit chasing Bea's every step. "You're a fucking idiot if you don't take every chance now, Bea. If you don't take *me*!" The blonde burped, and bits of fecal matter shot from her mouth. "You're what, thirty? You've got maybe another year or two before your looks begin to fade and you're no longer relevant. Before you're done!" She gagged and tipped her head to spit a glob of dark brown to the ground.

Bea backed away faster, flicking a speck of something disgusting from her t-shirt with a shiver.

"Come back, Bea! No one cares about you and that stupid French bitch or that fucking teenager. Take me or I'll block you, and then everyone else will block you. You'll be done!" The last word came out in a slur as Kaitlyn vomited up a gutful of excrement. She stood there up to her knees now, blowing like a tiny, blonde, shit volcano.

Bea spun, running right past her two dumbfounded partners, up the rockfall ladder out of the sixth bolgia in a burst of supernatural speed, and straight across the seventh bolgia, and then the eighth, not stopping until, wracked with remorse, she gave up her flight somewhere over the middle of the ninth bolgia and crumpled to the ground.

Only one ditch away from the entrance to the Ninth Circle.

Chapter 28

THE EIGHTH CIRCLE
Part II

Bea lay there, body stretched out on the cool stone bridge. At some point after the hyperventilating ceased, she'd rolled onto her back, her limbs fanned out like at the end of a yoga class—in corpse pose.

She stared at the sky above, which no longer appeared as a pink Monet painting. While she'd been running, it had morphed into a sheet of solid charcoal. No clouds or movement. No weather. Yet, the landscape was still lit by some mysterious neutral light. Everything was visible yet shadowless, as though they existed in a strange diorama.

Bea suspected this was the true appearance of the entire place, and that she'd crossed some threshold in understanding where she no longer saw the illusion. Toni would no doubt tell her this was a good thing, but Bea just thought it was creepy. And she didn't prefer it.

Her partners soon caught up, stopping to flank her. Jesse held out a hand to pull her up. "Come on, Bea. I know that was gross." The kid shivered. "So gross. But it's behind us now. Shake it off. Let's keep moving."

Bea didn't respond. Didn't move.

Jesse dropped her arm.

From her position on her back, Bea could see the pit's higher circles rising above them. The bridge across the bolgias appeared so much longer and steeper than it had seemed when they'd come down it. The first terrace where their balloon had landed was barely visible. The Parisian café and little cup of espresso she'd been craving now seemed unreal, like it had never happened. As though she'd always been here, on her back on a stone bridge, looking up at a blackboard ceiling.

Toni squatted down. "You tried your best to help her, *chérie*. The poor soul could not see her way out. It is not your fault."

See her way out. Perhaps a coincidental choice of words, but she didn't have the energy to consider further.

"I don't understand it." Bea spoke to no one in particular. "That could just as easily have been me standing there. Her question was valid. Why did *I* get this gig? In life, I was no different than her."

"That's bullshit." Jesse planted her feet apart and crossed her arms at the chest. "I didn't know you before you died, but I can't believe you were ever that ignorant. Or that your ambitions were so empty."

This time, when Jesse and Toni both shot out their hands, Bea reluctantly sat up and let them pull her up. "I don't know about my motives. Certainly, I had to make a living, but I'd convinced myself I was trying to help people live their best lives." What the fuck did that even mean? *Live their best lives.* It was nothing more than another damn hashtag.

Toni gestured them forward, and they continued along the bridge, crossing the rest of the way over the ninth bolgia. Maybe it was the dark sky, or maybe their proximity to the Ninth Circle and whatever awaited them there, but their pace slowed.

"Let it go," Jesse said, walking backward in front of the

others, facing them as she spoke. "I know you're comparing yourself, but you're nothing like her. I remember that woman. I was still alive when it happened, and it was all over the news. That fool died trying to look impressive for the internet."

Bea stopped in her tracks, flinging her arms in the air. "So did I!"

Turned out, that was a hard reaction to counter, and though Bea hoped one of them would, Toni was silent while Jesse merely dropped her head and eventually resumed walking forward.

Which hurt.

But soon there was a hand pressed to the small of Bea's back, and a soft French voice beside her. "As I've said before, I do not know why you were granted this opportunity, *mon ami*, but I'm sure there was a reason. Maybe, in your heart, you wanted to learn these lessons, even before you fell from the balcony, and someone or something heard that. Maybe it was the call to find your brother that leant a certain possibility. Maybe, as you said once, you were simply the right person at a tipping point in the history of this place. Does it matter?"

As they neared the far side of the ninth bolgia, Bea risked a glance beyond the edge of the bridge. She hoped to see a lovely new vista that might remove some of the chill she now felt, and, for a moment, something flickered in her vision. A beautiful, soaring orange bridge, sunlight reflecting on a bay below. Flickered... and gone. Replaced by a sooty canyon. Something horrible moved down there, a huge creature wielding an axe. The sounds of hacking and dismembering were clear, as were the shrieks of extreme pain. Bea couldn't remember which fraudulent group this ditch contained, but she quickly averted her eyes and refocused on the path ahead.

Toni kept talking as they passed beyond this ditch and began their walk across the tenth and final bolgia. "Whatever the reason. Whatever you had been in life, you are a different person now. I see it. I've watched you grow and learn, seen your empathy blossom and your goals change. I've seen the golden glow of your soul." She took hold of Bea's hand and continued to hold it as they walked. "I know we didn't succeed in all the ways you wanted, and I am sorry for that, but know that you make me proud."

Bea leaned her head against her guide's shoulder, the closest they'd yet been on this journey. "I could say the same about you, you know."

A soft breath escaped Toni's mouth. "I apologize for judging you at the beginning."

"Ah, so you *were* judging me," Bea chuckled because it no longer mattered.

"I was. But I was wrong about you."

"That's okay. I was wrong about myself."

They were now a third of the way over the tenth bolgia, just minutes away from the Ninth Circle, and the darkness sank lower, seemed to seep into their bones. Even Jesse slowed to let them catch up, soon taking hold of Toni's other hand.

Bea forced herself to not start chanting, *Lions and tigers and bears, oh my.*

"Do not let it frighten you. We are moving over the last ditch, where the Falsifiers are kept," Toni said. "It is the home to the worst of liars. Speakers of evil untruths and wicked words. If there truly were a devil, the souls here would've been his voice on earth."

"Jesus," Jesse said. "What's going on down there? I can't bring myself to look."

Toni didn't respond, and Bea had a more urgent question anyway. "I'd really like to know what to expect in the Ninth Circle. We're almost there, Toni, yet we've never talked about it. What happens from here?"

"Yeah, good point," Jesse added. "Forget the tenth bolgia, let's get the itinerary for what's coming up."

There was a tremor in the teen's voice that Bea hadn't heard before, and she couldn't blame the kid. Her own vocal cords were pulling tight. "Toni?"

Almost across the last ditch, the old queen paused her step. "Um…"

Something seemed off, and a chill started at Bea's ankle, a tickle really. She rubbed that ankle with her other foot and heard a crunch. "Huh?" Looking down, she found a piece of paper clinging to her leg, as if blown there by wind, though the air was dead calm. She reached for it and opened it up, smoothing out the wrinkles.

Even in the gloom over the tenth bolgia there was enough of the strange light to read what was there. It was the front page ripped from a newspaper, *The Underworld Times*. Of course. Bea rolled her eyes at the cheesy thing, but the headline nevertheless grabbed her attention, and her hands went weak as she read it:

MARIE ANTOINETTE FAILS YET AGAIN.
AFTER HER LATEST ATTEMPT, THE CURRENT
COUNT STILL STANDS AT ZERO SOULS SET FREE.

Jesse, who'd been reading over Bea's shoulder, was the first to find her voice. "That's not true, though, is it, Toni? We're in the fraud circle. It's another illusion, right? The Game knows how close we are, and it wants us to lose hope." The kids' eyes grew round with worry. "Right? It's not true."

The French queen didn't respond. She stared out over the inky, mysterious depths of the last bolgia, her arms wrapped around her torso.

"How recent is this article?" asked Bea. "Tell me it was from a century ago. It's just an ancient, yellowed newssheet floating around the pit with long-outdated information. Is that it?"

But Bea already knew the answer. Guilt was written all over the lying monarch's face.

Why the hell had she ever trusted otherwise? Why did she ever believe that a woman famous for her selfishness and neglect would be anything *other* than deceptive? Right now, Bea was as pissed at her own gullibility in believing the French queen as she was at Marie herself. They'd all been so fucking betrayed and never saw it coming.

Words failed as her jaws clamped together and she studied her so-called guide's face.

Toni sucked in a breath. "I never lied to you, *chérie*. You made an assumption."

"No. I heard what you said to Master Minos way back at Le Cirque. I was your hundredth and last person."

"You misunderstood. My task was never to get one hundred souls out of Hell. It was to get one soul out, and I was given one hundred tries." She took a step forward. "You're not the hundredth person I will have gotten through, Beatrice. You're my last chance."

Bea had known she'd been carrying a weight on her shoulders since early in this journey—the weight of her brother and of Marie and her four children. She'd had no idea just how *much* weight, though, and a tiny coal of resentment began to smolder and smoke.

This queen, who now appeared so diminished in stature, dropped her voice to a near whisper. "Please don't fail me now, Beatrice."

The resentment caught fire, combusting into a pyre of anger like she'd never known. Every freaking step of the way she'd believed this person was a sage of wisdom. She'd trusted her, and put not only herself, but her brother, Jesse, Benny, in fact, a damn good portion of the inhabitants of Hell at risk because of that.

Bea's body shook and her mouth worked on silent words before she finally pushed them out. "Don't. Fail. *You*?"

Marie raised her hands, her own words now coming fast. "You can do this, Beatrice. You can save all of us. You are so very strong. I've never seen anyone do what you've done and get so far."

These words did not help ease the sickness in Bea's gut. She remembered the Queen's hesitancy to go down a certain path in the Third Circle. No doubt she'd lost one of her assignments there, someone she must have particularly cared about. Were her failures scattered throughout the Nine Circles? Which raised another question. "Just how far did you get with everyone else?"

No response.

"Marie, exactly what is the farthest you've taken anybody before me? I want to know."

The Queen hung her head. "I have never before gotten anyone through the Gates of Dis."

Jesse and Bea gasped in stereo—and whatever remaining hope Bea had at getting out began to slip away. Yet, looking back, it explained so many of Marie's reactions along the journey. Her utter shock at Bea's success at the Gates. Her failure to answer so freaking many of Bea's questions.

"You've lost all those people," Jesse said, fear and defeat deflating her tiny body.

Marie appeared equally small. "All I ever do is lose people."

A series of Marie's memories flashed through Bea's mind, showing her the truth of the statement, but it did little to quell her anger.

"So how did Bea get through?" Jesse asked, touching Marie's arm in a gesture of comfort Bea could not bring herself to offer. The kid was stronger than her. "What made *her* different?"

Marie shrugged. "I've suspected it had to do with her brother. After he was captured and taken into Dis, her motivation was so high that she found a way. She faced the fear none of my other assignments could face." She straightened her spine, suddenly appearing proud again as if she'd figured out the perfect teaching method. "I suspect that, without his dire peril, Beatrice would have failed, too, and I'd have lost my last chance to be with my children."

"Whoa, whoa, whoa!" Bea's muscles coiled so tight with rage it was painful, and what little empathy she'd felt at the Queen's memories burned to cinders in a flash. Her limbs almost moved on their own to release that anger all over the Queen's face. "You're standing there acting like it's a *fine* thing my brother was almost ripped to shreds, because it meant *you* might now get your precious prize?"

Marie realized what she'd said and she reached out to Bea. "*Non*, that's not what I—"

"Go to Hell!" Bea flung herself at this traitor of a mentor, forcing every ounce of rage straight through her arms and shoving Marie backward to the edge of the bridge, her back slamming against the stone railing. She was vaguely aware of Jesse yelling for her to stop, and the kid's words sank in just enough to keep her from pushing the Queen over the side.

Instead, they stood there, panting at one another, Bea's hands still at Marie's throat.

"Let her go!" The teen ran up, pulling Bea away. "We need her."

"Thing is… we don't."

Jesse opened her mouth to speak when Marie put up her palms. "Hush, child. Beatrice is right. My motivations from the start have been purely selfish. I should have cared as much for the people I was supposed to lead out of this place as I did for my own desires. *They* should have been my priority." She glanced at Bea and paused. "Or maybe I did truly care but convinced myself otherwise. In any case, I now understand that the reason for my failure is that I am not worthy of leaving, and all of my charges have suffered as a result."

Jesse reached for her. "But that's not—"

"Bea, I am aware I have no right to ask it of you, but please lead Jesse out. Unlike me, you are more than capable of it. I know this in my heart." She hopped up onto the stone wall.

Jesse cried out in panic and ran forward. "What are you doing?" The teen glanced back. "Bea, what is she doing? Stop her!"

Bea stood frozen there in the middle of the bridge, the massive pile-up of anger, shock, and resentment leaving her immobilized.

"But your children," Jesse pleaded, taking action where Bea could not.

"My children? I am not worthy of their sweet souls. I have failed them." She looked at some horizon in the distance, her voice soft and sad. "I have failed everyone. All my people. And I am so deeply sorry." She glanced down at the ditch below before locking eyes with Bea at last. "This is my place."

The Queen relaxed into a backward dive off the wall, gentle and accepting, to the darkness below.

"Oh my god!" Jesse shrieked, running to look over the side.

Frozen, Bea stared at the void where Marie's body had been moments before. Still, it was anger and undiluted shock that remained forefront in her emotions.

The sobbing teenager ran back, gripping Bea's hand in despair and tugging her toward the edge. "Come on. We have to go get her."

Bea shook her off. "We're better off without her."

The look of hurt on Jesse's face nearly gutted Bea again, but it made no difference. They were lost with or without their guide. And Bea couldn't handle looking anymore at the face of the woman who'd kept silent while her brother had gone through so much, knowing there was little to no chance of saving him. She shook her head. "Let's keep going. We'll figure out the rest on our own."

The teen stood still. "We have to get her back. You caused this when you attacked her. You didn't even let her explain. You were so damned angry."

"Yes, I was angry! Her lies put us all at risk. Me, Dante, you. More importantly, she gave us hope we had no right to believe in. Do you not care about that?"

A shadow of disappointment crossed the girl's face. "Do you really think you'll be able to escape this place if you simply ignore what just happened? If you don't try to fix it? Are you feeling particularly enlightened right now? You're completely consumed with anger and, yet, you think *now's* a good time to step into the Ninth Circle? She just wants her kids back, Bea. Her *kids*!"

Jesse was probably right—of *course* she was right. But, at the moment, the only image playing on the cinema screen of Bea's mind was Dante, carried above an angry mob deep into the horrors of Dis. And she refused to care about a selfish old queen and her spoiled freaking progeny.

She shook her head at Jesse and started forward toward the Ninth Circle.

"Bea!" the kid shouted behind her. "I'm not going with you. I'm going down there to get Toni!"

Bea glanced over her shoulder to see the teen standing on the wall of the bridge. "Her name's Marie."

The kid gripped the satchel with white knuckles. "Please. Come with me."

But Bea declined, tipping her head to indicate Jesse should come along with her, and turned away toward the path.

Just slow enough to see the blur of movement as Jesse jumped.

Chapter 29

UNKNOWN LOCATION

Right Now

Perhaps she still walked the last stretch of bridge over the tenth bolgia. Or maybe she'd already stepped down off the ramp and crossed into the Ninth Circle. There was no way for Bea to know. In the moments since her world had tipped sideways, since she'd lost the last of her companions, since she'd traded every bit of understanding, every ounce of hope, every true feeling of connection for the fury that had become her entire focus, total darkness had descended over the pit, obliterating all light and sound. A darkness as black as midnight in a room with no windows or lights. A silence as deep and relentless as the shadow now growing inside her.

Bea picked her way along, feet sliding more than walking as she felt her way forward. She reached out with both arms, feeling around the void like a blind woman in an unfamiliar house. There was no time to regret her actions just yet as she focused on making her way.

Wrong. There was plenty of time. An eternity, in fact, for regret and fear to seep into her imagined bones, to fill her phantom lungs, as she fumbled in the dark alone. So alone.

A sensation began at the base of her throat, a tickle really, which she soon realized was the beginning of a scream. She would *not* let it out, fearing that, once it started, it would never *ever* stop.

But it popped out as a whimper anyway when her fingers bumped into something.

She yanked her hand back and held still, holding her breath. When nothing further happened, she reached out again.

The hard, flat surface felt like a common plaster wall, cool and smooth to the touch, so she trailed her fingertips along it, following until she came to a corner, around which she discovered the most beautiful thing she'd ever seen—light.

Her pupils shrank at the sudden illumination, but soon relaxed as she moved down a narrow hall toward the warm glow. Voices beckoned from the room ahead, laughter and conversation. Bea picked up the pace, trotting the last few feet as she entered the living room of... her Boston apartment.

She choked out a sound that was half-gulp of air and half-gasp of joy. Here were the beloved matte-black walls, her favorite white leather sofa, the row of floor-to-ceiling windows looking out over the twinkling city lights below.

The voices she'd heard were from a television talk show playing on her big flat screen across the room. "We will return right after the break," a voiceover said as the channel went to a car commercial.

A totally regular earth-based channel, she thought as she released another giddy hiccup.

Bea twisted to the direction she'd just come from to find, not a black void, but her bedroom, lit warmly by a table lamp, and the edge of their big bed just visible around the corner. This might be another illusion, of course, but it proved too personal to have been created by some mass group subconscious. For example, there, at the base of the hallway wall, was the scuff mark Bea had caused with a runaway vacuum. She'd been planning to repaint it for months, but had never gotten around to it. And, there was the tiny piece of masking tape covering up a light switch near the bedroom, which needed to always remain in the down position lest someone accidentally turn on the kitchen disposal. No, this was way too specific to be a mere façade.

A tentative smile began to pull at her mouth as she allowed herself the tiniest bit of hope. Was it possible that she'd...

God, she was afraid to even voice the thought in her head.

Moving back through the living room, she ran her fingers along the edge of the couch as she let herself speak the words out loud. "Did I make it out?"

Maybe getting through the Ninth Circle was just a matter of making it there in the first place. Being brave enough to step into the horrifying unknown. And, if so, where was she now— the homes in heaven likely didn't have scuff marks or bad wiring—perhaps she'd been sent back into the world fully incarnate again, her death erased, a new timeline where she might continue living. *Time is irrelevant.* Is this what that meant? If it were true, when, exactly, in time was she? More precisely, was she still with...

"Did you make it out of *where*, babe?" Angel stepped out of the kitchen, a dish towel slung over one broad shoulder.

Her jaw dropped. She stood gaping like a fish at the most handsome man in the whole world, even dressed as he was in torn jeans and faded black t-shirt.

Bea glanced down at her own attire—gone were the white shirt and generic jeans, now replaced by low-slung pink sweatpants and a cropped gray tee with the words *Yes, I really do care*, written across the front.

"Bea? Is everything okay?" He must've wondered at her stupefied expression.

She flew to him, wrapping her arms around his body in the tightest of hugs. Breathing deeply of his scent and feeling his muscles flex beneath her grip, she wondered how she ever could've put anything ahead of their relationship. How she'd ever thought his love was not enough. His love, her friends' love, her parent's love... Dante had been there, too, in all of them. How had she not seen that?

Warmth spread throughout her body along with a sensation of fullness, and she couldn't wait to share her love with everyone she knew. To make up for all the time she'd wasted while alive before, thinking herself so isolated and empty. Now, all she wanted was to pour this sensation out of herself and into everyone around her, an endless, overflowing connection.

She was getting his shirt wet and he pulled back, holding her by the shoulders with concern in his eyes. "What's going on? You took the longest damn nap in the world, sleepy head. I was just about to come wake you up. Did you have another bad dream?"

Her nod was slow. "I... I guess? It sounds silly, but I thought... I dreamt I was in Hell. The Nine Circles like in that old story, *Inferno*." But she *was*, wasn't she? Bea touched her hair, her arms. Glanced at the ankle that had once been broken. There was no evidence of her travels through the Underworld, but there wouldn't be of course, because she'd learned how to heal.

"Oh, no, not that one again. I'm so sorry." He pulled her into another hug, rubbing her back.

Again?

"It's the worst of them, I know. Same one you had the whole week you were in the coma in Paris." He released the hug and tucked a loose strand of hair behind her ear. "I can't imagine how horrible it was to be trapped in that nightmare for so long. But what a small price to pay for the fact that you survived that horrifying fall. I'll gladly take it." He placed a kiss to her forehead and went back toward the kitchen.

She followed him like a puppy, mumbling mostly to herself. "A coma?" Maybe she'd wrongly dismissed that early hypothesis she'd considered way back in the Grecian ruins. Or what she'd *dreamed* were Grecian ruins.

"I've said it a thousand times and I'll keep saying it for the rest of our lives. Thank God for that hard head of yours." He flashed his perfect smile as he put away the last coffee mug from the drying rack, but then that smile faded. "And thank God for the scaffolding you got caught on two flights down. Jesus, Bea, you came so freaking close to... And right after we'd had that horrible fight and almost broke up. To think... Well, it didn't happen, luckily." He shook his head.

Scaffolding? She tried to remember the fall, but all she pictured was a sea of swirling stars overhead.

He draped the dish towel over the oven handle and turned to study her. "The doctors warned us your recovery would take a while, remember? They said you'd be fatigued and would sleep a lot." He grinned. "Check and check. And they said they wouldn't be surprised if the nightmares continued for a while, too. You've been through a trauma, babe. It's been two months now; it might be time to start thinking about counseling to help you process. Let's talk about it this weekend." He stepped forward and cupped her cheek. "In the meantime, I've got to go shower and get dressed for my business dinner, remember? I won't be out late, I promise." He planted a knee-melting kiss on her, then headed to the bedroom, calling back over his shoulder before disappearing around the corner, "What do you plan to do tonight? Anything good on Netflix?"

What *did* she plan to do on her first night back? The idea of binging a TV show made her a little queasy. Call her parents? Her friends? Her stomach rumbled. Eat! Oh my God, she planned to order everything. Every. Fucking. Thing.

She trotted back into the living room in search of her cell and the local food delivery app. Her iPhone was right where it always was when not in her hand, on the end table. She grabbed it as the television caught her attention. "We now return to *The Spectacle*, with your host, Nadiyah Germain."

Her attention whipped to the screen. "*What*?"

Sure enough, there was her best friend, thick black curls bouncing on her shoulders and model-long legs crossed gracefully beneath a strong yet feminine pale pink skirt suit.

"Nadi? Holy shit. When did you get this gig?" Bea whispered as she dropped her phone back onto the end table and came around to perch on the edge of the sofa. Damn, she'd apparently missed so much during the time she was, one way or another, gone.

Two gray-haired white men, both wearing glasses, sat on chairs across from Nadi, one with a pointy Van Dyke beard and hawkish, piercing eyes, the other sporting only a mustache. His kind, grandfatherly eyes twinkled as if he held back a private joke.

Nadiyah introduced them. "Today, we have the privilege of talking to two of history's most famous psycho-analysts and philosophers. Please join me in welcoming Sigmund Freud and Carl Jung."

The studio audience applauded, but Bea rolled her eyes. Okay, so *The Spectacle* was not a serious interview show, because these were obviously actors playing the long-deceased men. Still, she was curious to see what Nadi's approach to entertainment would be. Proud of her bestie for whatever form of programming this was, Bea sank back into the soft cushions of the sofa, wishing she already had her food in front of her because this promised to be interesting.

"Dr. Jung, before we went to commercial break, we were discussing the notion of whether Hell might be a real place. In other words, whether the Judeo-Christian concept of an actual fire and brimstone destination is at all a plausible concept. Your colleague, Dr. Freud, dismissed the notion altogether. Your thoughts, Dr. Jung, please."

A chill shot through Bea's spine at the coincidental topic, but her eyes remained glued to the screen as Dr. Jung began to speak, the spark in his eyes still shining. "Having had a near-death experience myself, Nadiyah, I am forced to disagree with my old mentor. I know for a fact there is some form of life after death, as my own soul has experienced it, albeit briefly before I was revived from my heart attack."

"And how would you describe that experience?" Nadi asked.

"I don't believe the particulars of my story are what is relevant, as I presume everyone will experience something slightly different, yet all pulled from a universal subconscious. I believe we, as humans, have manifested our world together, including an agreed upon, collectively created—yet very real—Afterlife."

A swish of silken skirts and the scent of powder turned Bea's head, but nothing moved in the room.

"Nonsense," said Freud. "Any images one might see flashing through their mind in the moments just before death ends all consciousness are no different than the ones haunting their dreams during sleep. Symbols of deep-seated fears or old wounds their mind is afraid to look at in true form. Other times, the imagery is nothing more than random scraps from their daily life."

"Sometimes a cigar is just a cigar," Nadi quipped, and the audience laughed. "Seriously though, can you give us an example?"

Bea really didn't want any examples. The interview had suddenly become agitating. She glanced around for the television remote.

"Of course," Freud continued. "Let's say someone went on holiday to Paris shortly before their death. Perhaps, in their dying mind, they imagine they've floated away from their body to now hover before a patisserie window with rows of *pain au chocolat*."

Bea shot up from the couch, feeling short of breath and

dizzy. A French mime wearing stripes and holding a video camera stood briefly at the edge of her living room until her vision resolved the image into a white sofa against a black wall.

"Let's take a case study, shall we?" the Viennese shrink said, his Schwarzenegger accent beginning to grate on her nerves.

Where is that damn clicker, Bea thought as she shuffled magazines on the coffee table and slipped her hands between the couch cushions, but to no avail.

"Excellent idea, professor," her bestie urged.

"Shut up, Nadi." Now she was talking back to the TV as she continued her quest for the remote, looking behind the sofa.

"Let's talk about Beatrice Allegra," Freud said.

Bea froze to the spot, her throat clenching shut.

"The poor young woman believes she's had quite an eventful post-death experience," the man continued. "Believes she's been walking through Hell on a mission to find her dead brother. An absurdity, of course. No such real place exists."

"I beg to disagree," Jung jumped in. "The concept of the Nine Circles of Hell as originally described by the poet Dante Alighieri in the fourteenth century has become the standard depiction of the Underworld for most of the western world ever since. It makes sense that the universal subconscious would create a very real presence there and—"

"Rubbish. There is a much easier explanation than your fairytale of mass hallucination. To begin with, the woman did not die. She was in a coma for a week and her brain pulled up relevant imagery from her life to populate her dreams. Let's examine the facts. She was on a trip to Paris and staying at a hotel above the *Place de la Concorde* when she fell. Not surprisingly, her brain produced a guide on her journey in the form of none other than Marie Antoinette. My lord, Beatrice even created such an in-depth persona of the old queen that she imagined flashing back to periods of the French woman's younger life. Classic projection."

"Interesting," Nadi agreed. The damn traitor.

Bea found her voice. "No. I knew Marie's history because we're all connected, asshole. Especially those of us who are... were... non-corporeal." She stuck her tongue out and made a raspberry noise at the screen.

"*Eloquent,*" she heard Jesse tease with a giggle.

Bea whipped her head left and right, but the girl wasn't there.

"While on her supposed journey there, Beatrice ran into her physicist brother's idols, including Professor Patel. Her whole journey was riddled with symbols of her social media career. As a matter of fact," the old man said, stroking his pointy beard, "remind me, what was the title of her very first YouTube entry?"

"Ah, yes," Nadi said and then laughed. She *laughed!* "*Life After Death. Getting Through Hell One Step At A Time.*"

Bea's breathing grew shallow and she struggled to catch enough oxygen. She turned toward the hallway to the bedroom, the sound of the shower having shut off. *Angel.* Angel was in there and he'd explain away this craziness. He'd set everything right again as it was only a few minutes ago.

"Even just moments ago her boyfriend made a comment about therapy, and, suddenly, here we are, two psychologists discussing her case," Freud had to go and add.

"So, you're saying she was dreaming this whole journey while she was in the coma?" Nadi asked.

"*Was* in? Who's to say she's not *still* in the coma?" he replied.

Bea took a step down the hall, panic shaking her limbs as a man crossed from the bathroom toward the bedroom, a towel wrapped around his hips. "Angel?"

The figure stopped and looked toward her. *Not* Angel. Rather, the long-haired golden man from the winds.

She gasped and backed up, a whimper escaping her lips as the man turned away and continued into the bedroom and out of sight.

"What is happening?" Bea tip-toed further backward into the living room, her hip bumping into the end table.

"Well, are you, Bea?" Nadi's voice whipped her attention back to the TV. Her best friend spoke directly to her, staring at her through the screen. "*Are* you still asleep?"

Her cell phone rang on the table next to her leg. Bea began to reach for it, but yanked her hand back from the Moto Razr.

"Where are you, Bea?" her best friend continued. "Are you awake? Look around and tell me what you see?"

Something shifted on her body, and Bea looked down to see plain jeans and a white t-shirt. The walls of the apartment began to crack and crumble. Demon French cameramen in black-and-white costumes stepped through the gaping holes which, this time, stayed in place.

"Angel!" she called out, the fear of losing him again unbearable. "Angel, help me!"

But the apartment continued to fracture, and, suddenly, the wood floor was gone and her feet were slipping on ice.

She stumbled then stood. Then slipped again, and then stood again. The entire room, along with the TV, disappeared, but the broadcast continued beneath her feet. A frozen lake of ice as far as the eye could see from horizon to horizon acted as an endless television screen.

Nadi's face, as big as a football stadium, kept talking. "Are you awake?"

Bea slipped once again, landing hands and knees upon the ice. She stayed there, imagining herself now to be the tiniest, frozen, little ant.

Nadi's questions became a plea. "I love you, Bea. Please open your eyes for me, sweetheart, and see. ARE YOU AWAKE?"

Bea reached out and touched one little pixel of her best friend's face, tears dripping onto the ice and freezing there as Nadi disappeared and the image morphed into the massively sized logo of Brimstone TV.

Chapter 30

THE NINTH CIRCLE

Soon, even the Brimstone logo faded away, leaving a cold, gray slate of ice below and a cold, gray slate of sky above. Bits of soft color dotted the depths of the frozen lakebed, bodies in awkward positions with mouths and eyes open as if iced over in mid-sentence. Or mid-scream.

Some were nearer the surface and Bea could make out their features. Others were at greater and greater depths, and appeared as no more than pale smudges. These were the souls representing the sin of treachery. Betrayers of friends, family, or country. Cruel destroyers of those who had depended on them. Traitors, child molesters, despots. The one nearest her blinked—the souls here were awake and aware of their situation—which gave Bea a shiver more powerful than the freezing temps of the Ninth Circle ever could.

As the unbearable cold of the ice seeped through her feet into her legs, Bea spun a slow circle in an effort to get her bearings. Vague forms, amorphous shapes of a slightly darker shade of gray, ringed the horizon all the way around. Possibly distant mountains. Possibly nothing more than layers of atmosphere.

Church bells sounded behind her, a slow, steady gong as if marking the start of a solemn event.

Or someone's passing.

She whipped around to find a massive, copper church bell. It hung vertically in the open air, attached to nothing, swinging as the clapper struck the sides, the sound echoing across the lakebed.

Tick tock, Beatrice.

Whispers came from the dark all around her, the words repeating and overlapping, from nearby and far away, a chorus of voices. Men, women, children, the scratchy words of a demon, the deep vocals of a game show announcer.

Tick tock.

She lifted her chin to the bell, unafraid now of the sound, as more objects popped into the air one-by-one before her—a kitchen timer, an hourglass, a grandfather clock, a wall clock in the shape of a plastic cat with its tail swinging to mark the seconds.

Soon, there were hundreds of floating timepieces, all attempting to remind her of the supposed cosmic obligation she owed her twin.

This time, she did not turn away; she did not cower against the sound. The Universe did *not* work like that, she now understood. It did not keep score, did not collect debts. Humans chose to do that all on their own.

Below her feet under a layer of ice, something caught her eye—a tiny gold spark flickering from the chest of a woman frozen in an impossibly arched position, her hair forever tangled around her face.

The spark was barely there, like a candle flame sputtering to catch hold. Bea allowed her eyes to roam over the surface of the lake and found the same human glow struggling for oxygen in all the bodies. Even these ugly souls, who had caused so much pain in their lifetimes, still held the possibility of understanding. They were not yet broken machines ready for recycling. And the stronger, brighter light in Bea's own chest responded to them, glowing within her body like a child's comforting nightlight. Like a beacon in the dark for the lost.

Still, the voices whispered their collective suggestion that she give up and stay, and she wondered if the voices of Toni and Jesse were among them. She worried if their own golden sparks were still shining or in the process of growing dim somewhere in the Eighth or Ninth Circles.

Turning away from the bells and clocks, she looked out over the vast cold landscape. "Where are you guys?" she whispered to her lost companions—the companions she'd abandoned in a fit of her own massive identification with anger.

As if in answer, light from her gut shot down through her legs out toward a distant horizon in two sparkling tracks.

Curious.

Bea lifted her gaze to address the voices coming from nowhere and everywhere as her limbs warmed and loosened, heat fueling her like a shot of bourbon. "Time is irrelevant," she said, jerking a thumb at the timepieces behind her, though, in truth, she still wasn't exactly sure what that statement meant. "Nothing has come due for me. Nothing in the Universe is out of balance."

The voices quieted to a murmur and then... nothing.

"I'm not some lost and broken girl. I know who I am and want I want. What I truly need. Yes, I want connection—with my brother and many others as well—and yes, I still want to be seen, but that desire is based on feeling full and wanting to share the sensation, not feeling empty. I am no longer *half.* I never was."

The only remaining sound was the slide of Bea's feet over the ice. No monitors rose up to announce some new twist in The Game.

She waited until she could stand it no more. "So, what's

next then, huh? What do you want from me now?" Would she stand there in the center of the Ninth for eternity? Maybe she would follow those two bright tracks running from her feet into the dark distance. Perhaps they would lead her to Toni and Jesse, somewhere out there in the void.

But, in the empty space around her, a slow clap started. One pair of hands was soon followed by more, and then the pace picked up, becoming full-blown applause—loud, almost deafening, as if she were a rock star taking a bow in a sold-out stadium.

Next, a quick series of booms and crackles sounded over her head and she looked up. Fireworks lit the sky as far as the eye could see, and, in the center of the colorful spray, the words "Congratulations Beatrice!" was spelled out in a fantasy of pyrotechnics. The rockets gave a sense of warmth overtaking the previously frigid bottom of the pit.

Rotating in a slow circle to view the rainbow of fireworks above, she discovered the bell and timepieces had disappeared, now replaced by the entrance to a long red carpet, velvet ropes lining each side to keep the boisterous crowd back.

And quite a crowd there was. Masses of people on either side of the carpet fought to get close to the ropes, pushing to get around the paparazzi and their flashing cameras.

The pops of light nearly blinded her as she stepped onto the glamourous path, her tennis-shoed feet leaving a trail of glowing footprints as she moved toward her adoring fans.

"Bea, over here!" An entertainment television host wearing a navy suit and expensive tie thrust his microphone in her face. "Do you mind telling everyone how it feels to win The Game?"

Before she could answer him, a woman with glossy red lipstick and jet-black hair, pulled Bea into another interview. "Any thoughts on where you'll end up now that you're about to get out of here?"

"Get out of here?" Bea asked. Everything was happening so quickly she hadn't had a moment to consider what came next. The woman pointed toward the end of the carpet where a big white door with a shining chrome knob awaited her. "The exit's right there, doll. Can I just add how envious we all are? Well deserved, though, Ms. Allegra. Well deserved."

There is no exit.

Bea dismissed the thought as she shook the woman's hand and moved on, beginning to enjoy the smiling faces beaming at her. This is exactly what she'd hoped for—to be an example for the people of Hell. To show them what was possible and that anyone could leave this place. She'd always said her goal as an influencer was to show people how to live their best life—well, their best *Afterlife* in this case—and everything she'd done had led to this. From her first vlog entry to her nearly one million followers on Instagram, and now this... billions of followers right here in the Underworld. *Billions!*

"Hey, Bea!" A woman wearing the ripped white rags of the Seventh Circle, her bare legs coated in red from the knees down, waved a phone in the air. "Will you take a selfie with me?"

"Of course!" Bea beamed as she trotted over to the woman who stood on the opposite side, vaguely aware that the golden light no longer lit up beneath her steps. She leaned her head next to the woman, confirming that the phone was held at perfect selfie height for the most flattering angle as she smiled big.

"Thank you!" the woman of the Seventh said as she squealed with joy at her prize.

Bea moved further down the carpet, stopping to chat with an agent waving a contract and offering representation. She tried to read over the contract, but her teeth had begun chattering as the cold of the Ninth began to seep back into her bones. Hadn't it been warm only a few moments ago?

Rubbing the goosebumps on her arms, she kept moving. The path to the door seemed to get longer with each freezing, stiffening step. "Over here!" a man shouted, holding up an exquisite deep blue gown he wanted her to wear on his upcoming runway show.

Damn, she'd look good in that.

She paused in her step on the way to him, though, since she could have sworn she saw Benny in the crowd over his shoulder.

But when she looked again, he was gone.

Somebody else called for a selfie, and as she stared into the image on the phone held just above her, there was her friend and makeup artist, Melanie, standing right behind her and shaking her head, eyes sad even as she popped a big pink gum bubble.

Bea whipped around. "Mel?"

The face of a confused stranger looked back at her.

Bea continued on toward the door, which finally came within reach though her steps had grown slower with stiffness. Familiar faces in the crowd taunted her. Faces that shouldn't have been there—Professor Patel, Angel, Nadi, her parents— each one appearing just long enough to register displeasure before dissolving just as quickly. Gone was the glow from her solar plexus, the feeling of completion in her gut, as she stepped up to the door, a bright red EXIT sign hanging above it.

She reached for the doorknob.

There is no exit. Please see yourself out.

"There is no exit." She dropped her hand. "Not like this, anyway."

If the book was to be believed—and her gut told her it should be—this was another trick. And even if it weren't, what would she find on the other side of the door? That was a question she hadn't given much thought to on this journey because it seemed an obvious assumption that, if one were able to get out of Hell, one should immediately take steps to do that.

Of course, she'd mostly figured she'd be walking out of here with Dante by her side. Also Toni. And Jesse.

Bea turned back toward the crowd now gaping silently at

her from both sides of the carpet. At some point in the last couple moments, she'd become frozen and empty inside, already missing the golden tracks, the feeling of her soul's light calling out to others. She glanced over her shoulder once more at the door with its big block-lettered sign. What would she find on the other side that wasn't already right here? She stepped back from the door, and a faint golden glow lit the ground beneath her foot.

As the crowd took a communal gasp at her movement *away* from the exit, she snapped her head up. A hush spread across the masses while they waited for her next move.

She lifted her voice in a shout. "I assume you're still broadcasting," she said to what she'd long since given up believing was an actual production company or governing body in Hell, though she still didn't understand what exactly it was. "Well, guess what? I'm not going through that door behind me. I assume it's going to be more tricks and games and I've decided I'm not playing anymore."

The crowd hung on her every word, but she didn't care an ounce. "Anyway, I don't have to leave this place in order to find happiness and find my way back to Angel, or back to my parents or friends. Because I have them all right here," she said pointing to her heart.

She had other loves to find as well. Loves right here in this corner of reality. "Where are you, Toni and Jesse? I'm so sorry I abandoned you," she whispered, and her torso bloomed in gold as two bright tracks of light shot down through her legs and feet and flung out across the ice. A grin spread on her lips as she looked up toward a starry sky. She raised her voice to whoever was listening. "Want to know what I'm going to do next? Well then, broadcast this!"

Running out across the carpet and, soon, the bare ice, she followed the glowing double lines. Soon a third, thinner track made an appearance, thinner because it disappeared into a greater distance, and she knew in her soul it was the track that led to Dante.

She moved with supernatural speed, yet still aware that her footfalls now landed on pink and white blossoms and that a Monet sky was overhead. Not a fraudulent illusion created by a mass subconscious, but a very real sky, full of atmosphere and moisture, in a real place in the Universe that she was manifesting. *Please see yourself out.*

The view outward from her path also changed as she ran, first through a larger Zen Garden. Then the ground became cobblestones, and she raced through the Left Bank of Paris, and, later, her steps fell on a Boston sidewalk as she sped past familiar cafes and bookstores.

Please see yourself out.

She could stop running at any time and would simply be in those locations. Maybe back in time with her death erased, maybe in a parallel Universe or self-manifested reality. Maybe a different version of the Afterlife, "Heaven" perhaps. It hardly mattered; either way, she'd be free. Whoever she wanted to be with would be there.

Seeing things in multiple dimensions, Dante had said. *Aware of all possibilities or timelines at once.*

Yet she chose to keep running, right here in this place. And laughing and crying every step of the way forward, propelled along those parallel golden tracks toward Toni and Jesse somewhere out there in the void.

"I'm on my way to you," she whispered, wondering if their connected minds would still read each other at this distance. *No pain, only love*, was the message she sent out with her heart, *no reason to suffer.*

It must have reached them because something in her gut shifted, lifted in response, and, soon, two blurs of color were headed her way.

She recognized the strawberry blonde curls and straight black mohawk long before they came to a stop in front of her.

311

They wrapped each other in a group hug, mumbling apologizes over one another. But the apologies hardly mattered, as they each understood... well... everything.

"So crazy," said Jesse as she pointed to the glowing spiderweb of light that flowed between and through the three of them.

"It's not just us, *mes amies*," Toni said, a breathless catch in her voice. "Look."

They stood atop a high rolling hill, lush green grass beneath their feet, and higher snowcapped mountains behind them, which Bea thought was likely Toni's touch. Before them, though, lay the vast population of Hell. Billions of souls spread out like a thousand galaxies, each their own spark of light, and every single one connected to the others in an infinite network of glowing golden threads. A neural net, pulsing with human connection, no soul separate from any other. No soul ever alone.

"That's where the broadcast is coming from. From everyone," said Jesse.

Sure enough, the imagery of Hell, all the various forms of suffering, even of the gameshow itself appeared as little thought bubbles over the heads of the people.

"If we could just get everyone to turn it off and see the truth like we are. To stop creating their own pain." She turned toward Bea. "It's exactly like the book said. The book *was* the key. How do we tell them all?"

Bea didn't know the answer to that, but if she looked hard enough, reached out from the center of her own soul, she realized she could locate individuals and peek in on them.

She spotted Dante, moving through the catacombs on his way to collect Ronna from her slumber.

Searching in another direction she found Benny, and he startled as if feeling the tickle of her contact.

There was hope in reaching them.

"I see my parents," said Jesse, pointing at a spot in the distance. "But they're alive, so... I don't understand."

Bea, too, could peek in on Angel going through his workday, her parents holding hands on the living room sofa as they watched a movie. Nadi and Mel, at dinner with their boyfriends, talking about Bea and laughing at good memories. "I think we're connected to everyone. I don't think it matters where in time or place we are."

"Time is irrelevant," Toni mumbled, and Bea noticed the Queen staring off to the side.

Just beyond where they stood was an opening to another place, and Bea recognized from her studies of Paris that they were looking at the grounds of Le Petit Trianon.

Three young children stood there, the oldest of them holding the fourth child, an infant, in her arms. And, in the far distance, across the expanse of green lawn, stood a tall blond man, his waiting smile luminous.

Axel.

"Hello, *maman*," one of the boys said to Toni. "Are you coming back to the house to play with us now?"

Toni's shoulders shook, her hands going to cover her face.

Bea and Jesse stepped up to her.

"Go with them now, Antoine," Bea said.

That only made her guide—her friend—cry more.

She turned to Bea and wiped her eyes. "I've wanted nothing more for so long, but how can I receive this gift when I did such horrible things to the people of France when I was alive? Such neglectful things. I do not deserve this."

Bea took her hands. "Because you are a human who was in human pain when you made those choices. And you have punished yourself for nearly three hundred years." Bea moved closer and touched her forehead to the old queen's, her voice soft. "You have loved well, my friend. And you are loved in return." Bea pulled back just enough to run her hands through the warm ribbons of light encircling them and reaching to the children and beyond. "You *are* love, you see. We all are. Now, go to them."

313

Antoine hugged first Bea and then Jesse. She started to step off toward her children when she looked back at the remaining twosome. "Where will you both go now?"

Various options floated through her mind, and Bea was aware of different entryways opening around her. All she had to do was step through one, but her feet remained in place.

Behind Jesse, a view of Times Square opened up and the girl glanced at it only briefly.

"I think we're not quite done here yet," Bea said. "We've got choices when we're ready."

Antoine nodded, her smile soft. Then she walked toward her children, who took her hands as they moved across the gardens of the chateau, yellow sunlight bouncing off all their matching curly heads.

Bea and Jesse spun back to study the souls suffering before them. "What do you want to do now, kid?" Bea asked.

"Not a kid," Jesse scoffed before sliding into a grin. "Let's go get your brother."

Bea chuckled as she looked over the sea of sparkling lights, picking out not only Dante, but Sanjay and Madame B., and Benny and Ronna, the man in the winds, and the kids in the Third Circle. Even Kaitlyn and Wolfgang. "Let's go get them all."

Epilogue

Jesse and Bea sat at a round café table underneath a baby blue sky somewhere, theoretically, in the Sixth Circle, though, to them, it looked nothing like it had before. Happy NPC characters moved up and down the sidewalk a few feet away and a recreation of the Eiffel Tower rose up in the distance.

They were now seriously pro at manifesting their reality in this place and, right now, what they wanted to manifest was lunch. It wasn't as though they *needed* to eat anything, of course, but they could and the food here was delicious. A young waitress with twinkling eyes and a big smile set bowls of pasta in front of them. She wasn't a real soul, just another created figure, but Jesse still gawked, her teenage cheeks turning pink.

Bea set aside the food and flipped open the computer. Jesse preferred to just stick with the smart phone she'd created. As a few of the only people here who realized it was the citizens of Hell who were subconsciously controlling the broadcasting system, they were no longer interrupted in their social media use.

They both typed in the details to join a massive zoom-type meeting they'd scheduled, for which they'd been putting out the word over the last few weeks on all their Underworld socials. Bea had no idea if anyone would tune in, and was soon stunned as hundreds, then thousands, then *tens* of thousands of human souls from the pit joined the call. "Holy crap. I guess this really *is* my new gig, isn't it?" she said, making sure her mic was still muted. A moment of doubt crossed her mind. "Same as the old gig?"

"Nah. You're still an amazing influencer, that part's true. But, this time, you're using your superpowers for good." Jesse twirled a forkful of pasta and then gestured with it to Bea. "So, carry on, Wonder Woman."

Laughing, Bea unmuted herself and started the meeting. "Hey, everybody, it's Bea."

"And I'm Jesse," the teen chimed in before devouring a mouthful of spaghetti right there on camera, no avatar in use.

"Dante and Ronna here, too." Her brother's face shared another tile on the screen, he and Ronna waving from their own beautiful choice of setting.

Bea waved back. "Thanks, everyone, for joining us today. I'm so glad you did. We'll be doing these calls as often as need be," she said. "So, fasten your seatbelts and open your minds. Because, boy, do we have a *lot* to show you."

ACKNOWLEDGEMENTS

As with all novels, and particularly a debut novel, it takes a village (in this case, a small city) to bring it fully-formed into the readers' hands. The idea for this came after a random discussion with a friend about the classic story *Inferno* by Dante Alighieri. My fantasy-loving brain decided it would be a fun ride to recreate that original depiction of the Nine Circles of Hell into a modern-day version. Thus launched my journey of over four years to complete this book.

Along the way I had mountains of invaluable help and support. To that end, I want to thank first of all my critique partners Deborah Ahern Evans, Kate Forest, and Nancy McCarty, who read and edited numerous versions of the story, and spent hours brainstorming with me. This book would absolutely not exist without their creative brains and emotional support.

Thank you to my beta readers John Strauss, Sharon Roszia, Michelle Gardner, Raistlin Bittues, and Gloria Guzman. A special acknowledgement is due, too, to Luis Tovar Lemus, whose cheerleading pushed me across the finish line to finally act on publishing.

Even with all that help, the final product would not exist if it were not for the brilliant assistance of Judi Fennell, who line-edited the crap out this thing ("sooooo many adjectives!"), formatted it, and basically held my hand through the self-

L.M. Strauss

publishing process. Thank you, too, to my spectacular cover designer and map illustrator Rena Violet—your art makes me giddy with happiness, and to my proofreader extraordinaire, Michelle Gardner.

Lastly, my utmost gratitude to my spiritual teachers: G.I. Gurdjieff, Eckhart Tolle, Daniel Schmidt, Thich Nhat Hanh, and Michael Singer.

And to John (my husband), and Sharon (my mom), for everything, every step of the way.

ABOUT THE AUTHOR

L.M. Strauss writes adult contemporary fantasy and adult fantasy romance (under the name Elle M. Strauss). When she's not writing books, she's a fine art photographer and digital artist who specializes in book cover images. She lives in a 200-year-old farmhouse in the countryside near Philadelphia with her husband and two children of the four-legged, fur-covered variety (well, her husband has just two legs and only a little fur).

You can find out more about her books at www.LMStrauss.com.